A VISION in VELVET

MISSING!!

GALLAGHER CORA'S CLOSET

"Juliet's writing is creative and wickedly imagin—
—*Once Upon a Romance*

JULIET BLACKWELL

New York Times Bestselling Author of *Tarnished and Torn*

OBSIDIAN

$7.99 U.S.
$9.99 CAN.

ISBN 978-0-451-24090-3

> S > EAN

PRAISE FOR THE NOVELS
OF JULIET BLACKWELL

THE WITCHCRAFT MYSTERIES

Tarnished and Torn

"This series never disappoints."
—Mysteries and My Musings

"Blackwell has another winner . . . a great entry in a really great series." —*Romantic Times*

"Blackwell mixes reality and witchcraft beautifully . . . fascinating. . . . [This] book sparkles with Blackwell's outstanding storytelling skills." —Lesa's Book Critiques

In a Witch's Wardrobe

"A smashingly fabulous tale."
—*New York Times* bestselling author Victoria Laurie

"Funny and thoughtful, *In a Witch's Wardrobe* is an easy read with an enjoyable heroine and a touch of witchy intuition." —The Mystery Reader

"A really entertaining read. . . . I look forward to the next installment." —Cozy Crimes

"A wonderful paranormal amateur sleuth tale. . . . Fans will enjoy Lily's magical mystery tour of San Francisco."
—Genre Go Round Reviews

Hexes and Hemlines

"This exciting urban fantasy murder mystery . . . is an entertaining paranormal whodunit."
—Genre Go Round Reviews

"*Hexes and Hemlines* carries you along with an unconventional cast, where nothing is out of bounds. Extraordinarily entertaining." —*Suspense Magazine*

continued . . .

"I love the mix of vintage clothes, magic, and a lingering possibility of romance combined with mystery."

—Fang-tastic Books

A Cast-off Coven

"If you like your mysteries with a side of spell-casting and demon-vanquishing, you'll enjoy the second title in Blackwell's Witchcraft Mysteries." —*Romantic Times*

"This awesome paranormal mystery stars a terrific heroine." —Genre Go Round Reviews

Secondhand Spirits

"An excellent blend of mystery, paranormal, and light humor, creating a cozy that is a must read for anyone with an interest in literature with paranormal elements."

—The Romance Readers Connection

"It's a fun story, with romance possibilities with a couple of hunky men, terrific vintage clothing, and the enchanting Oscar. But there is so much more to this book. It has serious depth." —*The Herald News* (MA)

THE HAUNTED HOME RENOVATION MYSTERIES

Home for the Haunting

"This story, with the usual characters as well as some new faces, is fascinating and keeps readers thinking that there is more than meets the eye." —*Romantic Times*

Murder on the House

"*Murder on the House* is a winning combination of cozy mystery, architectural history, and DIY with a ghost story thrown in, and somehow manages not to feel overstuffed."

—The Mystery Reader

Dead Bolt

"Juliet Blackwell's writing is like that of a master painter, placing a perfect splash of detail, drama, color, and whimsy in all the right places!"

—*New York Times* bestselling author Victoria Laurie

"Cleverly plotted with a terrific sense of the history of the greater Bay Area, Blackwell's series has plenty of ghosts and supernatural happenings to keep readers entertained and off-balance." — *Library Journal*

"Smooth, seductive. . . . Fans will want to see a lot more of the endearing Mel." — *Publishers Weekly*

If Walls Could Talk

"A terrific blend of suspense and laughter with a dash of the paranormal thrown in make this a great read." — TwoLips Reviews

"Kudos and high fives to Ms. Blackwell for creating a new set of characters for readers to hang around with as well as a new twist on the ghostly paranormal mystery niche." — Once Upon a Romance

THE ART LOVER'S MYSTERIES BY JULIET BLACKWELL WRITING AS HAILEY LIND

Brush with Death

"Lind deftly combines a smart and witty sleuth with entertaining characters who are all engaged in a fascinating new adventure." — *Romantic Times*

Shooting Gallery

"If you enjoy Janet Evanovich's Stephanie Plum books, Jonathan Gash's Lovejoy series, or Ian Pears's art history mysteries . . . then you will enjoy *Shooting Gallery*." —Gumshoe

"An artfully crafted new mystery series!" — Tim Myers, Agatha Award–nominated author of *Slow Cooked Murder*

"The art world is murder in this witty and entertaining mystery!" — Cleo Coyle, national bestselling author of *A Brew to a Kill*

Feint of Art

"Annie Kincaid is a wonderful cozy heroine. . . . It's a rollicking good read." — Mystery News

Also by Juliet Blackwell

THE WITCHCRAFT MYSTERY SERIES
Secondhand Spirits
A Cast-off Coven
Hexes and Hemlines
In a Witch's Wardrobe
Tarnished and Torn

THE HAUNTED HOME RENOVATION MYSTERY SERIES
If Walls Could Talk
Dead Bolt
Murder on the House
Home for the Haunting

A VISION IN VELVET

A Witchcraft Mystery

Juliet Blackwell

AN OBSIDIAN MYSTERY

OBSIDIAN
Published by the Penguin Group
Penguin Group (USA) LLC, 375 Hudson Street,
New York, New York 10014

USA | Canada | UK | Ireland | Australia | New Zealand | India | South Africa | China
penguin.com
A Penguin Random House Company

First published by Obsidian, an imprint of New American Library,
a division of Penguin Group (USA) LLC

First Printing, July 2014

Copyright © Julie Goodson-Lawes, 2014

OBSIDIAN and logo are trademarks of Penguin Group (USA) LLC.

ISBN 978-0-451-24090-3

Printed in the United States of America
10 9 8 7 6 5 4 3 2 1

To Mary Grae

Botanical sorceress, artiste, friend . . . and so much more

Acknowledgments

Thanks to my editor, Kerry Donovan, for her keen critiques and unstinting support of my books. And to my agent, Jim McCarthy, whose counseling and cheerleading keeps me going in this crazy business — so glad you've got my back!

Special thanks to Arlene Johnson, clothing conservator, for putting up with my incessant questions. And to the herpetological wonders of the California Academy of Science.

As always, many thanks are due to my sister and writing partner, Dr. Carolyn Lawes, especially for her cogent interpretation of the history of witchcraft in Salem. And to the wonderfully talented, irreverently funny, always-inspiring writer friends, without whom I would be curled up in a corner: Sophie Littlefield, Rachael Herron, Nicole Peeler, Mysti Berry, Victoria Laurie, and all the Pens and the Thursday morning gang. To the entire Mira Vista social club and its unofficial leaders, Sara Paul and Dan Krewson . . . who also happen to be Oscar's real parents. To my friend Anna Cabrera, for all your support and love and organizing; to Pamela Groves, Jan Strout, Shay Demetrius, Suzanne Chan, Kendall

Moalem, Susan Baker, Bruce Nikolai, Karen Thompson, Claudia Escobar, Wanda Klor, and Bee Green Enos, for being so supportive of my writing. Thanks are due, as ever, to my sister Susan and my incredible father, Robert. And to my son, Sergio, who makes me proud every day. And to Eric—for all the meals, the wine, the dancing, and the love. And a special nose-bump to Oscar the cat.

Finally, in memory of all those women and men who have stood accused of witchcraft—as though it were evil—and persecuted and brutalized by those who don't, or won't, understand.

Chapter 1

Sometimes it's hard to distinguish between an antiques dealer and a hoarder.

Sebastian's Antiques, a tiny shop on a narrow side street off San Francisco's Jackson Square, was so crammed with furniture, paintings, carvings, mirrors, rugs, dolls, miniatures, and tchotchkes that it was hard to know whether its proprietor, Sebastian Crowley, was the owner of a vast treasure trove, or simply the unfortunate overseer of a musty, oversized closet full of junk.

Not that I was pointing any fingers. After all, my primary motive for opening Aunt Cora's Closet, my vintage clothing store, was to indulge my love of fabulous old garments . . . some of which no doubt qualified as "junk" to those who didn't share my passions.

"'Course, the trunk alone is worth a fortune," said Sebastian Crowley as we inspected a very old, very damaged wooden chest.

I was skeptical. The chest's metal hinges were so corroded with rust I doubted they could withstand repeated openings, while the wood sides, bottom, and lid were pitted and crumbling. "It came across the country on the overland route, all the way from Massachusetts. Back with the pioneers, come to settle the new land."

"Was this during the Gold Rush?" Like many newcomers to the West Coast, I was a little fuzzy on California's history. For such a young area of the country, it had a colorful and tumultuous past.

Crowley frowned. "Yeah, um ... not sure 'bout that. As I was saying, the trunk's a beaut, but it's what's *inside* that's gonna knock your socks off."

He heaved open the lid to reveal two neatly folded stacks of clothing.

I drew back as my nostrils were assailed by the intermingled odors of mothballs and cedar. One quick glance, and my heart sank. It didn't take a close inspection to see these garments had fallen victim to the vicissitudes of age that combine to shatter cloth: rot, moths, and moisture. I keep a seamstress on retainer at Aunt Cora's Closet to address the minor repairs needed by many of my vintage acquisitions—small tears, lost buttons, frayed cuffs—but at the end of the day I stay in business by selling clothes my customers can actually *wear*. The items in this chest should go directly to a museum-grade clothing conservator. Either that, or straight into the trash can.

Sebastian lifted a simple white shift and shook it open. The aged, yellowed cotton cracked and split along the folds, sending small poofs of dust into the musty air.

"Well, I'll be *danged*," Sebastian murmured, studying the shredded garment with a furrowed brow.

It was an expression I'd already grown familiar with. In the half hour we'd spent together, Sebastian's expression had been a mixture of surprise and confusion, so perhaps that was simply the way he viewed the world. Tall and gaunt, the antiques dealer was in his late sixties, with a weak chin and raised bushy eyebrows that reminded me of Ichabod Crane, a character in one of my favorite childhood stories, "The Legend of Sleepy Hollow." He dressed well; I had to give him that: a nice white linen shirt under a tweed jacket. But his wire glasses had a tendency to slip down his large, hooked nose, and he had a habit of pushing them back up. Since everything in the shop was covered in dust, his nose was now covered in gray and brown smudges. I tried not to stare.

"They looked fine when I bought the trunk. . . . I didn't think to inspect them. I'll be *danged*."

"Cloth is tricky," I said sympathetically. "If it's not preserved properly, it falls apart with age. Antique pieces were made of natural fibers like cotton, linen, wool, or silk. Eventually, they break down and return to the earth. Dust to dust and all that. It's rather poetic, in a way."

The sour expression on Sebastian's face made it clear that he did not share my appreciation for poetry. He shook his head. "That pretty little thing sold me a trunk full of worthless clothes. Son of a *gun*."

I wondered how much he had paid for the trunk and its contents, but refrained from asking. I'd been burned once or twice myself. It isn't a pleasant feeling, but it's not unusual in our line of business.

"Tell you what: How 'bout you give me eighty bucks for the whole kit 'n' caboodle?" he suggested, his voice regaining a touch of the salesman's swagger. "Get it out of my way."

"I'm sorry, Sebastian," I said with a shake of my head. "I'd like to help you out, but I can't use these. The fabric is just too compromised."

"Nip here, a tuck here, it'll be right as rain. You'll see."

"It would take a lot more than a nip and a tuck, I'm afraid. Maybe a professional conservator could help, but for my purposes they're beyond repair."

"*Humph*. Try to do someone a favor, and what do I get for my trouble? Ripped off, is what." Sebastian made a face as if smelling something unpleasant and said in a falsetto: " *'My uncle needs money; he's selling off all his antiques. Can't you help him out?'* Sweet young thing comes in here and twists me around her little finger. I'm just too nice a guy, is what."

Next time, try thinking with your brain, I thought, but I did not say it aloud. We stood side by side for a moment, staring at the open trunk.

That's when I felt it. Something emanating from beneath the stack of linens.

I have a special affinity for clothing. For textiles of all kinds, actually. It's hard to explain why or how. I'm not sensitive to what most psychics are, such as metal and stone, though maybe that's because I'm not a psychic. I'm a witch. A powerful witch, too, though not always on top of her magical abilities . . . I never finished my formal training in the craft, so I am still learning as I go along. I can brew with the best of them, but divination and most psychometrics escape me.

But clothes? Clothes, I can read. They absorb the vibrations of the people who have worn them and emit a wisp of that human energy. Before moving to San Francisco and finding a community of friends, I had lived a lonely and isolated life. The sensations I picked up from cast-off clothing had offered solace and connection to others, and old clothes had become not just a passion but a profession.

Even given my particular sensitivities, though, I wasn't normally able to hear a piece *calling* to me. But there were vibrations coming from something in that trunk. Strong vibrations.

Sebastian slammed the lid shut, muttering under his breath, "Worthless piece of—"

"*Wait.*"

His eyes flew to mine.

"Mind if I take another look?" I asked.

"Why, surely. You take all the time you need." A calculating gleam entered Sebastian's watery blue eyes as he lifted the trunk lid with a flourish. "Don't see specimens like this every day; am I right? Work a bit of the ol' magic on them, and they'll be good as new."

I gave a start of surprise, which I turned into a shrug when I realized the "magic" he was referring to was just a turn of phrase. And frankly, I could brew for a week nonstop and still not reconstitute those decaying threads. Even my strongest magic didn't work that way.

But when Sebastian opened the trunk, I heard it again. Something was in the trunk, calling to me. I heard it, *felt* it, deep in my gut . . . and in a tingling in my fingertips.

"May I?" I asked.

"Just don't hurt anything or you bought it. Like the sign says." He jabbed a finger in the direction of a large sign, grimy with age, hanging above the register: YOU BREAK IT, YOU BOUGHT IT.

It wouldn't take much more than a strong gust of wind to damage these pieces, I thought. Gingerly, I lifted the top garments from the trunk and set them aside: men's clothes in one pile, women's in another. My practiced eye recognized these yellowing white cotton shirts, petticoats, and bloomers had once been fine, quality garments; but now they were falling apart. The linens beneath them were in somewhat better condition, but still too far gone to sell. Taking care to disturb the clothes as little as possible, I dug deeper.

My fingers touched something soft and fine, like the coat of a baby bunny. I peeked in: velvet.

"What's this? Do you know?" I asked.

Sebastian shrugged. "I didn't look through it, to tell you the truth. The girl who brought it in said her uncle was desperate for cash, and the whole trunk came across from Boston back in the day, with the pioneers. Probably some cockamamy story. Tell you what. I have too big a heart; that's my problem. She sold me a few decorative items that might be worth something, so I just took this as part of the deal."

"Would you mind if I examined this velvet piece?"

Sebastian rubbed his hands together. "How 'bout you buy the lot, and it's yours? Think about it: This trunk came from Boston with the pioneers! Just imagine the history, the stories it could tell. There's bound to be something really great in there."

"I thought you said that was a cockamamy story the seller made up."

"Doesn't mean it couldn't be true."

"So if the trunk came across the prairies all the way from Boston, how come it's still packed? Why wasn't it opened and the clothes worn?"

"The owners died on route."

I glanced up at him, surprised.

"Leastways, that's what the gal said." Sebastian stuck out his receding chin. "She said the way she heard the story, her relatives were in a party of wagon trains coming overland, and this trunk and a few other items belonged to a family who died before they got here. Buried somewhere en route. I guess their stuff was picked up and carried the rest of the way by other relatives and eventually ended up here in San Francisco. Listen, I tell you what I'm gonna do: seventy-five bucks and the trunk's yours, contents included. You can't beat that."

I hesitated, calculating the available floor space at my store. The shop was already jammed with racks upon racks of dresses, coats, skirts, jackets, and blouses and shelves upon shelves of hats, gloves, purses, and shoes. There were umbrellas and parasols, shawls and scarves, and a sizable selection of secondhand jewelry. I also had a weakness for antique kitchen gadgetry, which meant a growing collection of vintage cooking items now crowded a cupboard in one corner. Much of the inventory turned over quickly, but the quirkier items collected dust in nooks and crannies and display windows. So crowded had the shop become in the last few months that my friend and coworker, Bronwyn, had threatened to pack up her herbal stand and leave.

Which was why I sympathized with Sebastian Crowley. Honestly, left to my own devices, my shop would look as bad as his.

"I can't take the trunk, but I'll take the clothes." It was possible we would be able to salvage something from the shattered garments: a few buttons or bits of lace. We might even be able to copy some of the designs to make re-creations. And there was something about that velvet item....

"Hundred bucks."

"You said seventy-five!"

"That's for the trunk and its contents. Contents *without* the trunk are a hundred."

"That's ridiculous."

"Hey, you know how this works!" Sebastian was referring to auctions, where patrons bid on numbered lots that contained numerous items. If you wanted one particular item, you had to take the whole lot. Afterward, you were stuck figuring out what to do with the rest of the stuff. Problem was, few of us junk-hounds were able to toss the worthless items into the nearest Dumpster. "One man's trash is another man's treasure" were words we lived by, which explained why so many of our shops resembled Sebastian's Antiques.

"These clothes really aren't worth anything, Sebastian. Let me give you fifty for the clothes, and you keep the trunk."

"Seventy."

"Fifty-five."

"*Sixty*-five, and you help me carry this beautiful, historic trunk out to the curb. Tomorrow's trash day."

I studied the chest one more time. If it really had come across country on the overland route—and it certainly looked old enough—it seemed wrong for it to meet its end in the gutter.

"Oh, fine," I said with a sigh. Giving in to the inevitable, I handed him three twenties. "Sixty, and you help me carry it out to my van."

Sebastian beamed. "Pleasure doing business with you, Lily Ivory."

"That's *it*," declared Bronwyn as my friend Conrad and I dragged the heavy trunk through the front door of Aunt Cora's Closet.

Bronwyn was a proud fiftysomething Wiccan with frizzy brown hair, which today was adorned with a garland of Shasta daisies.

"You were given fair warning, Lily. I am hereby tendering my notice to vacate these premises. Forthwith and forsooth and all that. Maybe Sandra next door has room for my herb stand in *her* store."

"I'm not going to *keep* it," I said, trying to keep the chagrin from my voice. "I just want to find it a good home."

"You make it sound like a lost kitten," said our young coworker, Maya, with a laugh. "When in reality it's . . . a creepy old trunk."

I had at last returned to Aunt Cora's Closet after stops at Goodwill, the Salvation Army, and two garage sales. As a result, in addition to Sebastian's trunk I was in possession of several large bags of clothing. Fortunately, most of these would require little more than washing and steaming or ironing to be ready to sell for a neat profit. Still, I was disappointed; back when I first started my business, a person could pick up a slightly tattered example of a 1940s skirt suit for a song and 1930s satin cocktail dress for not much more. Even labeled items from Oscar de la Renta and Armani used to find their way into my basket at bargain prices. No longer. The competition for quality vintage items had become fierce.

"Really, Lily, I don't know where you think you're going to put this thing," said Bronwyn.

"It's historic," I said. "It came across the prairies. On a wagon train."

Bronwyn and Maya looked skeptical.

"Really," I said.

"That may be, but it's *big*."

"And ugly," Maya chimed in.

"And smelly," Bronwyn continued.

"*Dude*, it's sort of . . . gross." Conrad nodded. This from the homeless guy who lived in Golden Gate Park and spent the better part of each day on the curb outside of Aunt Cora's Closet, soliciting spare change.

"All right. All right. I get the point," I said, realizing that if I wasn't careful, soon I would become like Sebastian, grumbling about being too nice to people . . . and to objects. "But let's at least look through the clothes and see what we've got. Then maybe I can clean up the trunk and put it on the community bulletin board. Surely *someone* will want such a historic piece."

"I could call the Oakland Museum," offered Maya. "If it really did cross the prairies on a wagon train, maybe they could use it in one of their Gold Rush displays. You could donate it, get a tax donation."

"Now we're thinking!"

Bronwyn smiled indulgently—fortunately for me, she was far too loving to hold a grudge. "Well, what are we waiting for? Open it up!"

I lifted the lid, and the strong odors of mothballs and cedar wafted out.

"*Whoof!*" said Bronwyn, waving a hand in front of her nose.

My miniature Vietnamese potbellied pig—and ersatz witch's familiar—retreated to his bed and hid his sensitive snout in the monogrammed purple satin pillow Bronwyn had given him. Oscar was one spoiled pig.

"Considering how bad they smell, the mothballs should have done a better job, don't you think?" asked Maya, grimacing.

"The mothballs are probably a recent addition. Before that . . . well, the cedar keeps insects at bay, but it's not one hundred percent effective. And these clothes have been in here a very long time. But I'm not worried about moth damage as much as rot. Look at this."

I reached in and, using two fingers of each hand as gently as possible, lifted the shift that Sebastian had unfolded in his store. It cracked further along the creases, sending more tiny puffs of dust into the air.

Bronwyn and Maya gasped, and I couldn't help but smile at their reactions. Neither had been particularly interested in textiles, or any aspect of fashion for that matter, when I met them. But there was something about vintage clothing. . . . The blending of tangible history, supreme craftsmanship, and fine lace could be addictive.

"What a *shame*," said Bronwyn with feeling.

"Are they all that way?" said Maya.

I shrugged. "One way to find out."

I lay the first item on the counter and removed another: a man's shirt that was in even worse shape than the shift. Next was a linen shirtwaist in slightly better condition, though not by much.

"Look at those beautiful buttons!" Bronwyn exclaimed. "Dollars to doughnuts they're bone."

"I'll bet my mom could find a use for them," said Maya.

"Let's set them aside," I agreed. Maya's mother, Lucille, was an expert seamstress—a crucial asset for a vintage clothing store. Lucille had recently established a cottage industry mimicking vintage dress patterns. She sized up the beautiful old designs to fit today's women, who were larger and much healthier than their grandmothers. From these designs, she created charming old-fashioned dresses that were also machine-washable—a huge advantage over most vintage, for which only the most expensive dry cleaning would do.

I removed more items from the trunk, but these, too, were beyond repair. Still, we examined each one carefully. Joined by several customers, we *ooh*ed and *aah*ed over the tiny handmade stitches, the bits of exquisite lace and fine embroidery, the surprisingly petite dimensions of adult men and women back in the day. As usual when I dealt with historical items, I kept imagining what life must have been like; in this case, the courage—or foolishness—it took to leave a city such as Boston and set out for the unknown. What had the trunk's original owners died from? I wondered. Disease? An accident?

At last I reached the velvet I had felt calling to me in Sebastian's shop. As I held it up there were several audible intakes of breath.

It was a deep gold velvet cape with a purple silk lining. Gold brocade ribbons ran down the interior seams and along the hem, and purple and gold fringe decorated the neckline. A silk-lined hood hung down the back, a large tassel at its crown. An ornate brass frog toggle fastened the cape at the throat. Where the rest of the trunk's contents had been typical of the merchant class in the nineteenth century—quality construction with modest decorative touches—this cape was something else. It was also much older and appeared to have been fashioned for royalty.

It was not in great shape: The silk lining was shattered and hung in strips, there were numerous moth holes, the velvet had faded unevenly, and there was a large tear at the seam along the left shoulder. Yet even with all that . . . it was an amazing garment.

Unable to resist, I whirled it around my shoulders and only vaguely noticed as Oscar careened toward me, alarm in his pink piggy eyes. I fastened the brass clasp at the neck.

And then . . . I was no longer in the shop.

I felt a shock of freezing cold wash over me, followed by a river of heat. As though in a dream, I saw fuzzy shapes and heard sounds, unintelligible yet very real. As the images coalesced, I realized a mob was surrounding me, pointing fingers, faces distorted in anger and fear. They were jeering, yelling, calling out . . . curses? I couldn't quite make it out; the sounds were like a recording being played at the wrong speed. It reminded me of being underwater. . . . The lights bobbed and flickered, and sounds were muffled and distorted.

It was nightmarish. What were they saying? I concentrated, straining to hear, trying to make out their words. . . .

"Lily? *Lily!*"

Chapter 2

The concern in Bronwyn's voice cut through the visions and brought me back to the present with a shock. Her hands were on my shoulders, shaking me gently, then nimbly undoing the clasp at my throat. The cloak puddled on the floor.

"Are you all right? What in the world . . . ?"

"Yes, of course. I . . ." Relief washed over me as I realized I was in my shop, surrounded by friends. I swayed on my feet. "Just a little . . . dizzy. I think I forgot to eat lunch."

"Your blood sugar's probably low," Maya said, moving toward the kitchenette in the back room. "There's some pomegranate kefir in the fridge."

"That's a good idea," Bronwyn said. "The body needs fuel, you know."

I wrinkled my nose but took a sip of the yogurt drink Maya held out.

"Better?" Maya asked.

I nodded. A customer brought several purchases to the cash register, and Maya and Bronwyn turned away to ring her up now that they were satisfied I was okay.

Picking up the velvet cape, I folded it over my arm and held it close to my chest. In all my years of dealing with vintage clothing, I had never encountered anything like this. Clearly, this was no ordinary cape. What was the nature of its power? Was it positive or negative? Good or evil? Only one thing was sure: I had to learn more about it.

And until I knew its story, it was vital no one else try it on.

I crossed over to the counter, picked up the phone, and dialed the number for Sebastian's Antiques. I got voice mail but didn't leave a message; once we closed up for the night, I would go back to Jackson Square and have a little chat with Sebastian about the cloak's provenance. With any luck he kept decent records, so I would be able to track down the woman who sold him the trunk—and its strange contents—and talk to her directly.

Out of the corner of my eye, I saw Conrad sink onto the velvet bench near the dressing rooms. He leaned forward and cradled his head in his hands.

"Are you all right, Conrad?" I held out the bottle of kefir. Conrad did look a mite peaked, but it was hard to tell if it was out of the ordinary. His eyes were habitually red-rimmed, due to the illegal, or ill-advised, substances he imbibed.

"Dude, I haven't been, like, sleeping well?"

"Insomnia?" It wouldn't be surprising. It amazed me that Conrad, along with so many "gutterpunks," as the homeless young people called themselves, got any sleep at all. I had slept in the forest many times, but an urban park? No matter how thickly wooded, I doubted I'd be able to relax enough to get my REM sleep.

"I got a prime sleeping spot, but, dude, it's gnarly. I keep waking up from sort of, like, bad dreams? Prob'ly 'cause of, like, I have a lot of work to do. The Con's not used to it. Not my thing."

"What kind of work?" Bronwyn asked.

He looked around, his face blank.

"Does it have something to do with the clipboard tucked under your arm?" Maya offered. She hadn't much cared for Conrad at first, but he had won her—had won all of us—over with his desire to please and the sense of protectiveness he felt toward Aunt Cora's Closet.

After a moment, realization dawned. "*Dude!* Yes! We're collecting names for this petition. City plans to kill Ms. Quercus, and we're, like, totally against it."

"An execution? Really?" Maya asked.

Conrad nodded.

"Are you sure?" Bronwyn said. "By the city?"

"Totally."

That sounded odd. There were occasional executions at San Quentin, a maximum-security prison across the bay, but the city didn't control San Quentin; the state did. Not to mention, the executions were well publicized and engendered loud protests, but I hadn't heard a thing about this one.

"Could I see the petition?" I asked, and Conrad handed me the clipboard.

The petition, written in red ink in Conrad's surprisingly neat handwriting, read: *I don't want the city to remove Ms. Quercus, as she deserves to deteriorate at her own pace rather than having her demise hastened unnaturally.*

"It's a woman?" Bronwyn asked, reading over my shoulder.

"It says 'Ms.,'" Maya pointed out.

"She's a friend of yours?" Bronwyn asked Conrad.

"What'd she do?" Maya said.

"Nothing," Conrad said. "She's innocent."

"That's what everybody on death row says," Maya muttered.

"The innocent are sometimes unjustly convicted," Bronwyn argued.

Conrad nodded.

I suspected there was more to this story. "Con, who, exactly, is Ms. Quercus?"

"Not a 'who,' dude. She's, like, totally a tree."

Now I understood. Among the Bay Area's numerous charming quirks was the frequency with which people protested the cutting down of trees. I had never heard of such a thing before moving here.

"So are you tree sitting Ms., uh"—I glanced at the petition—"Quercus?"

"Nah, dude, can't. She's, like, an ancient oak, but rotten on the inside, I guess. So she's, like, dying, which is totally sad, but it's also, like, the circle of life. Besides . . . you ever seen how much life is supported by a dying tree? Woodpeckers, all sorts of squirrels and lizards, critters hollowing out burrows around the roots. Even frogs. Plus mushrooms! Dude, you'd never believe the mushrooms."

"Are these 'magic mushrooms,' by any chance?" Maya asked.

"Nah, dude. At least . . . I don't think so." He frowned, as though in concentration. "Never tried, actually. Not the Con's style."

I'd finally put it all together. "So you're saying that the city wants to take the tree down because they're afraid it will fall over and hurt someone?"

He nodded. "This tree lady came by and told us Ms. Quercus can't be cured, but it might take her a while to fall apart completely. So that's when this other scientist dude says, how come we can't just put a fence around her, keep people back in case she falls or a branch goes? And me and my friends are like, *dude.* She still has leaves; she's still a beauty. Besides, I totally sleep under her, no problem. I love that tree. She's . . . she's special."

"How do you know it's a 'she'?" Maya asked, one eyebrow cocked.

"Dude."

Maya, Bronwyn, and I shared a smile. I took the clipboard from Conrad and signed his petition. I was all for woodpeckers and other critters keeping their arboreal homes as long as possible. Besides, surely the city had more productive ways to spend its money. Conrad was right: Why not put up a fence and let nature take its course?

"I'm next," Bronwyn said.

"Hand it over." Maya sighed.

"So how do you know her name?" I couldn't help but ask.

"That tree lady came to take a look," said Conrad. "She told us all about her kind—they're called Quercus . . . something or other. I can never remember the full name, but the Quercus part just stuck."

Conrad paused and perused his petition, full of several new names.

"Okay, then. Thanks for the support. The Con's got to mosey on down the way and pick up some more signatures. And, dude, let me know if you need help carrying this trunk out to the alley for garbage day. See you around."

"Bye."

As he turned to leave, tingles went up my spine and the back of my neck felt cold. Watching Conrad's back, I suddenly felt as though I was back in . . . *wherever* I went to when I tried on the cloak. I wasn't a big one for premonitions, but I'd been working on my magical skills, so perhaps I was developing new sensibilities. Whether it was that, or something about that velvet cloak, or something else entirely, I wasn't sure.

But one thing I knew for sure: Something was wrong.

"Conrad, *wait*."

He turned back toward me, eyebrows raised in question.

I hesitated, looking around the shop. No one else seemed to have noticed anything unusual. Several customers were absorbed in their search of the racks and shelves of clothing. Bronwyn had returned to her herbal stand, where she was mixing custom tea blends, and Maya was straightening the changing rooms. Frank Sinatra crooned softly in the background, and as always, the air in the shop was scented with the sachets I changed out every week, filling black silk squares with rosemary and rue, or juniper and rose petals . . . whatever herbs or flowers were abundant and in season.

I was safe and sound in Aunt Cora's Closet, my refuge. So why did I feel like something was seriously amiss?

"Conrad, you mentioned you were having bad dreams?" He nodded and gazed down at the clipboard.

"And you've been sleeping under this oak tree you're trying to save?"

"Dude."

I searched my memory for what I knew about oak trees. In European folklore they were said to be home to the woodsfolk, who could be vengeful if their trees were razed. The California live oak was a different breed from the European version, with a small spiked leaf instead of the oak's classic five fingers. But I had never heard of any species of oak being associated with nightmares.

And this oak tree probably wasn't, either. More likely, Conrad was suffering the effects of a life spent ingesting too many drugs and too little food, compounded by a lack of sleep.

But then again . . . I rarely had premonitions. And I was too smart a witch not to pay attention when I did.

"Would you show me the oak tree you're talking about?" I asked. "I'd like to see it."

"Um . . . Ms. Quercus? Sure. When?"

"Five minutes?"

"Dudette, tell you what. I'll stroll down Haight for more signatures, and if you don't catch up with me, I'll meet you near the horseshoe pits and show you to the tree. She's not far from there."

"Perfect, thanks."

The bell on the front door tinkled as new customers arrived, and Conrad went to ask for their signatures on his petition.

I quickly riffled through the remaining items in the trunk to be certain there was nothing else out of the ordinary, but the velvet cape was the only oddity. I stared at the cape a moment before rolling it up and bringing it upstairs to my apartment over the store, where I placed it in a wicker basket and covered it with a black cloth that had been washed in rosewater and consecrated. Then, just in case, I surrounded it with stones—quartz, Apache tears, and tiger's eye—cast a quick binding spell, and left it under the watchful eye of Oscar before returning to the shop.

I tried calling Sebastian's Antiques one more time, hoping to make an appointment to talk with Sebastian, but still no one answered. I realized I would have to take my chances and try to catch up with him later.

"Bronwyn, Maya, do you have a moment?" I said, and they joined me at the register. "I took the cape upstairs for safekeeping. Until I've had the chance to study it, I'd prefer no one else knows anything about it, okay?"

"Of course, Lily," Bronwyn said.

"I know it sounds a little odd . . ." I began.

"No more than a lot of what goes on around here," Maya commented. "Pretty much par for the course, in fact."

I smiled, grateful for their support. "I know I've been gone all day, but would you two mind if I took off again? I want to see this Ms. Quercus character for myself."

"Have fun," said Bronwyn.

"We've got plenty to sort through," said Maya. "I'm itching to see what you found at the thrift stores."

"Thanks, y'all."

I glanced over my shoulder as I walked out the door. Happiness washed over me as I took in the sight of Aunt Cora's Closet brimming with vintage clothes and bustling with customers and friends. Part of me longed to stay and sort through the new acquisitions with Maya and Bronwyn—not only did I enjoy their company, but we always turned these moments into a fun treasure hunt.

Still, it was also a lovely day for a walk in the sunshine. San Francisco's climate was temperate, though it could be plagued by fog and chill blowing in off the ocean. The spring and fall months, I had learned, were by far the most beautiful, as summer days often were shrouded by heavy blankets of fog.

I walked down Haight Street, passing head shops, a few other secondhand clothes dealers, restaurants and pubs, the Booksmith, and plenty of tourists basking in the hippie hangout of yore. The neighborhood was still filled with young people, like Conrad, who had left their homes in rural Nebraska or downtown Detroit or sunny Florida in search of love and open-mindedness in the City by the Bay. Unfortunately, they also found some of the highest rents in the country and a tight job market. Add the lure of cheap drugs and alcohol, and too many ended up spending their days begging for spare change on the streets of the Haight and their nights sleeping in doorways or in Golden Gate Park. They were frequently dirty, smelly, and pushy to the point of obnoxiousness, but my heart went out to them. I had searched for a home for too long myself not to be touched by their plight.

Just after Amoeba Records I crossed Stanyan and entered Golden Gate Park, turning right on a curved path toward the horseshoe pits. A couple of boys were playing tag in the grassy field, their young parents sprawled on a picnic blanket. A teenage couple sat on a bench, heads together, hands clasped tightly.

Just then there were two loud popping sounds, like balloons bursting.

A moment later, a pair of women, clad in skirts and heels, ran past. Hot on their heels was a man dressed in a business suit. Not your typical joggers.

Sometimes my body senses things long before my brain catches up. My lips trembled, and I felt another prickling sensation, as if an army of ants was crawling along my arms, then down my spine. I caught a wisp of the cloying, sickly sweet scent of death.

Carefully, I proceeded toward the noise, passing through a small wooded area and entering a clearing dominated by a massive oak. Its thick branches spread wide, dipping close to the ground as though inviting children to climb. The tree's immense trunk was encircled by orange traffic cones and city-stamped A-frame wooden signs warning people to keep back.

Conrad was kneeling by a prone man near the base of the tree.

Two bright red stains marred the breast of the man's white linen shirt. Bushy eyebrows were raised as though in surprise; a smudge of dirt marred the bridge of his bespectacled nose.

Sebastian Crowley had been shot.

Chapter 3

"Duuuude," Conrad exhaled in a harsh whisper, looking up at me as I approached. His eyes looked wild with fear and shock; there was blood on his hands. "He's right where I usually . . . I mean, this is the exact spot where I've been sleeping."

"Conrad, what happ—"

Sebastian groaned. I rushed over to kneel beside him. He was still conscious, but just barely.

"Sebastian, what happened? Who did this?" I grabbed the scarf from around my neck, wadded it up, and held it against his chest to stanch the blood. Conrad shrugged off his T-shirt and handed it to me. The blood soaked through both quickly.

The antiques dealer gurgled, sounding like he was choking. I realized he was trying to speak and leaned in close.

"Witch."

I reared back, shivering all the way to my core, as though someone had placed an ice-cold hand on the back of my neck.

"Sebastian, tell me, *who*? Who did this?"

He closed his eyes, no longer responsive.

"Conrad? What happened? Did you see anything?"

"I didn't see a thing. I was like, walking toward the tree, and I totally thought the dude was just napping, until I saw the . . . uh . . . blood."

I glanced up and saw a woman with a baby carriage staring at us. She clapped a hand over her mouth and rushed away. An elderly man averted his eyes and hastened off as well. But others approached, forming a loose half circle in front of us and gawking as if unsure how to help. Oddly enough, they did not cross the invisible barrier formed by the orange plastic cones, and for a moment I felt as though we were putting on some sort of macabre performance-art show.

"Call nine-one-one!" I called out to no one in particular.

"I left my phone at the office," one man said, speaking with a slight accent I couldn't quite place. He was a large man, with thinning sandy hair and goggle eyes that appeared even wider than normal with shock. He and the dark-haired man next to him wore lab coats, and official-looking lanyards hung around their necks.

"I don't carry a phone," I said. "Someone, anyone, a cell phone?"

"Take mine," said Conrad, pulling the device from his pants pocket.

The man was homeless, but had a cell phone? I grabbed it and dialed.

"Did you see what happened?" I asked the goggle-eyed man as he came to kneel by Conrad, as though to lend moral support. I held the phone to my ear as the number rang; a recording told me to hold on the line.

"I didn't see anything. . . . Kai and I were supposed to meet a colleague here to take a look at the tree. Nina's the tree expert. . . . She should be here, unless . . ." He scanned the area, apparently looking for her.

"I'm Lily Ivory. I own a shop on Haight Street. You work nearby?"

"We're scientists at the Cal Academy. That's Kai . . . and oh, there's Nina. Good; she's okay."

"Dude," said Conrad. "That's the tree lady."

I glanced up to see a tall young woman had joined the other man in a lab coat. Though she appeared strong and broad-shouldered, all three were so pale I wondered if they ever left their laboratories.

"You still on hold?" asked Conrad. "Why don't I go see if I can wave down a park ranger or something? I'll go out to the main road."

"Good idea. Thanks, Con," I said. I felt Sebastian's neck for a pulse, but though he was still laboring to breathe, I couldn't find even a murmur of a beat.

"I think I'm going to be sick," said the man.

I couldn't blame him. A trickle of blood from Sebastian's chest was pooling on the soil beneath him. I noticed the dirt had been churned up and recalled Conrad mentioning that animals liked to burrow near the ancient oak tree. Unless someone had been digging for something . . .

"Nine-one-one, what is your emergency? Hello?"

My voice was shaky as I gave the operator our location as best I could: a clearing north of John F. Kennedy Drive, down the path toward the horseshoe pits. Directions were tough in Golden Gate Park, which was full of meandering lanes and woods and fields. I told her someone would be out on the road to wave the emergency vehicles in. She told me to stay on the line; paramedics were on their way.

"Take a deep breath, hold it. Then let it out slowly, to the count of eight," I suggested to the man kneeling beside Sebastian, trying to distract him while we waited. "What's your name?"

"Lance. Lance Thornton."

"And what's the Cal Academy, exactly?"

"The California Academy of Sciences. It's sort of ... well, part natural history museum and part scientific research facility. It's not far from here, right across from the DeYoung Art Museum."

"I don't know the area that well. I moved here a while ago, but I . . ." I trailed off as Sebastian's labored breathing ceased with a final rattling gasp.

I felt another icy sensation flow over me, then lift, all at once, from my shoulders.

As I reached out to feel for a pulse in Sebastian's neck, his head turned toward me . . . eyes open and staring.

The breath caught in my throat.

Since moving to San Francisco, I had encountered too much violent death. But I had never been present at the actual moment of transformation, had never knelt beside someone and heard their last breath, witnessed their passing from this dimension to the next.

I almost told the 911 operator not to bother with the paramedics, to send the coroner and homicide inspectors instead, then decided that it wasn't my place. I did say the victim was named Sebastian Crowley, that he had been shot, and that he appeared to be deceased. She asked a few clarifying details about that last statement, then again told me to remain on the line until the police arrived.

"Poor Sebastian," I whispered.

"You know him?" asked Lance.

"Just barely."

Holding the phone to my ear, I focused once more on Sebastian's now lifeless body. This time I noticed something sticking out of his jacket pocket. I leaned closer: It was a small rectangle of cheery purple paper stock emblazoned with the slogan *Aunt Cora's Closet—It's Not Old. It's Vintage!*

My calling card.

"You wanna tell me why the victim had your business card in his pocket?" demanded Inspector Carlos Romero of the San Francisco Police Department.

The paramedics were the first to arrive; then the medical examiner had been called in, and the photographer and forensics team had begun working the crime scene. I was simultaneously relieved and chagrined when I saw which homicide inspector had been assigned to Sebastian's murder. Carlos and I were on a first-name basis. Our visits were inevitably connected to death and mayhem—murder with a magical edge. Because there was more of that than one might expect in this beautiful City by the Bay.

The inspector was only a little taller than me, but the way he carried himself suggested he could inflict some serious damage were he so inclined. He wore his standard uniform of a thigh-length black leather jacket, starched white shirt, and khaki chinos and had already taken statements from Conrad and Lance Thornton, as well as from several other bystanders. No one, it seemed, had witnessed the shooting.

Carlos had saved me for last.

"Out with it now. And don't hold anything back."

"I met Sebastian Crowley—"

"The victim?"

My stomach churned. "Yes, the victim. I met him at his shop earlier in the day, and—"

"Time? Purpose of the meet?"

"Around ten this morning," I said. "And the purpose of the 'meet' was to buy clothes."

"Did you?"

"Yes, I bought a trunk of old clothes."

"I'll need to check it out."

I nodded. It wouldn't be the first time the SFPD had confiscated some of my inventory. "It's at the shop."

"Find anything out of the ordinary? A fortune in jewels and gold coins, anything like that? Motive for murder, maybe?"

"It's not a pirate's treasure. Just a bunch of old clothes, not worth anything, really. They're falling apart, scarcely fit for the rag pile."

"What about the trunk itself? Did you check the lining? Look for a false bottom?"

I shook my head. "The trunk's kind of old and smelly, mainly of value to an antiquarian. You're welcome to it." I'd happily surrender the trunk—for all I cared, the SFPD forensics team could tear it apart looking for hidden treasure. But even though Carlos was a friend and even though I realized it might be evidence or provide a motive of some sort . . . I decided not to mention the strange velvet cloak quite yet. That cape and I had a date to get to know each other better, just as soon as possible.

After all, Carlos had his skills, but I had mine. And anything associated with that particular garment, I feared, was more in my realm of expertise than his.

"Would you like me to call and ask Bronwyn and Maya to set the trunk aside?"

"I'd appreciate that."

He handed me his cell as a crime-scene tech walked up to ask a question. I quickly dialed Bronwyn.

"Aunt Cora's Closet," Bronwyn singsonged as she answered the phone. "It's not old. It's vintage!"

"Hi. It's me. Listen, a police officer will be swinging by the shop before too long to pick up the old trunk. Let him have it."

"Okay," Bronwyn said slowly.

"I'll explain later," I said. "Another thing: There's a

bundle of stinging nettles at the top of the stairs to my apartment. Do you know what I'm talking about?"

"Yes, of course," she said. "They keep your apartment locked down."

"Take those and distribute them around the shop's front and rear doors. And keep an eye out for anything, or anyone, unusual. Just be on guard."

"What happened?"

"It's probably nothing to do with us. But the man who sold me that trunk has been . . . killed."

"Lily . . ."

"I'm with the police right now. It probably . . . probably has nothing to do with us," I repeated. "I just want you to keep an eye out."

"All right. Anything else?"

I glanced at Carlos, standing just a few feet away, and lowered my voice. "When the officers get there . . . don't mention that other item I tried on earlier, okay?"

"Understood," Bronwyn said. "Will you be back soon, do you think?"

"I hope so," I said, and thanked her before hanging up. I walked over to the inspector and handed him his cell phone. "Carlos, what happened to Sebastian . . . it probably has nothing to do with that trunk, but—"

"Probably not. But I still need to look through it. Standard procedure."

"Of course, that's fine. What I was going to say is that if Sebastian was killed because of that trunk and someone tracked it to Aunt Cora's Closet . . ."

"That crossed my mind as well. I'll send a car by, have them keep an eye on the place. And you might want to do . . . whatever it is you do in these sorts of situations."

I nodded.

"So let's summarize," Carlos said. "You meet the victim, Sebastian Crowley, at ten this morning at his antiques store in Jackson Square, where you buy a trunk of worthless old clothes. You then return to your shop with the trunk and said worthless clothes, then decide to take a walk in Golden Gate Park, where you stumble across the antiques dealer's body at the base of a tree."

"Then I called the police."

Carlos pressed his lips together for a long moment while he studied me.

"Why'd you buy the trunk if you thought it was"—he glanced at his notes—"'kind of old and smelly'?"

"I'm not always a shrewd businesswoman."

He raised one eyebrow.

I shrugged. "Crowley was going to throw it out, and I ... I felt sorry for it."

"What, are you saying this trunk *talks* to you? You communicate with furniture now?"

"Of course not." The cape, on the other hand ... maybe. "But Sebastian said it came across the prairie with the pioneers, and ... I don't know, I couldn't bear to think of it sitting out on the curb waiting for garbage day. So I gave him sixty bucks for it. I thought maybe I'd find something inside, and Maya was going to see if a museum might want it. It's a tax write-off."

Carlos smiled. "Remind me to sell you the contents of the back of my closet sometime."

"Now, *that* would be interesting."

"And you came here to this tree, why? Because of the protestors?"

"Yes. My friend Conrad told me about trying to save the tree, so I thought I'd come take a look. It was that simple."

"It's hard to believe anything's simple where you're concerned, Lily. It's awfully coincidental that both you and Sebastian Crowley would end up here after meeting earlier in the day, don't you think?"

"Not in the cosmic sense. All sorts of strange things happen every day."

Carlos looked cosmically unconvinced.

I tried again. "Maybe . . . I don't know. Maybe Sebastian was a tree lover, and he heard about Ms. Quercus being condemned and came to take a look. Just like I did."

"Ms. Who?"

"The tree. Conrad calls it Ms. Quercus."

"May I ask why?"

"I think it has to do with the kind of tree it is—its Latin name, I guess?"

"I never would have pegged Conrad as an arborist. He know a lot of Latin?"

"I think he got it from a woman who came to assess the tree. Does it matter?"

"You know me. I'm a curious guy. So, tell me more about this Conrad fellow. I've seen him at your store. He tells me he's been sleeping here under this tree lately. What's his connection to the victim?"

"He doesn't have one, at least not that I'm aware of." There was a harsh glint in Carlos's dark eyes. Realization dawned. "I'm sure he's not involved in this, if that's what you're asking."

"How are you so sure?"

"Because . . . because it's *Conrad.*" I would no sooner accuse Conrad of shooting someone than I would myself.

"Unless I miss my guess, he lives on the street and he uses. Maybe he, or one of his friends, they get feeling jumpy, and they see a guy walking by, nicely dressed, demand his wallet, things get out of hand . . ."

"No," I said.

Carlos shrugged.

"Carlos, seriously: *no.* You should look at *me* as a suspect long before Conrad. He wouldn't hurt a fly—literally. I've seen him carefully shoo insects out of the store to escape Maya's wrath."

Our eyes held for a long moment. He blew a long, noisy breath through his nose.

"Why would Crowley have your business card in his pocket?"

"As I said, I gave it to him this morning. . . ."

"At his shop."

"Right."

He nodded and consulted his notebook, then went over my timeline once more. There were about three hours between the time I left Sebastian's shop and when Conrad found him. Three hours in which he came—or was brought—to Golden Gate Park and was shot under the outstretched arms of Ms. Quercus, condemned oak tree.

I felt as jumpy as spit on a hot skillet, but I tried to clamp down on my impatience as I watched Carlos ponder his notes. Among other things, I was itching to wash up and to cast a protection spell over Aunt Cora's Closet. Unless I missed my guess, that extraordinary garment might have something to do with all of this. It was too much of a coincidence to find Sebastian shot to death right after experiencing the strange visions from a cloak he had sold me earlier in the day.

I reached up to fiddle with my ponytail and realized with a sickening jolt that my hands were still stained with Sebastian's blood. As were Conrad's . . . Surely Carlos didn't truly suspect him. Did he?

"We'll keep an eye on Aunt Cora's Closet for the next couple of days," said Carlos. "Until we figure out the connection between you, the trunk, and the victim. If there is one. It could just have been a random attack. Patrol went by the victim's store and says the door was unlocked and the register had been emptied out. Place was such a mess it was hard to tell if anything else had been taken."

"But why would someone rob Sebastian at his shop, then bring him here just to . . . kill him?"

Carlos's dark eyes rested on mine for a long moment. "An excellent question."

Not that I was the best judge, but I didn't believe robbery had been the motive for Sebastian's murder. Not only would a robber not march Sebastian all the way out here, but he'd have to be pretty desperate to target Sebastian's Antiques in the first place. The Jackson Square neighborhood was full of high-end antiques stores, the kind that sold vast dining room tables for tens of thousands of dollars and petite pencil cups for several hundred. Why would a criminal rob the one shop on the lane that looked as though it had been abandoned for years? Especially if that criminal was hard-core enough to kill?

"Anything else you might be 'forgetting' to mention? Now's the time," Carlos said. Although the inspector and I were on good terms and had worked well together in the past, we'd also worked at cross-purposes on occasion. Carlos was a professional and held himself apart. We were alike that way.

I shook my head.

"How about the guy who helped you with Crowley?"

"Lance?"

"You know him?"

"No. We just met over . . . over Sebastian."

"Yet you're on a first-name basis?"

"We introduced ourselves."

"When was this?"

"While we were waiting for help to arrive. I was trying to calm him down, so I chatted with him. He looked a bit beside himself."

"Never met him before?"

I shook my head.

"You sure?"

"Of course I'm sure. I'm sure I would have remembered meeting him before. He's . . . a little unusual-looking."

"Was he alone?"

"He was with a couple of coworkers, um . . . Nina and Kai were their names." I tried to remember what they looked like, but all that came to mind were a couple of very pale visages in lab coats, the woman tall, the man in heavy glasses. "Lance told me they all work at the Cal Academy of Sciences. They were coming to check on the tree. Apparently, it's supposed to be cut down."

"A dying tree. A death tree."

Every once in a while Carlos broke out of restrained cop mode and got poetic. I found it a little bit charming and a whole lot disconcerting.

"Were they on the scene when you arrived?" he continued.

"Maybe, but I . . ." I paused and searched my memory. "There were a few people here before me, but I was focused on Sebastian. Now that I think about it, the killer could have been standing right there with a smoking gun and I wouldn't have noticed. I'm sorry. I guess I wouldn't make a very good cop. It was all a little . . . shocking."

"Huh."

"Is Lance a suspect?" I thought back to the stricken look on the man's face. I hadn't seen anything to suggest Lance and his colleagues were anything other than hapless passersby. And what was the likelihood a trio of scientists from the Cal Academy would be walking through the park armed and bent on murder? I hated to deal in stereotypes, but how often do scientists form street gangs?

Carlos shrugged. "You know my motto: Until I find the killer, my own *grandmother* is a suspect."

"I'd really like to meet this nefarious grandmother of

yours someday," I teased in a weak attempt to cut the tension. "She sounds like a fascinating woman. Maybe I could riffle through the contents of *her* closet."

Carlos gave me a tiny half smile and returned to the crime scene. I had been dismissed.

Chapter 4

I had hoped to see Conrad when I returned to the shop, but he wasn't in his customary spot on the curb. It wasn't unusual for him to disappear for hours, or even several days at a time; still, I wished I could speak with him further about what had happened. I had the sense that the police in general—Carlos in particular—weren't finished with him yet.

After explaining everything to Bronwyn and Maya, we closed the shop for the day. I locked up behind them and cast a special spell of protection over the store. Unfortunately, though my witchy charms were strong, they weren't foolproof. I couldn't lock down Aunt Cora's Closet completely because it was, after all, a retail establishment. If I cast too strong a spell no one but an equally powerful practitioner would be able to enter. That would wreak havoc with customers searching for 1950s cocktail dresses.

I knew that if someone wanted to get in badly enough, they could find a way. It had happened a few months ago, and I still felt vulnerable. It was not a nice feeling. But it was one I had to deal with.

After casting, I crossed the shop into the back room and climbed the stairs to my small apartment over the store.

"Mistress!" Oscar greeted me as I walked in the door. "Where have you *been*? I'm starving!"

My familiar was a gobgoyle—half goblin, half gargoyle—who appeared as a pig when in public. At home he was his natural scaly gray-green self. He had been given to me as a witch's familiar, but he wasn't an ordinary familiar. He wasn't my ambassador to the world beyond or the embodied extension of me and my powers. Instead he was just . . . Oscar.

At the moment said pseudo familiar was staggering about as if on the verge of fainting from hunger.

"I'm sorry I'm late, Oscar," I said. "Didn't you eat the snack I left for you?"

"You mean the *apple*? You call that a snack?"

"Apples are good for you."

Oscar made a very rude noise, but when I glared at him he grimaced, which was his gobgoyle version of a smile.

"It's your turn to make dinner, mistress. I would have cooked something, but you said you wanted to."

He's right, I thought guiltily as I headed for the kitchen. "I'll get right on it. How's roasted chicken sound?"

"With cheese and potatoes?"

"How about a salad?"

Oscar sighed.

"I'll let you grate the cheese for it," I said, and he sprang onto the kitchen counter.

I've never had a pet, so when Oscar first came to live with me, I forgot to feed him once or twice—what with running around town after suspicious spirits and all, it plumb escaped my mind. So I set about teaching my familiar how to cook a few things for himself, and though he was an enthusiastic chef, his specialties consisted ex-

clusively of some form of carbohydrates combined with
cheese: grilled cheese sandwiches, mac and cheese, potatoes au gratin, cheesy baked potatoes. In an effort to in-
ject a few vegetables into our bodies—Oscar claimed his
kind didn't need anything green and leafy, though I
wasn't buying it—I had called dibs on making dinner tonight.

So although I was anxious to learn more about the
velvet cape, I decided to put it off until after dinner. A
hungry gobgoyle was not a happy gobgoyle. Besides, after what Conrad and I had found in the park . . . well, a
little time to regroup would help calm and center me and
restore my energy.

I rubbed an organic free-range chicken with olive oil,
garlic, and fresh herbs from my terrace garden, then
popped it in my old Wedgewood oven. Afterward I
started pulling together the ingredients to make a Caesar salad—one of the few leafy dishes Oscar would eat,
as long as I put enough parmesan cheese on it. I handed
him a head of romaine, which he dutifully washed and
put in the salad spinner as I'd taught him; then he tore
the crunchy lettuce leaves and tossed them into a huge
hand-thrown blue ceramic salad bowl.

"How do you know how to make that dressing?" Oscar asked as I started mixing lemon juice, a raw egg, a
dash of Worcestershire sauce, and anchovies in a large
glass measuring cup.

"My grandmother taught me. She claimed that Caesar salad had been invented in Mexico. One of the north-
ern resort towns—Tijuana or Rosarito, if I remember
correctly."

"Is that true?"

"I have no idea," I admitted with a chuckle as I mea-
sured out a cup of green-gold extra-virgin olive oil. "Apparently, a *lot* of people claim to have invented Caesar
salad. Graciela also said Thomas Alva Edison was Mex-

ican—that's why his middle name is Alva. I think it's best not to fact-check one's grandmother."

Oscar smiled his ugly gobgoyle smile. "Oh, mistress, I forgot to tell you! I bought you a present."

"A present, for me? That's so sweet, Oscar. I'm . . . I'm so surprised. What's the special occasion?"

"It's my birthday."

"What?" I stopped chopping garlic and stared at him. It had never occurred to me that my familiar had a birthday. Though of course he did. He had a mother, after all. "It's your *birthday*, Oscar? Why didn't you tell me?"

"We don't do that."

"How old are you?"

"We don't talk about that."

"Okay, little guy, if you say so." I laughed and let it go. As someone with my own share of secrets, I like to respect others' privacy.

Oscar retrieved the present from his cubby over the fridge. It was wrapped in a surprisingly sleek way, in fuchsia-colored tissue paper with a raffia bow, sprigs of rosemary and rue crossed atop it. Really lovely.

"Thank you, Oscar. But if it's your birthday, shouldn't I be giving *you* a present?"

"You humans! I'll never figure all y'all out." Oscar had recently taken to mimicking my accent and was developing a pretty authentic Texas-style twang.

"Your kind don't get presents for their birthday?"

He waved his hand and cackled. "'Course not. We *give* presents on our birthday. Makes much more sense."

"Well, I surely do appreciate it. Thank you so much."

"Rip it open!" My familiar urged me on impatiently, but I opened the package with care. When I was growing up, my mother had insisted I open gifts painstakingly so she could reuse the wrapping, and it had been a struggle to restrain my enthusiasm to rip into the brightly colored paper. As an adult I found myself sympathizing with my mother. In her honor, I peeled back first one side of the paper, then the other, taking care not to tear the pretty tissue.

Inside was a manila envelope addressed to Oscar.

I paused and looked at my familiar, wondering what on earth it contained.

"Open it!" he repeated eagerly, his big glass-green eyes fixed on the present.

Peeking inside the envelope, I saw what looked like small squares of cloth. Patches to repair rents in my vintage clothing? I tipped them out onto the kitchen table.

"Labels?" I asked, examining them. One was marked "Valentino," another "Versace," another "Balmain." There were dozens. "Couture labels?"

Oscar nodded. "Aren't they awesome? Got 'em off the Internet, real cheap."

"But . . . I don't understand."

"You sew 'em into any old dress, and then people think they're *designer* dresses and pay you gobs of money for 'em. Guy sold 'em to me says an Estevez dress can go for six hundred and fifty dollars. Not sure who Estevez is, but apparently the man can make one heck of a dress."

"Oscar, this is very sweet of you, but . . . that's fraud."

"Come again?" He tossed the last of the torn romaine into the bowl. As was usually the case when Oscar and I cooked together, we had enough salad to feed an army, and there was half a head of lettuce littering the floor as well.

"Sewing false labels into dresses constitutes fraud."

"They're not false! They're real labels!"

"I mean, sewing a label into a dress where it doesn't belong. . . . That's a crime."

"But you could make a load of money."

"I can't make money by fooling people into thinking their dresses are something they aren't."

"Yes, you can."

"I meant to say I *won't*."

"I don't see the problem. Your customers'll think they've got a collector's item for a great deal, and you make buckets of cash. Everybody wins."

While I pondered how to explain this to my morally dubious familiar, I studied the labels more closely. As far as I could tell, they appeared to be genuine and had probably been removed from unwearable clothing or minor items such as scarves. I was no expert, but I'd learned a lot about vintage clothing since I'd been in the business. These labels belonged to garments that were well out of my league. Not only were originals hard to come by and extremely expensive, but they required a level of care I simply could not provide. I might see the occasional Chanel or Oscar de la Renta come through my doors, but nothing like a Madame Grès. That was museum-quality stuff.

"You don't like my present," Oscar grumbled.

"I love that you thought to give me a present, Oscar. It's just . . . it concerns me that it's possible to buy designer labels on the Internet. That could lead to some serious vintage clothing fraud. But thank you so much for thinking of me on your birthday. And happy birthday!"

He picked at his scaly claws, clearly offended.

"Wait a minute—you know what occurs to me?"

Oscar shrugged, still grumpy.

"It occurs to me that a birthday requires a birthday cake. How about it? Chocolate cake with coconut icing?" Oscar had been on a coconut kick ever since we had watched *Cast Away* during an impromptu Tom Hanks film festival with Maya and Bronwyn one night after closing.

I didn't have to ask twice. Like Bronwyn, my familiar couldn't hold a grudge. Not if there was food involved.

"Real coconut? Not from a package?" He leaped up to perch on the kitchen counter. It was a bad habit I'd

tried to break him of—like standing on the stove while
he cooked, apparently impervious to the heat—but needless to say, I'd failed in my attempts.

"Is there any other kind?"

"Oh, and, mistress? Another thing."

"Yes, Oscar?"

"Don't forget you're taking the GED on Saturday."

"I'll be there."

"It's just that you kept forgetting to register, remember? So I thought I should remind you."

"Thank you. I haven't forgotten." How could I? My
friends, and Oscar, were practically hounding me about
the subject. All because a fit of absentmindedness had
led me to miss the exam once. And I had forgotten to
register for the next one until it was almost too late.

They knew the truth: I didn't want to take it. I was
afraid of algebra.

Fortunately, I had no such fear of cooking. I brought
down my old battered tin canisters of organic flour and
cocoa from a high shelf and took out some whole milk in
the old-fashioned glass bottle and a couple of brown
eggs I'd bought at the farmers' market.

"Want me to drive you to the test?" Oscar asked.

"No." I mixed the dry ingredients, then combined
them in a large mixing bowl with the milk and eggs and
turned on the mixer, enjoying the old machine's familiar
cranking sound. "Wait. You know how to drive?"

"'Course I know how to drive! I just had a birthday.
I'm no kid." Oscar stuck one long bony finger into the
batter and brought a chocolate dollop to his mouth.

"But—"

Suddenly my heart sped up, I could hear pounding in
my ears, and I smelled roses. Not long ago, I might have
been afraid I was experiencing a seizure of some kind.
But I now knew the signs: a certain sexy, grumpy psychic
named Sailor must be nearby.

There was a smart rapping on the door of my apartment.

Last week, in a gesture of trust I could scarcely believe myself, I had given Sailor a key to Aunt Cora's Closet, as well as to my apartment above the store. Still and all, he always knocked. He was a gentleman that way.

I hurried to open the door, then stepped back, embarrassed by my own eagerness.

"Well, aren't you just a sight for sore eyes," Sailor growled, setting down his motorcycle helmet and taking me in his arms. He smelled of fresh laundry, leather jacket, and that indefinable scent that was just . . . Sailor. He had dark eyes and hair, was tall and lean but strong, and I was obsessed with a different body part every time I saw him. Lately it was his forearms. They were broad and capable and covered with dark hair.

We kissed for a long moment, the connection deepening until he pushed me gently up against the wall, leaned into me, and—

"Ahem," said Oscar from the kitchen, his arms folded over his scaly chest.

Oscar liked Sailor, even had a bit of hero worship for him, but he wasn't fond of what he called "PDA," or public displays of affection. The fact that we were in my apartment and not on a crowded street didn't matter. If Oscar could see something, he considered it "public."

"Ever hear the saying: Don't count your change in front of the poor?" Oscar groused.

"Sorry, little guy," I said with a smile. In fact, my familiar had stolen that saying from me.

Sailor shot him a dirty look. "Maybe it's time you moved out, found your own place."

Oscar's eyes grew so wide you could drown in their bottle-glass green depths.

"Mistress," he breathed. "Mistress, tell me you're not planning on making me—"

"Of course not," I said, hitting Sailor lightly on the shoulder. He just grinned. "You bully, don't be mean." I turned to my familiar. "Oscar, as long as I have a home, you have a home. And even if we didn't have a place to live, we'd be each other's home. We're family."

Oscar's bony shoulders sagged in relief, and he moped back into the kitchen to turn off the mixer, mumbling as he went, "Batter's prob'ly past ready."

"You can't say things like that to him," I scolded Sailor in a low voice. "He's sensitive."

"He's a gobgoyle."

"He's a *sensitive* gobgoyle. Now we'll have to spend the whole night making it up to him."

"Don't worry so much. As soon as I make him one of my famous grilled cheese sandwiches, all will be forgiven."

True. As much as Oscar liked me, he *adored* food.

"Speaking of food, something smells delicious." The aromas of rosemary, oregano, marjoram, and thyme wafted through the apartment, filling the air with the delectable scents of herb-encrusted roasting chicken.

"It'll be ready in half an hour. Join us for dinner?"

"Twist my arm," said Sailor as we headed toward the kitchen.

I had been deliberating on something since shortly after finding poor Sebastian. I had tried playing by the rules, but it hadn't gotten me very far. Given how often I seemed to land in the middle of homicide investigations, I was beginning to realize I should get comfortable playing by what Graciela used to call "witches' rules." We weren't out to hurt anybody, but sometimes we needed to color outside the lines. And it was all much easier with an accomplice.

"Super. And after dinner . . . I need a favor."

"Uh-oh. Why do I think this favor doesn't have anything to do with us rolling around in bed?"

I felt my cheeks burn. According to folklore, witches

can't blush. So either I wasn't one hundred percent witch, or the folklore was wrong, which was often the case. History and customs were easily muddled over time, given the very human tendency for exaggeration and misinterpretation.

"Let me pour you a drink."

"Now I'm really worried," he said, but he followed me into the kitchen and leaned against the tile counter while I poured a shot of amber tequila into a handblown shot glass.

"A man was found dead this afternoon . . ." I said, as I began to butter and flour the cake pans.

"You killed him?"

I gasped. *"What?"*

"You need help disposing of the body?" offered Oscar from his cubby over the refrigerator.

"My *stars*, why would you say something like that? What is *with* you two?"

Sailor shrugged. "I'm just saying, if you did kill somebody, you probably had cause. A demon of some sort?"

"No," I said. I glanced at Oscar, who was looking at me with interest but mimicking Sailor's shrug. These two seemed to have faith that if I had done such a thing, it was justified. Or else they just didn't care that much. Then again, Sailor and Oscar adhered to a different sort of moral code from a lot of folks. Perhaps that's why they hung around the likes of me. It was enough to make a witch worry.

"If it's not a dead body . . . does this have to do with the cape?" asked Oscar.

"Oscar, I thought we agreed we weren't going to mention that to people," I reminded him.

"Sailor's not people."

"Sailor's curious," Sailor said. "What cape?"

"Um . . . yes. So, earlier today I purchased an old trunk full of clothes from an antiques dealer named Sebastian

Crowley. And later in the day he was found dead under an oak tree in Golden Gate Park."

"I don't get why you bought worthless clothes from the likes of that guy," grumped Oscar, "stuff he prob'ly stole anyway, and then you don't like my present."

"Why do I have the feeling I missed something?" Sailor said.

"I do appreciate your present, I just can't use it," I said to Oscar, then turned to Sailor. "Oscar gave me a present today. A collection of designer clothing labels."

"That sounds . . . imaginative. Why labels?"

"Mistress can sew them into the clothes and ratchet up her prices! It's genius!" Oscar said.

"It's fraud," I insisted.

Sailor nodded thoughtfully. "Not a bad idea."

"What?" I said. "Are you saying you endorse an act of fraud?"

He grinned, as if to say "gotcha," and Oscar cackled.

I glared at the two of them. "As I was saying, before I was so rudely interrupted, a man died in Golden Gate Park today, not long after I bought a trunk from him."

"I hope we get to the good part soon," Sailor said in a dry tone that reminded me of how sardonic he'd been when I first met him . . . and how it used to put me off. No longer.

Oscar nodded in agreement.

"Y'all are awful—you know that?" I said. "A man *died* today. Think about his poor family."

"Didn't have no family," said Oscar.

"What? How do you know?"

"Sebastian Crowley, right? Didn't have family. No great loss to the world, just sayin'."

"You knew him?"

Oscar smiled, which always looked like a grimace. "You're kiddin' me, right?"

"Crowley was the go-to guy for a certain kind of antique, if you catch my drift," Sailor explained. "His business practices were . . . shady, to be kind. Why'd you buy a trunk from him? That's inviting trouble. Is it still here? Have you cast an extra protection spell?"

"The police took it this afternoon, in case it could tell them anything related to the murder." I stared back and forth between Sailor and my familiar. "So you're saying Sebastian was a practitioner of some kind? Why don't I know about this? I'll bet *Aidan* knows about this."

Aidan Rhodes was the local witchy godfather of sorts, a powerful practitioner who knew everyone and everything magical in the Bay Area. He had also been Oscar's master until gifting the critter to me. Aidan and I had worked together in the past, but I trusted him about as far as I could throw him. Aidan always had something up his enchanted sleeve. Still, to be fair, he had probably saved my life on more than one occasion.

"You're on a, whaddayacallit? A need-to-know basis. Like in the top-secret military. Like James Bond. *Dun de de DUN de de duh . . .*" Oscar started humming the theme from the James Bond franchise, and I feared an 007 marathon was in my immediate future.

My familiar had been catching up on popular culture lately, giving me the distinct impression I wasn't keeping him busy enough. When he wasn't hanging out in Aunt Cora's Closet, trying to spy on women in the changing room or being petted by the customers and cradled by Bronwyn, he spent a lot of time watching DVDs or reading mysteries and eating bonbons at home. Not that he complained; it was a tough job, Oscar was fond of saying, but *somebody* had to do it. Still . . . as my mother used to say: "Idle hands are the devil's workshop."

Of course, in my case she had meant it quite literally.

"Anyway, maybe Sebastian Crowley wasn't a great guy, but murder is wrong, no matter who the victim is," I said. "Besides, among other things, it means there's a murderer out on the streets running loose."

"You know what I'm really not enjoying about this conversation?" said Sailor. "Other than the obvious, which I've already mentioned. What I'm not enjoying is that your next observation will be that *you*, somehow, are the one who will have to track down this murderer."

"There's more," I said.

"Imagine my shock," Sailor said. "The cape, I presume."

"The cape," Oscar echoed.

"The cape was in the trunk. When I put it on . . . It's hard to explain, but it was as though I had been transported to another time and place. Not a particularly welcoming time and place."

"Where is this cape?" Sailor asked. "Let me see if I can sense anything from it."

I brought the basket to Sailor, took off the black silk cloth, and set it before him.

He pressed his lips together, his eyes half-closed, in an expression of displeasure I knew only too well. Since we'd gotten together, I saw it less frequently—in fact, he even laughed from time to time. But now I saw the old Sailor, the supremely dissatisfied, scornful man for whom I had fallen head over heels.

Sailor said nothing, but took the gold velvet garment out of the basket and held it to his chest. His eyelids fluttered closed and he breathed deeply, then stood stock-still. Oscar and I watched and waited in silence.

Finally, he let the cloak fall into the basket and shook his head.

"Nothing?" I asked.

"No. But that's not unusual for me with textiles. And . . . as you know, lately things just haven't been the same."

When I first met Sailor, he was a powerful psychic.
Unhappy, grumpy as all get-out, but extremely sensitive
to vibrations and even able to communicate to the world
beyond the veil. But ever since he'd had a falling-out
with Aidan, his old "boss," things had changed. He was
still intuitive, but something was blocking his psychic
abilities. Either that, or Aidan's patronage had given
Sailor an extra boost that evaporated when they split. It
was unclear what was going on, but it was plain to see
that Sailor was frustrated—even embarrassed—by it.
After years of not wanting his psychic abilities, he had
realized they were an important part of him.

Sailor and Oscar shared a look; then Sailor let out a
loud breath.

"Okay, you see a vision of something nasty when you
put on this cape. So maybe it once belonged to someone
in a violent or threatening situation. That could leave an
energy trace—perhaps enough of a mark that someone
like you can feel it. Big deal. You often get sensations
from clothing, don't you? I mean, that's the whole thing
with Aunt Cora's Closet."

"Yes, but this is different. It isn't just sensations or
vibrations; when I put the cloak on, I felt transported
somewhere, somewhere from the past. So finding Sebastian Crowley dead at the base of an oak tree right afterward, well, that seems like quite a coincidence. Maybe
someone was after this cloak? And on top of everything
else, the police seemed suspicious of Conrad."

"Conrad? He wouldn't hurt a fly."

"That's what *I* said. But he was the first on the scene,
with blood on his hands. And he told the police that he
always slept there, and . . . I haven't seen him the rest of
the afternoon. I'm afraid they've been interviewing him."

Our eyes caught and held for a moment.

"So let me guess," said Sailor with an exasperated sigh.

"Now you want to track down the source of this cape and try to figure out its connection with the oak tree."

"And here I thought you couldn't read my mind," I said, trying my best to be coquettish.

Sailor poured himself another shot of tequila and raised it in salute to Oscar. "One thing I can say for your mistress, Oscar. She's as mad as a hatter."

"Ain't she just?" said my familiar, pride in his voice.

Chapter 5

"One of these days you're going to have to explain how I go from looking for a drink and a kiss at your place, to breaking into an antiques store," Sailor whispered as he used a slim bit of metal to defeat the ancient lock on Sebastian Crowley's shop. "Especially one that's still a crime scene."

"Well, for one thing, you were looking for more than a kiss. I can tell you that much."

He grunted softly and tilted his head closer to the locking mechanism, as though he was listening for something. Latex gloves covered his long, graceful fingers.

The narrow alley at Balance and Gold Streets was illuminated only by the milky glow of a streetlamp. After a warm day, thick fog had settled like a blanket over the city, giving the air a damp, heavy feel. A dripping sound overhead echoed in the silence, and though I knew it was my imagination, I could have sworn the old brick buildings on either side were leaning in toward us.

"This might not be the best time for this discussion," Sailor continued, "but I'm worried about the direction our relationship is taking. Seems to me I find myself helping you commit felonies—especially of the breaking-and-entering variety—more often than I'd like."

"Hey, I cooked you dinner. Doesn't that count for something? And I'm a witch, not a spirit. I can't walk through walls. So when it comes to breaking in, I have to rely on entirely normal, everyday methods. . . ."

"Like talking your boyfriend into helping you."

"Right." I felt a little thrill run through me at his use of that word. "Um . . . You're my boyfriend?"

"I certainly hope so. Otherwise I'd be hard-pressed to explain what I'm doing here."

I leaned down and gave him a quick kiss on his forehead, feeling like a lady rewarding her knight.

"Trying to distract me?"

I laughed softly. "I really do appreciate this, Sailor. If not for you, it would just be me and my Hand of Glory here in the alley in the middle of the night. Even *I* would find that scenario a little creepy."

"At some point we should talk about how you run around town with no thought to your own safety. You—"

He stopped speaking as the locking mechanism clicked, and he pushed the door open. With a triumphant bow, he gestured that I should go on in.

The shop was musty and crowded, just as it had been when I was here earlier in the day. But now there were signs of a struggle: shards of glass and ceramics littered the floor, a grandfather clock had been knocked on its side, and a stained-glass lampshade was split into several colorful pieces. The register sat open, empty of any paper money. It had all the markings of a simple robbery gone bad . . . except for the fact that Crowley had been killed under an oak tree clear across town in Golden Gate Park.

"What are we looking for?" Sailor asked in a low voice. He remained near the front of the store, keeping an eye out for passersby through the plate-glass display window.

"Anything, really . . . Something that might give us a clue as to what's going on. Also, I want to see if I can unearth the name and address of whoever sold him that trunk. Sebastian mentioned it was a woman—"

"That narrows it down."

I ignored him. "She was the niece of an old man and sold him a number of other items from the man's estate. You and Oscar mentioned that Sebastian kept careful records."

"Records of who owed what, mostly." Sailor raised his eyebrows and cast a glance around the disorganized store. "This guy mostly laundered money for criminals. I'm not sure he ever actually *sold* anything."

"He sold something to me."

"Other than a worthless trunk full of worthless clothes and one possibly disastrous cape to you. Ever occur to you that this was no accident of retail?"

I bit my lip as I riffled, as carefully as I could, through the papers atop Sebastian's crowded desk. It was such a mess I couldn't imagine my search would disturb much of anything. There were stacks of unpaid bills and articles ripped out of newspapers, receipts, catalogs, and advertising circulars. Nothing that seemed significant. In the drawers were old index cards, a mélange of dried-up pens and stubby pencils, and a half-empty plastic bottle of Old Crow bourbon.

Frustrated, I sat back in the desk chair and blew out a loud breath. Where would someone like Sebastian have kept a telltale ledger? Probably not here at his desk, which would be the first place a person would look. His shop was such a jumble, it could be anywhere.

Like most antiques stores, Sebastian's was jammed with bureaus, standing lamps, old oil paintings and baroque frames, and hundreds of decorative tchotchkes. There was a sculpture of the goddess Diana, a couple of marble pillars topped with busts, and a pair of stone wings that looked like they had fallen off a statue. Any of a hundred drawers could be hiding a ledger, unless . . . On the other side of the shop, I noticed several leather-bound books atop a walnut rolltop desk sitting up against the side wall.

Could the ledger be hiding in plain sight?

I crossed the shop and took the books down one by one: a volume of poems by Robert Louis Stevenson, *L'Étranger* in the original French by Albert Camus, Dickens's *A Tale of Two Cities,* and a few other novels I wasn't familiar with. And among them, one unmarked leather-bound ledger, full of long columns, like an old-fashioned accountant's book.

Full of handwritten names and dollar figures and a series of symbols I didn't recognize.

Sailor was looking over my shoulder, his face angry. "Worse than I thought. I knew this guy was bad news, but this . . . ?"

"What is it, exactly?"

"It's a score book. He was keeping track of magical folk, what they owed. Not only in dollars, if you know what I mean."

"For whom?"

"Can't say for sure. But if I were a betting man, my money would be on your buddy Aidan."

My heart sank. I was never sure what to think of Aidan. Part of me was grateful to him for what he'd done for me—and my father—but I knew he used his magic to manipulate others and gain power. That was not only ethically questionable; it was dangerous in a man as magically powerful as he.

"So you think the trunk was part of a payment of some sort?"

"Maybe."

"Then why sell it to me for sixty bucks?"

"You paid *sixty bucks* for an old trunk full of worthless clothes? Remind me to show you some andirons I've been hauling around."

I smiled. "Carlos said the same thing."

"First Aidan, now Carlos. I've said it before and I'll say it again: You have terrible taste in men."

"Don't I, though?"

"Do I have to tell you what I think about you palling around with a homicide inspector?"

"If you'd give him a chance, I think you'd see he's a really good guy."

"*He's* the one who won't give *me* a chance," said Sailor. "And one of these days—mark my words—he's going to catch you at something. Whether he likes you or not, you know as well as I do that he won't hold off on applying the law just for you."

"Anyway, going back to what we were talking about . . . I bought the trunk because I felt something powerful within it. Vibrations that ran through me as soon as the lid opened."

"The cloak?"

I nodded. "Also . . . I don't know, I sort of felt bad for Sebastian. He didn't seem like he did much business here."

Sailor let out a bark of a laugh. "You are something else; you know that? Let's get out of here. Take the book, and we'll look through it more carefully at your place."

"I think this latest sale, from Bartholomew Woolsey, might be the man we're looking for," I said as my index finger lay on the top line. "See; it indicates he bought a trunk for twenty dollars, right here."

"Okay."

"Let's go find Mr. Woolsey."

"No."

"What do you mean, *no*? You're my partner in crime, remember?"

"Yes, 'partner.' I know that only too well." He checked

his watch. "But it's after eleven. If this mystery man is some kind of magical predator, you'll need to go in prepared. If he's just some schmuck who found himself with a trunk of worthless old clothes and a magical cape that he didn't recognize, then you'll wake him up and scare the hell out of him."

"Then what do you suggest?"

"Crowley told you the old man—"

"Woolsey."

"Okay, Woolsey, presuming you're correct about the records. Crowley told you Woolsey needed money, right? Contact him tomorrow morning. Pretend you're in the market for junk, and say you heard he's got stuff for sale. Act like a pushy vintage dealer. You know," he said with a shrug. "Just be yourself."

"Not a bad idea."

"Thank you. You know what else isn't a bad idea? Bed."

I meant to study the ledger when I got back home, but Sailor distracted me. I woke early and started to pore over it with my morning coffee, but then Sailor woke up and distracted me some more.

Hell's bells, having a sexy man in her bed wreaks havoc on a witch's concentration.

But as soon as the hour was decent, I called the phone number listed beside Bartholomew Woolsey's name. Among other things, I wanted to talk to him before the police did. If this had anything to do with Sebastian's death, I would have to share the information with the police.

A young woman answered, then passed the phone to her uncle. Bartholomew Woolsey sounded elderly and genial but a bit vague, and I sure didn't pick up on any kind of "magical predator" vibe, as Sailor had put it. Still, my powers of perception are compromised over phone lines.

I could hear the young woman coaching her uncle to

say "yes" to my offer to buy some clothes. They bickered. Finally, she took the phone back.

"I'm Bart's niece, Hannah," she said. I wondered whether this was the "sweet young thing" Sebastian was sure had taken advantage of him. "Yes, definitely you should come by. Bart's got a whole closetful of old clothes you could look through. How about eleven o'clock?"

"That's perfect, thanks."

At nine thirty I went downstairs and prepared to open Aunt Cora's Closet as I always do: by sprinkling saltwater widdershins, or counterclockwise, then smudging with a sage bundle doesil, or clockwise. I said an extra chant of cleansing, just in case the trunk—or the cape—had left behind any trace of bad juju. Then I lit a white candle on the glass counter by the register, flipped the sign to OPEN, and was pleased to see that Conrad was already sitting on the curb outside the store.

I asked him to wait, then ran upstairs to make a fried egg sandwich, wrapped it in a paper towel, poured a glass of orange juice, and joined him on the curb while he ate.

"How are you doing?" I asked.

"Dude," he answered.

"Did the police, um . . . did they keep you overnight?"

He nodded and dug into the sandwich.

"I'm so sorry," I said. "But they released you, so they must be satisfied?"

He shrugged, then spoke with his mouth full. "Didn't sleep at all last night. Can't even sleep at the tree anymore; cops have it cordoned off. Wouldn't want to anyway, after . . . I can't believe what happened to that poor dude."

I nodded. *Dude.*

"Conrad, did the police say anything about you being a suspect?"

He shrugged and continued eating. I feared if I

wanted more information, I was going to have to get it from the source: Inspector Romero.

Bronwyn arrived just before ten, accompanied by her friend Duke, a retired fisherman. I was glad to see him; not only did he make Bronwyn glow more than I'd ever seen her—and she'd been happy *before*—but I'd also noticed that having a man in the store, especially one of a certain age, seemed to encourage other males to enter what was more typically seen to be the haven of young women. Besides . . . given what had happened, the more people around, the better.

At ten thirty I told Bronwyn I was headed out for an appointment, which she took in stride. I was spending less time than ever at the shop, which didn't make me particularly happy, though I did enjoy the search. The hunt for really cool clothes never stopped. If it wasn't estate sales and auctions, it was garage sales and thrift stores, or soliciting older folks in their homes and helping them to clean out their attics, basements, and closets.

I hoped today's visit with Bartholomew Woolsey was as simple as my typical visit to an elderly man with a closet full of old clothes. Probably, he had no idea he had been in possession of a cape with such . . . interesting vibrations.

Probably.

In case I was wrong, I prepared several amulets and packed up the ingredients for protection spells. I carried a jar of brew in my satchel with which I could hastily draw a magical circle, if needed. Just in case Bartholomew Woolsey was *not* just a hapless guy unaware of the contents of his historic trunk.

Maya came along to help with the clothes; she had a way with seniors, and made a point of collecting their stories and writing down their oral histories. I tried to talk Sailor out of accompanying us, but there was no way he was going to stay behind. I decided that on the off chance that Woolsey really was bad news, it would be helpful to have Sailor along so I was sure I wasn't putting Maya in danger.

Woolsey's address was an apartment in a surprisingly graceful historic building on Broadway in Pacific Heights. A doorman let us in, called ahead, then ushered us into the elevator and pushed the button for the fourth floor.

As we *wooshed* up, Maya looked at me, eyebrows raised. "I thought you said he was desperate for cash."

"That's what I was told. Who knows? Maybe he's . . ." I shrugged. "Maybe he owns his apartment but can't make the condo fees?"

The hallway to Woolsey's apartment featured crown molding, muted taupe carpet, and what appeared to be original, handblown amber sconces. It smelled like scented candles and cleanliness. It was hard to believe anyone who lived here was selling off possessions for cash.

A woman about my age answered our knock on the door. She was attractive, tall and strong-looking, wearing athletic clothes: orange Lycra shorts and a bright blue stretch tank. Could this be the woman Sebastian had referred to as a "pretty little thing"?

"You must be from the thrift store," she said upon opening the door, her blue eyes puzzled as they raked over our trio. I doubted we were what she expected of a thrift store crew.

"Yes, I'm Lily, and this is Maya and Sailor. Thank you for having us."

"I'm Hannah; I think we talked on the phone. I'm helping my uncle Bart get cleaned up in here. He's been a little . . . challenged."

She opened the door wider and invited us into a warren of pathways through stacks of newspapers, books, and plastic bags like giant balloons. Collectibles and antiques were gathered in organized groupings: ceramic figures, silver pieces, painted plaques. I thought Sebastian Crowley's antiques store looked like a hoarder's lair, but Bartholomew Woolsey's place was even worse. At least it assured me that I was not, in fact, a hoarder myself.

"Ignore the mess," Hannah continued. "It's a work in progress."

It wasn't as closed-in smelling as Sebastian's shop had been, but I noted the distinctive musty smell of old books. I saw the reason why as I turned the corner: a dining room table sat amid — and under — stacks and stacks of old books.

Huddled with their heads together over a book- and paper-strewn table were two men: one white haired and elderly, the other boyish and scholarly looking, complete with an argyle sweater-vest and wire-rimmed glasses.

Both looked up as we entered.

"Uncle Bart, these are the people from the thrift store."

"Oh ..." He glanced down at the watch on his wrist. "Already?"

"It's eleven o'clock, Bart," Hannah said. "Remember? I told you they were coming."

"Hello, Mr. Woolsey. It's nice to meet you. I'm Lily Ivory. We spoke on the phone earlier. . . ."

"Yes, yes," he said. His hair stuck out here and there on his balding head, and his eyebrows were bushy. Tall and apparently once quite strong, Bart had kindly, crinkly blue eyes behind aviator lenses that looked out of place — if not for the modern eyewear, he might have been the kindly shoemaker in a fairy tale, complete with an open vest over his striped shirt. "I remember. I don't get a lot of visitors. Except for Williston, of course. Williston's a professor over at . . . where was it?"

"UC Berkeley," said the young man as he stood and

shook our hands. "But please, call me Will. No need to be as formal as Bart. Nice to meet you."

Darn. I had hoped to speak with Bart Woolsey alone to see what information I could glean from him about the trunk.

The good news was he didn't seem dangerous. The bad news was I doubted this visit would be particularly fruitful, murder-solving-wise. Then again, you never knew. As they say back in Texas, every fish ever caught had its mouth open.

"Did you want to see the clothes?" Hannah urged from the hallway.

"Yes, thank you," I said. "Maya and Sailor would love to check them out. I actually . . . I was hoping to speak with your uncle for just a moment."

Smooth, Lily, real smooth. Fortunately, Hannah didn't appear to care very much what I did. "Okaaaay." She dragged out the word as she led the way out of the room. Maya followed. Sailor cast me a long look before joining her.

"Hannah, don't . . . don't throw away anything until you ask me," Bart called out after his niece, craning his neck to watch her walk down the hall.

A muffled, "whatever" floated back from the direction of the hallway.

"She wants to get rid of all my things," Bart said, his voice anxious.

"I think she's just trying to help you sort through all your . . . um . . . everything," I finished lamely.

"I agreed to sell some of the old clothes that don't fit anymore, but there's a lot of other stuff I don't want to . . . I'll be right back," he said as he rose and hurried out of the room.

I was left with the young professor.

He smiled and shook his head. "Poor old guy. He's a sweetheart, but he does have a bit of a problem."

"You mean the ... uh ..."

"The hoarding. I mean, whether or not he's really a pathological hoarder is hard to say. It's not like there's a lot of filth, or neglected animals or anything. Just lots and lots of ... stuff."

I nodded. There were framed pictures covering almost every inch of wall space, stacks of newspapers and manila folders and notepads. Besides the books, knickknacks filled the tops of mismatched side tables and bookshelves. Not exactly a Zen aesthetic, but as a collector myself, I understood the impulses that led to such a state.

"I know Hannah's trying to help, but I fear it's making things worse," Will continued. "Hoarders need to be part of getting rid of their things; otherwise they can end up feeling alienated and out of control."

"You teach psychology?"

He laughed. "No, I'm a professor of religious studies, actually. I was just spewing a little pop psychology I learned from too much late-night television. I don't actually know anything. Feel free to ignore me—my students always do."

I returned his smile. "So you're working with Bart? As a ... professor of religious studies?"

"Seems odd, right? But I'm part historian, part anthropologist. . . . My specialty is the lives of early settlers in religious communities in the United States."

"Like the pilgrims?"

"Yes, the pilgrims, Puritans, Shakers, Mennonites, Amish. Among others. Bart has an impressive lineage; his family's been in the United States for generations. And he's got tons of paperwork, far more than you normally find passed down through families. You don't come across this sort of thing very often among Americans, especially not here in California."

A million questions sprang to mind, but I didn't get

the chance to ask a single one. Bart walked back into the room.

"I love my niece," Bart said, clearly agitated, "but she's bossy. Don't you agree that she's bossy?"

I didn't know what to say to that one. Luckily for me, Bart didn't wait for a response.

"The other day she sold a bunch of stuff to an antiques shop. Right out of the blue. I didn't say she could." Bart looked at me, his rheumy blue eyes questioning. "Do you think that's right? I've still got my mind, no matter what she might think. Last night I actually slept through the night, first time in years, and now I feel sharp as a tack."

"She means well, Bart," said Will. "Remember, you agreed that I would help you go through your papers and books, and she's helping with the clothing and household items."

"I guess so," said the older man as he returned to his seat at the table. "What are you two talking about?"

"I was just telling Lily about my research and how you're sharing your family history with me."

"You believe that?" said Bart. "Man's being paid by the taxpayers to study something like this. Why anyone would be interested in my genealogy besides my family, I'll never know. In fact, the family doesn't seem to care. . . . Hannah's more interested in cleaning out my closets than learning about her ancestors."

"I should get out of your hair," Will said, gathering up a stack of papers and a couple of books. "And let you two have a visit. Nice to meet you, Lily."

"Same here."

Bart saw Will to the door. It was easier to speak about yesterday's events without a witness; worried we'd be interrupted soon, I started in as soon as Bart came back to the table.

"Speaking of the things Hannah has sold," I began. "I

wanted to ask you a few questions about a trunk that she brought to Sebastian Crowley's shop."

"Do you have it?" he said, sitting up straighter. "My niece sold it by accident. I'd like it back. I tried calling Sebastian, but he never picked up."

"I, uh ..." The vision of Sebastian under the tree washed over me. Should I tell Bart Woolsey about Sebastian Crowley's death? Was it my place? I couldn't believe I didn't think of this beforehand. What should I say to the man? "No, I'm sorry. Actually, the police have the trunk."

"The police? Why?"

"They thought it might be connected to a crime. I ... Mr. Woolsey, I — "

"Please, call me Bart."

"Bart, did you know Sebastian Crowley?"

"A little. I've known him for years, through a cousin who buys and sells antiques. Not like we get together to play pinochle or anything. Why?"

"I'm sorry to be the one to tell you this, but he was found in Golden Gate Park yesterday. He had been attacked."

"Attacked? Is he all right?"

"No, I'm sorry, he's not. He was killed."

Chapter 6

"Oh. Oh my. Poor guy." Bart looked down at a stack of papers he held in shaky hands. "Though . . . Sebastian really was a bit of a character. I imagine he's made some enemies through the years. Have the police talked with his clients?"

"Clients?" I asked, wondering whether Bart might know something about Sebastian's occult activities, the ones to which Sailor and Oscar had alluded.

"He always bragged about buying things cheap, claiming they were worthless and then turning around and selling them for a fortune. There was one time . . . what was it? Something about telling the owner of priceless Limoges ceramics that they were cheap knockoffs. Then he made a bundle off the deal he finally brokered. Dangerous stuff. Trust an old man when I tell you: Greed can drive people to extremes."

I nodded. Maybe it was as simple as that, I thought. Maybe Sebastian had dealt on the wrong side of things one too many times and had made a dangerous enemy — the kind who packed a gun. This might be liberal California, but it still didn't seem all that difficult to obtain a firearm. Even if you didn't actually intend to *kill* someone, in a moment of rage, what could be easier than pulling a trigger?

The one thing that still made no sense, however, was that Sebastian was found under a tree across town from his ransacked shop.

When it didn't seem as though Bart was going to volunteer any further information, I added, "Could I ask you where the trunk came from?"

"That trunk ... Well, now, let me see...." He nodded and continued with sorting through a stack of papers. His attention seemed to wander. I wondered precisely how long this cleanup process was going to take—and how long it had already gone on. "Seems to me that trunk came on the overland route, with relatives coming here from Massachusetts to settle in California."

"What year was that?"

"The caravans, had to be during the 1850s. I believe it was my great-grandfather on my father's side.... His name was Woolsey as well. Very old name."

I was almost certain the visions I had took place much earlier than the 1850s. I wondered how the cape was connected—if it was at all.

"Wasn't gold discovered in forty-nine? So, your relatives came to California during the Gold Rush?"

"Yes, that's what I was told. But according to family lore, some of the items in that chest had been in the Woolsey family for decades, maybe centuries. I'm the last of the name. Can you believe that? Never had any children. Luckily, all the latest generation are girls. That's good. They won't carry the name."

"You don't want the name to continue?"

"No male descendant in the Woolsey clan will ever be able to find true happiness in love."

"Oh ... really?" I said lamely. I was unaccustomed to old men talking about finding love; it was a conversational gambit I associated with teenage girls more than men Bart's age.

"No happiness in love? Why is that?"

Just then Hannah came into the room and rolled her eyes. "Not going on about that again, are you, Uncle Bart? Listen, I'm going to put the kettle on for tea. Lily, would you like tea or coffee?"

"I'd love a cup of whatever's easy," I said.

"Maya and Sailor are looking through a pile of things on the bed," said Hannah. "I just culled them from his closet. Bart doesn't have much occasion to wear tuxes these days, do you, Uncle Bart?"

Bart seemed distracted, as though he was only registering a fraction of what we were talking about. He and Hannah might drive each other crazy, but I was glad Bart had family; in my line of business I met a lot of older people who didn't seem to have anyone at all. It was a constant worry to think of them alone in this world, especially when their mental faculties began to slow and confusion set in. When they started goin' 'round the bend, as we used to say back home.

Hannah disappeared into the galley kitchen. Bart seemed intent on his search through the documents, as though newly on task. I started inspecting the spines of the books piled on every horizontal surface: Right in front of us was a stack focusing on early US history, including several volumes on the Salem witch trials.

My eyes landed on a gold-edged, slim volume of *The Crucible*.

I had read the play in one of my last high school classes, before I was forced to drop out and flee my small hometown of Jarod, in West Texas. I remembered sitting in English class, trying to become part of my chair, not moving, in hopes that my classmates wouldn't connect the story with me. But it didn't take much. After all, my peers had been calling me *witch* since I was eight years old. They snickered and turned in their chairs, then continued to torment me in the halls, pointing their fingers in accusation and malice. I tried explaining to them that they were proving Arthur Miller's point: that the witch hunts were an unfair hysteria that led to terrible injustices. Unfortunately, that argument was far too rational for their closed minds.

I looked up to find Mr. Woolsey staring at me. "You know that story, of course."

"Yes, I remember it well."

"It's a dramatization, but it's based on true history. If you don't believe me, just ask the professor. Where . . . where'd he go?"

"He had to leave, but he said he'll see you again soon."

"Oh, yes. That's right. I don't think he liked . . ." His voice dropped to a whisper, and his eyes slewed over to the swinging door that separated the kitchen. "A lot of people don't like me to talk about the curse."

"The curse?"

"I have suffered under a curse all my life. Many generations ago, my ancestors were among the Puritan settlers in what would become Massachusetts. I presume you've heard of the Salem witch trials?"

I nodded and hoped I looked outwardly calm, though my heart skipped a beat. When you're a witch, these things were not just fascinating yet gruesome historical tales. They were examples of the persecution and violence that powers like mine, and those of my ancestors, have inspired in those around us. Their memories ran in my blood.

"Salem wasn't the only place that sort of thing occurred, I'm sorry to say. The people in my family's settlement, they believed in witches, too. After all, *'Suffer ye not a witch to live.'* If you believe in heaven and hell, and God and the devil, you must therefore believe in witches."

"But Saint Augustine argued that while witches might be guilty of idolatry, the belief in their powers was tantamount to heresy. In short, he argued that anyone who feared witches didn't have enough faith."

He barked out a rusty laugh. "Very good. Very good. But I think it's safe to say my family didn't listen to Saint Augustine, even if they'd known about what he'd said, which I'm sure they didn't. It was a different world back then. They didn't exactly sit around with religious scholars debating the meaning of the Bible. Small-mindedness was the way of it; most people were raised to believe what they believed, and if anyone challenged those thoughts, they were cast out."

"Or killed."

"Yes, or even killed."

"And . . ." I paused, wanting to choose my words carefully so I wasn't leading him to say anything. "Was the trunk from that time period in your family's history?"

"The trunk's old, not sure exactly how old. But the clothes, yes, I think there were one or two items in there that might have been much older. And there was my family Bible, of course, but I kept that."

He held my eyes, as though expecting me to interrupt or disclaim what he was saying, perhaps to decry it. But I knew my history in this regard.

"And, back from that time, ever since then," continued Bart, "there's been a family curse that no male descendant will ever find true love."

I tried to keep my expression neutral, but I doubted I'd succeeded.

"I know it sounds silly. But this is our fate."

"And yet you're here to tell the tale," I said. "So there must have been some affection in your family line."

"Procreation is not the same thing as true love; surely you know that. In fact, marriage and partnership without love, isn't that the most painful thing of all? Never to know the solace and comfort of someone who cares more for your own welfare than their own? Someone who thinks of you first, who believes the sun rises and sets on your head?"

Now I was reading the titles of the books stacked on the table in an attempt to distract myself from this line of thought. I didn't want to think too much about love and all it entailed. It was too frightening, making me wonder—not for the first time—whether Sailor and I had something real, or if I was fooling myself. Could a misfit like me ever find true love?

With effort, I wrested my thoughts away from Sailor and focused on what Bart was confiding in me. Truth was, I didn't know a lot about ancient curses, and part of me doubted their existence. Not that I didn't think there were witches powerful enough to cast through the ages, because I knew different. Though we witches are mere mortals, our power comes from our connection to our ancestors, to the living streams of power that pass through the veils of time and space.

No, what I really doubted were modern humans who understood enough of their own past—and that of their family—to understand what the curse was, who had cast it, and why. In the old days, such tales were handed down from generation to generation, the family history recounted and retold over and over through the ages, so people felt a rock-solid connection to the generations that had gone before. But today? In modern-day San Francisco? Children no longer sat at the knees of their grandparents, hanging on every word of their family lore; instead, most were able to recite the detailed features of whatever video game they were playing. As the professor had noted, it was rare to find an intact family history in these parts.

Since few people knew much beyond their grandparents' names, the knowledge of ancient curses seemed almost inconceivable.

"So how might a person go about breaking this curse?" I asked.

Bart let out a hoarse bark of laughter. "If only I knew! I have spent all the adult years of my life in the pursuit of just such magic. Recently, I . . ."

"Uncle Bart," said Hannah as she walked into the room with a tray holding a gleaming silver tea set that looked to be antique. The only piece that didn't match was a little porcelain sugar bowl. "Enough with all that. Remember, we talked about this. People don't want to hear old folktales about such things."

"The professor does. The taxpayers pay him for this sort of thing. You believe that?"

"Oh, darn it, I forgot the cream," said Hannah, as Sailor and Maya joined us at the dining room table. "Could you go check the fridge to see if you have any, Uncle Bart?"

Bart heaved himself up from his chair and shuffled off toward the kitchen. Sailor hurried to clear a space at the table for Hannah to put down the tray. When the door swung closed behind her uncle, Hannah spoke in a low voice.

"I swear, like it's not bad enough that he spent every dime he has looking to cure this 'curse.' Half the family won't even talk to him anymore, or want to institutionalize him. But the thing is, he's a sweetheart, as you can see. Just . . . deluded."

"So you don't believe in ancient curses?" I asked.

She rolled her eyes again and started pouring tea from the silver pot into delicate, eggshell-thin china cups. "I think if he'd lived like a normal person, he would have had no trouble finding love. He was born into a wealthy family, and he wasn't a bad-looking guy. And he's a decent fellow, very sweet, in fact."

"Was your father a Woolsey too?"

"You mean, was *he* able to find true love?" She laughed

softly and handed me a teacup. "I don't believe in speaking ill of the dead, but my father wasn't nearly as sweet as my uncle. He had other priorities. Anyway, love isn't some concept out of the blue; it's something you work at with communication and determination." She handed Maya a cup of fragrant Darjeeling. "Right?"

Maya shrugged. "I'm not the person to ask. That's for these two." She gestured to me and Sailor. I was busy avoiding eyes and was back to reading the spines of the books. But Hannah was probably right. Despite my propensity for seeing magical interventions everywhere I went, I would have put Bartholomew's tales down to the imagination of an old man . . . if there hadn't been a murder, and that darned cape, associated with an old trunk he had sold to Sebastian.

Actually, *she* had sold those things.

"Hannah, could you tell me anything about the trunk you sold to Sebastian Crowley?"

"Anything, like what? It was just an old trunk. Smelled funky. I wanted to toss it, but my sister said it might be worth something, so I took it down there with a bunch of other things. If he wants it back, though, I mean, whatever. Sebastian only gave me twenty bucks for it. No big deal."

"So you don't know anything about its history, where it came from?"

She shook her head. "You'll have to ask my uncle if you want that sort of information. He's the family historian. He might be vague about what's happening here and now, but he's got a million old stories about the family."

As if on cue, Bart walked in and joined us at the table.

"I looked, but I think we're out of cream," he said. "I may have used the last of it on my strawberries this morning."

"That's okay. Thanks for looking. One thing I'll say

for the Woolseys; they always lay a nice tea service, right, Bart?"

He nodded and dropped several sugar cubes into his cup of tea.

"I just love the little sugar bowl," I said.

"Do you? I couldn't find the silver one, so I just used this. Bart has a million of these things."

"Family stuff," said Bart. He shook a finger in Hannah's direction. "It'll all be yours one day if you play your cards right. Yours and your sister, Nina's."

"Thanks, Uncle Bart," said Hannah. "But as you know, I have other interests."

Bart snorted loudly. "You call those snakes an 'interest'? How are you gonna find yourself a husband hanging out with snakes all day?"

"I work at the East Bay Vivarium, in Berkeley," explained Hannah.

"Vivarium?" asked Maya.

"It's a reptile store."

"You sell snakes?"

"And lizards and frogs and turtles. And some really cool spiders. Creepies, crawlies, and critters, we like to say. And in answer to your question, Bart, just who do you think hangs out at a reptile shop? I guarantee you, other than the mothers dragged in by their curious children, I'm usually the only woman in the store."

"You'd be better off studying your family's history," insisted Bart.

"You want to pay me to be the family historian, okay. Otherwise, I'll keep my job, thanks. I happen to love snakes, and I'm not going to apologize for that."

"You *go*, girl," said Maya.

"Thank you," said Hannah with a smile. "A fellow snake enthusiast?"

"Noooo," said Maya with a firm shake of her head.

"Can't stand them, actually. But I admire people who go after what they want."

"Fair enough. Anyway, Will doesn't seem to be put off by it at all."

Bart grunted in reply and loudly blew on his hot cup.

Ten minutes later, we finished our tea, agreed on a fair price for the clothes based on Maya's estimate, and hauled two big black plastic bags of clothing out of the apartment. Maya carried one, Sailor the other, while I got off easy with nothing but the vintage sugar bowl Hannah insisted I keep.

We were saying our good-byes at the door when something else occurred to me.

"Bart . . . you mentioned you didn't sleep well?"

"I sleep, but I have terrible dreams. They wake me up. . . . It's the ancient curse; I'm sure of it."

"Oh, Uncle Bart . . ." Hannah sighed.

"But you said you slept well last night?" I asked.

"*Yes.*" For the first time since we'd arrived I saw a small smile on his face. "I've been plagued with bad dreams for years. But last night, I finally had a good night's sleep. It does wonders for a person."

I was willing to bet that last night was the first night in years he'd been without his family's historic trunk. And without that velvet cape.

Chapter 7

Sailor, Maya, and I said our good-byes and lugged our
new acquisitions into the elevator and out to the van.

Sailor climbed into the back, leaving Maya to ride
shotgun. I fired up the engine and started across town,
debating how much to share with Maya. Both Bronwyn
and Maya, the "normal" friends I felt closest to, knew
and accepted that I was a little . . . different. But unlike
Bronwyn, Maya hadn't expressed much interest in learning more about my witchy ways.

"What's all this about an ancient curse?" Maya asked
after a few moments.

"It's probably nothing," I said lightly, waiting for her
to give me a cue that she wanted to know more. "A lot of
people who experience bad luck blame it on a curse. No
big deal."

"Think so?" she said, clearly skeptical. She glanced
back at Sailor, who lifted one eyebrow in a signature sardonic move.

I watched him in the rearview mirror and felt a small
pique of envy; I wished *I* could get away with a move like
that.

"Then why do I have the feeling you will soon be running around town searching for a way to break the curse and in the process encountering all manner of individuals of a sinister nature?" Maya continued.

I heard a faint snort from the back of the van.

"I have no idea what you're talking about," I said. "I have no intention of doing any such thing. I have quite enough on my plate as it is, thank you very much."

Maya and Sailor burst into laughter.

"She's cute when she fibs," Maya said to Sailor.

"She's always cute," Sailor replied.

I glared at both of them.

When I pulled up in front of Aunt Cora's Closet, Conrad was still sitting at his usual spot on the curb. He helped us carry the bags into the store.

Sailor drew me aside. "Why don't I go check out the tree, see if I feel something?"

"Please don't," I said with a shake of my head. "The police may still be there, and even if they aren't . . . I know it takes a lot out of you."

I didn't add "lately," though we were both thinking it.

"This is driving me crazy." Sailor blew out a frustrated breath and ran a hand through his hair. "I'm meeting a few old friends later. One of them will know something. One of them *always* knows something."

"Sure you want to do that?" I asked, knowing how much Sailor hated to ask others for favors. A loner by nature and circumstance, he had no true friends other than me, just professional colleagues. I didn't know much about his world—Sailor wasn't the only one with loner tendencies—but did know that the circles he moved in kept close tabs on favors owed and received. Repaying a debt was not optional, though one rarely had a voice in just how that debt was to be repaid.

"Yes, but I hate to leave you alone," he said.

I smiled. "I'll be fine. There's more than enough new

inventory to keep me occupied. Between the washing, pressing, and pricing, I'll be too busy to get into trouble."

Sailor snorted but said with a smile: "Yeah, right."

"And then I'm going to look through that ledger some more and try to figure out what Bart knew, if anything, and then . . . I'm not sure."

"Maybe you should reread *The Crucible*. Just think, it might turn up on the GED. Speaking of which, aren't you supposed to take that on Saturday? Want me to go with you?"

"Why is everyone so eager to escort me to the GED?" I asked, annoyed. "I'm perfectly capable of getting to a simple exam all by my lonesome."

"Just don't get distracted by another yard sale. *Ciao, bella.*"

He gave me a brief kiss, climbed on his motorcycle, and roared off. I decided to head over to Booksmith a few blocks away. There I found a gently used copy of *The Crucible*—complete with yellow highlighting and what appeared to be insightful, handwritten comments in the margins. *Thank you, lit major, whoever you are,* I thought.

I flipped through the book as I walked slowly back to Aunt Cora's Closet, hoping it might throw some light on the situation I was facing. If the velvet cape dated from when Bart's family lived in a Puritan settlement, it could explain the unsettling images I had seen when I put it on. But I still didn't have any idea how it might be connected to a malevolent oak tree, much less to Sebastian's violent death.

If things were quiet when I got back, I would let Maya and Bronwyn handle things while I slipped upstairs to try on the cape again. Maybe this time, knowing what to expect and surrounded by peace and calm, I would be able to understand the voices that swirled around me. I picked up my pace, eager to get started.

But just as I approached the store, a small tour bus pulled up in front. The bus door swung open and a steady stream of tourists poured out, eager to check out San Francisco's famous "Haight-Ashbury." Snapping pictures and chatting excitedly, a large throng of women went into Aunt Cora's Closet.

Looked like communing with the cape would have to wait.

By the time I walked through the door, dozens of women were flipping through racks of clothing and pulling items off shelves. Maya and Bronwyn scurried about, showing some into changing rooms, helping others find just the right piece of jewelry to accessorize a blouse. It was a scene of cheerful bedlam, and I immediately waded into the fray.

"Where y'all from?" I asked a woman who was inspecting an eyelet sundress from the 1970s.

"Honey, we're from all over," she replied. "Louise and Rose are from Kansas City, Becky is from Fresno, and Lisa is from Redding. Jenny and I are from Salem."

"Salem?" I asked, wondering if this was yet another coincidence. How often could the Salem witch trials come up in one day? "You came all the way from Massachusetts?"

"Salem, *Oregon*. Not the wicked *witch* Salem," she clarified. "This dress isn't going to fit me, is it?"

"Sorry to say, this style is not very forgiving," I replied in my most diplomatic tone, feeling relieved that these customers, at least, were not from "wicked witch" Salem. "If it's even just the slightest bit too small, it will be terribly uncomfortable. Have you considered something more like this?" I held up a loose-fitting shift in a gorgeous paisley print.

For the next hour or so, the tourists kept Bronwyn, Maya, and me on our toes. Instead of contemplating an enchanted cape in peaceful solitude, I was caught up in a flurry of consulting with customers, helping size garments, and ringing up sales. Oscar was, once again, a huge hit, and I kept having to shoo him away from the changing rooms. There was no denying it: He was a bit of a peeping pig.

Clutching dozens of recycled Aunt Cora's Closet bags filled with their purchases, the tourists finally climbed back onto their bus, and Bronwyn, Maya, and I took a well-deserved break.

"I've never sold quite so much quite so quickly," Maya said, propping her feet on the counter. "I think we broke some kind of record."

"I must have sold five hundred dollars' worth of herbal salves and lotions," Bronwyn said happily. "I feel like I owe somebody a commission or something. Who were those women?"

"They were from a tour company," I said. "I should look into that."

"At least send the tour company owner a muffin basket," Bronwyn suggested.

"Wouldn't that be considered a kickback?" Maya asked. For all her offbeat ways, Maya had a strong law-and-order streak.

"Kickbacks are illegal. Muffins are just yummy," Bronwyn explained. "Hey, did you know carrot cake is technically a muffin?"

"I did not know that," Maya said. "For some reason, that makes me very happy."

We were silent for a few minutes, enjoying the peace.

"Time for a bit of housekeeping," Bronwyn sighed, getting to her feet. "Have you seen the mess in the changing rooms?"

"Count me in," Maya said. "Lily, I think we have some space to put out more stock. Those women made quite a dent."

"Good point. I'll start pricing new items." I said, realizing that once again, I would have to put off communing with the cape.

Pricing merchandise wasn't the sort of task I could delegate to Maya or Bronwyn. It was a never-ending job that was equal parts fact-checking (how much had I paid for it?), research (how much was it worth on the open market?), and judgment call (how much would my customers pay for it?). Usually I approached pricing analytically because I was, after all, running a business and needed to make a profit so I could pay my bills. At times, though, I went with my gut, pricing a high-value item below market because I just didn't like it that much and wanted to get rid of it, or pricing a lower-value item above market because I loved it and wanted the person who bought it to appreciate it.

Once I'd determined a price, I entered it into the computer system and wrote up a tag. The tags were dated so we'd know when stock had been around a while and if it needed to be marked down. Finally, the tag had to attach to the garment in a way that wouldn't hurt the fabric, which was especially tricky with silks and satins. Fragile pieces required special care: I threaded the price tag onto a ribbon and hung it around the hanger.

"This coming Saturday is the GED, isn't it?" said Bronwyn casually as she swept up some potpourri that a customer had knocked off a shelf.

"Yup." I hoped my monosyllabic response would convey that I didn't want to engage in this conversation.

"Need a ride?"

"Nope."

"You sure? You missed it last time. . . ."

"That was due to an unavoidable time conflict."

"Yes, it was crucial that you made it to that estate sale," Bronwyn said dryly. "Because yard sales are once-in-a-lifetime opportunities."

"I'm a vintage clothing dealer. If I'm not Johnny-on-the-spot, I lose my chance to buy something."

I heard Maya snort as Bronwyn gazed pointedly at the numerous bags of clothes we'd recently acquired that had yet to be sorted, washed, and priced.

"Okay, okay," I conceded. "Maybe I should slow down on the acquisitions, at least until we clear out the backlog."

"And the exam?" Bronwyn asked.

"You're a persistent one, aren't you?" I groused.

"That's one of the reasons you love me," she replied.

I surrendered. "One of the *many* reasons. I promise I won't duck out on the exam this Saturday in favor of an estate sale."

"Or in favor of anything else," Maya clarified.

"You two!" I exclaimed. "Yes, all right, *fine*. I promise."

"Need help boning up on anything?" Bronwyn asked.

"I'm good, thanks."

"Okay. Great, then."

I turned back to my work, and Maya and Bronwyn continued tidying up the shop floor.

"I'm a reasonably intelligent woman, you know," I said, now unable to let it go.

"Indeed you are," Bronwyn said.

"I've read through the reading lists Maya gave me. I'm rereading *The Crucible* right now, as a matter of fact. And I've traveled extensively."

"More than most people even," Maya agreed.

"Surely I can pass a test aimed at the average high schooler," I said. "Who, if I may be so bold, is nowhere near as well read or as well traveled as I."

"Nowhere near!" gushed Bronwyn as she removed a magenta satin swirl skirt from the classic T-shirt rack and hung it back among the skirts.

"So I should do just fine."

"Just fine," said Maya. "Except for the algebra."

Just then Susan Rogers breezed in. Susan is a journalist who writes for the Living section of the *San Francisco Chronicle*. We met not long after my shop opened. After spending a day at the store shopping for vintage gowns with her niece's wedding party, Susan wrote a glowing feature article praising Aunt Cora's Closet. Oscar had even gotten his picture in the paper, which he somehow matted and framed and hung on the wall behind the register.

"What's this I hear about algebra?" Susan asked after greeting us all.

"I think I might have dyscalculia," I said with a sigh.

"I had that once. A simple course of antibiotics and it cleared right up. Nothing to be ashamed of."

I laughed. "No, no. 'Dyscalculia' is a condition wherein a person has problems understanding numbers. It's like dyslexia, but with numbers instead of letters."

"Clearly the *verbal* section will be no problem for our Lily," said Bronwyn with a proud smile. "But sorry, Lily: I don't buy the learning disability. You have no problem calculating prices," she said with a nod at the clothing I was tagging. "Or completing tax forms and doing the payroll."

Of course Bronwyn was right. I didn't like dealing with the bureaucracy that comes with owning a business—who did?—but I didn't find it challenging, just boring.

I was okay at geometry, because visualizing is second nature for me. But algebra was another story. All those X's and Y's floated around in my mind like so many helium-filled balloons; there was no context, no anchor. Algebra reminded me of looking into my crystal ball—not only did I not *see* anything, but I was afraid I wouldn't know what I was looking at even if I *did* see something. It didn't mean anything to me.

"I'm doomed," I whined. "Why do I even *need* a diploma? I wish I'd never started this stupid quest." I put my head on my arms on the counter and groaned. "It's all y'all's fault. I was fine before."

One ill-fated lunch a couple of months ago, Bronwyn and Susan had discovered that I'd never finished high school. They'd been surprised and encouraged me to get my GED. Maya had been coaching me in literature and social studies, which I quite enjoyed—it was a revelation to catch up on what I had missed while practicing conjuring spirits, learning the proper method of melting dragon's blood resin, and memorizing the Calendar of Revelry.

Math proved to be an entirely different beast.

Bronwyn's nine-year-old granddaughter, a math whiz, had been tutoring me in the algebra she found so simple. Imogen was a good, patient teacher, but I was a hard nut to crack. It was humiliating.

Bronwyn came over and started rubbing my back. "There, there. Don't fret. Think of the young people! You're setting a sterling example. Lily Ivory doesn't quit. When the going gets tough, she gets going!"

I lifted my head enough to give her the stink-eye. "Did you read that on a Marine recruiting poster?"

"In a locker room, actually. The *boys'* locker room." With a wink and a pat, she returned to the shop floor to help two new customers find unlikely, but charming, mixes and matches.

"How about y'all give me a proper send-off, come to breakfast on Saturday, the morning of the test? I think I might need some cheerleading. I'll cook."

"I'm game," said Maya.

"Me too!" said Bronwyn. "Especially if you make your famous French toast."

"You're invited, too, Susan. Oh, hey, you'd be the person to ask about this," I said, glad to change the subject. I brought Oscar's present out from a shelf under the counter. "What do you make of these?"

I tipped the manila envelope and sprinkled the labels onto the glass counter: Lilli Ann, Helga, Armani Privé, Molyneux.

Susan studied them and then lifted her expressive eyes to mine. "Fraudulent labels?"

"I think they might be originals," I said. "Taken from authentic garments and sold over the Internet."

"Wow, a Madame Grès!" Susan gasped. "Looks like an early one. I didn't even know these *existed*! You think someone would seriously try to pass off a mass-produced dress as a 1940s-era Madame Grès?"

"There's a sucker born every minute," I said. "Tell me more about Madame Grès. I've heard of her, but can't remember the details."

"Gladly—usually folks try to get me to shut up about this sort of thing," Susan said, and settled in to lecture. "Madame Grès was a French fashion designer from the 1930s. Her first love was sculpture, and she incorporated classical Greek elements in the way she draped material. She liked to construct the dresses directly on the models—celebrities such as Marlene Dietrich and Greta Garbo."

"Imagine accidentally sticking Greta Garbo with a pin," said Maya.

"I vant to be alone," Bronwyn mimicked with a laugh.

"Sometimes she built bras and girdles into the dresses, which if you think about it is a *fabulous* idea," Susan continued. "No foundation garments peeking up from the neckline, no falling bra straps, no tugging at underwear. All one piece, very glamorous."

As often happened in Aunt Cora's Closet, our talk had turned into an impromptu mini class on vintage fashion. Customers joined Bronwyn and Maya as they gathered around to listen to Susan.

"I saw a fabulous exhibition of her work at the Met in New York City not too long ago," Susan continued.

"They said her pleats were so carefully tailored that she could compress something like three *yards* of fabric into fewer than three inches of pleats. Not to disparage your wonderful store, Lily, but an original Madame Grès is extremely expensive, and her designs are found mostly in art and fashion museums, or private collections."

"I wonder where these labels came from," Maya said. "Why would someone rip one out of a valuable gown?"

"Sometimes they're taken from lesser objects, such as scarves or even belts," said Susan. "Or from ruined items. Not everyone fortunate enough to afford a Madame Grès appreciated what they had. But to sell labels like this, when their obvious purpose is to commit fraud . . ." She trailed off with a shake of her head.

"Who would do such a thing?" said one customer.

"That seems pretty sleazy," said another.

"Where did you get them?" Susan asked.

"I, um . . . A friend of mine found them and bought them for me. A very well-meaning friend."

Oscar glared at me, pink piggy eyes narrowed.

"When it comes to vintage clothing, it's caveat emptor—let the buyer beware," said Susan with another shake of her head. "Especially where expensive collectibles are concerned. Don't spend much unless you're sure of what you're getting."

Our little group examined the labels, groused and chatted a bit more, then dispersed. Susan and I were left alone at the counter while I gathered the labels and dropped them into the envelope.

"You should make those into a display," Susan suggested. "Teach your customers about different designers and labels fraud."

"That's a great idea," I said. "I'm just not sure when I'd find the time. I'm behind on laundry and steaming, I haven't carved talismans in forever, and my garden's in desperate need of tending. And I have to take that stupid test this Saturday."

Susan smiled. "It's good you're taking it, Lily. All joking aside, I'm very proud of you. We all are. Hey, want *me* to take the labels and make a display?"

"Really? That would be just peachy. Thank you."

"No problem. It'll give me an excuse to do a little research on designer couture. Maybe I'll write an article about it for the paper—my editor loves this sort of thing."

"Hey, you do a lot of antiquing, don't you?"

"Sure do. Why? You in the market for something in particular?"

"Not really. But are you familiar with Sebastian's Antiques, off Jackson Square?"

"Sebastian's? It doesn't ring a bell. Why?"

"The owner of the shop . . . Sebastian Crowley . . . was found the other day, shot to death in Golden Gate Park."

"Oh my Lord, what a terrible thing!"

Bronwyn left a trio of sisters in the communal changing room with a stack of bustiers and an armful of full peasant skirts. She came over to join us, shaking her head.

"Scary, isn't it?" Bronwyn said. "Poor Lily found him, with Conrad."

"*No.*"

"*Yes!*"

Even though we were discussing a tragedy, the two women were always so expressive that it made me smile. Then I recalled that I hadn't finished looking through Sebastian's log and wondered if it could tell me anything more. A cursory inspection had revealed mostly unintelligible symbols, but maybe if I stared at them hard enough I might recognize a name or a reference. It could happen.

The bell over the front door tinkled merrily as a cus-

tomer left the store. Waving good-bye, I noticed a police
cruiser—they call them "radio cars" here in San Francisco—roll to a stop in front of Aunt Cora's Closet. I
waved at the pair of uniformed officers to wait a moment, then brought them each a piece of the cake I had
baked for Oscar's birthday.

This did not please Oscar. Not only was he selfish with
his baked goods; he also had an antiauthoritarian bent
that made him suspicious of the police. As did several
people in my orbit, now that I thought about it. Sailor,
Conrad, Aidan . . . I should probably take some time to
think about that soon.

I had already warned Maya and Bronwyn to be on the
lookout, but I really doubted anything would happen
during the day with people coming in and out. I decided
I wouldn't allow anyone to remain in the store alone, and
I would ask Conrad to keep an eye out as well.

Much later, after closing Aunt Cora's Closet, straightening the merchandise, and bidding good night and
blessed be to Maya and Bronwyn, I set up a powerful
protection spell at the front door. I was anxious to get
upstairs and do the one thing I wanted—*needed*—to do:
commune with that strange velvet cape.

At dusk I took a boline—the curved knife I used for
gathering botanicals—hung a woven basket over my
arm, and started collecting herbs from my terrace garden. Rue, agrimony, and devil's pod for protection; juniper and wolfsbane and a bit of bleeding alder for
concentration. Then I consulted my Book of Shadows.
When I opened the big old red-leather-bound book, it
had a musty smell that reminded me of Bart's place.
And, like his apartment—and Sebastian's shop, for that
matter—it was chock-full of what I thought of as trea-
sures, but others might consider junk: recipes, techniques,
articles, quotes, a few scratchy old photos.

As with any Book of Shadows, of course, spells and incantations filled most of the pages.

The parchment was soft with age and frequent turning. It had been my grandmother Graciela's book for years before she gave it to me. From time to time a new spell would appear, or a quote I hadn't remembered reading before. I could only assume that the Book of Shadows had a life of its own. If ever I had to run from fire, I imagined I would carry Oscar in one arm and this book in the other. I had many other items I would be sad to lose, of course, but only my familiar and this tome were irreplaceable. In stark contrast, my crystal ball—a stunning specimen with a gold base encrusted with jewels—I would happily consign to the flames. It was far more frustrating than helpful in my unskilled hands.

Flipping through my Book of Shadows in search of anything referring to ancient curses, I happened upon a notation I didn't remember seeing before. Written in Graciela's spidery writing, it was suggestions for keeping a person tethered to the here and now. My grandmother always included a plant she called *ongles de sorcière*, or "sorcerer's fingernails," which Californians more commonly referred to as ice plant. In the Bay Area I had noticed it used as a drought-tolerant planting along freeways. Funny how a plant could be common landscaping material on the one hand and a powerful ingredient for brewing on the other. I should gather some next time I spotted it. In fact, if my Book of Shadows was suggesting it . . . perhaps I should plant some in my garden.

After full dark, the portals began to open more fully.

Oscar stayed close by, doing his witch's familiar duty even while still grousing about *somebody* being too good for a little simple vintage fraud.

Ignoring him, I laid out a clean white cloth on the kitchen counter. On it I placed my athame, or spirit blade; a length of blessed rope; a kind of vinca known as Sorcerer's Violet, and dried stalks of Verbascum dipped in tallow. I had already showered and washed with lemon verbena soap and wore an all-white ensemble. *"Blanco o negro,"* I could hear my grandmother saying in my head. "Black or white clothing. Color can disturb the energy of the spell."

Using my ancient stone mortar and pestle, I methodically ground the herbs, blended them with the salt, and carefully drew a circle while reciting my incantations.

Finally, within the safety of the circle, and with Oscar at my side, I held the old velvet cape in my arms and felt for its vibrations.

They were there, reaching across the generations, across the centuries. Powerful, intense. Almost painful.

Finally, taking a deep breath and clearing my mind, I locked gazes with Oscar and drew the cape around my shoulders. With trembling fingers, I fastened the clasp at the neck.

Chapter 8

And just as before, I was back there. Wherever "there" was.

I tried to fight the panic that swept over me, my heart hammering and my breathing coming in harsh, labored gasps. Feeling out of breath, I was reminded of a recent, horrifying episode, when I was being "pressed" in the traditional torture for a witch. And yet another time, when I felt myself drowning in the bay.

Those moments of terror came back to me in an excruciating, steady stream, enveloping me in their twisted embrace.

I was witnessing a burning.

A woman was chanting as she stood atop the pyre, tethered tightly to a stake. Empty, black eyes. A smiling, mumbling mouth. She was strangely beautiful, but horrific. In fact, she looked a little bit like me, pale with long dark hair and strong cheekbones.

And she was staring straight at me. *Deliverance* . . . I could hear her in my head. Over and over, she was crying out: *Deliverance*.

And then the burning. I reached out toward the flames. I felt agonizing heat on my fingers, scorching, the still-smoldering ashes being lifted and dumped into a box with symbols on it. I could see it all as though I were behind the camera. After a moment I realized it was me—I was the one collecting the ashes.

I inspected my hands. The pads of my fingers were charred and blistered. Ignoring the searing pain, I picked up the box filled with ashes and ran deep into the woods. But someone was chasing me, growing nearer....

"Mistress!"

I awoke on the floor of my apartment, flat on my back, a worried gobgoyle standing over me.

"How long have I been out?"

"About half an hour," he growled. "I started to worry, so I undid the clasp. Hope that was okay."

As I sat up, the cloak slipped from my shoulders, pooling on the floor.

My fingertips still burned. I held them up. They were covered in ash.

"Gak!" Oscar pulled back, appalled. "What did you *do*? Don't you know you should never bring anything back with you? *Never*. It's very dangerous, mistress!"

"I didn't mean to," I said, awkwardly rising from my position on the floor without using my hands. Taking care not to touch anything with my hands, I brushed aside the line of herbs and salt with my foot to open the circle.

"Oscar, would you please fill my cauldron about a quarter full of spring water?"

He did as I asked, hauling my heavy iron cauldron onto the stove. I washed my hands carefully in the pot, watching as the ashes clouded the water and turned it a grayish white. When I pulled my hands out of the water and inspected my fingertips, I realized they weren't actually burned. Despite bringing back ashes with me, I had merely dreamed the injuries.

Still ... I've never had fingerprints. Those ridges so

common to the rest of the world were missing on the pads of my fingers. When I was a girl the doctor had told my mother it was a known genetic condition called *dermatopathia pigmentosa reticularis*. But he also said I exhibited none of the other attributes common to that syndrome. Only the lack of fingerprints.

"That's one heck of a cape," said Oscar. "Where'd ya go?"

"I'm not sure. Somewhere they were burning witches. Could it have been . . . Salem, Massachusetts?"

"They hung witches in Salem, no burning."

"True. So, I wonder what I was seeing?"

He shrugged. "Travel cloaks are like that. It's always hard to tell where you are when you just drop in like that. That's one reason I've never liked them."

"Travel cloaks? What's a travel cloak?"

He snickered and waved his big hand at me, as though I were making a joke.

"Seriously, Oscar. What's a travel cloak?"

"You gotta be kiddin' me. I thought you were textile sensitive."

"I am. But lest we forget, I don't know much."

"Wow. Okay . . . here's the deal: Travel cloaks are like, if you're powerful, you put them on and go to a different dimension. You know, like when you crawl in a dumbwaiter."

"In a dumbwaiter?"

He nodded.

"I've never crawled in a dumbwaiter," I said.

"No? You should totally try it. There's one at the Fairmont Hotel that's *awesome*. Wanna go?"

"Maybe later. So just to clarify: You're saying this is a magic cape of some sort. . . ."

He rolled his eyes. *"Duh."*

"Bear with me for a moment, please. Will this cape take me just to one particular place, or anywhere I want to go? Is it just taking me along for the ride, or am I subconsciously directing it? How does it work?"

He cradled his head in his hands and spoke slowly and distinctly, as though to a child: "If a magical person has one made, then it's for that person and they can use it to travel back to where they want. Only to places they've gone. They can't change anything; they just witness it. But other people could put it on, and the only travel you can do is to the places the owner of the cape's already gone. Like you have to use their ticket to ride, sorta. Unless you're a familiar like me, of course. I got skills, so's I can go anywhere I want."

"And does a person actually travel? I mean, are you actually there, or is it a mental thing?"

He stared at me with his big green eyes. "Now you're kiddin' me, right? A person can't, like . . ." He started to cackle. "What? Fly through the air? Like those pictures of witches on brooms? *Hahahaha!*"

I adore my familiar. I really do. But I was about ready to throttle him at the moment.

"I'm so glad I provide you with such amusement. Really, I am." I decided to change the subject. "Hey, I have another question for you: Do you know anything about oak trees?"

"I'm not that big of a nature guy. I like it right here in our nice apartment, in the city."

"I wasn't suggesting we live in one. I was wondering if oak trees were associated with anything, I don't know, an evil of some kind."

"Like the chained oak of Staffordshire?"

"I'm sorry?"

"The Earl of Shrewsbury, boy, he was a real piece o' work. Anyway, he was mean to the wrong beggar one night, so the beggar says"—Oscar dropped his voice to be sinister and even more gravelly than usual—"'For every branch on the old oak tree here that falls, a member of your family will die.' And that very night, a big storm blew in, and one of the branches fell, and the earl's brother died real suddenlike. The next day the earl ordered his servants to chain all the branches together to keep another one from falling."

I was so entranced with Oscar's story it took me a moment to realize that it really had nothing to do with what I was asking.

"I was thinking more along the lines of an oak that could, maybe, hold something evil within it?"

"Well, they're famous for holding a grudge. They're real avengers—that's for sure—and they live a long time so they're real patient when it comes to getting revenge. Like this one time in Somerset? Father and son weren't respectful of the oaks and cut down a whole coppice."

"Coppice?"

"Like a copse. A thicket o' trees."

I nodded and committed the word to memory. Just in case it came up on the vocabulary section of the GED.

"Anyhoo," said Oscar, as though frustrated at my interruptions. "When the father and son went back in, after new growth had started, another tree dropped a big old branch right on 'em! When the youngest brother came to help, he could hear the trees rustling: They were talkin' to him right then and there, warning him off."

"And then?"

Oscar shrugged. "The youngest brother inherited the farm, and whenever he went past the great oak by the gate, he always asked permission to go into the forest, so trees never followed him or dropped branches on him and he lived happily ever after."

"So your point is . . . ?"

"They've got long memories and are resentful as all getout. Just ask the woodsfolk. 'Cept . . . on second thought, you'd better not. The Good People are . . . touchy. And if you touch *their* trees . . ." He shook his head and sucked in a loud, slow breath.

"So I hear. But you know them, right? You've been introduced?"

"Yeah, but . . ."

"I'd love to have a talk with them."

The woodsfolk, or Good People, adhered to a strict set of rules, not the least of which is that they would not interact with anyone to whom they had not been properly introduced. But I'd been meaning to establish some sort of relationship with them for a while, and what better time than now, when they might be able to tell me what happened to Sebastian? If they had witnessed what had happened, they could solve this mystery just that fast.

"Tell you what," I said. "You make the introduction, and leave the rest to me."

At which Oscar *again* guffawed, this time literally slapping his knee.

"I take it you don't like that idea?"

He laughed some more, a rusty chortle that had a lot in common with a hiccuping car.

"Okay, then. I'll leave the talking up to you."

"If you're serious about this, then we gotta go at dawn. It's the best time to talk with them. And you gotta take a gift."

"What kind of gift?"

"Hmmm." Oscar looked around thoughtfully, as though seeing whether I had a decent candidate for gift giving. "Too bad you don't have any babies lying around. They like babies."

"I am *not* going to sacrifice a baby to the woodsfo—"

"It's not like they'd *eat* it or anything! They just like to raise 'em. And they do better than a lot of *cowan* parents."

"Let's just say I don't condone kidnapping, as a general rule."

Oscar shrugged, as though considering the source. "They like gorse blossoms. They make 'em into faery gold."

"I'm fresh out of gorse blossoms at the moment. Maybe . . . I don't know, maybe I could find some down at the flower market?"

"They also like bread, cream, butter. Honey."

"Okay, that's doable."

"Unless they *don't* like it, in which case they'll see it as an insult."

"How can you tell which it is?"

"Can't."

"That's a little confusing."

"Yeah. They're a confusing lot. First off, we don't know whether this tree is even owned by the woodsfolk, and if it is, are we talking wee folk, like the fae, or brownies, or gnomes, or who knows who . . . ?" He trailed off with a heavy sigh, rolling his eyes. "And they're all so *touchy*. There's the Seelie court and the Unseelie court; some are scared of rowan, and some hate bread. All I can say for sure is they don't like complaints *or* compliments. And they don't like to be thanked 'cause they think it lets you off the hook, and they like you to be beholden for any favors."

"Okay . . ."

"And never, *ever* look them in the eyes; they like their privacy. And don't use their names. They're like demons that way. If you know their names, you can invoke them and either force them to do what you want or, ya know, they kill you or maim you or whatever. Prob'ly it's not worth the risk."

My mind was reeling. "Anything else?"

"They prob'ly won't talk to you anyway. They really don't like humans, and if they haven't showed themselves to you already, what with your herb garden and your powers and all . . . they prob'ly won't. Just be sure to wear your clothes inside out, and bells."

"Bells?"

"They don't like the tinkling. Except for a few that really do."

I stared at him for another moment.

"Either way, wear 'em. And be sure to wear the clothes inside out; that's important. Oh, there's one good thing," Oscar added finally.

"What's that?"

"They can't lie. They can confuse, but they can't lie. So if they saw what happened with Sebastian, and we ask them the right way, they'll have to tell us."

"Oh, well, that's good then."

Oscar shook his head and let out a world-weary sigh. "I sure hope Sebastian Crowley's worth it. It would be a lot more fun to go check out the dumbwaiter at the Fairmont."

"Could we pick up the pace, please?" I asked my familiar.

I looked over my shoulder to see Oscar with a book in one hand and a single dish in the other. Oscar hated cleaning the kitchen, but he loved eating. Since I did most of the cooking, I insisted he at least help by clearing the table. But in the time-honored way of immature creatures who didn't want to do what they were told and yet didn't want to get in trouble, he was completing his tasks at such a sluggish pace that I was tempted to jump in and take care of it.

"Put the book down *now*, Oscar, seriously. I would like to read too, you know. We can relax as soon as we finish here."

I had long since cleaned up my magical supplies but was busy scrubbing the lasagna pan.

"So he really did keep careful records after all," said Oscar.

"Is that Sebastian Crowley's ledger?"

Oscar nodded absentmindedly and placed the dirty plate on the counter, so far over that it teetered on the edge. I lunged for it.

"Huh," he said. "So if whoever killed him really was looking for the trunk, he could have looked in here and seen your name. Good thing Sebastian wrote it down wrong."

I rinsed the now-spotless lasagna casserole dish, placed it in the drainer, and dried my hands.

"What do you mean he wrote it down wrong?"

"Instead of Aunt Cora's Closet, he wrote down Aunt *Flora's* Closet."

"Let me see," I said, looking over Oscar's shoulder. I had overlooked that last night, assuming it had read Aunt *Cora's* Closet. "Aunt Flora's is a florist out in the Richmond."

"*Aunt Flora's Closet?* Someone ripped off your name?" Oscar's eyes narrowed. "Of all the low-down, dirty . . ."

I shook my head. "No, it's nothing like that. I've spoken with the proprietor. They opened about the same time I did—it was purely coincidental. I've gotten phone calls for them from time to time and mail occasionally."

Our eyes met for a long moment. I hurried over to my crowded desk in the living room and looked up Aunt Flora's Closet in the Yellow Pages.

I dialed the number, but of course I got voice mail. After all it was past nine o'clock. The florist probably closed hours ago.

I nearly left a voice mail, but for the life of me I couldn't think of a message that didn't sound crazy. Then I thought about calling Carlos, but what could I possibly say to *him*? That I had been reading through a dead man's private account book, which I had stolen when I broke into said man's shop, and that the trunk might have special significance, and a case of mistaken identity might have sent the perpetrator to a florist out in the Richmond? Oh, what tangled webs we weave.

Oscar seemed to read my mind. "They friends of yours, mistress?"

"I wouldn't say friends, but the owners are very sweet couple, originally from Japan. I hope . . ."

"Tonight's a nice night for a drive. Wanna swing by there, just in case? Maybe drop off some stinging nettles, and then we could go check out the dumbwaiter at the Fairmont!"

"I don't know about that last part . . . but the stinging nettles are a great idea. Just in case."

I packed up several herbs and plants, as well as a talisman and a small black silk bag full of rye seeds and an old key. I could leave it with them like a witchy care package. Probably it was unnecessary, but . . . one never knew.

My familiar was extremely good at keeping his true self a secret from strangers. He shifted into his miniature potbellied pig form as we descended the stairs to the store, then out the front door to my vintage cherry-red Mustang, which I park in a driveway around the corner. Doglike, Oscar loved riding in the car, and at first he would jump from the backseat to the front and back again in his excitement. Finally, halfway to our destination, he settled. He hunkered down low in the passenger's seat and transformed back into his natural state so we could talk.

"So, what's your theory about Sebastian's death?" I asked him.

He shrugged. "Business deal gone bad? He ran with some *nefarious* characters."

"Like Aidan?"

"*Ha!*" He let out a loud laugh, then slapped his hands over his mouth, looking decidedly uncomfortable.

"It's okay. Aidan can't hear us," I said. On second thought . . . "Can he?"

Oscar was still muffling himself, his green eyes almost comically huge as he stared at me.

"So if Sebastian was killed because of a deal gone bad, why would they have forced him to the oak tree?"

"Killing tree."

"What?"

He shrugged and looked out the window.

"Oscar, tell me what you said."

"Sometimes there are killing trees. Trees that just sort of . . . invite death."

Well. That was something to ponder. But it still didn't account for Sebastian being brought there to be shot. Killing tree or no, why not just murder the man in his store and be done with it?

It took us twenty-five minutes to drive across town to the section called the Richmond. The neighborhood was mostly stucco two-story homes, with a few retail zones. Aunt Flora's Closet was in one of these small shopping areas, sandwiched between an Irish pub and a dry cleaners shop with signs so outdated they looked vintage.

The parking lot was jammed with emergency vehicles, their flashing lights bright and frenetic in the sooty black of night.

Chapter 9

My heart pounded in my chest as we rolled on by. Oscar stared out the window, gawking at the police milling about the florist shop. I saw a uniformed officer talking to the owner, who was holding an ice pack to his head.

"Don'tcha wanna stop, mistress? Find out what happened?"

"I can't," I said as I continued down the street and around the corner, driving steadily away from the scene. "I just . . . I can't get involved with this, not after they found Sebastian with my card in his pocket."

"So you met with Crowley yesterday, bought a trunk from him, and then someone else wanted that trunk badly enough to kill for it? You lucked out that he wrote down the wrong name."

Had the owners of Aunt Flora's Closet been hurt on my account? In my place?

I drove the remaining few blocks to where the street ended at the Pacific Ocean. It was windy and cold, as usual, by the water. The night was dark, the gray of the sky meeting the gray of the water with barely a line. A few tiny lights in the distance indicated boats passing by, far offshore.

Other than two other cars at the other end of the long narrow parking lot, we were alone.

"This isn't your fault, mistress," said Oscar.

I remained silent, looking out at the lights in the gray distance.

"Did you hear me?" Oscar put one large, scaly hand on my shoulder.

Finally, I managed a nod.

"Prob'ly we should put some extra protection on the shop."

"I already did. I could cast an even stronger spell, I suppose."

I had done that once before, and it hadn't gone all that well. Unfortunately, the by-product of reducing risk is quelling creativity. The staff and customers seemed unable to function normally. And that didn't even begin to address the fact that I was casting on people who were unaware, something about which I had more than a few ethical qualms.

But Oscar was right. If someone had gone after Sebastian, and then Aunt Flora's Closet, why would they spare me? I tried to think back. Was there any way they would know it was *me,* the proprietor of Aunt *Cora's* Closet, who had purchased the trunk? It would have been odd for a florist to buy a trunk of clothes, wouldn't it? So if someone knew the city and realized there was a store with a similar name that specialized in antique clothing, would that bring them to my doorstep?

It wouldn't take a genius. But it would take a few logical leaps, and in my limited experience, thugs were rarely the brightest porch lights on the block.

"I'm guessing this whole thing's put the kibosh on checking out the Fairmont's dumbwaiter?"

"Afraid so, little guy. I've got to get back home and . . . call Carlos, I guess."

I limped back toward Aunt Cora's Closet, wanting only to get up the stairs and into the sanctuary of my apartment. As I was unlocking the shop door, I noticed another radio car slowly pulling past and exchanged a wave with the officers. Surely between the vigilance of the cops, my staff, and Conrad, in addition to my protection spells . . . we'd be okay, wouldn't we?

My heart dropped as I remembered that the owners of Aunt Flora's weren't so lucky.

Once upstairs, I made my phone call.

"I tell you what," said Carlos. "My heart skipped a beat when I heard the name. I thought it was your place at first. Anyway, I'm off duty, believe it or not, but it looks like a botched robbery."

"Is . . . is everyone all right?"

"The owner hit his head on the doorjamb trying to chase after whoever was in his shop, but he'll be fine."

I felt relief wash over me. "Thank goodness. Did they lose much?"

"Not from what I can tell. But like I said, it's not my case. I investigate dead bodies, not robberies."

"Speaking of dead people . . . I think there's a connection with this robbery and what happened with Sebastian," I said. "Aunt Flora's would be easy to mix up with my place. I think they were after the trunk."

"Yeah, I wondered about the name. But I've had the forensics team all over that old chest, and they've found nothing of interest. The Aunt Flora thing looks like a standard robbery. Any particular reason, other than the similar name, you think these two entirely disparate cases are related?"

"I can't say for sure. But maybe you can match forensics, something like that."

"Here's what's weird," Carlos said, and I could hear the tapping of computer keys in the background. "No suspicious fingerprints came up in Crowley's shop."

"Wouldn't a professional have wiped down the prints?"

"Sure. Or, I hear there are people in this world born without fingerprints."

I wasn't sure why this one thing about me stuck in Carlos's craw. I was born without fingerprints. But that wasn't my fault. I had always been like this. It would be a boon, I supposed, if I had a criminal bent, but it made certain bureaucratic tasks, like providing a thumbprint to get a driver's license, a real bear.

"So," I said without much hope, but I had to ask. "Have you found out anything new about Sebastian Crowley's murder?"

"I can't tell you anything more than what was in the papers."

"I mean—you don't really suspect Conrad, do you?"

"You know I can't discuss something like that with you. But I'd like you to go with me to visit Parmelee Riesling."

"Is that a . . . winery?" I asked.

"Not a 'that.' A 'who.' Parmelee Riesling is, by all accounts, the West Coast's premier textile conservationist. She agreed to analyze the contents of the trunk for the SFPD."

"Oh, that's jim-dandy."

"Is that genuine, or are you making fun?"

"I get that a lot. Sorry. It's a Southern thing. It was genuine—I think it's a great idea. I would love to speak with her. I trained briefly with a textile expert in Prague. It was fascinating."

"And here I thought you just bought and sold junk."

"It's not junk. It's vintage. And yes, Mr. Skeptic, there is a lot of science that goes into textile conservation. I'm nothing like an expert, obviously, and I deal more with everyday items than true collector's clothing. But I still find it fascinating. So why are you speaking with a clothing conservator?"

"Our boys looked the trunk over, but they're not exactly up on their fashion IQ. I had everything sent over for her assessment, just in case there's anything in the clothing that might connect to Crowley's death. I know it's unlikely, but it's worth a look."

"That's a good idea. I'd be happy to go."

"Great. I have no idea what to say to the woman. I'm not exactly up on my fashions myself. You might have more informed questions."

"Okey-dokey. Oh, by the way, I . . ." I realized I couldn't keep the ledger to myself. I'd thought it might provide me with clues that the police wouldn't be able to understand, but I had to admit they might be able to find something I hadn't. Besides, I could just make a photocopy of it before turning it over. "I have something to give you. A ledger that Sebastian kept of his clients and whatnot."

"A ledger."

"Yes. Sebastian Crowley's ledger."

"Uh-huh. How is it you happen to have Sebastian Crowley's ledger and you forgot to tell me about it until now?"

"Do you want to see it or not?"

Carlos blew out a breath, and I could practically see him pinching the bridge of his nose. "I'll pick you up at your store tomorrow, quarter to noon, and we'll go see Ms. Riesling. Bring the ledger."

"Okay, sure. See you then. Thanks for asking me."

I hung up and was met with the scowl of an overly curious, entirely disapproving gobgoyle.

"You've got a date with a *cop* now?"

"It's not a 'date.' He's trying to figure out what it was about that trunk that someone is after."

"*Duh.* They're after that cloak. Travel cloaks aren't

dime a dozen, you know. By the way, prob'ly you shouldn't bring it to the tree tomorrow. Better to leave it here. Just to be on the safe side. G'night." And with that, Oscar climbed up into his cubby above the fridge.

He started snoring in about ten seconds flat.

I envied my familiar his ease with the sandman. I was exhausted, but sleep eluded me for a long time. All I could think about was the nice couple that owned Aunt Flora's Closet, and Sebastian, and the face of that woman upon the pyre ... and the horrifying burning sensation on the pads of my fingertips.

They tingled now, just thinking of it.

Oscar woke me an hour before dawn. I threw on yesterday's 1960s striped sundress—inside out—matched it with a reversed coral cardigan, and grabbed a cocoa brown wool car coat for warmth. One thing about San Francisco weather: You learned to be prepared for temperatures ranging from cloudy fifties to the sunny eighties.

This morning was chilly and damp, as was typical, when Oscar and I crossed Stanyan, entered Golden Gate Park, and made our way down the meandering path to the suspect oak tree.

The "do not cross" tape was still up, but there was no SFPD or park security presence. Interestingly, though, there were no homeless people, either. Probably Conrad and his crew had abandoned the police-ridden scene for less threatening sleeping areas. I wondered whether they'd be back, and whether they'd continue their campaign to save the tree—Ms. Quercus, as Conrad called her.

Looking at its massive branches, black against the gray moonlit sky, it was hard to believe the tree was on its last legs. Oaks were like that: so substantial and hulking that they spread their broad arms and seemed to invite the world to come sit under them; but when they fell, they fell hard.

Now that we were here, I didn't know what I hoped to accomplish exactly. The only thing I was sure of was that it was no coincidence that Sebastian Crowley had been found here not long after I had been with him. With my card in his pocket, no less.

Had he been digging for something . . . ? And the police, I presumed—or someone else?—had continued digging; the earth at the base of the tree was disturbed, big clods of clay dirt overturned. I knelt and placed my hand on the earth, trying to feel for something, anything. I wasn't gifted at reading minerals, but it was worth a shot.

Nothing. Maybe I should take Sailor up on his offer to try to read, just in case. Even with diminished abilities, he'd do better than I.

"I don't like it," said Oscar.

"What is it?" I asked.

He shrugged. "Were these mushrooms here when Sebastian was killed?"

"I don't remember seeing them. But you know how they are; they can spring up overnight."

I remained kneeling at the base of the tree, looking very carefully in the dim light.

"Oh! There goes a frog!" I pointed as the chubby fellow hopped out of sight.

"You know what they say: Mushrooms are 'toadstools,'" said Oscar with a little sigh, apparently less enthralled with the wildlife than I. "Though why toads need stools, I've never figured out."

"I don't know either. More importantly, I also don't know how any of this would have anything to do with Sebastian's murder." I leaned back on my heels and gazed up into the branches of Ms. Quercus. "I guess I was just curious. . . . I thought maybe I would notice something out of the ordinary."

"Did you know in German the word *Todestuhls* means death's chair?"

"They're also called *Hexensessel*, or witch's chair, so I guess we shouldn't get too carried away. So in *Todestuhl*, does the word refer to toads or to death?"

Oscar nodded. "Right."

"No, I'm asking—"

There was a rustling in the tree. I tried to peer up, but all I could see was the outline of black against the pre-dawn sky. What did I expect to find that the police hadn't already discovered and confiscated? I inspected the trunk of the tree with my flashlight to be sure there were no magic symbols or other markings that might be out of the ordinary.

Another rustling. Squirrels, no doubt. Or birds. Or any one of the animals that Conrad had mentioned dwelt in the branches of dying trees. The circle of life, all of that.

But then I could have sworn one of the low-hanging branches took a swipe at me. The rough edges of its leaves scratched the side of my face.

I jumped back, swearing a blue streak, and landed on my butt in the mud.

Oscar came running. "Mistress? Are you all right? The woodsfolk say to stay away from this tree. It's no ordinary arboreal specimen. I'll tell you that much."

"How do you mean? You talked to them already? Aren't you going to introduce me?"

"I didn't get specifics, but Ms. Quercus here is no ordinary tree."

Something poked me in the back. I spun around to see what looked like a common, innocent little branch sticking out from the massive trunk. It swayed slightly.

"You're saying the tree's alive?"

"All trees are alive."

"Yes, of course. I mean . . . sentient?"

Oscar stared at me. "Don't know what that means."

"Conscious. Like . . . like the apple trees in *The Wizard of Oz*."

Now he started snickering. Oscar and I had snuggled on the couch last week and watched the movie, which I had heard of all my life but had never seen. Oscar thought it was the funniest thing he'd ever seen. I found it horrifying—especially the flying monkeys and the evil witch and the trees that threw apples. Oscar informed me that I had lost my sense of humor and that I clearly needed his help to find it again. He could well be right.

Still shaking his head, he wiped tears from his eyes with his oversized hands. "Those apple trees. That was somethin'. But yeah, in a way I guess you could say it was like that. Except this one . . . This is a different deal entirely. It's a source of"—he dropped his gravelly voice—"*evil*."

"Are you saying the *tree* killed Sebastian Crowley?"

"No, of course not. It wouldn't kill like *that*. How would a tree use a gun?"

Somehow that wasn't as comforting as one would hope. Besides, I thought with a sick feeling deep in the pit of my gut, someone had gone after the proprietor of Aunt Flora's. Someone very human, unless I missed my guess.

Another rustling sounded up in the far reaches of the tree.

"Grrrrr." Oscar started to growl, making a rasping sound like an old saw. I rarely heard him make such a sound—it was the kind of noise that reminded me that Oscar could be fierce when provoked.

He was peering up into the branches, his muzzle set in a ferocious cast.

"What is it?" I whispered, trying to see what he was

looking at. As before, all I could see was a web of dark lines crisscrossing the rapidly brightening sky. "What do you—?"

Oscar scrambled up the tree trunk and disappeared into the branches.

There was a great rustling sound, more growls. Small branches snapped. I was showered with leaves, twigs, and acorns.

Then sudden silence.

"Oscar?" I called out in a fierce whisper. "Oscar, are you okay? Where are you?"

The otherworldly pink light of the dawn seemed to close in on me. I looked around, feeling as though I was being watched or that I was doing something wrong. It made me realize how rarely I had to go it alone these days, what with Maya and Bronwyn and Sailor and Oscar and others. . . . I was no longer a solo act.

Another long moment passed, the silence much more sinister than the earlier commotion.

"Oscar?" I whispered again. When there was still no response, I threw caution to the wind and yelled as loud as I could, *"Oscarrr!"*

I passed the beam of my flashlight around and through the branches, but it was light enough now to see without it. Unfortunately, with or without the flashlight, I saw nothing more than wood and leaves.

My familiar was gone.

Chapter 10

"Oscar!" I shouted again.

"Lily?" came a voice from behind me. I whirled around to see Conrad standing with a couple of his friends. "Lily, what are you doing here? No one's supposed to cross the police tape; *dude*, a man was killed here just yesterday." Apparently, he forgot I had joined him shortly after he found the body.

"I..."

"Where's Oscar?" Conrad looked around the clearing. "I heard you calling for him."

I looked back up into the tree, hoping for a glimpse of my familiar.

Conrad looked up too, then back at me with a worried expression on his face.

"I think I ... I lost him."

"Where did you last see him?"

"I..." I trailed off, realizing that to the normal world Oscar appeared as a miniature potbellied pig. And it didn't stand to reason that a pig could have climbed a tree. "Right around here," I improvised. "I lost sight of him here at the tree."

"I'll help you look," said Conrad. "Though I gotta say, you shoulda had him on a leash. I know pigs are smart, but they're sorta like dogs, right?"

At those words, I hoped to hear a disgruntled Oscar somewhere, as he hated being compared to a dog. But still there was nothing.

"Here, Oscar!" Conrad started yelling, looking under benches and behind trees. I handed him my flashlight as he started to literally beat the bushes. "Here, piggy piggy pig!"

I blew out a breath, closed my eyes, and tried to reach out to Oscar psychically. I wasn't good at this, but I hoped if I could focus enough I might be able to piggy-back on our connection. So to speak.

Nothing.

Calm yourself, Lily. Obviously, Oscar was up to something. My familiar had lived a very long time—for centuries, probably—without my help. He knew what he was doing around magical events, most of the time much better than I did. He was probably . . . I don't know . . . probably communing with the tree, or maybe he found something to eat. Didn't tree sitters bring picnic baskets up into the branches of the trees sometimes?

"Conrad, were there sitters in this tree?"

"What? Nah, dude. I told you. We can't sit in it on account of the rot. You could totally, like, fall, or even hasten the tree's death. The tree lady said it could go on like this for another five years, dude. A slow death. That's the way they do it."

Another pair of young people meandered by, hair tousled and eyes still sleepy, looking like they just woke up. But then again, I guess when you live in Golden Gate Park you always look like you just woke up. I had spent nights out in the open from time to time, and the sleeping wasn't the worst part—it was awakening to no toilet, no shower, no privacy. I was sure it wasn't good for anyone's mental health.

"Okay, everybody, listen up!" yelled Conrad. A small crowd of gutterpunks gathered around him in a loose semicircle. Suddenly, the vagueness seemed to drop from him; the Con was large and in charge. "We've lost a pig. Everybody, fan out and look for him."

"What's it look like?" asked one young man.

"Yeah, what's it look like?" asked a young woman.

This question seemed to stump Conrad, and just that quickly, the vagueness was back.

"It's, uh . . . he's sorta pink, a little bit? And . . ."

Conrad glanced over at me as though seeking rescue. I was about to describe Oscar's porcine form when one of the cleverer men offered:

"Dude, if he's a pig . . . well, if anyone finds a pig of any sort we should probably say something. How many pigs could be running wild in Golden Gate Park?"

"*Excellent* point, dude," said Conrad. "Any kind of pig sighting at all, you yell, okay? And, dudes, don't be afraid or anything. He's, like, a totally friendly little pig."

While Conrad made his speech, I couldn't stop searching the tree. I looked up as surreptitiously as possible, wondering, yearning, trying as hard as I could to clamp down on my incipient panic. The sun was now pouring soft golden light down onto the park, and the new growth at the top of the tree was clear to see: bright green leaves among the darker mature ones. So the tree might be dying, but it was still producing new life, still performing photosynthesis, taking in nourishment. As Conrad had pointed out, trees did not die easy.

The clearing was now awash in calls of "Heeeere, piggy piggy" as the gutterpunks enthusiastically crashed through bushes and between the trees. I supposed it was possible that Oscar, seeing the witnesses, had climbed down the other side of the tree and transformed into his piggy form and would appear any second.

But my heart fluttered as I gazed at the tree, whose

broad, low arms were perfectly clear in the morning light.

They now appeared sinister to me ... and full of dreadful secrets.

Hours later—after searching fruitlessly and calling incessantly—Conrad insisted on walking me back to Aunt Cora's Closet.

"Dudette, I don't mean to embarrass you, but your clothes are totally on inside out. I do that sometimes," he said with an understanding nod. "Get dressed in the dark, easy enough to screw up. I like the bells, though. You sound like music when you walk."

Aunt Cora's Closet was open for business when we arrived. Two early-bird shoppers were browsing; one was flicking through antique negligees, the other trying on a fringed buckskin jacket in front of the three-way mirror.

"Lily, *there* you are!" Bronwyn gushed, enveloping me in a coffee- and muffin-scented hug. "I don't believe I've ever opened the shop without you before! Where have you been? I didn't see any signs that you had cast your usual morning spell. . . ."

"I—" I had held it together the whole time in the park and on the walk home. But for some reason, upon seeing Bronwyn's face, I lost it. I wasn't crying, since I don't cry. But I started gasping for breath, unable to rein in my emotions.

Before I could get ahold of myself, two prom dresses flung themselves off the rack. A shelf fell down on one side, sending its contents—hats and gloves—tumbling to the floor. The bell over the front door started ringing incessantly, as did the ones circling my wrists.

The two customers witnessed the destruction, looking confused and startled.

"Dude?" asked Conrad.

Bronwyn spun around, watching as things crashed and

flew. Finally, she looked back to me, realization dawning in her eyes. "Conrad, what happened?"

"Dude, she totally, like, lost her pig? And now she's losing her shi—"

"Thank you, Conrad. That's fine. Why don't you slip outside for a moment while we gather our wits? Do us a favor by keeping any customers out for a moment. We'll reopen in a few."

Her words were accentuated by a nineteenth-century gown that flew off its display on the wall and careened across the store. A hatbox flew in the opposite direction, and a pair of umbrellas skittered along the plank floor.

"Lily, listen to me," Bronwyn said, her voice low and very calm. "You have to get ahold of yourself."

Oscar. I couldn't stop thinking about him, couldn't stop panicking at the thought that he was gone. I took a step in one direction, then another, spinning around without knowing where I was going. I was gasping for breath, my heart hammering in my chest; I could feel its wild fluttering through my veins.

The two customers fled the store, one after the other rushing out into the cool, sunny morning.

"Lily," repeated Bronwyn firmly. She took me in her arms again, this time more as a restraint than a welcome. "Listen to me, Lily. You're going to hurt something, or someone. *Calm down.*"

Her words finally sank in. I felt myself start to quiet.

"*Breathe.* Take a deep breath, hold it for four, release for eight." She breathed in deeply, demonstrating. I tried to match my breath to hers. After a moment, things stopped flying around the store as I regained control.

"Oscar is . . ."

"I know. Conrad told me. He got loose in the park? Did something scare him off?"

She knew it wasn't like him to run. He stuck by my side—he was my familiar, after all. That's what he did.

Unless he had a very good reason not to. Or unless he wasn't able to . . .

I felt the panic rise again and forced myself to breathe, as Bronwyn had instructed me. It wasn't going to do anyone any good if I carried on like a sinner in a cyclone.

"Okay, let's think this thing through logically," said Bronwyn as she poured heated water over some herbs in a tea bob and handed me a steaming mug. "Drink this."

It was a measure of trust that I took the hot drink from Bronwyn without asking. Usually a witch didn't accept random herbs from another person. Somewhere in the back of my head I realized that I had come a long, long way from that lonely, friendless witch who'd wandered into town not even a full year ago. I didn't have to deal with things alone anymore.

But how could I tell her that Oscar was no ordinary missing miniature potbellied pig?

I wanted Bronwyn to understand the level of my fear and frustration and why Conrad's friends' efforts to help were useless. But there was a reason we magic folk keep certain things from nonpractitioners. Even though my friends had come to accept me and the things I did, I was still human and remained within their frames of reference. If I introduced them to the idea of magical creatures . . . well, I didn't know what would happen exactly. But I had the definite sense it wouldn't be pretty. It would rock their world, upset their parameters of reality and knowledge. And not in a good way. I didn't adhere to Oscar's generalized disdain for cowans, but I did agree with one thing: Sometimes ignorance was a blessing. Knowing too much about what existed in the world wasn't going to do them any favors.

"How long has he been gone? Should we check the pound?" Bronwyn ventured now that I was calmer.

"I—"

There was a commotion at the front door. Bronwyn

and I looked over to see Maya in a brief tussle with Conrad right outside the front door. We could hear her explaining to him that she wasn't a customer and so should be allowed to enter. Finally, he acquiesced and she dashed in.

"What's going on?" she asked. "What's all this about a missing pig?"

I swallowed but seemed unable to speak. Luckily, Bronwyn stepped in for me.

"Oscar and Lily took a walk through Golden Gate Park this morning. And Oscar appears to have gone missing."

"When? Where? And what's been done to find him?"

"We're just working that out now," said Bronwyn, her voice overly composed, as though afraid to set me off again. "Look, among all of us, we've got a lot of friends. We'll send out search parties, put up flyers. How long could it take to find a lost pig, for heaven's sake? And Oscar's so smart. And adorable, and . . ."

Her chocolate-brown eyes took on a faraway look, and I realized that it just hit her: *Oscar was missing*. Her little Oscaroo, the piggy she doted on.

"I don't understand how this could have happened," said Maya. "He wasn't on a leash?"

I shook my head. "He always stayed with me."

"Did he see something, chase something? Did he smell food, maybe?"

Everyone was clear on exactly how far Oscar would go for food. In some ways it made perfect sense that he had chosen his piggy form as his normal form.

I shook my head.

"Well, I'm not going to just sit around here," said Maya. "Let's go find him. He's a pig; how hard could it be to track him down?"

"You used to call him 'the other white meat,'" Bronwyn pointed out. We were all upset.

"That was before. Now ... well, now he's just ... he's Oscar," Maya said with a little hitch in her throat. "I'll call my friends, my cousins. We'll cover every inch of that park. He can't have gotten that far."

Actually, searching every inch of Golden Gate Park was a bigger job than it might have sounded. Similar in shape to New York's Central Park, it was a full twenty percent larger. Three miles long, half a mile across. It was more than one thousand acres of public ground smack-dab in the middle of the city, stretching from the Haight to the Pacific Ocean. There were lakes, playgrounds, museums of art and natural history, a Japanese tea garden, an AIDS memorial, soccer fields and baseball diamonds, botanical gardens. And plenty of people sleeping under trees. It was even said to have its very own ghost, a traffic cop who would occasionally stop people for speeding. It was a glorious, vast park.

With, apparently, one very nasty tree.

"Tell you what," I said. "I'll go check with the city, and then I'll go back to search in the park. Maya, if you want to search as well, Conrad knows where he disappeared. Bronwyn, would you please stay and watch over the store? We don't all need to panic, and for all we know, he might just walk right back in here."

Bronwyn was crying by now, her eyelashes spiked with tears. She nodded and sniffed. "Yes, he's such a smart pig. So smart, he'll probably be trotting in any moment."

"I'll go start telling people," said Maya.

"And I'll make some calls," said Bronwyn. "And get the coven involved."

"Great," I said, trying to quell the guilt I felt at accepting the help of so many well-meaning people when I knew full well there was something entirely supernatural going on. "I ... I'll check in, let you know if I find anything."

I slipped out. As I turned to close the door behind me, I could see Maya and Bronwyn with their heads bent low over the counter as they wrote up a list of people to contact for help and places to look. They might as well have been planning the Invasion of Normandy.

"Dude," said the Con. He was sitting in his usual spot on the curb, but now he was holding his head in his hands. "Dude, I am so, like, bummed about poor Oscar. I was thinking, Lily, you know how I told you I was having nightmares? Like, when I slept under that tree? And not just because I thought a branch might fall on me, but like, real nightmares?"

"Yes?"

"You don't suppose . . . you don't think the nightmares could have had anything to do with the little guy going missing, do you?"

It stunned me that Conrad, dear, vague, out-of-it Conrad, was the person closest to understanding the truth. Because *yes*, I did think that those nightmares had something to do with Oscar going missing. And with those strange visions that I'd had when I put on that cloak.

The cloak. Could it help me somehow, tell me something? So far all I had seen was the memories attached. But if those memories were somehow related to Conrad's nightmares, which were connected to the tree and to Sebastian's murder, then . . . what? What did any of this have to do with Oscar's disappearance? And how could I use it to get my pig back?

I didn't know, exactly, but I was fixin' to find out.

I had lied to my friends—I wasn't headed to check with the city or to search Golden Gate Park. Instead, I hopped in the car and headed for the San Francisco Ferry Building, which housed the temporary offices of Aidan Rhodes, witchy godfather, occasional friend, and Oscar's former master.

*   *   *

I parked downtown near the temporary Transbay Terminal and walked the several blocks to the Ferry Building. Along the way the city's siren blared, long and mournful. I never got used to it—it went off every Tuesday and always put me in mind of old WWII movies about Londoners running for air raid shelters. One of these days I was going to ask a native why it blew. Probably it was some obscure local reason, like the way everyone thought Lombard Street was the crookedest street in the world when, in fact, Vermont Avenue between 20th and 22nd Streets, near McKinley Square, had even more switchbacks.

The Ferry Building stood right on the shore of the bay, at the base of busy Market Street, and was marked by a tall clock tower. Built long ago, it had been one of the busiest hubs in the country before the Bay Bridge was built, connecting San Francisco to the East Bay. Afterward, it had fallen on hard times. But following the 1988 Loma Prieta earthquake, a freeway was demolished and the dilapidated building was transformed into a series of kiosks and small stores specializing in local products, from oysters to honey to ceramics—all of which were extraordinarily attractive and phenomenally expensive. It was also known for offering plenty of interesting dining options, from trucks to stands to permanent restaurants. Whether early in the morning or right before they closed, I had never seen the Ferry Building less than packed with people and buzzing with happy energy.

A few months ago, Aidan's office in the Wax Museum had burned down. It was a shame that the museum had to shut down for repairs—I was sure people lost jobs and money—but happily no one I cared about was hurt, and the neighboring businesses were saved. But since Aidan liked to be in the thick of things, he found temporary office space in the Ferry Building.

I was just glad not to have to brave a gauntlet of wax

figures in order to visit him. I had never enjoyed them, but now the nightmarish memories of those characters liquefying, their slippery wax flooding the floor and pouring down the stairs, burning our feet, their features melting and slipping . . . *ugh*.

Passing by flower vendors and mobbed food trucks was far preferable.

The offices were on the second-floor mezzanine, where an open walkway looked down over the crowds below. A security guard sat at a dais set up at the top of the stairs, but she was usually absorbed in whatever she was reading on her smartphone. I never paused, and she never tried to stop me.

Aidan's was one of many nondescript offices, distinguished only by the pure white long-haired cat that often sat outside his door. But not today.

I lifted my hand to knock, but the door opened before I had the chance.

"Lily! It is always *such* a pleasure." He spoke with warmth, as always. Aidan is impossibly good-looking, with brilliant periwinkle-blue eyes, gleaming golden hair, and just a hint of manly whiskers. Being near him, I found it hard not to notice his looks, but also his aura, which glittered so brightly even nonsensitive types tended to stop and stare when he walked by.

As always, I felt mixed emotions when in Aidan's presence. To be absolutely honest, it was easier to dislike him when I wasn't caught up in his aural spectrum. I wasn't sure how to interpret the feelings I had for him; they were complicated, a muddle of kinship and fear, gratitude and wariness. And even, let's face it, attraction. He had come through for me in the past, and I believed he was fond of me . . . in his way. But I wasn't foolish enough to think he wouldn't throw me under the bus if he needed to. Aidan wasn't one to let anyone stand in his way.

And he was powerful in more ways than one.

"Oscar's missing," I blurted out. At my own words, I felt the panic rise like bile in my throat. A leather-bound book flew off a bookshelf and landed in the center of the room, narrowly missing him. "Sorry!"

Aidan looked alarmed. I wasn't sure whether his re-action was due to the book or the news of Oscar missing.

"Come in, come in. Have a seat."

He made a gesture to the security guard at the top of the stairs and closed the door behind me.

"You need to calm down," Aidan said unnecessarily. "Someone like you could wind up taking down the bridge if you get too out of control."

"You're exaggerating." I hoped.

A crystal ball crashed to the floor and the cat yowled and jumped to the bookcase.

Aidan raised an eyebrow.

I collapsed onto a red leather chair that seemed to be an exact duplicate of the one in his old office. In fact, the entire office seemed to be a re-creation of that former locale: the same plush furniture, velvet curtains, Oriental rug. Dark woods, sumptuous fabrics, all very Victoriana. I noticed his bookshelf was becoming increasingly crammed with a rare collection of volumes and ephem-era regarding magical history.

"I thought your collection of books had burned?" I said, by way of distracting myself for a moment. I had to get control of my emotions if I wanted to be of any help to Oscar. *Oscar*.

"Indeed it did," he said with a shake of his head. "Such a shame. But I've been working at rebuilding my library. It's amazing what a person can find for sale on the Internet these days. Most people don't even realize what they have."

"Isn't most of this information available online any-way?" I was no expert, but lately Maya had been showing me just how much information was available via the Internet, if a person was so inclined. I didn't much care for computers for the same reason that I didn't carry a cell phone: I don't trust all that energy charging over electronic wires, all those electrodes or ions or whatever, rushing around. I feared there were ghosts in those machines. But I had to admit, when the alternative was coming begging hat in hand to Aidan to look at his printed *Goetiea*, it was much easier to look up random demons by way of a search engine. Especially when I could just ask Maya to do it for me.

"Are you here to borrow something from my library?"

"No." I took a deep breath and let it out slowly. "Do you know anything about Oscar disappearing?"

"When and where did he disappear?"

"This morning in Golden Gate Park."

"I don't know anything about it, no."

"Do you have any way of tracking him?"

"I'm no psychic; you know that."

"True, but you always seem to know where *I* am. . . ." He smiled.

"I guess I was hoping for some witchy form of a Lo-Jack chip," I continued.

"Sorry." He shook his golden head. "Tell me what happened."

I gave him the short version, including acquiring the trunk with the suspicious cloak, learning about Bart's supposed curse, and finding Sebastian under the tree.

"The woodsfolk must know something about this," said Aidan.

"Oscar was trying to make contact with them right before he disappeared."

"So he's probably with them now. They have a way of taking people into their world temporarily. And time is different there, so he might think he's been there only a few minutes."

"But Oscar seemed to think he saw, or heard, something in the tree. He went up after it. I lost sight of him in the branches, and then he just . . . disappeared. Wouldn't the woodsfolk have taken him down into the ground somehow?"

He nodded. "At the base of the tree, yes. And they prefer redwoods around here."

"That's what I thought. I really think something's wrong, Aidan. There's something about that tree. . . ."

"You're telling me you think this tree is haunted somehow?"

"Not haunted per se," I said, only realizing it as I spoke. "But . . . possessed, maybe? Is that possible? Oscar seemed to have a bunch of stories about trees seeking vengeance, that sort of thing."

"Possible, certainly. As living creatures, trees can be used as stand-ins. Not possessed, exactly; they act more like holding cells. If a creature wasn't able to maintain human form, for example. Or, if something were somehow captured and imprisoned."

"Imprisoned. How would that work?"

"Typically, something essential about a creature could be fed to the roots of the tree, with the proper spell casting, of course. The tree could soak up the powers, essentially holding the creature within."

"Until . . . ?"

He shrugged.

"What if the tree died, or was cut down?"

"The creature would die as well."

Well, that seemed easy enough. Except . . .

"If . . . if Oscar is in the tree somehow, then if the tree is cut down . . . he would *die*?"

Chapter 11

Aidan nodded.

I felt myself losing control again, my heart pounding.

"How is this even possible?" I demanded. "How would Oscar have been absorbed by the tree?"

"I don't really know, Lily. And we're still not sure that's what happened. But I will look into it."

"It's *Oscar*, Aidan," I said, and another book flew off the shelf. "I can't stand to think of anything happening to him. . . ."

"And I just told you, I will make inquiries. I'll let you know. In the meantime, I suggest you try to fill in the history of that cape you mentioned and maybe get to know the cursed man."

His familiar jumped on the desk, strutting along, and I leaned back. Noctemus and I didn't get along that well. For one thing, I was allergic to cats. For another, I didn't much like her attitude. Also, I feared we sparred a bit over Aidan, which I found rather disturbing. After all, I didn't want Aidan like that, did I? And besides . . . Noctemus was a *cat*. It was just plain weird to be vying with a fluffy pet, familiar or no.

"Listen, Lily," Aidan said, coming around to stand in front of the desk, half sitting on it in front of me. His voice was low and very gentle. "Oscar probably went somewhere to speak with the Good People. Like I said, time is different there."

"How different?"

"There are stories of people reappearing after two, three centuries."

I blinked. "You have to get him out, Aidan. I'll do . . . I'll do anything. Really."

"Oooh, those are dangerous words, my rash little witchy friend. You should know that."

"If Oscar's with the woodsfolk, though, that means he's okay, right? They wouldn't hurt him, would they? I mean, isn't he sort of one of them?"

"Sort of . . ." He pushed out his chin and tilted his head.

"And so you can go and speak with them, and they'll release him. Right?"

"Just as long as . . ."

"As what?"

"As long as he doesn't eat anything. It's like Persephone and Hades. She was okay until she ate those pomegranate seeds."

What were the chances Oscar would eat something if it were offered to him?

Another book flew off the shelf.

"Simmer down, Lily. We have no idea what happened—for all you know he might have simply wandered off, looking for new adventures. Did you have any indication he wasn't happy?"

I thought back. "He was . . . bored sometimes. But he seemed happy enough. He likes my cooking."

Aidan smiled. "I'm sure. But these creatures are quirky, unpredictable."

"You're the one who gave him to me in the first place."

"Well, I certainly didn't assume you, as a smart witch, would fetishize the poor little guy."

"I just want to make sure he's all right. If he doesn't want to stay with me, well, that's his choice."

"Here's someone who might be able to help fill in some of the history surrounding the curse and the cape." He wrote something on the back of a business card. "Go talk to him. And in the meantime, for the sake of us all, try to stay calm."

That was a lot easier said than done.

Once, when Aidan had given me the name and contact information of someone who could help me, I had hesitated. When I found him, he was a brooding man in motorcycle boots, scowling at everyone in the bar. He had intimidated me. But I had gotten to know him. Sailor. My Sailor.

So even though part of me, trained through a difficult childhood not to ask strangers questions about the magical world, still held back, another part of me decided to look up the name Aidan had written on his card.

And this time, it turned out I already knew the man. I had met him the other day at Bart's apartment. I supposed it made sense that circles of acquaintances would start to overlap; after all, how many experts in witchcraft history could there be in the Bay Area? I found a pay phone and placed a call to Williston Chambers, professor of religion, UC Berkeley. He seemed happy to hear from me; he told me he had class in fifteen minutes but suggested I come by at four during office hours.

Before leaving the Ferry Building, I braved the jostling crowd—and the exorbitant prices—to stock up on the ingredients to make Oscar's favorite foods: creamy mashed potatoes and five-cheese mac and cheese. *Never again*, I thought to myself, never again would I deny him

carbs in a misguided attempt to force him to eat vegetables. I also bought Scharffen Berger chocolate for chocolate-chip cookies. After all, wouldn't want the cookie
jar to be empty when he made his way back home.

I had just pulled into the driveway I rent near Aunt
Cora's Closet when I spotted an unmarked police car
pull up to the curb. Carlos Romero. *Shoot.*

I had forgotten we had a date with a clothing conservator.

"You ready? She's expecting me," said Carlos, checking his watch.

"Um . . ." I had been itching to get back to the store,
but this was more important. "Yes, I suppose I'm freeish.
Just let me go grab my bag." These days the medicine
bag tied around my waist wasn't sufficient. I never went
anywhere without my portable witch-in-a-bag: bottle of
all-purpose protective brew, tiny jar of cemetery dust,
lungwort, and mullein. When things calmed down, I really should consider selling these bags over the Internet.
I would make a fortune.

"Don't forget the ledger."

"Right you are. The ledger. I'll be right back."

Bronwyn was still watching over things at Aunt Cora's Closet; as I'd feared, Oscar hadn't wandered back
into the store while I was away, and my remaining
wouldn't help. At the very least, I should go meet with
the clothing conservator and see if she could shed any
light on the things in the trunk. It was all tied together,
somehow.

Also, Aidan's promise made me feel optimistic. He was
probably right—I had asked Oscar to arrange an introduction with the woodsfolk myself, and my familiar had tried
to tell me how complicated it could be. For all I knew, he
was hanging around with the Good People, swapping stories while negotiating terms. Or however this was done.

I would see Oscar again soon. I just had to keep believing that.

The conservator's office was located in the Asian Art Museum, right across from City Hall. The museum was one of those countless Bay Area cultural attractions on my list of places to visit, but this was the first time I'd managed to get here. As usual when entering a museum or historical building, I was agog at the art and artifacts, but also a little overwhelmed by the sensations. As we passed an exhibit on the Indian royal palaces, I could hear whisperings and felt a brushing sensation flutter past my cheek, a breath on the back of my neck.

Museums are full of ghost-ridden objects, their spirits traveling through the ages; this is one reason some people find them to be energy draining. The ghosts are misplaced and don't understand where they are, especially when housed in a strange new building. They reach out to attach to other human energies, feeling for understanding. It can be exhausting for people sensitive to such sensations. Like me. Unfortunately, ghosts latch on to me, sensing my strange energy, but I can't understand them. It's frustrating for all parties involved.

Carlos and I took the stairs up to the second floor and found Parmelee Riesling's workshop and office right past a display of fine ceramics.

"You're late," she said upon opening the door. Riesling was barely five feet tall, round, with a dark brown pageboy haircut and huge round glasses that magnified her eyes, giving her a buglike countenance.

"I apologize," said Carlos, checking his watch. I glanced down to see the time: It was three minutes past noon. Apparently, Parmelee was a real stickler for punctuality.

"Who's she?" the conservator demanded, her eyes on me, piercing.

"This is Lily Ivory. She's a special consultant to the department."

"Humph," she harrumphed, and turned to lead the way into her workshop.

I was still reeling a bit to hear myself described as a "special consultant" to the SFPD as we followed Riesling into the large, windowless room. There were four massive worktables, two covered in felt, the others in a slick plastic. Beside the regular lights, I noticed, were infrareds. Light was one of the biggest risks to delicate textiles.

"Don't touch anything," dictated Riesling as she led the way. "Your fingers carry oils, and oil goes on to trap dust deep within fabric. Roll up your sleeves—I don't want anything to catch threads. No bracelets, necklaces, rings, tags, and anything else sticking out from your clothes."

She looked over her shoulder at me and gave me a long once-over, raking me with dark gray eyes. Suddenly, she reached out and clutched my skirt, rubbing the fabric between two forefingers. "Midsixties, probably North Carolina, indigo dye lot on cotton blend. Nice example of simple American craftsmanship."

"I, um . . . thanks," I finished lamely.

"You should take better care of it; you've got dirt on your backside. Also, it's inside out. And take off those bangles."

"Yes, ma'am," I said, cringing inwardly to hear "ma'am" come out in two full syllables. My Texas twang tended to return with a vengeance when I was nervous or dealing with authority figures.

"Aside from the obvious—no markers, food, or smoking—there must be no direct contact with pins, iron, wood, newsprint, newsprint paper, note cards, non–rag cardboard, unwashed clothes, plastic films, acidic tissue papers, labels, or Scotch Tape. They all have detrimental effects. What kind of consultant?"

I almost missed her question, so caught up was I in her monologue and everything I was seeing: mannequins dressed in historical costume, intricate silk embroidery, ancient needlepoint.

"I'm, a, uh . . . I own a vintage clothing store."

"A what?" she said with a frown.

"A . . . vintage clothing store? In the Haight."

She harrumphed again and muttered under her breath as she led us to a small room with yet another worktable, on top of which rested the contents of the trunk, each laid out separately on the table.

"What we have here is an example of nineteenth-century clothing of the merchant class," she began. She spoke for another ten minutes straight without a pause. Carlos and I were receiving a crash course in the history and conservation of cloth, whether we wanted it or not. Then again without pausing to indicate she was changing the subject, she demanded: "Why have you brought this here, and why are the police so interested in a trunk full of junk?"

"We just wanted to be sure it really was junk," Carlos said with a shrug. Unlike me, he did not seem particularly flustered by Parmelee's officiousness. "So you're saying there's nothing here worth killing for, at least not that you can find?"

"There's nothing here worth anything, really. Clothing of this age is always fascinating, but these are so far gone I won't even allow them in the same room as the valuable textiles, lest mold spores or insects get loose."

"Insects?" For the first time Carlos looked uncomfortable.

I smiled at the thought of seemingly fearless San Francisco homicide inspector Carlos Romero being afraid of insects.

"Nothing too scary, Carlos," I whispered. "Mostly little moths."

Parmelee fixed me with another of her scathing looks. "And beetles. Spiders . . . any number of possibilities."

"But that's normal, right? We're looking for something odd, out of place."

"The only odd thing I've found is some strands of velvet."

"What would that indicate?" Carlos asked.

"That there was something else in the trunk. Something made of deep gold velvet. Given the age of the textiles, I would say it would have been an outer garment, a coat or cloak of some sort."

Carlos fixed me with a look, which I steadfastly tried to ignore.

"Can you tell anything else about it?" I asked.

She shook her head. "Just seems odd it was taken when everything else was left intact. Also, I had an expert look at the trunk itself. It's much older than these clothes. He dated it all the way back to the Puritans, and see here?" She pointed at a subtle design on the metal fasteners. "Apparently, that was the signature of a metalworker from New England."

"New England? Whereabouts in New England?" I asked.

"Massachusetts." Parmelee shrugged, unimpressed. "It's old, all right, but in terrible shape. Its only real value would be to collectors of Salem mementos. Believe it or not, there are a lot of—"

"Hold up one minute," said Carlos, a hand raised. "Salem? As in Massachusetts? As in . . . witch burnings?"

"They were hung, not burned," I felt compelled to mention.

Carlos dismissed my clarification. "Whatever. You're saying these clothes are from there?"

"Or that area," said Parmelee. "This metalworker is a known guy, always left a signature. And Salem was, and is, a real town, you know. It existed long before there were witchcraft trials and long after books were written about it. Those trials were an anomaly in the history of an otherwise unremarkable town. But . . . people get excited by the name and the history. So if you want to make money off this thing, I'd play up the possible Salem connection."

Carlos nodded thoughtfully for a long moment; then his dark eyes slewed over to me. They held many questions and the knowledge that more was going on than I had let on.

"Who collects this sort of thing?" he asked finally.

"I'm sure I don't know," Parmelee said. "Prior to my relocation to San Francisco, I spent a decade working on the Royal Collection at Hampton Court Palace and Kensington Palace, in London. I was lead conservator for the Princess Cassie Dress Collection and oversaw the conservation of the Ardabil Carpet. While there, I managed the largest textile wash bath in the world, constructed explicitly to handle the majestic sixteenth-century Belgian tapestries of the royal collection. I displayed Queen Victoria's first official public gown as well as all those of Queen Elizabeth II, and the ancient wrappings of a three-thousand-year-old mummy."

She paused and fixed us with the stink-eye. "All of which is to say: Witchcraft isn't exactly my realm of expertise."

This grand proclamation seemed to silence even Carlos.

"So . . ." I said in an effort to break the tension, "have you ever considered selling the contents of *your* closet?"

As we left Parmelee Riesling's workroom and descended the stairs toward the museum's main hall, I could feel the heat of Carlos's eyes on me.

"Interesting woman," I said. "Very . . . intense."

"Hey, I wouldn't make fun. She oversaw the biggest

textile bath in the world." His voice rose and he used a falsetto with a decidedly clipped British accent: "And she has *personally* seen to Queen Victoria's frilly under-things."

I laughed.

"Funny, though," Carlos added, "about whatever golden velvet thingee disappeared from the trunk."

"Yeah. Hard to say what was in there, when. It's an awfully old trunk."

"Mmm."

In the lobby, a big group of children on a field trip laughed and ran after one another while their teacher tried to settle them down. I noticed what looked like a fascinating museum gift shop and longed to go in; I'm not much of a shopper, with the exception of garage sales, thrift stores, flea markets . . . and museum gift shops.

But I had the distinct impression Inspector Suspicious here wasn't up for a side trip. Besides, something else occurred to me.

"So, Carlos, did you really expect Riesling to find something among those crumbling items so valuable it would provide the motive for Sebastian Crowley's murder?"

"Not especially," he said as we exited the building. The surprisingly austere plaza in front of City Hall was filled with homeless people, tourists, and men and women in business suits. Government workers spilled out of the nearby federal, state, and city buildings, as well as Hastings Law School, and lined up at food trucks and coffee carts for lunch. "But I thought it might be interesting for your investigation into his death."

"*My* investigation?" I blushed. "I'm sure I don't know what you're talking about."

"I know something odd is going on," said Carlos. "The way he was murdered, brought there under the tree . . . It

makes no sense. We thought maybe he'd buried something at the base of the tree, but all they found was a
rotted old box. Empty."

"Rotted old box? What did it look like?"

"Nowhere near the size of the trunk. About the size
of a shoe box."

"What was in it?"

"Nothing. It had fallen apart, wasn't even a box anymore, so if there had been something in it, it was long
since lost."

"Were there insignia on it, any markings?"

Carlos looked at me oddly and nodded slowly. He
took his phone out of his pocket, brought up his photos,
and showed me a picture.

I blew it up as far as I could to see the detail: strange
little symbols. Carlos was right; it was disintegrating so
there were only shards left. But unless I was very much
mistaken, it was the box I had seen in my vision.

"You recognize it?" Carlos asked.

"Maybe."

"Maybe?"

"I'll . . . I'll have to look into it. I might . . . I might recognize it. I'm not sure. I have no idea what the symbols
mean, though."

"Want me to forward the photo to your phone?"

"Yes, but I don't have a cell phone."

"What do you mean you don't have a cell phone?"

"Just that: I don't have a cell phone."

"Huh. This to do with the witchy thing?"

"I guess you could say that, yes. Cell phones mess with
my vibrations."

"Huh."

"Not *everyone* has to have a cell phone, you know. It's
not a requirement for being human."

"You sure about that?"

"Not really. You're right; I'm feeling more and more

like a freak. Witchcraft is one thing, but not having a cell phone? That's just plain bizarre."

Carlos smiled, and I responded in kind.

"Could you send it to my e-mail? I'll ask Maya to get it out of my machine for me."

"Sure. So, do you know anyone who could help with this?" Carlos asked. "Riesling mentioned calling in a historian of some sort, a witchcraft expert. If you don't know this history, do you know anyone who might?"

"Maybe. Actually, I met a man the other day. . . ." I hesitated, not wanting to mention I met Professor Williston Chambers at the house of the man who owned the trunk of clothes. Carlos probably wouldn't have appreciated me talking to Bartholomew Woolsey on my own initiative; while he asked for my help from time to time, it really irked him when I "ran around talking to his suspects."

"A man?" He roused me from my thoughts.

"Yes. A professor over at UC Berkeley. He researches the history of religious settlements, including, I would imagine, places like Salem."

"Sounds fascinating. Probably worth your while to go talk to him."

Our eyes met and held for a long moment. "So, you think this is a case of witchcraft?"

"Maybe. Maybe someone who *thinks* they're performing witchcraft. You know as well as I do, people can come up with all sorts of excuses for crazy behavior."

"So . . . you set up this meeting with Parmelee Riesling just for me?"

He shrugged again and squinted in the sun, looked off up Larkin Street.

"You see that corner?" he asked, pointing toward Larkin and McAllister, where there was now a flourishing community garden. "Years ago, a homeless guy was knifed right there, in broad daylight. His throat slit by another homeless guy, who was under the illusion that his victim was the incarnation of the devil. Rookie beat cop wasn't more than ten feet away, but wasn't able to stop it in time. There was ... blood everywhere." Carlos paused for a moment and cleared his throat. "Hard to imagine a human body contains that much blood. Poor guy died before he got to the hospital."

"And the rookie cop?" I asked gently.

"He was never the same." He looked back at me. "Witchcraft or no, crazy or not ... I just want the killing to stop. Go talk to this professor. Here, use my phone."

"I ... As a matter of fact, I already have an appointment with him this afternoon. Want to join me?"

Carlos blew out a long breath and shook his head. "No, thanks. I'm already skirting the boundaries of what's decent; if I push this too far, I really will be the department's official woo-woo guy. Just let me know what he says."

"Will do."

As Carlos drove me back to Aunt Cora's Closet, he said: "About that oak tree in Golden Gate Park, the one the body was found under ..."

"Yes?"

"I thought I would mention that the Parks Department has it slated for removal."

Chapter 12

"What? *When?*"

"As soon as the SFPD releases the crime scene, I would imagine."

"Can you stop it? Carlos, it's very important that the tree not be cut down. Not yet, anyway."

He fixed me with his laser cop look. "Why?"

"It's . . . This is one of those situations you're always curious about but that, in the end, you might rather not know about."

"Try me."

"There's . . . There might be something trapped in the tree."

"I take it you're not talking about a little kitten that can't get down."

"If only it were that simple." Oscar might well be with the woodsfolk, as Aidan had suggested. But if not . . . "It's something that might be trapped in the essence of the tree. It's a little hard to explain . . . but I need some time to figure it out. If the tree's cut down . . ." My voice faltered. *Oscar.* I cleared my throat. "If the tree's cut down, it could be too late. It might kill some ... body. Something. Somebody."

We had stopped for a light at an intersection, and Carlos stared at me with his dispassionate cop expression on his face.

"The tree will kill somebody?"

"No ... Cutting it down might kill somebody. Maybe."

"Uh-huh."

"Why are you looking at me that way?" I demanded, irked. "You just told me two seconds ago that you think there might be more to this case, that there might be something occult going on."

"I realize that. I wasn't looking at you thinking you were crazy. I was thinking ... I was thinking that you must get tired of dealing with this crap. You're not even getting paid for it."

Our eyes held and locked for a long moment. Finally, I nodded.

"Yes, it can be a little ... overwhelming."

"Don't forget to take some time for yourself or you'll burn out. It's important."

Good advice, but just about now I didn't have a lot of time. If Oscar was in the tree and Ms. Quercus was scheduled to be razed, I—*Oscar*, really—was under the gun.

"You can drop me here," I said when we got to the Haight, in front of Coffee to the People. I wasn't wild about the folks at Aunt Cora's Closet seeing me climbing out of an SFPD car, even an unmarked one. It made Conrad nervous, and with everything else going on, it made sense to play it cool. Besides that, I was starving. I realized I hadn't had anything to eat since last night. And I was suddenly desperate for coffee.

"Don't want to be seen with a cop?"

"Just caffeine deprivation," I assured him, wondering whether it ever hurt his feelings. He was so sure of himself, but one never knew. "So, about the tree, please promise me you'll get them to wait. It's essential it not be taken down yet. Just for a little while, until I figure this out."

"I'll do what I can, but I can only come up with so many reasons for them not getting down to business. I'll claim we're still collecting evidence or some such. With outdoor crime scenes, things can go on for a while."

"Thank you, Carlos."

"Here to serve. Here to serve," he said. "Now, hand over that ledger."

I did so. He flipped through it, his dark eyes intent. Then he looked back at me. "What's it mean?"

Time to fess up.

"I don't understand the symbols myself. But there are some names there. . . . I talked to Bartholomew Woolsey. He's the one who sold the trunk to Sebastian. And look." I pointed to the notation for the sale of the trunk. "He wrote down Aunt *Flora's* Closet instead of Aunt Cora's. I think . . . I think that's what happened. Someone must have read it."

"You're telling me you've spoken to the source of this trunk without letting me know you knew?" His voice rose the tiniest bit—which, in someone as calm and steady as Carlos, had an alarming effect. "You are coming very close to interfering with a homicide investigation, Lily. You should know better. I could haul you in for something like this."

"I thought . . . I thought I might be able to figure out the ledger, to see if there were clues that the SFPD might not notice. And Woolsey didn't really tell me much—just that it was a trunk from his family, that it came over with a wagon train during the Gold Rush." But Carlos was right. I should have handed it over immediately. "I screwed up. I apologize."

Carlos pinched the bridge of his nose.

"Um . . . I really hate to ask this," I said. "Especially under the circumstances, but I intended to photocopy the book before giving it to you. But this morning . . . well, it's been a crazy morning, and I didn't get a chance. Do you suppose . . . ?"

I trailed off as I realized Carlos was looking at me with a mixture of disdain, amazement, and anger.

"I wouldn't ask," I said, now growing peeved myself at his response. "But I still might be able to figure things out. I could still try to read it. What could it hurt? You know as well as I do that I'm often able to—"

"All right. All right. I'll scan it and e-mail it to you along with the photos of the box. Is there anything else I can do for you, Ms. Ivory?"

"I guess that's about it for now. Thanks, Carlos."

He grunted but did not meet my eyes. I climbed out of the car and waved good-bye, feeling guilty and frustrated.

Coffee to the People was such a quirky mix of past and present that it reminded me of San Francisco itself. Posters of Nelson Mandela, Harriet Tubman, and Mahatma Gandhi blended with calls to action against wars and notices of music gigs. The two regular baristas, Wendy and Xander, were behind the counter today, as on most days. Wendy was a large woman who styled her dyed black hair in severe bangs, à la Bettie Page, and tended to wear slips and lingerie as outer garments. She had a heck of a time looking through our merchandise at Aunt Cora's Closet, and she also happened to be a priestess in Bronwyn's friendly Welcome coven. Her fellow barista, Xander, was tall and lanky and always reminded me a little of a German skinhead, except that he was all sweetness and light, belying his outer appearance of painful-looking piercings and metal studs.

The café was so crowded today I wondered whether

they were hosting a poetry slam or an acoustic guitarist, as they often did.

"Lily!" cried Xander, holding up a poster. "Look!"

The hand-lettered sign included a cartoonish drawing of a pink miniature potbellied pig and read: HAVE YOU SEEN THIS PIGGY? HELP HIM FIND HIS WAY HOME! ANSWERS TO "OSCAR."

Xander had it set up on a special little side table with a huge jar that was already filled halfway with coins and a handful of dollar bills. A stack of bright pink flyers were there for the taking.

"Jiminy Cricket, this is amazing," I said. I'd been gone only a couple of hours and they'd already made up a flyer?

Unfortunately, unless I missed my guess, it wasn't going to help Oscar come home, of course. None of this would. But still, what a wonderful outpouring of support.

"The store's kicking in fifty bucks," said Wendy. "And then we'll add the contributions, and that will be a nice reward. I take it you haven't heard anything new? No progress?"

I shook my head, concentrating on keeping a lid on my emotions. "I haven't been back to the store for a couple of hours, but . . . I don't think so. I have some friends looking into it."

"Good. That's good," said Wendy. She seemed like she was holding back. "Um, one thing occurred to me: Are you sure it's strictly legal to have a pig in the city limits?"

"I don't . . ."

"Not that *I* care, of course. Or any of us. And he's already been in the paper and all, so probably if it were an issue, it would have come up already. I just wanted to be sure he hadn't been nabbed by the cops. . . ."

"A pig caught by the pigs!" Xander said with a bright smile, apparently pleased with his own joke.

"Please don't refer to police officers that way," I said.

I found dealing with the authorities sometimes difficult, even panic-inducing, but now that I knew a few personally, I couldn't easily jump on the police-bashing bandwagon.

"I thought it was funny," said Xander. He looked around Wendy at a few customers standing nearby. "Wasn't it funny?"

They shrugged and nodded.

"I get it," I said. "I'm just saying . . ."

"Anyway," said Wendy. "I just wanted to give you a heads-up. You want your regular latte, or is it time for chocolate therapy?"

"Chocolate. That's the best idea I've heard all day," I said.

A few minutes later she handed me a mocha and a bagel, my typical order. I remembered when I first started coming to Coffee to the People, back when I was still new to the neighborhood. I had gotten such a thrill out of finally gaining status as a "regular" here at the café. And now these people were going out of their way to try to help me and Oscar, rallying around, putting up posters, and contributing money to the cause. My heart swelled.

"Thanks, y'all, for everything," I said. "I really don't know how to thank you. I'll let you know just as soon as we hear anything."

I walked the few blocks back to Aunt Cora's Closet, hoping with every step, every footfall, that Oscar would be there when I arrived. Knowing him, it was still possible he had been playing a joke of some sort, and would sashay back to the store, flaunting his porcine strut as though nothing had happened. I would kill him. Hug him, then kill him. Or . . . like Aidan said, I supposed it was possible he was in some other magical dimension, as with the woodsfolk, and his sense of time had been lost. Perhaps that was all. Aidan would make contact with them, and Oscar would be home by suppertime. Pro-

vided he hadn't eaten anything. I could feel the panic
surging again and took another deep breath.

As I neared the shop, I started to chant: *Oh please, oh
please, oh please.* Not very effective as an incantation,
but it was all that came to me.

The flurry of activity at Aunt Cora's Closet made Coffee to the People's missing pig project seem understated.
There were helium balloons on either side of the door,
with a big banner featuring a blown-up photo of Oscar
taken from the long-ago newspaper article. And in huge
red letters: HAVE YOU SEEN THIS LITTLE PIGGY? Conrad
stood outside on the sidewalk, handing bright pink flyers
to passersby and explaining the situation.

Inside, there were at least half a dozen of Bronwyn's
coven sisters mingling with a group of art students in
paint-splattered clothing. Plus, the entire Jackson clan:
Maya's parents, sister, and several cousins. Her mother,
Lucille, came running over to give me a big hug.

"We came over just as soon as we heard," she said.
"We're going to hand out flyers. Maya's got a direct line
to animal control and the pound, and my niece has an in
at a local radio station, so she's trying to get it mentioned
on-air."

Again, I let my heart swell with the love and caring of
my friends and friends of friends. All these people trying
to help. If Oscar found out about this, there would be no
living with him.

If only it could actually help find him.

On the other hand . . . though I was sure Oscar was
being held by some sort of magical force, all this energy
and good karma might serve for something. Like the
power of prayer, the focused intentions of a large group
of people could make a difference—tip the supernatural
scales, as it were.

"Conrad, it's important to keep the pressure on the
Parks Department not to take down that tree. Maybe

while you're handing out missing pig flyers, you could talk about that too?"

"Okay. Good idea."

"How did the effort to save the tree begin in the first place?" I asked.

"The tree lady came by with those other scientist dudes."

"The ones who were there when Sebastian was killed."

"Right. They came by before, and the tree lady looked at the tree and taught us a little about it. And then that one dude, with the big eyes, he stopped by all the time and helped us understand why it shouldn't be taken down."

Just then the bell rang over the front door, and I was surprised to see Bart Woolsey walk in. He paused in the doorway and looked around, as most people did when they first stepped into Aunt Cora's Closet. Often I tried to study the place with fresh eyes, to see it the way new-comers did. The crowded shelves, the racks of clothing, the hat stands. Brilliant with color and bathed in a soft golden light at this time of early evening, the place always smelled of fresh laundry and sachets.

But today there was also a chaotic, partylike feeling, a table along one wall laden with tofu dippers and oat-meal-carob cookies—courtesy of the café and members of the Welcome coven—and the table set up specifically for the Great Piggy Search.

Bart's tired-looking, rheumy eyes fell on me, and he raised one hand in a little salute. Just then, a rack of dresses fell over as the crowd pressed in. Bart crouched down to help Maya right the rod. Clumsily, he tried to replace a trio of dresses that had fallen; their hangers stuck out helter-skelter at crooked angles from the rod.

"This isn't . . . I mean, is it always like this?" Bart asked as he came to stand near me. "It's not quite what I imagined of a vintage clothing store."

"I'm sorry; it's unusually hectic right now. I lost my pet pig," I said.

"A pig?"

"A miniature Vietnamese potbellied pig," interrupted Bronwyn, shoving a flyer into Bart's hands. "They're very intelligent and affectionate. . . ." Her eyes filled with tears, and Duke put his arm around her.

Bart glanced back at me, a questioning look in his eyes.

"I know it's unusual, but they're really a lot like dogs," I said, feeling disloyal even as I said so. Oscar hated being likened to a dog, but it was the only way to explain my attachment to what appeared as livestock to most people.

"Oh, I'm . . . sorry to hear that. I'll keep an eye out."

"I would appreciate that," I said. I had a sense I knew why Bart was here, but I had learned long ago not to put words into people's mouths—or ideas into their heads. Better by far to allow them to speak for themselves. He might be looking for a new smoking jacket, for all I knew. "Is there something I can help you with?"

"I . . ." He trailed off, as though fascinated by the overabundance of clothing.

"Did you want your clothes back?" Ever since we took them, I had wondered whether he was really ready to part with them, so I had kept them together in their bag. Will's words rang in my ears.

"No, not at all. I was . . ." Bart looked over his slumped shoulders, as though to determine whether we were being overheard. Folks milled around us, a few shoppers but mostly people involved in the hunt for one Oscar the pig. No one appeared to be paying the slightest mind to us or our conversation. "I was wondering if I could ask you about . . . the love spell. The curse."

"You mean the one you believe was cast against you?"

He nodded. "I've been asking around, and your name has come up as someone who might be able to help me."

"Is that so?"

He leaned closer to me and whispered, "Could you help me break the curse? I will pay you."

Since his niece Hannah had recently been selling off his possessions I wasn't sure what he was claiming he could pay me with, but I would leave that aside for the moment.

"I'm not really an expert in these areas . . ." I began.

"Sebastian mentioned you once. I just didn't put two and two together—I didn't realize who you were when you came to my apartment. You might be a vintage clothes dealer, but I believe you are an even more powerful practitioner."

I held his gaze for a long moment.

"I thought I felt it when I first met you," he said. "But I wasn't sure. I can't be sure of much of anything anymore. But through my life, through the course of my search for a cure, I've met many a practitioner. You have that feel."

"That feel?"

"Just a way about you . . ."

There was a ruckus at the front door when a large young man lugged in a huge plastic pig, its hide drawn into sections labeled with their butcher names: *loin, chops, rump roast, ham.*

"This isn't a treasure hunt," I heard Maya straining over the crowd to explain. "We're looking for an actual lost pig."

The man looked disappointed, but added his pig to a growing collection of ceramic and plastic pigs near the register. He took a flyer from Bronwyn and left.

"Anyway, the point is . . ." Bart was still talking. "Can you imagine what it feels like never to know true love?"

I studied the old man. His blue eyes were watery and red-rimmed, but I imagined they had once sparkled.

Hannah had told me Bart had been a handsome young man, and I could believe it. What would it be like to spend one's whole life searching for love only to find it elusive? Chances were great that Hannah was right: There was no actual curse and Bart simply hadn't been able to open up to love, for whatever reason people have—issues stemming from childhood, perhaps, or maybe even from a lifetime of being told you suffered under a curse and would never find happiness.

But what if he was right? What if there really *was* a curse through the ages, cast upon his family from the lips of a dying witch?

"I don't know that much about love curses, much less inheritable curses, but . . . I'll do what I can."

Now I saw something new in his eyes: hope. "You'll help me?"

"I'll look into it," I said. "I can't promise anything, but I'll look into it."

"Thank you! I can't thank you enough. Hannah and her sister told me not to bother. She said you wouldn't help. Do you want a deposit? I can give you money for expenses, that sort of thing."

"Why don't we see if I get anywhere first? If I have expenses, you can reimburse me."

"You can take more clothes if you want. Or sugar bowls."

"Thanks. But I don't actually carry that many men's clothes. We got some nice things from you just the other day, and as for kitchen items . . . you can see I'm running out of space."

He nodded. "How about looking for your pig? I could at least help with that."

"It's really not necessary. There are already so many—"

"I wasn't raised to expect a free handout. And besides . . ." He looked around the store. "It looks kind of fun."

I wasn't sure about the love curse, but it was clear poor Bart was suffering from the curse afflicting so many elderly in this country: He had nothing to do.

"Sure," I said. "I would appreciate that. The more eyes and ears out there, the better. Duke?"

The big retired fisherman was seated at the main table. He turned around in his chair. "What's up?"

"This is Bartholomew Woolsey. Bart, this is Duke Demeter. Duke, would you see how Bart could help?"

"Sure. Here; have a seat."

Bart turned back to me and dropped his voice: "And if you don't mind, could you keep this just between us? Maybe keep my name out of it if you're asking around?"

I nodded. "I'll be discreet."

"Thank you."

Bart sat down next to Duke. The two men looked similar in age. Perhaps this was the beginning of a beautiful friendship, I thought, trying to force my thoughts toward something pleasant. And then I noticed that two of Bronwyn's coven sisters were already welcoming Bart, their patchouli-scented purple gauze aflutter. One offered Bart a cup of steaming coffee; the other proffered a plate of cookies.

Unfortunately, none of this activity was going to help find my lost pig. That was a whole other kettle of supernatural fish.

I took a deep breath and tried to concentrate. What did I know so far? Bart Woolsey's niece Hannah sold a trunk of old clothes to Sebastian Crowley. Bart gave no indication that he had any knowledge of what had been in that trunk. Sebastian was subsequently killed under an oak tree that was causing Conrad to experience nightmares. Aunt Flora's Closet was attacked, possibly by someone looking for the trunk. A velvet cape—which Oscar called a travel cloak—within the trunk gave me visions of a witch burning. Bart Woolsey believed he was the victim of a love curse passed down through the ages. Oscar disappeared in—or near or around—the oak tree.

And I was one clueless witch.

At three I set out for Berkeley. It probably wouldn't take me a full hour to reach the university located right on the other side of the bay, but it was rush hour, so one never knew. Still, the real reason I left early was that I wanted some distance from the flurry of well-meaning activity at the store.

Just thinking of Oscar hurt my heart, leaving it feeling scraped and raw. The longer he was missing, the more I feared he was being kept against his will.

I often get lost when I cross over the Bay Bridge, so I followed Will's instructions carefully, taking the University Avenue exit off of 80 and then crossing town on surface streets. I half expected to see student protests and hippies, as though it were still 1969. In reality, I passed through a neighborhood full of Indian clothing stores, display windows jammed with jewel-toned saris and glittering gold bangles—I made a mental note to stop in one day, as though I needed more cool clothes in my life—and then drove by several blocks peppered with restaurants and cafés and health food stores.

University Avenue, handily enough, dead-ended at the UC Berkeley campus. I found metered parking and bought a ticket for two hours. Just in case.

Then I threw myself on the mercy of a student who showed me how to get to the religion department, which was housed in Evans Hall, along with the mathematics department. Mathematics made me think of algebra and how Oscar had encouraged me to go to the GED this weekend, offering to drive. How I hoped he would be back in time to offer again.

The door was ajar. I knocked lightly and pushed it in. "Professor?"

"Hello! Nice to see you again," said Will as he came out from behind a standard-issue beige institutional desk to shake my hand.

Besides the desk, the office consisted of one wall of bookshelves, a filing cabinet, and two chairs. Everything was neat as a pin; the desk blotter was empty of anything but a framed photo, a well-ordered stack of papers, and two pens that seemed to have been placed at the side with military precision. I wondered how Will managed to work in the chaos of Bart's apartment without either organizing or sitting on his hands to keep from diving in.

"Please come in. Have a seat," he continued. "How's Bart doing? Have you seen him?"

"As a matter of fact, I just left him at my shop. He stopped by and then stayed to help find a lost pig."

Will had returned to his seat behind his desk. He blinked.

"I have a . . . pet pig," I clarified. "A miniature Vietnamese potbellied pig."

"Oh?"

"It's sort of like a dog. It's gone missing."

"I've heard of that. Didn't George Clooney have one of those?"

"I think so, yes."

"I'm sorry to hear it's lost. You must be so worried. I have a couple dogs myself." He picked up a photo in an ornate antique frame and held it out to me. He smiled, a little embarrassed. "I don't have kids, so . . . they're my babies."

I looked at the photo—a goofy-looking golden retriever and a smaller dog of unknown heritage, grinning widely, tongues lolling—and returned it to him with a smile.

"Cute. I love dogs."

"Anyway," he said. "You didn't come here to ask about my canine companions. What can I help you with?"

"I was wondering . . . We met the other day at Bart's house, of course, but I was also referred to you by someone else, who suggested you might be able to answer some questions for me."

"Who might that be?"

"Aidan Rhodes."

"Ah. Aidan." Our eyes held for a long minute. "And now you're not sure what to think of me."

"Where I come from, we say someone like Aidan might be welcome to supper—but hide the silver."

Will grinned, showing straight white teeth. "I like that. Mind if I steal it?"

"It's not like it's mine. Belongs to plenty of Texans, I reckon. By way of warning, I wouldn't say it to Aidan's face, though."

"Believe me, I know better. Aidan was kind enough to answer some questions for a class of mine once. One of my students recommended him as a visiting lecturer. It was . . . fascinating."

"I'll bet it was."

"So, you're here because of Aidan, or because of Bart? Or something else?"

"I was hoping you might be able to tell me more about the history Bart was discussing yesterday."

"His family history?"

"Yes. But also . . . about the witchcraft trials in general. For instance, he mentioned his family was from a Massachusetts settlement that was . . . similar to Salem?"

"That's right. Salem was the location of the most famous witch craze in colonial America, but trials also took place elsewhere. Many elsewheres, in fact. Bart's family settled in a town called Dathorne. Nasty history there."

"So it was a generalized hysteria?" I should know more, but had always shied away from learning much about the witch hunts. The subject was too frightening, too painful.

"I wouldn't call it 'hysteria,' exactly," he said slowly, as though searching for words. "In my work I describe it as a confluence of events and attitudes that led inexorably toward an extreme response—"

"Such as putting a bunch of women to death?"

"And several men as well," he said with a nod. "But yes, that's the kind of extreme response I'm talking about. It's hard for the modern mind to understand the seventeenth-century mentality. The Scientific Revolution was just getting underway in England, and the world-view of most American colonists was still very much medieval. They saw the universe as a battleground between the forces of good and evil, between God and the devil. And they didn't mean this metaphorically; they meant it literally."

"Weren't the colonists mostly uneducated and illiterate?" I asked.

"That's a common misconception. In early colonial New England especially, literacy rates were uncommonly high—much higher than in most of Europe at the time. The Puritans prized education and founded Harvard College only six years after settling the Boston colony."

"Then why . . . ?"

"In the Puritan world, the devil was constantly on the prowl to snatch vulnerable souls from the path of righteousness. Lacking a scientific explanation for natural events, they tended to interpret bad things—a crop failure, a baby's illness, a cow's milk drying up—as the actions of either God or the devil. Witchcraft was not the default explanation when something bad happened, but it was one possible explanation."

"So are you saying there weren't any actual witches in Salem?"

"The evidence for Salem suggests the accusations of witchcraft grew out of social conflict rather than the presence of actual witches. But this is not the same thing as saying there were no witches in colonial America; witchcraft has been present throughout history and all across the world. Women, mostly, often healers and botanists, who specialized in the rites and traditions that brought people comfort and health. They were the wisewomen, or cunning women."

Will reminded me of myself, insisting upon the positive aspects of the history of witchcraft. While I took in the professor's words, my gaze wandered to the window, which looked out across a stand of trees. Idly, I wondered if this would qualify as a "coppice." The word brought Oscar's loss back to me with a vengeance.

Will continued. "Women were considered more vulnerable to witchcraft, of course, since they were traditionally defined as morally and spiritually more fragile than men and therefore at greater risk of being seduced by the devil. The Puritans were trying to create a 'city on a hill,' a shining example of a godly community on earth. What greater prize for the devil than to disrupt God's people? So when conflict broke out, as it did in Salem and other places, a logical suspect was the devil and his minions—the witches."

"I understand." I watched Will and tried to assess whether he knew I was a witch, whether he might have a sense of such things, as Bart had mentioned about himself. That still shook me a bit. I wasn't used to being outed by someone who barely knew me, who wasn't part of the magical world. "But what I'm wondering is whether there might have been some true witches present at that time. Powerful women. Maybe someone who cursed someone else?"

He held my eyes for a long time. "There is a story of one woman. Bart's obsessed with her. Deliverance Corydon."

Chapter 13

"Deliverance? That was her name?" That word was ringing in my head when I snapped out of the vision I'd had with the cloak.

"Pretty, isn't it? A lot of the Puritan women had names like that: Chastity, Purity, Prudence. All the virtues. But Deliverance Corydon was a special case, obviously."

"How so?"

"For one thing, she was burned at the stake. That almost never happened in the American colonies. Witches here were executed by hanging."

My heart sped up. "Then why did they burn her? Were they out of rope, or was there some significance to the method?"

"That sort of question keeps scholars like me employed and writing treatises on the issue. I would argue that Deliverance Corydon was a very special case."

"How do you know so much about her?"

"The Puritans, bless their hearts, were world-class record keepers. Not only that, but they tended to store these documents safely, which means we have many

more from them than from others of the time. There are
letters, diaries, newspapers, church accounts, all kinds of
notations. And there is the transcript of her trial, of
course. It's a summary, not a word-for-word recording—
stenography was several centuries in the future—but it's
quite revealing. It describes, for example, how Deliverance was extensively interrogated about her familiar
spirit, which was, apparently, a frog."

"Really. What kind of frog?"

"I'm afraid they weren't that detailed, but I imagine it
was just a common toad of some sort." Will smiled. "The
accused were imprisoned while awaiting trial, and if any
animal wandered by—even an ant or a beetle—it was
assumed they were the witch's familiar. The human mind
is infinitely creative."

"Anything else out of the ordinary in her interrogation?"

"Not really. She had a witch's mark, which was common among those accused. Usually they were moles or
birthmarks that were thought to be without feeling, and
marks of the devil. Hers was shaped like a crescent moon
and was on her neck. Like a hickey."

"I was wondering . . . This might sound a little gruesome, but do you know what they did with the bodies of
witches after they were killed?"

"Not gruesome at all! A fascinating question!" Will
stood and began pacing behind his desk, as though too
excited by my query to remain seated. I imagined him in
a lecture hall, speaking to a class of rapt students, and
wished, not for the first time, that I'd had the chance to
go to college. Maybe I could think of pursuing it after I
got my GED. As long as there was no math requirement,
I would quite enjoy it, I felt sure.

"Because a witch was a minion of the devil, her corpse
was considered polluted, and often there was a great
deal of debate about what to do with it. It couldn't be

buried in consecrated ground, for instance. One option was to bury the corpse outside the graveyard, literally on the other side of the fence. Makes quite a statement, don't you think? 'We reject you, in life and in death!' "

"Is that what they did to Deliverance?" I asked, wondering how on earth I would ever find a beyond-the-boundary colonial-era grave. Probably under a condo development by now.

"No, they chose another option. Fire was a traditional method of purification and had the added benefit of being thought to break residual spells. It was said—wait a minute. I have it right here."

Will pulled a thick tome off a shelf, flipped to the middle, and ran his finger down the page. "Here it is. 'The body of a witch being burned, her blood is prevented thereby from becoming hereditary to her progeny in the same evil, which by hanging is not.'" He snapped the book shut and grinned at me.

"In other words . . . ?" I asked, wanting to be sure I understood.

"Oh! Sorry. In other words, fire keeps the witch's sins from being passed on through her blood kin, should she have any." He put the book back, taking the time to adjust the spine so it was in line with the others on the shipshape shelf.

"What did they do with the ashes . . . the remains of the witch who was burned?"

"Usually they were thrown into a river to completely dissolve. Not unlike executed criminals today, who are given an anonymous burial in quicklime. The idea is to wipe out any trace of them."

"And that's what happened to this witch's remains? Deliverance . . ."

"Deliverance Corydon," he finished with a nod. "Actually, no. Deliverance received special treatment. Her ashes were put into a wooden box carved with symbols."

"This was in the historical record as well?"

"Yes. It was noted by a particularly devout young minister, who was also a bit of an artist. He even drew pictures of the box, thank goodness. It's the sort of thing that makes history fun, this kind of window into the past. I have an image of it somewhere. . . ." Plucking another book from his extensive collection, he thumbed through it and then handed it to me.

A shiver ran down my spine. The drawing of the symbols on the box containing the remains of Deliverance Corydon was a match for the photo Carlos had shown me . . . except that the box was now several rotted pieces of wood. But some of the carved symbols had survived.

"Where did the symbols come from? Was it something the Puritans came up with?"

Will shrugged. "Their meaning has been lost, but it was assumed to be a spell or protective markers of some sort. As I said, burning witches was unusual in colonial America, though more common in Europe."

"Could Deliverance's ashes have been transported to San Francisco?"

Will thought for a moment. "It seems highly unlikely . . . but possible, I suppose. Once a witch was executed, most folks seemed to want to forget all about it. It's possible someone kept the box, and it was handed down through the generations and taken with them when they moved. Over time, it's likely the family forgot what was inside, but really, who knows?" He shrugged. "The box would have been sealed with nails and wax, but wood does disintegrate. Depending on environmental conditions, it might take a few years, or several centuries. But eventually, it will rot away, faster if it's buried."

My mind raced as I tried to process all he was telling me. "Suppose . . . Suppose a box like this were buried at the base of a tree. Could it have disintegrated and the ashes soaked into the tree?"

"Um . . . can't help you there," he said with a slight smile, eyebrows raised. "That's botany; not my specialty."

"Sorry. Never mind. Tell me, were you studying the Woolsey family in particular? Is that how you found Bart? Or did he find you?"

"Woolsey was a reasonably common name. It was also the name associated with the most famous curse from the colonial era."

"The one Bart believes he suffers under?"

"He told you about that?"

"He actually asked me to help him get rid of it."

"Poor guy. Seeking true love at his age . . ."

"You think the desire for true love lessens with age?"

"Oh no, no, no, I'm no ageist." He sat back down behind his desk and adjusted his glasses. "I guess I just thought, well . . . I don't know. Half my colleagues are looking for love online and whatnot, and I guess part of me hoped it would get easier with age."

He smiled and shrugged again, and I was struck by his open and friendly expression. Will had the kind of nerdy good looks one saw a lot on college campuses: intellectual and intense, but eager and interested. I imagined he had more than a few young students falling for him.

"I discuss the Woolsey curse in a book I'm writing, titled, appropriately enough, *Ancient Curses*. I'm interested not only in how these stories originated and were handed down through the years, but also how they're kept alive by a modern society that claims not to believe in curses."

"Do you see a lot of hereditary curses active today?"

"No, not at all. Especially not in these parts. I'm from New England originally. Same country, different world. My family traces its ancestry back multiple generations. There it's more common to find an obsession with pedigree."

I had to smile. "Did you 'come out' at a debutante ball?"

He chuckled. "No, that's for young ladies. But I was the next-best thing: an escort to a deb. Not as much fun when it comes to wardrobe selection, sorry to say. But I looked pretty snazzy in my rented tux."

We didn't have debutante balls back in Jarod, Texas . . . though most of the girls in town would have given their eyeteeth to have taken part in one. Instead, we had regional beauty contests. As a young woman, my mother had been crowned Miss Tecla County; she was photographed wearing a rhinestone tiara and a silk sash, carrying a huge gold trophy inscribed with her name. The photo was published on the front page of the local weekly newspaper, the *Jarod Journal*. It was her moment of glory and the highlight of her life.

Needless to say, I had never been invited to participate.

"Anyway, if you're wondering about the curse Bart claims he has been carrying around, it was supposedly cast by Deliverance Corydon. It was recorded in the family Bible, which Bart still has—I've been angling to take a look through it, but he hasn't yet allowed me to. But this Deliverance is a bit of a mystery, to be honest. I've looked and looked but haven't found any reference to her or her family, which is odd. As I said, the Puritans were excellent record keepers, and her birth should have been recorded in the church and town records."

"Maybe she came to town as an adult."

"Maybe so. Still, she should appear *somewhere*. Tax records, census records . . . But I haven't found anything. Apparently, she lived alone on the outskirts of town."

"That was the case for many women accused of witchcraft, wasn't it?"

"Not all, but many. A woman living independently was not the norm at this time. Deliverance was also accused of fornication with several of the town elders."

"'Fornication'? I haven't heard that term in a while. Was she . . . a prostitute?"

"Doesn't appear to be the case. She was, by all accounts, a beautiful, powerful, independent woman who kept herself apart from others—just the sort the devil would go after."

"Which made her vulnerable."

Will gave a simple nod. "Which meant she didn't have many friends—and that made her vulnerable. Stray too far outside the bounds of what is socially acceptable, and you might as well paint a target on your back."

I sighed. Too often this was still true today. Would we humans ever learn from our mistakes?

"Anyway, what we do know is that Deliverance Corydon was accused of witchcraft, tried and convicted in a court of law, then sentenced to death by fire. As the flames roared higher, it is said she looked at her primary accuser, the magistrate in her case, Jonathan Woolsey, and cursed him and all his male descendants, declaring that they would never find true love or domestic happiness."

"She only cursed the males?"

He nodded. "Maybe because men had the authority in her society?"

I pondered that for a moment. "So, were there other women killed in Dathorne?"

"Yes, several."

"But Deliverance was the only one burned?"

"As far as we can tell. But there was another woman who was put to death not long after Deliverance. She was charged with stealing Deliverance's ashes."

The back of my neck tingled. "That's a charge?"

"As I said, the people of the time were concerned with the effects of earthly remains. There's also an illustration of the woman, who was called the Ashen Witch. Let me see. . . ." He looked up at his orderly bookshelves, rubbing his chin absentmindedly. "Yup, here it is. . . ."

He took out a large book labeled *New England Ghost Stories*.

"She's said to haunt the town still, especially the site of Corydon's burning."

He turned the book around to face me. There was a full-color illustration of a dark-haired woman in a gold cape, kneeling before a pile of gray-white ash. I studied her image and swallowed hard.

"Hey," said Will, glancing at the picture, then at me. "You know, ever since I met you, I thought you looked familiar. You're the spitting image of the Ashen Witch!"

He was right. I looked just like her. Not as pale, perhaps, but that could be due to the fact that she was, after all, a ghost.

"No one knows her real name, but according to the lore, she was a newcomer in town—already a big mark against her since outsiders were suspect—and was tasked with gathering up Deliverance's ashes. She started too soon after the burning and singed herself, but applied a poultice that healed her miraculously. And then she was found applying the marks on the box, and she tried to run away with it. The townspeople found it all very strange and accused her of being a witch as well. Further cementing their suspicions was that she and Deliverance Corydon were said to 'have the impression of one another'—meaning, they looked alike. Both had dark hair and pale faces."

"Seems there's a lot of that going around," I said. "So you're suggesting I look like Deliverance, too?"

Will shrugged.

"And so they killed the newcomer because she was a quick healer and wrote a few symbols?"

"And because she looked like the witch they'd just burned, yes." He nodded. "It made sense to them at the time."

I took a deep breath and blew it out slowly.

"Here's an interesting tidbit," said Will as he read through the story. "The Ashen Witch is shown here in her cape and was always referred to as wearing one—but she was not hanged with it. In fact, upon her arrest, the cape was nowhere to be found. According to the arrest warrant, 'said garment, perhaps enchanted, was assumed hidden upon her foreseeing her arrest.' *Huh*. Where do you suppose it went?"

I meandered slowly back through the campus, enjoying the scenery. It surprised me that the UC Berkeley grounds were so bucolic. Located as it was in the middle of an urban area, I expected big ugly gray buildings; there were a few, but the overall impression was of a graceful, historic site of higher learning. I passed by Hearst Mining Circle, and gathered eucalyptus branches to hang in my shower; the aroma they released with the steam was great for one's skin and lungs.

In front of Bancroft Library a group of five students bounced a Hacky Sack with their feet, laughing and chatting. As usual when I'm on a college campus, I couldn't keep from looking around at the students and thinking how lucky they were to be here, studying. I was willing to bet that most of them had families that loved them and homes to go for winter break, where they could sleep in to all hours and then awake to delicious-smelling pot roast and potatoes and bicker with their parents and siblings. Normal homes with normal problems.

I had begun to feel so good about myself and my situation in San Francisco. The success of Aunt Cora's Closet, Maya and Bronwyn and all our friends who hung around the shop; Sailor, and even Carlos and Aidan and Max . . . I had people here who accepted me, more or less, for who I was. And I felt that I was in a unique position to help my community, from time to time, by looking into magical murder and mayhem.

But then something like this came along and suddenly

I found myself linked across the centuries to an ancient crime against women. Had the velvet cape come to me on purpose? Was it meant to be a tie to those long-ago women, a connection that I was intended to discover? And who were these women? Were they simply caught up in the brutality of the time, as Will suggested, or could they have been bent on destruction?

And thinking of that . . . was Deliverance Corydon all that bad? She may have been a bit randy, and perhaps she ran around with other women's husbands . . . but was that enough to put her to death? And then to cast a love curse upon the house of Woolsey . . . Again, maybe it wasn't very nice, but it wasn't along the lines of cooking children, as witches were accused of in parts of Europe— or even in fairy tales, like Hansel and Gretel.

And who was the other one, the Ashen Witch?

My fingertips tingled. I looked down at my hands and rubbed the pads of my fingers with my thumbs. I couldn't forget the feel of those ashes searing my outstretched fingers.

I arrived at my car and climbed behind the wheel, but hesitated before starting the engine. I wasn't sure I was ready to face the folks at Aunt Cora's Closet, all those well-meaning people looking for my missing familiar. I pined for Oscar so; it was like a physical ache. If Oscar were with me now, he would be haranguing me to search for gargoyles on the Berkeley campus. He was always on the lookout for his mother, who apparently suffered under a curse that had transformed her kind into stone.

I wasn't up for such a quest without my little guy by my side, but there was something else in Berkeley that interested me. Bart's niece, Hannah, had mentioned she worked at the Vivarium, near the busy shopping district of Fourth Street. She loved all the "creepies, crawlies, and critters."

It wasn't far, and it would serve as a distraction. Why not?

Parking was why not, I realized as I circled the block for the second time. Berkeley's Fourth Street shopping district used to be a series of old factories, but it now featured upscale foodie restaurants and several small, very chic boutiques. A parking space was hard-won, but I finally found one without having to resort to using a magical charm I kept in my glove box for emergencies.

A block off the main drag, the East Bay Vivarium was tucked discreetly back from the street, surrounded by old Victorians and sweet clapboard cottages. A huge mural showing a lizard with its tongue extended, eating a fly, made it clear I was in the right place.

Before I even got through the door I noted the strange, dry smell of reptiles ... and the distinct odor of rodents that, I guessed, would serve as dinner. All around the shop glass-fronted cages held snakes and lizards, frogs and spiders. I read signs as I walked toward the central counter: There were sunbeam snakes, Indonesian tree snakes, yearling green pythons, emerald tree boas, uromastyxes, rainforest frogs, and a variety of chameleons.

I spied Hannah toward the back of the store. Today she was wearing slightly more formal athletic gear: black stretch pants, a stretchy bright yellow yoga top, and a hoody tied around her muscled, slim waist.

But the most interesting piece she was wearing, by far, was a large, oh-so-albino snake. I didn't much care for serpents, but of all animals—with the notable exception of one potbellied pig—they were the only creatures that could understand me. Snakes had saved my life—at least once, maybe twice—but nonetheless they still weirded me out. There was something deeply disturbing about the way they moved. This is where we derive the word "creepy," after all.

"Hi, Hannah . . ." I trailed off, trying to think of something nice to say about her snake. Happily, she beat me to it.

"Oh, wow, *hi*. I didn't really expect you to actually come! I invite people all the time, but they never actually *come*. Meet my friend Zelda."

"Zelda's the snake?"

"Isn't she beautiful?" she asked, and ducked her chin to give Zelda's yellow hide a kiss. "She's an albino Colombian boa. Very rare."

"Um . . . yes. So unusual."

"You don't like snakes?" she asked, half accusation and half question. "Then why are you at the Vivarium?"

"I actually came to see you," I said. "And I don't *dis*-like snakes, I just . . . I have a lot of respect for them."

She laughed. "Well, that makes sense. And it's a better attitude than those folks who come in here thinking they're buying an instrument to strike terror into the hearts of their neighbors. Matter of fact, I think some of our customers go for the tarantulas because they're hoping to kill off a mother-in-law or something."

Hannah was still smiling, but the thought gave me pause. What was to keep someone from buying one of these critters with the express purpose of hurting someone? Then again, I'd heard that tarantulas weren't as venomous as people thought. Not that I wanted to find out.

"We also have iguanas and dragons."

"Dragons?"

"Bearded dragons. They're a kind of lizard," she said with a gesture toward large lizards with ruffles around their neck. "They puff up if they feel threatened, make a big show. Aren't they cute?"

I smiled and nodded. Lizards were better than snakes—once creatures had legs, they didn't seem nearly so creepy. Still . . . "I think I'm more of a frog person."

"We have a bunch of those, too. Have you been to the new frog exhibit at the California Academy of Sciences?"

"No, I haven't. Is it worth seeing?"

"Oh, definitely. In fact, tomorrow night they're having a cocktail party. You should totally come! It's adults only. My sister works there so I can get in free, and I totally love going, but sometimes you can barely walk because of all the schoolkids. It's cool to be there with just adults. You should go."

"Maybe I will."

I thought back on what the professor had told me about Deliverance Corydon being accused of having a frog familiar. Frogs were popular as witches' familiars in the old days, probably in part because of their transformational abilities. Not that familiars were usually able to shift—Oscar was a rarity where that was concerned. *Oscar*. His absence had become a constant ache. How I wished he were snuggled in his cubby over the refrigerator at home. I could hear him now: *"A cocktail party? Awesome! I love frogs! And I'm a real museum booster, you know. I'm a card-carrying member."*

But right now everything depended on what happened with Oscar. I wasn't about to make plans until I had that little guy back in my apartment, eating and making a mess and talking loudly through movies.

"Anyway, what did you want to see me for? Is it about my uncle?"

"Yes, as a matter of fact. I—"

"He's harmless, really," she interrupted, talking while the snake curled around her arm. "He just . . . can't stop talking about that curse, so everyone thinks he's crazy. But he managed the family finances just fine most of his life."

"He said he's spent most of his fortune?"

"That's what he says." She nodded, her eyes shadowed. "If you want to know the truth, I think that's the biggest reason people in the family are angry with him. Like they thought they were going to inherit his money or something."

"But not you?"

She shrugged. "I figure it was his money in the first place, so if he wants to spend it all to dig up information on his family and this supposed curse . . . well, my dad spent his at the racetrack and in bars. At least the apartment Bart lives in is paid for, and he was sensible enough to set aside a dedicated account for the taxes and condo fees, so he won't be homeless."

"Well, that's good, then."

"As long as we can get that place cleaned up, that is, so he's not thrown out by the homeowners association. Which, frankly, I think is pretty bogus. I don't really get condos. Don't you think it's strange to pay for a place and then have the condo committee tell you what you can and can't do?"

"I hadn't really thought about it, but I suppose so," I said, thinking that close neighbors wouldn't much enjoy my middle-of-the-night incantations or the smells of my brews, the more exotic of which could be a little noxious. It was best I lived by myself, with no immediate neighbors to bother.

"Then again, I'm not a homeowner, so what do I know? Anyway . . . is there a problem with the clothes? We could negotiate on the money if they aren't worth what you paid. You were really generous, but to tell you the truth, it was a help just to get them out of there."

"No, it's nothing like that. A deal's a deal. But could you tell me about selling things to Sebastian Crowley? What made you reach out to him in particular?"

A shadow passed over her eyes. "Oh, Uncle Bart told me about . . . what happened. That is so odd, isn't it? That I could be talking to someone one day, and the very next day he's *shot*? It's . . . disconcerting. Really sad."

I nodded. "Yes, it is."

"So, I tried a few antiques dealers in Jackson Square, but they're pretty snooty. Really, I didn't know anything about how to go about selling something like that. . . . I asked Uncle Bart, but he didn't want me to sell the items anyway, so he's not a lot of help."

"So your uncle didn't mention Sebastian to you himself?"

"I mean, Bart's known Sebastian for a while, but like I said, he's not up for me selling his things, or giving things away." She petted the snake. "It's a battle every time I go over there—you know, he's pretty upset about the trunk."

"He can probably have it back as soon as the police release it."

"What are they doing with it?"

"They were checking it out, in case it served as evidence in Sebastian's death."

"Really? So it'll be one more piece of junk for his apartment. Think how gorgeous that place could be if he'd let me clean it up." She shrugged, which gave the effect of Zelda-the-yellow-snake levitating on her shoulder. "But as they say in mindfulness training, you can't control anyone else. We all make our own choices."

"I'm sorry if this is a personal question, but . . . You're the only family member who is in contact with your uncle?"

"Pretty much. I mean, my sister goes over every once in a while, when I drag her there. She always claims she's too busy with work, because she's a scientist over at the Cal Academy, and I'm just a lowly clerk in a reptile store. But I always tell her that working here has taught me lots about . . ."

Hannah kept talking, but I wasn't listening. She mentioned that earlier, but it hadn't really registered. . . . Her sister worked at the Academy of Sciences?

"What does your sister do at the Cal Academy?"

"Nina? She's a botanist."

"Do you happen to know one of her colleagues over there? A fellow named Lance Thornton?"

"Yeah." She made a little face. "He gives me the willies."

"How so?"

"He's always staring. Those goggle eyes . . ."

And then, as though embarrassed to have made such a personal comment, she added: "I mean, I guess he's nice enough. He's just odd. A lot of scientists are. I think scientists are like artists: willing to take low pay to pursue what they love. They work long hours, passionate about something no one else cares about. I guess it makes sense they end up being sort of misfits, right?"

And then she kissed Zelda-the-albino-boa again.

Chapter 14

As I got in my car I thought to myself that a lot of young people are willing to give away more information about themselves than I ever would. But then again, perhaps it wasn't so much youth per se, as having grown up in a safe and secure situation. What with my childhood, I wasn't even sure about eating food from unknown sources, much less telling my family history to some woman wandering in off the street.

All the way home, inspired by Hannah's mindfulness training, I tried to concentrate on the here and now and on not controlling anyone. The fact was that, like Aidan said, Oscar could be anywhere. I wasn't really his mistress; he was free to go. It would surprise me if he left me, but he might well have his own reasons for doing so, as Aidan implied.

Still, I paused in front of the door to Aunt Cora's Closet, hoping to see some sign that my missing pig had returned. But the signs were still up, volunteers still milling about. No indication of the celebration I felt sure would accompany Oscar's return. In fact, it was almost six o'clock, but the store still appeared very much open for business.

When I entered, I discovered why: Some of the volunteers—my money was on the coven sisters—had organized a potluck dinner. They appeared to have no intention of closing down Lost Pig Central anytime soon.

With a heavy heart, I forced myself to walk in with a smile.

But I spent the rest of the evening trying to ignore Oscar's monogrammed purple silk pillow, pathetically empty.

"I can't believe you waited so long to tell me about Oscar," Sailor said later that evening.

We were seated at Sailor's cheap laminate kitchen table, eating take-out from one of the best noodle shops in town. Roast duck and dumplings and seared bok choy and noodles with black bean sauce—the food sent up a bouquet of mouth-watering aromas. Despite this, I was picking at my food and trying in vain to work up an appetite. I hadn't eaten a thing at the potluck, but I still wasn't hungry.

Sailor's apartment was in Chinatown, down a little alley into which tourists rarely ventured. Everything smelled of spices and the faint whiff of a ghostly perfume that lingered, evidence of a long-ago perfume factory here in Hang Ah Alley. Once you got past the ghost of a murdered gambler on the landing right outside Sailor's door, it was a nice place. Urban, but cozy. A neatly made bed, stacks of books, an old TV with a DVD player. The kitchen had only one plate, one bowl, and one set of cutlery, so Sailor was eating straight out of the box with the free wooden chopsticks, which he wielded with mastery.

Normally, I had to practically sit on my hands in order not to offer to fix the place up for him. It wouldn't take much: a nice set of dishes, some pots and pans, curtains in the window, a pot of basil on the counter and some rosemary at the front door for good luck. For that matter, I could outfit the place with the vintage kitchenware I kept acquiring, cleaning out a corner of the store while making Sailor's place into a home.

But things were still new between us, still tender. The last thing I wanted to do was send him screaming to the hills about being beholden first to Aidan, now to me. He hadn't asked me to decorate or contribute to his comfort. That was why we usually hung out at my place, which was full of herbs and the smells of baked goods, with a snug couch and bed and a funny, smart-alecky familiar. . . .

Oscar—or the *lack* of Oscar—was precisely why we weren't at my apartment tonight. The shop was one thing—we kept busy and Oscar wasn't part of every fiber. But upstairs, in my place . . . all I could see was his empty nest in the cubby above the refrigerator, the TV remote control sticky with whatever it was he was eating last, the scratches his claws had left on the brass bedstead. My apartment had become a home with Oscar there; without him, it was nothing but sad.

"The folks I talked to the other day couldn't tell me much more than what we already know: that Sebastian had made a lot of enemies over the years. But now this thing with Oscar makes me think it's a lot more complicated than simple revenge. Unfortunately, we both know I'm not as sensitive as I once was." Sailor looked at me a long moment, as though searching for words. "Now that I'm not with Aidan, I need to reestablish my equilibrium. I need to spend some time with my aunt, not only to help her out while she recovers, but to try to figure this thing out."

"I thought you didn't want the powers in the first place."

"I didn't. I still don't, not really. But . . . I tell you what, after what I've seen and felt, it's a little hard to go back to a nine-to-five job."

Sailor was searching for his place in the grand scheme of things. I was familiar with the dilemma.

"But that said," he continued, "I'd be happy to go to the tree and see if I can pick up on anything."

Ironically enough, now that Sailor was willing to read for me whenever I wanted, I cared so much for him that I hated to expose him to such things. I knew how hard it was for him to experience the evil thoughts and impulses of demons and spirits. Besides, since his powers of perception had diminished, I wondered whether he was also less able to keep himself safe. The way he "felt" things was to let them in; without a strong guard, he could well put himself in danger.

"Unless you can talk to the woodsfolk, I'm not sure you can help. You're better with spirits and the like, right? This is more of a haunted tree situation."

"Haunted by a spirit?"

"I don't think so. It's possible that . . . I'm thinking maybe the ashes of a woman who was burned at the stake for witchcraft were buried at the base of the tree, and . . ." I trailed off and shook my head. Saying it aloud made it sound even more far-fetched than it already did in my mind. "I mean . . . Oscar's disappearance might not have anything to do with the tree at all. Aidan suggested that the Good People brought Oscar down for a chat. After all, I asked him to introduce me. I insisted, in fact. . . ."

"It's not your fault," Sailor said quietly. "And even if I can't help directly, I'd like to go to the tree with you. How about we go by there in the morning?"

I shrugged again and played with a dumpling, concentrating on holding the chopsticks just right so I could grasp the slippery piece without squeezing so hard that it skittered along the table. I remembered doing just such a thing once while visiting Hong Kong, and how an old woman at the table had laughed and showed me how to hold the sticks properly. That was back before I had roots and a community. Back before I was embroiled so deeply that I'd do just about anything to keep my loved ones safe.

Though I loved my new life, I felt a fleeting pang of nostalgia for those days of not having to worry about anyone but myself.

"Aidan says time passes differently down there, but that Oscar could return anytime . . . unless he eats something."

Again, our silence hung heavy with thoughts and fears. Hard to imagine Oscar turning down a faery feast.

"Or he might just have moved on of his own accord," I continued. "Aidan said he might have just gotten bored and . . ."

"Oscar wouldn't leave you."

"I didn't think so either, but Aidan said—"

"I don't care what Aidan said. And you shouldn't either. Even if Oscar was ready to leave you—which I don't believe for a minute—he couldn't just take off. He's still beholden to Aidan."

"How?"

Sailor shrugged. "Aidan keeps sway over people. You should know that by now."

"Speaking of which, you never told me how you broke free of him—why did he let you come back to San Francisco after banishing you?"

"I guess he saw the error of his ways. And then once his office burned, he had bigger fish to fry. Hey, guess what I rented?"

He held up a DVD of *Bell, Book, and Candle*, starring Kim Novak, Jimmy Stewart, and Jack Lemmon. Sailor was changing the subject, as he did every time I asked him how he was able to return to San Francisco, and to me. As with so many people—and creatures—in my life, when it came to Sailor, a lot of questions went unanswered. We magical folk relished our secrets. We were trained from an early age to respect one another's right to privacy, but it was tough to get close with so much left unsaid.

We sat on the bed to watch the film. Sailor wrapped his arm around my neck, and I rested my head on his shoulder. His scent wrapped around me: clean, slightly citrus, spicy but fresh. Despite—or perhaps because of— his sardonic ways and dark outlook on the world, Sailor had always made me feel safe, even before we were romantically involved.

The movie was a hokey, early-Hollywood look at witchcraft, and—amazingly enough—it actually got a few things right. It was supposed to be funny, but I wasn't laughing.

I started thinking about Oscar again.

"Hey," Sailor whispered. "Stay with me."

"Sorry. It's just that—"

"Shh," he said, putting a finger on my lips. "I know how important that little pig is to you. I swear to you I'll do everything in my power to bring him home. Between the two of us, we're sure to figure something out. I didn't find out anything useful today, but I put out some feelers. I'll go talk to my aunt Renna tomorrow, see if she knows anything, or has any leads for us. She might know something about the woodsfolk—she seems to know something about everything. In the meantime, try to keep your mind off of it."

"How am I supposed to do that?" I asked.

His mouth came down on mine, and for the next while, I didn't think about Oscar or enchanted trees or the woodsfolk or the death of an antiques dealer I barely knew.

But later, as I lay in Sailor's arms, the lights of Hang Ah Alley sifting in through the dusty windowpanes, all I could think about was Deliverance Corydon, and the

Ashen Witch, and whether they could somehow help me get my piggy back.

"I changed my mind," I told Sailor in the morning. "If you wear one of my talismans and I go with you, will you try to read the tree?"

"Yes."

"You're sure? You really don't mind?"

"Let's take the bike. I bought you a helmet."

He tossed the headgear to me. He had tied a red ribbon around it in a bow.

"That's so ... sweet. First Oscar buys me a present and now you. Y'all are going to positively turn my head."

Sailor smiled. "You just go on ahead and let it turn. We'll keep you in line. You warm enough to ride?"

I nodded, excited at the prospect of becoming a Motorcycle Mama.

"Let's go talk to the trees and see if we can't figure this thing out."

The first thing I noticed when we arrived in Golden Gate Park and walked to the clearing at the oak tree was that the crime-scene tape was gone. I wondered whether the police had officially released the scene, or if it had been taken down rather more informally. Did this mean Carlos wasn't able to keep it an open crime scene? And if so, would the tree be razed soon?

The clearing was full of young people—most of them appearing homeless, like Conrad—standing around watching, chatting, eating. One played the flute, another strummed—badly—on a guitar. A few had dogs with them, just as scraggly and hungry-looking as they were. I noticed bright pink signs asking *Have you seen this lost piggy?* stapled to several trees, and there was even evidence that one had been stapled to the big oak but then torn off. Only the corners remained.

A man was crouching by the base of the tree. Dressed

in a stained white lab coat, he didn't fit in with the rest of the ragtag group of young people.

"Lance?" I called. "Hi . . . Do you remember me?"

"Yes. You . . . you were here that day." He looked up at me with a glum expression in his big eyes. "With . . . with the body."

I nodded. "Yes. I'm Lily. What are you doing here?"

"Probably the same as you," he said, eyes flickering rather nervously to a point just beyond me.

I turned around to see that Sailor stood at my back, arms crossed over his chest, glowering. With his motorcycle boots and black leather jacket, he looked formidable. I elbowed him, and he backed away to give us some privacy. I wanted Lance to talk to me, not to be intimidated into silence.

"I just wanted to come take another look," I said, trying to sound sympathetic. "It was all such a shock."

My ploy seemed to work; Lance nodded and spoke eagerly. "I was trying to figure out what he might have been looking for under the tree. I know it seems strange. I mean, I didn't even know him from Adam, but . . . I've never seen a man die before." His voice caught on his final words.

"That's right. The ground was disturbed, wasn't it?" I said, noticing the scent of damp, freshly turned earth. But I thought back to finding Sebastian; the ground was moist here, so wouldn't his hands have been noticeably muddy if he had been the one digging? Could he have interrupted someone while they were looking for something, and had been killed for his trouble?

"The police dug up part of some old box the other day; you think that's what he was looking for?" Lance asked. "It seemed worthless, probably something that was here since before."

"It's really hard to know. I, um . . ." I thought about how to mention the connection through Hannah. "You know, it turns out an acquaintance of mine is the sister of one of your colleagues. I think the last name's Woolsey?"

"You know Nina Woolsey?"

"Not really, no. But I know her sister, Hannah, a little."

Lance shrugged. "I study amphibians. But Hannah likes snakes more than frogs, so that's the way that goes."

Unsure of how to respond, I just nodded. Then something occurred to me. "My friend Conrad mentioned that you were trying to save this tree. Do you know anyone at the Parks Department?"

He shrugged.

"I just thought maybe ... since the Cal Academy of Sciences is so influential with regard to conservation and the environment, that sort of thing ... and if Nina's a tree expert—"

"She's not really a tree expert; she just knows a lot about them."

I nodded. "It's just that this tree is slated to be cut down, and I was hoping to get someone to—"

"Cut down? Cut *down*? When?"

"I'm not sure. I asked a friend to try to delay it."

"They can't cut it down! It's home to ..." He trailed off and looked up into the branches. I followed suit. "To squirrels and birds and ... and all sorts of things. There's still life left in it. Look at the new green on those far branches. They can't just cut it down."

"I agree. I'm hoping to stop it. Do you have any pull, do you think, as a member of the Cal Academy? Maybe Nina ... ?"

"I don't know, but I'll try. It was ... nice to see you," he finished rather lamely.

"Same here."

"Oh, we're having a big event tonight at the Cal Academy of Sciences. Cocktails, and frogs, and other things. You should come."

"Actually, Hannah mentioned it to me yesterday. Sure, I'll try."

He loped off in the direction of the main road.

"You've got a date now?" Sailor asked as he came to join me.

"Yes, Sailor. I'm going to throw you over for Lance, the bumbling scientist. He's just my type."

"Don't even joke about that. The party's tonight? I can't go with you. I promised to take my aunt to a family event—where, among other things, I was hoping to ask around for any information leading to a certain lost pig."

"That's okay," I said. "I'd rather you follow up with your family."

"I don't want you going alone."

"You're seriously afraid I'll run off with Lance?"

"No, but with everything going on lately, I don't like the thought of you running around town without me."

"I have to be without you *some*times. And lest you forget, I'm a pretty powerful witch." I was painfully aware that I was omitting one fascinating tidbit: that Lance worked with Bart's niece, Hannah's sister. I still wasn't sure how that fit in, but it seemed significant. But if I told Sailor, he would insist on coming with me.

Sailor went to stand very close to the massive trunk of the tree, stretching his arms out as though he were going to hug it.

"You're right about this tree being odd," he said. "It doesn't take much to figure that out. Here's what's strange: I sense something ancient."

"It's a very old tree."

"Not as old as what I'm feeling. I'm talking . . . *ancient*."

"Dude and dudette!" Conrad's voice rang out as he came to join us under the tree. He looked at Sailor; his voice dropped and his words rang with earnestness.

"That's really beautiful, man, to see you express your love for the tree like that. A lot of guys wouldn't feel secure doing something like that out in the open."

Sailor muttered something under his breath.

"Yes, Conrad, you're right," I interjected. "It's a lovely thing to see a man open up and hug a tree if he feels like it, isn't it? Especially a big manly man in his motorcycle gear."

"True that." Conrad nodded. "Was that the scientist dude I saw leaving right now?"

I nodded.

"He's the tree lady's friend. He knows a lot about frogs, which is *awesome*. Frogs transform from fish into land animals in, like, metamorphosis. It's like when I found out caterpillars become butterflies. It, like . . ." He put his fingers to his brain and blew it up, making the sound of a gunshot. "Blows my mind, dude."

I cringed at his gesture. What with a man being shot under this tree not long ago, it didn't seem wise to tempt the fates.

I looked up into the branches of the tree. It looked so innocent by the light of day, broad, strong arms reaching out as though to embrace and welcome all who would shade themselves under its leaves. To provide a home to squirrels and nesting birds, trails of ants and scores of passing insects. Its low crooks seemed to beckon for a tree house to be built, for someone to make their home here among the branches, or at least a child's clubhouse.

Its bark was split here and there in an intriguing pattern of gray and black streaks, with lighter core wood peeking out. If a person looked long enough into that bark, they could start to see pictures. A house here, a bird's leg there. A face.

I studied it for a long while, wondering whether, if I

concentrated hard enough, I might make out a monkey-like snout or batlike ears.

But I saw nothing beyond wood and bark, cool and silent as any other tree.

Just as I was getting ready to open Aunt Cora's Closet for the day, up walked a man with a pig.

Not Oscar. Some regular, big, fat farmyard pig. It had huge black spots on an otherwise pink skin and snorted loudly while stomping its little cloven hooves.

"I heard the story on the radio," the man said. He was about my age, with the weathered look of someone who worked out of doors. Dirty blue jeans, a John Deere ball cap, and a Raiders T-shirt. " 'Bout how you were lookin' for a pig."

Sailor and I stared at the man and the pig for a long moment.

"We're looking for a miniature potbellied pig who ran away," I said. "Not looking to *buy* a pig."

"Really?" The man looked crestfallen. "*Shoot.* We got foreclosed on. We're living with my mother-in-law in her mobile home out in Niles Valley. Temporary. I was hoping Miss Nelly here might have a good home with all y'all."

"Where are you from?" I asked, noting his accent.

"Tennessee. Came here a coupla years ago; thought I might do okay with a little piece of land my wife's family had. But with the way things are now, we weren't able to hold on to it. Now I don't even have anyplace to keep the pig. If I come back with the pig and no cash . . ." He shook his head and let out a weary sigh. "I was hoping we could find a good home for Miss Nelly and maybe collect the reward."

"Surely there are lots of people who would buy a . . . Miss Nelly."

The man shrugged. "It's my girl's seventh birthday tomorrow. I was really hoping to come home with the doll she wanted from the store."

I took pity on him, shelled out some money, and assured him I would find a good home for his pig.

After I saw the man out, I noticed Sailor was sitting on the velvet bench near the dressing rooms, a mocking look on his face.

"What?" I said, feeling defensive and wondering how I was going to explain this latest acquisition to my coworkers when they arrived.

"First you make a date with the bumbling scientist, and now you're accepting strange pigs from perfect strangers. And you wonder why I worry about leaving you alone. If this is what goes on right under my nose, just imagine what trouble you could get into all by your lonesome."

I smiled despite myself and held his gaze from across the store, over racks of frothy negligees and frilly prom dresses. I straightened, holding on to the leash of my new pig with as much dignity as I could muster.

"You're just jealous because you don't have a new pig. And here I was, planning on giving him to you as a gift. Surely one of your relatives . . . ?"

"Just because I have a big extended family doesn't mean I want to take your cast-off pig. We're more the *urban* gypsy types."

"I thought maybe somebody lived on a farm somewhere. Maybe I should ask Carlos. I'll make some phone calls. In the meantime . . . I don't know, maybe I could keep her in the alley? She's a little . . . fragrant."

Sailor helped me to urge the creature out to the alley behind the store, where I tied her to a post. She snorted and looked up at me with sweet eyes. I'd never been a pig fan—never thought about them much, to tell the truth—but now that Oscar was in my life I felt I had a new appreciation for the beasts. Still and all, I needed to find the poor thing a real home, and soon.

I left the back door open so I could keep an eye on her.

"You do realize, don't you, that there are probably ordinances against this sort of thing?" said Sailor. "Livestock in the city and all that."

"Wendy mentioned that yesterday—she was wondering if it was legal for me to keep Oscar here. How would I find out something like that without making somebody suspicious?"

"Maybe put Maya on it? She's awfully good at ferreting out information."

"Good idea. I'll have her do that, maybe, while she finds this little beauty a new home."

"That last will be easy enough. Bacon is very popular."

"*Shhh*. Miss Nelly might hear you. She'll go to a petting zoo or something. Not . . . you know."

Sailor gave me a lopsided grin. "I've seen you eat meat, you little hypocrite."

"Not once I know it up close and personal. I refuse to eat meat if I know its name. And besides . . . ever since Oscar's been in my life, pork has been off the menu. But you're right—I suppose I should just go vegan and have done with it."

He chuckled. "Well, now that you have a temporary replacement pig, I'm afraid I'm going to have to leave you. In all seriousness: Promise me that you won't go to that cocktail party alone tonight. Just in case."

"It will be mobbed with people."

"Still."

I nodded. "I'll see if the gang will go with me. Bronwyn and Maya . . . maybe Duke would be interested in coming along."

"Sounds good. I'll see if I can find anything out from Renna or any of the rest of the clan. Call me after the party?"

I nodded and we said our good-byes.

Mere minutes after Sailor's departure, Aidan walked through my door.

Chapter 15

As usual with Aidan, the bell over the door failed to chime; as usual, he strode in and assessed the inventory like he owned the place. But unusually, he was accompanied by his feline familiar, Noctemus.

"Lily, it is always such a pleasure to see you here among your things. To tell you the truth, when you first came to town and set up shop, I didn't understand your choice of retail. But now it seems just right, just perfect for you. All these silks and satins match your vibrations perfectly."

"Um . . . thank you?" I said, not sure how to respond. I watched Noctemus strutting around the floor and worried she would leave long white hairs on the merchandise. "Did you find out anything about Oscar? What did the woodsfolk say?"

"I haven't been able to speak with them yet."

"What do you mean, not yet? Aidan—"

"There were some unexpected developments. I told you, these things are never easy. The Good People are very . . . touchy."

"So I hear. Did you find out anything at all?"

"Apparently they're short on gorse blossoms this year."

"Excuse me?"

"That's as far as the talks have gotten."

"Aidan, I have to get Oscar *back*. It's driving me crazy. Among other things, I can't even do magic like I could when he was around. He helped me open the portals."

"I could give you a loaner."

"A loaner?"

He lifted Noctemus toward me. She hissed at me. I reared back. "I told you, I'm allergic to cats."

"I have a few others that might do the trick. Let me just see. . . ." He took an ancient-looking leather-bound notebook out of his breast pocket and started thumbing through the crumbling old parchment pages. It reminded me of a much smaller version of the ledger Sailor and I had taken from Sebastian's antiques store. I wondered whether Carlos would come through with the photocopy for me.

"Ah, here's one. Manifests as a dog. Do you like dogs?"

"I love dogs, but what am I going to do, just take any old familiar? I already have one, one I love."

He flipped through a few more pages, a tiny frown of concentration between his eyebrows. "Mm-hmm . . . No, not that . . . Aha! A goat, maybe? They're quite clever. . . ."

"Are you trying to tell me you don't think we'll be able to get Oscar back? That's not possible, Aidan." He continued to search the book, ignoring me. I leaned closer to him. "Listen to me, Aidan. I am not giving up on Oscar; you hear me? I am *not* giving up on him."

Things started to fly around us in the store. Aidan held up his arm just in time to deflect a plaid miniskirt on a hanger. It bounced off his forearm.

"All right. All right. Calm down. I'm just saying . . . it's not impossible, no. But it will be tough. And extremely expensive."

"Expensive as in cash?" I immediately started adding

up in my head: my savings, a money market account, some stocks. If necessary, I would use my magic to get more. It was an ethical gray area, but at the moment I didn't care. Whatever it took.

"Costly, I should say. I really think right now what you need to do is calm down and have a little faith."

"How am I supposed to have faith when two minutes ago you were trying to foist off a goat on me, for land's sake."

I tapped my foot, tried to keep a lid on my emotions, and gathered my thoughts. "All right, let's change topics for a moment. What can you tell me about hereditary love curses?"

"You and Sailor not doing well?" he asked, overly interested.

"This has nothing to do with us; we're fine, thank you very much. I was asking for someone else."

"I offer a very reasonably priced package deal."

"I guess I assumed you were expensive."

"That's a relative term. What's true love worth?"

Good question. Now that I thought about it, I wondered whether Bart had already tried going to Aidan in search of a cure. Aidan advertised for this sort of thing, after all. And, according to Sailor and Oscar, Sebastian Crowley might have been keeping tabs on some of Aidan's clients for him.

But I'd promised Bart my discretion. And I didn't trust Aidan. What if—

There was a loud snorting sound from the rear of the store. Miss Nelly had come in as far as she could, given her lead. She appeared to have gotten lonely.

Aidan turned back to me, one eyebrow raised. "A pig in the alley? Really? And you're looking down your nose at a goat?"

"It's a long story. . . ." It was just past ten in the morning, the shop wasn't even officially open yet, and already I felt weary.

Aidan seemed to notice the defeated tone in my voice.

"Why don't you try to forget about this for a bit?" he suggested. "Maybe take the day off, go to the ocean with your 'boyfriend.' I take it you two are still enamored of each other?"

"None of your business."

"Oh, I think it's very much my business. You deprived me of a very good, very beholden psychic. Now I'm just hanging out here, all alone, without anyone to help me...."

"Cry me a river, mister. You've got plenty up your sleeve."

Aidan grinned, his blue eyes sparkling.

"Hey, speaking of Sailor," I continued. "Are you doing something to block his sight?"

"Pardon?"

"You heard me."

"Sailor's abilities are diminished?"

Only then did it dawn on me that Sailor might not want me to mention this sort of thing to Aidan, his arch-nemesis.

"Just leave him alone, will you?" I said.

Aidan smiled his enigmatic smile, picked up his cat, winked, and left.

To my surprise, Maya, Bronwyn, and Duke all wanted to attend tonight's event, entitled Cocktails and Frogs, a Leaping Good Time. Even Conrad accepted my invitation to join us. He had been doing so much work with the campaign to find Oscar, hanging around the store every day, and I'd been feeding him. He seemed more with it lately; whether it was the result of having regular meals

and a purpose, or simply not being on as many substances, I wasn't sure. Either way, I was enjoying his company.

So the whole entourage was going. Whether I would
find out anything regarding Lance or Bart's nieces I
didn't know, but frankly, an evening spent with friends,
cocktail in hand, checking out a natural history museum,
sounded like the best idea I'd had in ages.

Better by far than sitting at home trying to ignore Oscar's empty nest.

But I was still beside myself, wondering if there was
any way to communicate with the woodsfolk. Aidan was
a bust so far, Sailor was checking with his aunt Renna,
and my voodoo friend Herve didn't have this kind of
relationship with the Good People. But there was one
other person who might know something . . . and I'd
wanted to introduce her to Bronwyn for some time now,
anyway.

"Bronwyn, you know I've mentioned my new friend
Calypso to you? I've been thinking you two should
meet," I said later in the day, when Missing Pig Central
was in full swing and Maya had plenty of company in
the shop. "Any interest in taking a drive and meeting
her?"

"This is the woman with the gardens and the beehives?"

"The very one."

"I'd love to!"

"I'll stay here with Maya," offered Duke. "And Miss
Nelly."

I had taken a fair amount of ribbing over the pig in
the alley, but Maya thought she would be able to find a
place for it soon. In the past couple of days she had gotten to know the local animal shelters, vets, and animal
control officers that dealt with every sort of domesti-
cated animal, as well as livestock.

"Thank you, Duke. That would be great." The SFPD radio car still rolled by from time to time, and the shop was full of Bronwyn's coven sisters, Starr and Wendy among them, as well as several of Maya's cousins, and her parents. I felt sure she was safe.

The drive out of San Francisco was sunny, though a wall-like bank of fog lingered just off the mouth of the bay, as though trying to decide whether to roll over the city or to recede. For now, at least, the sun glinted off the water as we passed over the majestic Golden Gate Bridge. Bronwyn and I spoke of anything besides Oscar as I drove; Aidan's warning still rang in my head, and though I was pretty sure he had been exaggerating, I didn't want to take any chance of losing my temper and accidentally causing some damage to the iconic bridge.

After a windy drive along Highway 1 we finally came to an unmarked turnoff onto a dirt road and squeezed the car through an opening in a tall, thick hedge. The big yellow Victorian farmhouse had creamy white trim, a huge wraparound porch, and was surrounded by lush gardens on all sides. Rose trees lined the path to the front door, a calico cat slept on a porch swing, and there was a large attached greenhouse to the back.

Bronwyn gasped and clasped her hands over her chest. "It looks like something out of a fairy tale book."

"I know, right? I always think of a picture in a calendar, especially with the cat curled up on the porch swing like that."

Before we even pulled to a halt, Calypso opened the front door. She was a tall, elegant woman in her late fifties, her silver hair swept into a bun. Her eyes were kind, her smile warm. She had that deep, resonant calm that I had come to associate, since I had moved to the Bay Area, with people who meditate. Or perhaps she was just supremely happy in her own skin.

She gave me a big hug. This sort of thing made me feel

awkward—I'm not really a hugger—but Bronwyn stepped up and moved in for a hug as well, even before I'd introduced them.

"I'm Bronwyn," she said. "It is *such* a pleasure to finally meet you! My goddess, I am already enamored with you—this place is incredible!"

Calypso laughed a deep, husky laugh, returned the hug, and offered her a tour. As they made their way arm in arm toward the gardens, I realized I had been right: They were clearly sisters of the heart.

Half an hour later, we wound up in the kitchen, where Calypso heated water in a copper kettle, while Bronwyn shared several samples of her herbal blends.

"Well," said Bronwyn, "I know Lily wanted to speak to you in private, so how about I take my tea into the greenhouse? I'm sure I could entertain myself out there for hours!"

She left Calypso and me at the kitchen table, made of rustic oak worn smooth with the hands of those who had sat here over the years.

"Is it Aidan?" Calypso asked before I had a chance to begin. She and Aidan had history, as they say. I didn't know what had happened between them and wasn't sure I *wanted* to know. But one thing was sure: She knew the man better than I did—perhaps better than I ever would.

"I'm not sure, to tell you the truth. It's a little complicated, and I don't want to bore you with all the details. But the most important thing is that my familiar has gone missing."

"I'm so sorry to hear that. A cat?"

"No . . . a miniature potbellied pig."

"*Really*. Huh. Surely he can't have got far without being seen."

I hesitated. Oscar wasn't "out" to very many of us. As far as I knew, only Sailor, Aidan, and I were aware of his true form. And one or two bad guys he'd gone up against, but I was pretty sure they assumed they'd imagined his natural form due to stress, once they thought back on it.

"You don't have to tell me," Calypso said, her eyes kind. "But I can't help unless I know what kind of creature he is. And I won't betray a confidence; nor will I be surprised."

I nodded, sipped my tea, and made a decision. "Oscar isn't a regular familiar. He was a gift from Aidan. In his natural form, he's sort of a cross between a goblin and a gargoyle. He's . . ." Precious, is what he was. If I had been able to cry, I'm sure my eyes would have filled with tears.

A fern frond tapped my shoulder, distracting me. I looked up to see the delicate hanging plant twisting lazily in the breeze from the open window, its trailing arms reaching out.

"Oscar's a shape-shifter, then?" Calypso said. "How amazing. I wasn't sure those truly existed—I've never actually seen one."

"He's real, all right. But he's disappeared, and I think something magical is going on." I told her the story of the tree, and Sebastian's death, and Oscar's disappearance.

"You say the last time you saw him he was up in the tree?"

I nodded.

"And it's a California live oak?" She brought a large book of trees over to the table and showed me a picture.

"Yes, that's the one. *Quercus agrifolia*." That must have been where Conrad and his friends got the name, Ms. Quercus.

Calypso nodded. "*Agrifolia* refers to the sharp points on the leaves, as opposed to the oak trees pictured in most European art, for example. They can live for hundreds of years."

"I have the sense this one's pretty old. Its trunk is massive. Are there any stories associated with oak trees that you know? Any folklore I should consider?"

She sipped her tea, fragrant of cinnamon and apple. "There are several stories out of Europe, mostly about trees taking vengeance. There's the chained oak of Staffordshire, for example. . . ."

"I heard about that one. But nothing closer, nothing with regards to the *Quercus agrifolia*?"

"Around here it's the redwoods that really attract that kind of folklore. They send up faery circles, that kind of thing. And of course you know about the dangers associated with sleeping under flowering *brugmansia*. But no, I'm not familiar with oaks being particularly supernatural."

"What if, for example, a person's ashes were buried at its base and soaked into the tree . . . ? Could that person's energy become part of the heartwood?"

Again, I found myself transfixed by Calypso's steady gaze. She seemed to pause before she spoke, which had the effect of making me listen that much harder.

"Trees are living, responsive beings. I know many people would argue with me, but they have souls and personalities, just as do the footed creatures. But because they draw sustenance and are connected so directly to the land, they are affected by it, just as we are by what we eat and see and experience."

I nodded.

"What kind of person are we talking about? Who did these ashes belong to?"

"I think . . . it's possible it was someone accused of being a witch, who was burned at the stake centuries ago."

"Yes, I suppose that could be. I've heard of a few cases in which a spirit seeks sanctuary in the heartwood of a tree. Or in the case of hanging trees, when sleeping people are haunted by the pain of those killed there. But becoming part of the wood . . . this person would have to have been very powerful. Have you spoken with the woodsfolk?"

"I haven't. Oscar was my only go-between with them. Could you introduce me?"

She shook her head. "I don't have that kind of power. Not anymore. I'm good with plants, but that's a whole different world. Aidan would be your best source for that."

"I know. But I can't trust him. He's trying to foist another creature on me for a familiar rather than helping to save Oscar. I don't know what's going through his head."

"Interesting. He must not think it worth the price to bring Oscar back."

"It's not his decision; it's mine. And Oscar's worth the price."

"But Aidan holds power over him. He's still the one in charge of your Oscar, even though you'd like to think he's *your* familiar."

"How does he keep him beholden?"

"He must hold a marker of some sort. Probably some part of Oscar."

"What do you mean, part of him?"

"How does one explain Aidan?" Calypso said, sipping her tea and looking out the window to the garden. "He's not a sociopath. . . ."

Oh goody, I thought. *At least there was that.*

"But . . . he's ruthless. He gets no joy out of hurting people, not like a psychopath, but he won't pull a punch, either. He does what he believes is necessary."

"Necessary for what?"

"To maintain control, his position of power. I don't know what he's after in the long run. I really don't. Like most of us, I doubt he knows himself. But in the short run . . . he's all about doing what's necessary to maintain his position."

I pondered Aidan's motives as I looked through the window. Outside in the garden, I could see Bronwyn wandering through the tall tomato vines. She seemed to fit right in here, in her flowing tunic, flowers in her hair. I always thought she fit in perfectly on Haight Street, but looking at Bronwyn now, I realized that she would probably fit in perfectly no matter where she was. With the possible exception of the suburbs.

"So tell me more about Oscar. He's a cross between a goblin and a gargoyle, you say? I've never heard of that."

"He's got gray-green skin, a monkeylike snout, big bat ears, humanlike hands but clawed feet."

"Are his wings feathered, batlike, or segmented like an insect?"

"He doesn't have wings."

"No wings? You're sure?"

"Of course I'm sure. I mean . . . wouldn't I have noticed them?"

"Sometimes they're subtle. They might blend in, get tucked in, sort of?"

I thought back. On the one hand, Oscar never ceased to amaze me. But I had held him often enough; surely I would have noticed such a thing.

I shook my head. "I really, *really*, can't imagine I would have missed them."

She rose and went into the front room, which was covered floor to ceiling in bookshelves. "Let me see . . . wings, witches . . . ah, here we are. Witch's familiars."

She thumbed through, looked in the index, and finally flipped it open and turned it around to face me. She tapped on a picture that looked rather like Oscar, though not quite. The skin was wrong, and the size was off. And it had nothing like Oscar's ugly, adorable expression. But overall . . . I could see it.

"Anything like this?" Calypso asked.

"Very much like that," I said.

"The cursed gargoyles—a sad case. I never knew it was true."

"So you're not only a botanist, but also an expert on gargoyles?"

"Oh, hardly," she said, waving me off with a chuckle. "Though I do climb Notre Dame every time I'm in Paris, just to see all those marvelous creatures up there, overlooking the city."

"Apparently his father was a goblin. When his mother shifted . . ."

"Oh." Calypso blushed prettily and chuckled. "Oh, my, my, *my*. The mind does reel, doesn't it?"

"I think it involved an egg and a faery circle."

"Well, I should think so."

"So, even though he's only half gargoyle, you think he should have wings?" I thought of how Oscar had cackled when he saw the scene with the flying monkeys in *The Wizard of Oz*.

"I'd be willing to bet on it. Wings are an *extremely* dominant gene." She got up and poured more hot water into our mugs. "If they're missing, there's a reason for it."

Chapter 16

"You're saying what exactly? That Aidan *took* Oscar's wings?"

Calypso stirred a dollop of honey into her tea but said nothing.

"Why would he take his wings? That's . . . horrifying."

"That would keep him beholden to Aidan. Right?"

I had known Oscar worked for Aidan. And then Aidan "gave" him to me, which seemed wrong at some deep level. But . . . I guess I had come to think that Oscar really cared for me, that he was with me for reasons other than being forced to do so. This made him sound like a slave.

"How do I get his wings back?" I asked.

She let out a silent whistle, her eyebrows raised as if to say, *No way.* "Aidan doesn't give up things like that. That's his leverage. And if word got out that he made an exception in your case, or in Oscar's, the others wouldn't take him seriously anymore. You know how the magical world is, Lily. Lots of saving face, making symbolic gestures, putting out the right image." She blew on her tea. "Frankly, I'm just as glad to be rid of the whole lot of 'em. Except for my plants, of course."

While we were speaking, a long frond of the hanging fern wound itself around her arm. So slowly I didn't notice at first, but now it had wrapped itself several times around and seemed to hold on in a loving fashion.

I spied Bronwyn strolling near the old-fashioned beehives, trying to peek inside one.

"I think I've kept you to myself long enough. I'll bet Bronwyn would love to compare honeys with you. She has a special source up in the Oakland Hills somewhere. Just one more thing: Where do you think Aidan keeps those wings?"

"Lily, listen to me: You can't go around stealing things from Aidan."

"He stole them from Oscar."

"Oscar probably forfeited them for some reason, in exchange for something. But be that as it may, stealing from Aidan is a definite no-no. I know you're strong, but . . . you're not that strong."

"I'm getting stronger every day. And at the moment, I've got plenty of rage. So, does he have a warehouse somewhere? Where does he even *live*?" For some reason this last thought had never occurred to me. Aidan was so tied up with the Wax Museum in my mind, I never thought about him actually sleeping somewhere.

Calypso shook her head. "I'm not sure I'd tell you, even if I knew. And I really don't have any idea."

"No clue where he might hide valuable items? If Oscar's not his only minion, he must be holding a lot of stuff somewhere."

"It's not always that kind of marker. Sometimes it's a secret, or something much more subtle."

"Okay, but . . ."

"All I can tell you is that Aidan always used to enjoy hiding things out in plain sight."

"In plain sight?"

"He finds it . . . funny. Entertaining, I suppose. Now, shall we go talk about bees?"

An hour later we bid Calypso good-bye and climbed into my Mustang. Just as we were about to leave, Calypso mentioned she had decided to start offering botanical classes again.

"I'd love to take a class like that!" exclaimed Bronwyn.

"Me too," I said, thinking how much fun it would be to talk plants and herbs for hours at a time.

"Funny you should mention that, Lily," said Calypso. "I was actually wondering . . . Have you ever considered teaching?"

"Oh, I . . . uh . . . not really," I stammered in reply.

"You have so much knowledge."

"Oh!" gushed Bronwyn. "What a wonderful idea! Lily, you'd be *wonderful*."

"I don't know about that. I'm still learning myself. I don't know what I could possibly teach to others."

"How about methods of brewing and spell casting?" offered Calypso.

"Or how you carve and consecrate talismans? Or make spirit bottles?" suggested Bronwyn.

"I think you are more accomplished than you know," said Calypso.

I could feel myself blushing. I knew a lot about plants, true, but Calypso could blow me out of the water, botanicalswise. Still and all, I supposed she was right: Though I still had a great deal to learn, I certainly knew more than your average bear about charms and brews.

"I worry about teaching people just enough to hurt themselves," I said. "Witchcraft can be dangerous, especially if someone attempts something and then turns out to have more power than they know. I say this from experience. Spell casting is all about intention and effecting change; what if someone is great at intention but gets the details wrong and hurts herself?"

"When you and I grew up, this was all secret knowledge, and for good reason, to keep people from doing exactly that—hurting themselves or others," said Calypso. "But these days, anyone can get access to this kind of information over the Internet if they look hard enough. The point of classes would be to train them properly, so they *don't* hurt anyone. And you don't have to teach the tough stuff, nothing that would be potentially harmful. Just casting spells of confidence and good fortune, that kind of thing."

"Oh, Lily," put in Bronwyn. "I really think you would be splendid."

"Just think about it," said Calypso with a warm smile. "I'll start the classes up again in September, so you have a couple of months to consider."

"Well, thank you. I'm flattered," I said. "And thanks again for sharing all your information with me. I really appreciate it."

As we pulled out, Calypso left me with one more remark: "Don't underestimate Aidan, Lily. It . . . won't turn out well."

That night, Bronwyn, Maya, Duke, Conrad, and I approached the Academy of Sciences building. I was stunned at the size of the crowd. Clearly, I had underestimated the appeal of a frog-themed cocktail party for the residents of San Francisco.

"I can't believe how long it's been since I've been here!" said Bronwyn. "When my kids were young, we used to come all the time. Duke, you and I need to bring the grandkids and make a day of it."

"That's a deal," said Duke. "Don't think I've been here since my Miriam was a tyke. Place was different back then."

"I take it it's a new building?" I asked.

"Yes. It says here"—Maya read from a brochure she had downloaded from the Internet—"that one critic called the building a 'blazingly uncynical embrace of the Enlightenment values of truth and reason' and a 'comforting reminder of the civilizing function of great art in a barbaric age.'"

The five of us gawked at the building.

"Huh," I said.

"Can't argue with that." Duke nodded.

"Well written," Conrad agreed. "Art as a civilizing function in a barbaric age. Dude."

"Check out the sod roof," said Bronwyn, pointing to the roofline. "Personally, I'm a little unclear on how that fits with Enlightenment values, but it sure fits in well with *my* values. Funny how the traditional ways are coming back in vogue, right?"

"'Coming back' might be a stretch," said Maya. "Not a lot of hobbit dwellings in the Bay Area."

"Hobbit dwellings?" I asked.

"Sod-roofed buildings remind me of Hobbiton." She smiled. "Or have I been reading too much Tolkien?"

"No such thing as too much Tolkien," Conrad said.

"I suppose it does look a little hobbitlike on the roof," I said. "But this place is massive. I've seen sod roofs used in parts of Africa and rural Europe—eventually, if they deteriorate, they simply go back to the earth rather than into landfills."

"Ashes to ashes, dust to dust." Bronwyn sighed. "Circle of life and all that."

Her words brought to mind Sebastian Crowley. I'd said something similar to him, and the thought had resurfaced when Conrad and I were discussing the old oak tree. The circle of life, things returning from whence they came . . .

As crowded as the terrace in front of the museum was,

the space inside was still more jam-packed. We stood in a clump at one side, trying not to jostle others. Looking about, I took in the crowd, which seemed to be made up primarily of upwardly mobile professionals.

"Oh my," said Bronwyn with a glance at Maya. "Look at all the handsome young men."

"Thanks, Bronwyn, but I'm fine just as I am," Maya said.

Ever since Bronwyn had started seeing Duke, she had become a world-class matchmaker. Maya and I had promised each other we would be patient with our friend's newfound interest in our love lives, assuming that Bronwyn was motivated by wanting us to be as happy as she was. To Bronwyn's credit, she was the first to say she had been happy to make her own way and was quick to acknowledge that a woman didn't need a man at her side to be fulfilled. Still, she wanted to see all her friends in happy relationships.

"I'm just saying, if a person were young and single, they could do worse than to find another young single person at a gathering like this. Shared interests and all that . . ."

"Shared interest in frogs?" Maya was young but jaded, a forty-year-old brain in a twentysomething's body.

"You don't like frogs?" Conrad asked. "Dude, I *love* the little guys."

"I've got nothing against frogs. I'm just not sure how much I could commit to the theme, conversation-wise."

The crowd in the building kept getting bigger, and our group backed off, finding a little breathing room in a corner near the corridor leading to the stairway.

"Stand back, my friends. Duke and I are going to fight our way to the bar," said Bronwyn, putting her arm through Duke's. "You three go on and check out the exhibit—we'll find you. Margaritas all around? Speak now or forever hold your sobriety."

"A beer, dude," said Conrad. "Any flavor."

"We can all go," said Maya.

"Nonsense," Bronwyn said briskly. "In a situation like this, the fewer the better. And I have skills—I waitressed for years, remember? I could balance five drinks at a time back then. And Duke can do the pushing."

Bronwyn and Duke headed off in the general direction of the crowd, while Maya, Conrad, and I followed the signs to the frog exhibit.

The exhibit was less crowded than the bar area, but not by much. Still, we had fun checking out the big, open areas, where all kinds of frogs hopped around on rocks and splashed in ponds and puddles. There were also huge glass enclosures, where rarer or more delicate specimens were displayed.

"Dude," Conrad said. "That's a lot of frogs."

"Suppose there's one here I could kiss and change into a prince?" asked Maya.

"If there is, I'm sure Bronwyn will send him your way soon," I said.

"Check out that one. The bright orange ones have psychedelic properties," said Maya, reading the exhibit brochure. "Listen to this, Conrad: See the little yellow-and-black frog over there? Apparently, it emits a certain chemical. If you lick its back, you'll start tripping."

"Dude! No way."

"Way. Brochures don't lie."

"Did you know that witches used to brew up hallucinogenic herbal concoctions?" I said. "According to some historians, that's how they 'flew.' "

"So the whole riding broomsticks thing was only metaphorical?" Maya asked.

"The result of pharmacological use and abuse," I said. "Or so they say."

"Given the misery of the lives of a lot of women—

witches or not—back then," said Maya, "you can hardly blame them for indulging in a little escapism."

Conrad pointed out the horned toads, sitting almost motionless and blending in with the rocks and plants at the water's edge. One large brownish one sat amid a number of ceramic toadstools. They made me think of the mushrooms at the base of Ms. Quercus. I knew mushrooms could spring up overnight, but could there be any significance to them appearing at the base of the tree?

After a few minutes, I noticed a young man staring at us from across the pond. Dressed in a lab coat, he appeared to be one of the academy scientists, and I realized I had seen him on that nightmarish day in the park: He was one of Lance's colleagues. His heavy-rimmed glasses, pale face, and buzz-cut dark hair suggested he had stepped out of a poster of a scientist from the early sixties.

As I watched the man watching us, Lance Thornton walked up to him. Lance was a mess, with the same yellowish stains on his lab coat as the last time I'd seen him. As always, his eyes were large and unblinking. Poor fellow, I thought; what would it be like to go through life with one's features arranged in a constant expression of astonishment? Rather similar to his research subjects, now that I thought of it. But surely that was a coincidence, rather like when dogs started looking like their owners.

"Lance," I called out with a wave. "Hello!"

He shuffled toward us, trailed by his friend.

"Oh, uh, hello again," Lance mumbled. "This is my colleague, Kai Hiccum. He was at . . . the tree, too. You know. That time."

"Yes, I remember. I'm Lily. Nice to meet you," I said.

"Dude," said Conrad, a few beats late, as usual. "Your name's Kai? Awesome. I remember you from that day,

under the tree. What a *trip*. Just call me the Con. And, Lance, my man, how you doing?"

Kai was staring at Maya. Then, all of a sudden, he smiled. I hadn't thought of him as handsome, but when he smiled, his whole face lit up.

"Thank you so much for coming," he said. "You don't drink?"

"Our friends are braving the line at the bar for us," I said, glancing over to the sea of people milling about the concession area. "The cocktails are a big draw, it seems."

"I'll go reconnoiter," said Conrad, and disappeared into the crowd.

Kai chuckled. "I have a bottle of scotch in my office, if I can tempt you . . . ? Unless you have your heart set on cocktails."

"Too strong for my blood," said Maya with a definite shake of her head. "I'm more of a margarita gal."

"Yes, I could picture you on a beach somewhere, margarita in hand," Kai said.

Maya's skin was a rich mocha brown, so it was hard to tell . . . but I could have sworn she was blushing.

"What a great way to bring in the public to the museum," I said.

"Kai thought of it," said Lance.

"While I'm happy to take the credit for the idea, all I said was that we have families with kids coming in and out all day long—I swear, divorced dads are our bread and butter," Kai explained. "But adults on their own? Not so much. So I suggested we stay open late one evening, serve alcohol, and watch the grown-ups turn out."

"I'd say your plan worked brilliantly," I said. "Hey, since you're the experts, could I ask you a question? I notice the mushrooms in the frog display. Why are toadstools associated with frogs?"

Kai shrugged. "To tell you the truth, I think it's just folklore. Though some mushrooms, like some frogs, have hallucinogenic properties. Maybe that's why. In fact I wondered . . . When Lance and I came across that poor man under the tree, that was the first thing I thought of, that maybe he had ingested some mushrooms and was either high or had poisoned himself. Or both. Until I noticed the, um . . ."

"Bullet holes," said Lance helpfully.

And with that our conversation stumbled to a halt. It occurred to me that Maya, Kai, Lance, and I might have been the least socially adept social group imaginable. Maya was capable of being charming and breezy around those with whom she was comfortable, but with men in general, it was a different story. And the two scientists were probably happier looking through a microscope than making small talk with strangers.

The four of us were gazing awkwardly about in silence when Bronwyn breezed up, balancing cocktails in both hands. Duke and Conrad trailed behind her, also carrying drinks.

"Order up!" Bronwyn announced, and after handing out the drinks, immediately started chatting up the scientists, putting everyone at ease. "I remember coming to the old Natural Sciences Museum with my daughter; we used to get lost on the way to the restroom every time."

"The new building is much better," said Lance earnestly. "People rarely get lost. Though sometimes down in the basement . . ."

"It's a real rabbit's warren down there," affirmed Kai. "Our director disappeared for a few days before we realized he was gone."

Kai looked so serious I wasn't sure if he was joking.

"Oh, look, Nina's here," said Lance.

I followed his gaze to see Hannah Woolsey, Bart's niece. She was standing with the tall, pale woman I had seen at the tree—Nina, I presumed. And with them was the professor, Will Chambers.

"*Hey!*" yelled Lance suddenly. Gone was the hapless, bumbling scientist. He looked outraged. "Don't touch those frogs!"

"Dude," said Conrad, holding his hands up in surrender. "Sorry. Sign says right here you can touch these little dudes, just not the other ones."

As Lance marched over to the display, I noticed that the back of his lab coat was stained worse than the front. What on earth did he do in his lab?

Lance yanked the sign down. "I don't know who put this up. This is *not* a petting zoo."

"Sorry, dude," Conrad said.

An awkward silence descended on our group.

"Um . . . I'm going to talk with Nina and Hannah," I said.

Bronwyn, Duke, Maya, and Conrad went to investigate the tree frog exhibit while I made my way across the crowded floor to the Woolsey sisters and the professor.

Hannah's eyes lit up in recognition. "Hey! You made it. How are you?"

"I'm okay. Thanks. How are you?"

"Great. Hey, you know Will, don't you?"

"Of course. Nice to see you here."

"Exciting, isn't it?" said Will. He was clutching a martini, and I realized that he and Hannah, both singles of a certain age, fit right in here at Cocktails and Frogs. It was like a slightly nerdy dating service.

"And this is my sister, Nina."

"Nice to meet you," I said, noting that despite her pallid complexion, Nina was as tall and fit-looking as her sister. They were like Amazonian stock. I stood up straighter, feeling gremlinlike standing beside them. "Great exhibit."

"Thanks," Nina replied. "I didn't really have anything to do with it."

I looked around for their uncle. "Is Bart here?"

"What, and take part in the real world?" said Nina in a snide tone of voice.

"Nina . . ." Hannah warned. "Be nice."

Nina rolled her eyes.

"I tried to get him to come," said Will.

"Uncle Bart doesn't get out a lot," explained Hannah with a shake of her head. "Though he told me he stopped by your shop. Could have knocked me over with a feather. He's never come to see me at the Vivarium."

"Probably 'cause it's creepy," said Nina.

"No creepier than all these amphibians," said Hannah. "After all, frogs are slimy and even poisonous sometimes. People think snakes are slimy, but they really aren't."

"Frogs are cute," Nina said. "Snakes aren't cute."

"*I* think they're cute," Hannah insisted.

"I'm not surprised," Nina said.

Will met my eyes, and we shared a look. I had always wanted a sister, but occasionally witnessing these relationships gave me pause.

"Lance mentioned that you're an arboreal specialist," I said to Nina.

"That's overstating the case. I actually work more with algae, but I'm a botanist, so I agreed to go out and look at that oak tree with Lance. For some reason he feels the need to save it."

"Is it salvageable?"

She shook her head. "It's rotten on the inside."

"I thought I saw new growth."

"There's some, yes, but not enough to save such a massive specimen."

"I went up to the redwoods not long ago," said Hannah, "and a lot of the biggest trees didn't have anything at the core at all. They formed what looked like round rooms; only the bark was alive. You could even drive through some of them."

Nina nodded. "Some trees can lose their entire core to fire or disease and still thrive, it's true. The redwoods are famous for it. But not California live oaks. They're a different species entirely."

"So you recommended it be removed?" Will asked.

"It isn't up to me. The Parks Department makes those decisions," said Nina. "I'm just a lowly scientist here at the academy. Lance was worried, so I told him I'd take a look, that's all. If they were taking down a healthy specimen, I might try to intervene, but as it is . . ." She trailed off with a shrug and took a sip of her manhattan.

"So . . . I saw you there, when Sebastian Crowley was found under the tree."

"You knew the stiff?" asked Nina.

"Who's this we're talking about?" asked Will. "Or tell me if I'm doing that annoying thing now where I'm asking about someone everyone else knows. . . . I am, aren't I? Never mind."

"Sebastian Crowley was an antiques dealer. Hannah sold something to him for Bart, and later he was found shot in Golden Gate Park."

"That's awful," said Will.

"Poor Sebastian," said Hannah.

"Take a drink," said Nina in a derisive tone. "You'll get over it."

"You didn't even know him," said Hannah, clearly shaken. "How can you be so mean all the time?"

"And you were, what, dating him?" said Nina. "That'll be news to poor Will here."

Hannah shook her head, pressed her lips together, and looked around at the crowd.

"Seriously, Hannah. It's not like he was a good friend of yours. What was he, some lunatic friend of Uncle Bart's? Did he promise to cure Bart's love curse or something?"

"He said he might be able to do something for Uncle

Bart, yes," said Hannah. "I know you don't believe in it, and I don't either, not really. But obviously Uncle Bart does, and I think people should stop being so nasty about it. I mean, some people believe in Santa Claus, but that doesn't make them crazy."

"It does if they're over the age of five," murmured Nina.

"*There* you are!" I heard Bronwyn's voice and felt a wave of relief as the gang appeared: Bronwyn and Maya and Conrad and Duke. We might be a motley, quirky bunch, but at least we liked one another. I knew bickering did not necessarily mean the sisters didn't love each other, but I found such exchanges exhausting.

"How were the tree frogs?" I asked.

"Lovely, really just splendid. Weren't they, Maya?" Bronwyn said.

"They're so sweet-looking, even the ones that can kill you." Maya smiled. "It really is a great exhibit. I can't believe I never come here. I'm gonna invite my cousins' kids so I have an excuse to come back."

"Kai would say you don't need an excuse," I said. "In fact, he might give you a private tour if you asked nicely."

"Cute," said Maya.

"You like Kai?" Nina said. "He's single. Want me to set something up?"

"*No.* No, no, no. No, thank you," said Maya, shaking her head. "She's kidding."

"Watch out, Nina," said Hannah. "Someone might call you a romantic. And here I thought you didn't believe in love."

"I don't believe in love *spells*, much less curses. Anyway, Kai's a good guy. Eccentric, but then aren't we all? Scientists are weird, no two ways about that. I'm sure not exempt from that. Hey, Kai!" Nina yelled, showing surprisingly good pipes, and waved with her free hand.

Maya looked daggers at me.

The two men came over, Kai eager and Lance hapless, as usual. Truth to tell, after Lance's outburst a few minutes ago, I was rethinking my assessment of him. Might the bumbling scientist bit be an act? I had sensed something was off about him from the start, but whether it was due to his social awkwardness or to something more sinister was hard to know.

"Dudes, there they are," said Conrad, slapping Lance on the back in a hearty hello. "That exhibit was really awesome, dude!"

Lance yanked back from Conrad's overly familiar gesture.

"Dude, your lab coat's all wet. You okay?"

"Of course," said Lance, then walked away so quickly he knocked over a potted palm.

"That's Lance for you," Nina said with a sigh. "Mr. Charming. I tell you what, Kai. We are a pathetic bunch of losers when it comes to social interaction, aren't we? We should form a club."

"We already have," said Kai with a shy smile. "We're the nerdy scientists, remember?"

"Oh, right," said Nina.

I noticed Kai's eyes slewed over toward Maya, who returned his smile.

"Hey, I'm single," said Will. "D'ya suppose the nerdy academics could join this club, too?"

"Sure," said Nina. "The more the merrier."

"Dudette," Conrad whispered to me in a loud stage whisper. "Like, do men get hot flashes?"

"Hot flashes?"

"You know, the way women do when they're, like, going through the 'change'? My mom totally had that and now . . ."

"Conrad, I'm not sure now's the time to talk about—"

"Dude . . . I feel sort of . . . funky."

Conrad crumpled and fell to the floor.

Chapter 17

His head knocked against the stone floor with a dull thud.

"Conrad!" I cried, kneeling beside him. "Conrad? What's wrong?"

He opened his eyes, his gaze unfocused. I put one hand on his forehead: His skin was wet and clammy.

"Duuuude . . ." He groaned. Then he closed his eyes and his head fell back.

Maya was already dialing 911 on her cell phone, and Bronwyn and Duke immediately departed to find whatever in-house first aid the academy might have to offer.

"Is there a doctor in the house?" I called out.

"What is it? What's wrong?" asked Nina as she knelt on Conrad's other side.

"I don't know," I said. "He was talking, then just collapsed midsentence."

She lifted his eyelids, first the right, then the left.

"Pupils dilated," she muttered, then held his wrist, timing his pulse with her watch. "Heartbeat rapid . . . Could he be on something? Drugs of some kind?"

"I . . . don't think so." I knew perfectly well that Conrad imbibed mind-altering substances. But he had never done so around me and had had only one beer this evening.

Conrad mumbled something, then giggled.

"The paramedics shouldn't take long," Nina said. "There's usually a crew stationed in the amphitheater out front during special events."

Sure enough, there was a commotion at the front door, and I gratefully ceded my place to the paramedics.

Twenty minutes later we arrived at the emergency room, and I was asked the same question over and over: "Is he on anything? Did he take anything? Anything at all?"

I wasn't able to answer them any better than when Nina had asked. I didn't think so, but I couldn't say so for sure.

I joined Bronwyn, Maya, and Duke in the waiting room, where we sat in glum silence. Maya was looking things up on her smartphone, Duke was gently stroking Bronwyn's hand. All I could think about was whether I had, once again, exposed my friends to danger. Conrad had been hurt because of me once before. Enough was enough.

After what seemed like hours, a doctor, middle-aged, bespectacled, and balding, emerged from the double doors. We all sprang from our seats.

"His tox screen came back with an interesting finding," said Dr. Burke. "He appears to have been exposed to a toxin that causes hallucinations."

"What kind of toxin? He didn't eat or drink anything unusual," I said, thinking back. The only thing Conrad drank was that one beer. That couldn't have been the cause, unless the bartender had somehow dropped a roofie in it, which seemed far-fetched. "Could it have been something he ingested hours ago?"

Dr. Burke shook his head. "It's a fast-acting toxin

that's absorbed through the skin. It's called *bufotoxin*. Has he been around frogs, by any chance?"

Uh-oh. "As a matter of fact, we were at the Academy of Sciences when this happened. They have a frog exhibit."

"Any chance he touched one?"

"Excuse me?"

"I noticed . . . I thought perhaps the young man was a drug user. Some people lick them for their psychedelic properties."

"Conrad did not lick the frogs. Land's sakes. He touched a few, but those were in the children's petting section. Surely they weren't dangerous." I looked at Bronwyn, Duke, and Maya. "Did he lick any frogs while he was with y'all?"

They shook their heads.

Dr. Burke smiled. "I'm not the frog police, folks. I'm only asking because the more I know what happened the better able I am to help your friend. Okay. Well, we'll have to keep him here overnight for observation. He also has a minor concussion, no doubt received when he fell."

"Could I speak with him?" I asked.

He shook his head. "You may peek in on him if you like, but he's not awake. The dose of toxin he received was very nearly fatal, and there could be more complications. But I'm confident he'll be all right."

We found Conrad in a hospital bed, hooked up to a dripping IV and several monitors. Someone had pulled the hair away from his face, and he suddenly looked very young.

"Conrad's an addict, Lily," said Bronwyn gently. "Isn't it possible he . . . ?"

"He was with us the whole time," I said.

"Not the *whole* time," Maya said. "He was with us at the exhibit, then left to help Bronwyn and Duke with the drinks."

"Yes, but he came right back with them—there wouldn't have been enough time, would there?" I asked.

"It was a bit of a mob scene," pointed out Bronwyn. "If he'd wanted to slip away for a few seconds, he could have managed it."

I shook my head. "Conrad wouldn't do that. Not while we were there. Someone did this to him."

"But why would someone target Conrad?" Duke asked.

I didn't know, and I certainly couldn't explain how this might be connected to a haunted, hateful tree under which a man was killed—a tree that might also have swallowed Oscar. Exasperated and afraid, I reminded myself to breathe in and out deeply and slowly.

Might Conrad have seen something I hadn't noticed at the crime scene? Or perhaps Conrad had seen something earlier, one night when he was sleeping there? Was someone was trying to silence him, afraid of what he might know?

Lance had been in Golden Gate Park when Conrad and I found Sebastian. Lance, the bumbling scientist who had shown a different side of himself tonight.

Then again, Kai had been there, too. And Nina showed up after we had gathered, and she'd been to the tree previously and knew Conrad. They all had been at the academy tonight before Conrad had fallen ill.

Outside, the evening was chilly. The marine layer—as the ocean fog is called—had settled over the city like a cool, sea-scented shroud. Maya handed me my keys— she had driven the Mustang while I rode in the ambulance with Conrad—and Bronwyn and Duke offered to drop Maya at her apartment. We said our good-byes in the parking garage.

I pulled Nina's card out of my bag. I imagined the cocktail party was still hopping, but I thought I should let her know what had happened with Conrad. I went back into the hospital and found a pay phone.

"Nina, I wanted to let you know that it looks like Conrad is going to be okay. And I was wondering whether I could talk to you about something."

"Now?"

"If you have time."

"Um, okay . . . shoot."

"I'd rather speak in person."

I heard her chuckle. "What is this, like in a mystery novel? 'Meet me at midnight down by the pier'?"

She was more right than she knew. "I'm just . . . not fond of talking on the phone."

I loathed phones because they didn't allow me to sense a person's energy. I was much less easily fooled when I could sense someone's vibrations.

"Okay, I guess. The party's still in full swing, but I was about to get back to work. I'm finishing up a report for Monday. Just call me from your cell when you get here, and I'll meet you at the employees' entrance."

"I don't have a cell phone."

There was a pause. "What?"

I rolled my eyes. Surely I wasn't the only person in California who didn't have one. "I said, I don't have a cell phone."

"Did you drop it? I dropped mine on the BART tracks once. Boy, was that a drag."

"No, I just don't own one."

"Oh my God, are you serious?" Nina seemed more shocked by this news than she had when Conrad passed out at the cocktail party.

I sighed inwardly. Eventually, I supposed, I was going to have to give in to the inevitable and start carrying a phone, strange electronic vibrations or no.

"I'm afraid so." I glanced at the clock. Eight thirty-five. "I can be there in twenty minutes. . . . Could we meet at nine o'clock at the employees' entrance?"

"Okay, sure," she said. "See you then."

I thought about calling Sailor, but decided against it. We didn't have to be attached at the hip, after all. And though I hated to admit it, I feared I didn't pick up on things as well with him at my side. Though he made me feel safe, sometimes safe is not all it's cracked up to be. And it wasn't as though I was meeting a stranger at the end of a dark pier, as Nina had suggested. I was going back to a museum full of visitors and staff.

On the drive, I made a point to pass by Ms. Quercus. You could barely see her from the road, but the upper branches extended high in their malevolent embrace, looking black against the moonlit sky. Nighttime in Golden Gate Park would lend itself to nightmares, I decided, trying to shake the sensation that I was being watched. Perhaps it was just the ghostly police officer. What had the poor fellow done in life to merit condemnation to forever issuing traffic tickets?

True to her word, Nina was waiting for me at the rear employees' entrance. The door was propped open, the light from within making it a bright rectangle in the otherwise dark stretch at the back of the building. She wore her lab coat and glasses; only faint remnants of her red lipstick remained. The cocktail party do had fallen, the locks now limp from their earlier curl. I could relate.

"Thank you for meeting me."

"Sure thing," she said as she led the way into the building. The door slammed behind us with a loud bang. "You have to sign in," she said as we walked past a desk space staffed by a huge, bored-looking security guard. His badge read: HI, MY NAME IS BUZZ.

I signed my name, clipped a temporary visitor's badge to the neckline of my dress, and followed Nina through the inner door to a long, featureless hallway.

"How's your friend?" she asked as we descended the stairs to the basement level.

"It looks like he'll be okay."

"Was it just too much to drink?"

"I don't think so — that's one reason I asked to speak with you." I glanced around, trying to feel or notice if anyone was present and could overhear. "Maybe we could wait until we get into your office?"

She looked back at me, a curious expression on her face. "Sure."

I smiled lamely, hoping she'd just assume I was quirky.

The lower level included a number of underwater exhibits, which cast everything in a bluish, ghostly glow. Fish, turtles, and jellyfish swam around lazily. Party sounds still emanated from the upper level.

"You got tired of the party?"

"I can socialize only so much. I'm happier in the lab. We have overnights here sometimes; people come with their kids. It's really fun, but by dawn I'm ready for solitary confinement. Speaking of which . . . here's my office."

Nina's office did have a lot in common with a prison cell: It was a windowless box. But the stacks of files and newspapers and reports reminded me more of her uncle Bart's apartment. The desktop was a jumble of pens, graph paper, forms, correspondence, and an old-fashioned letter opener. I wondered if she and Bart had more in common than she'd like to admit. On the other hand, a lot of creative types tended to live messy — or at least that's what I told myself when Aunt Cora's Closet threatened to get out of hand.

She had to clear a short stack of papers from a chair in order to offer me a seat.

"So," Nina said as she sat behind the utilitarian beige office desk. "What's up? Please tell me this isn't about my uncle. I really don't know — "

I cut her off. "Only tangentially. I really wanted to ask you about what happened to my friend Conrad tonight. At the hospital they said he was poisoned by bufotoxin."

Nina blinked. Stared. And blinked again.

"Was he licking the frogs?"

"No."

"Bufotoxin is secreted from some of the poisonous frogs. I mean, I'm not a herpetologist, but I know it's used by the frogs to paralyze animals that try to prey on them. But some people actually expose themselves to it on purpose, to enjoy the high. You don't actually have to lick the powerful ones—touching them can be enough to get you high."

"I'm aware of that. But Conrad was with me the whole night. Do you know if Lance . . ."

"Damn, if they trace it back to the expo . . . they'll be closing this whole thing down." Nina leaped out of her seat. "This is terrible. I've got to notify the director before it makes the news."

She rushed out of the room.

I remained seated, unsure of what to do. A long moment passed. I stuck my head out the door, but saw nothing more than a metal cart full of boxes in the long, empty hallway.

"Nina?"

I returned to my chair. Surely she would be right back. After a minute, the lights in the corridor flickered off.

I rose and faced the door, wondering whether the tingling at the base of my neck was a premonition or just the perfectly normal awareness that I was in the basement of a huge building, didn't know my way around, and the lights had just gone out.

I could still hear the party upstairs. The constant murmur of voices, background music, and the tinkling of glassware were reassuring. Maybe I should go up and join the crowd and deal with this another time. With Sailor by my side.

Just in case, I grabbed the letter opener from Nina's

desktop, stepped to the doorway, and peered down the darkened hallway again. Had I been set up? Was Nina somehow in on whatever was going on? Or was I grasping at straws now?

Probably the lights were on a timer, or a motion sensor, as an energy-saving device. That's all. These Californians and their environmental awareness . . .

Stroking my medicine bag for strength and protection, I stepped into the hallway and did a couple of jumping jacks, flinging my arms over my head, hoping a sensor would pick up on my movements and turn the lights back on.

It remained dark. Even the exit signs were extinguished. And now I heard a sound. Faint, barely there, just the whispering of cloth. But I heard it.

I started moving down the hall in the opposite direction of the noise. This was the way I came with Nina, so if I could just retrace our steps . . . Unfortunately, I couldn't see a danged thing. There was no natural light, and without so much as a glowing exit sign . . .

The elevator pinged. Its doors opened and light flooded out. No one was on it, but I ran toward it, glancing behind me in the hopes of glimpsing whether someone really was behind me.

The elevator doors closed right before I reached them. *Damn it!* I slapped the call button repeatedly, but it was already gone.

Now there was no doubt: I definitely heard someone behind me.

I backed blindly down the pitch-black, windowless hallway, hands in back of me trying to feel. Disoriented, I tried to remember whether the stairs were in front of me or behind.

I banged my hip and knee against the metal cart, which clattered to the floor. Grabbing it, I threw it farther down the hall as an obstacle to my pursuer, then ran.

I heard a crash and a grunt as my ploy worked. But then I ran into a doorframe. Pain lanced through my shoulder. Swearing a blue streak, I dashed around the corner and finally spotted greenish light coming out from under a door.

I ran to it and found the door unlocked. I dashed in. Lights were glowing on enough of the computers and equipment to bathe the room in a very subtle green light. There was no way to lock the door without a key, so I pushed a desk in front of it, risking alerting my pursuer to my location by the scraping noise. Then I searched the room madly for a phone. Nothing. *Dammit*. Everyone had cell phones these days. Modern technology would kill me yet.

Hearing someone at the door, I kept my eyes on it while backing up until I hit a metal enclosure, like a cage, that ran the full length of the room.

Was the cage for valuables? I wondered. Or something alive? The spaces between bars were too big for lab rats. I tried to peek in but couldn't see any monkeys, anything like that. What could they possibly keep in here? Aliens, probably.

Stop it, Lily. I was weirding myself out.

I had to pull myself together. I stroked my medicine bag, forced myself to breathe, and gathered my wits.

The thing about this cage, I thought, was it seemed to serve not only this room, but also the one on the other side.

Realization dawned on me just as someone grabbed my hair from behind and pulled so hard the back of my head banged against the bars of the cage.

Chapter 18

The attacker's arm snaked through the space in the bars and wrapped around my throat, squeezing.

Gripping the letter opener in my right hand, I reached up and jabbed at the arm that was trying to suffocate me.

I heard a grunt, but my assailant still didn't call out or withdraw the arm. But the grip around my throat loosened a little. I yanked back again with the sharp tip. Suddenly my hair was released.

I careened through the lab, dislodging a beaker, which shattered on the floor. I hauled the desk away from in front of the door, raced into the corridor, and bowled smack-dab into Nina.

We both sprawled on the floor of the hallway.

"What's going on? What are you doing?" Nina demanded, retrieving the flashlight she had been carrying. "Why are all the lights off?"

"I'm . . . I was . . ." Until that moment I wasn't entirely sure Nina hadn't been the one chasing me. Why she would, I had no idea.

The bloody letter opener lay on the floor between us.

The beam of her flashlight landed on it. Nina picked it up, questions flooding her eyes.

"What in the world's going on, Lily? Are you all right? Isn't this . . . mine?"

I nodded. "I took it off your desk. The lights went out, and I took it with me when I went to investigate, just to be safe. And then . . . someone started chasing me."

"Chasing you?" Nina stood, sending her beam both ways down the hallway. "Why would someone chase you? I don't even think anyone's here. Everyone's up at the party. Are you sure? Maybe you imagined it."

I shook my head, which hurt my throat. I put my hand up to it and pressed gingerly; it felt bruised. My scalp stung where my hair had been pulled so viciously.

"It was real," I said. "He was real."

"What did he look like?"

"I don't know. I couldn't see anything."

The overhead lights blazed back on. We both looked down the corridor. There was nothing to see but a boring hallway.

"If you didn't see whoever it was, could it have been a woman?"

"Maybe. A strong woman."

"Strong. Like me?"

I nodded. "I stabbed him—or her. In the forearm."

"Okay, this is crazy. Let's go check with security."

Up at the security desk, Buzz no longer looked bored. He had a phone to his ear as he fiddled with his screens and checked his computer.

Nina told him what happened.

"No kidding? There must have been some sort of serious power interruption, 'cause not only did the lights go out, but the cameras went out on that whole level at the same time. You okay?"

I nodded.

"We haven't had a breach in the building that we know

of. The party's just now winding down, so there have been folks all over the upper floors. And then you know how it is; scientists come in and out of here all night long. There are even some folks working on the new diorama upstairs. You sure you're okay?"

I nodded again. "Would you be willing to walk me to my car?"

"Are you sure you don't want us to call the police?" asked Nina.

What purpose would it serve? I hadn't seen who it was. I suppose they could search for someone with an arm injury, but how could they prove anything? And if I was right, that this was all caught up in something supernatural, their intervention would only make everything that much more complicated.

"I'm sure. Thanks. Hey, just one question: How long have you known Lance Thornton?"

"Lance? You don't think he's the one who chased you, do you? Lance wouldn't hurt a fly. He's been here forever, I think. He's odd, I know, but he's really great with amphibians."

I dragged myself home, feeling defeated. More than that. The attacker had knocked me off-balance, made me doubt my ability to take care of myself, thereby stealing my peace of mind. I needed to salve myself, to rejuvenate.

I mounted the stairs to my dark, quiet apartment. No Oscar. The feeling of tears stung the back of my eyes. How I wished I could cry and release some of this pent-up emotion.

"Where the hell have you been?" came a voice in the dark.

"Sailor! Hell's *bells*, you scared the living daylights out of me!"

He flicked on the overhead light. "Where were you? What happened?"

Sailor's eyes lowered to my neck. He reached out, and his hand hovered over the scratches and bruises that were starting to form. He frowned.

"I could feel you were in trouble, but I couldn't find you. I tracked you to the hospital, but lost your trail. Maya and Bronwyn told me you left the hospital when they did."

"I'm sorry. I—"

"I was so desperate I even went to Aidan to ask for help. And you know how crazy that makes me."

"I'm sorry."

"Where were you? Who hurt you?"

I took a shaky breath. "I don't know who, but it's been a heck of a night. I went back to the Cal Academy to ask someone who worked there about Lance. Nina and I were in the basement, but she went to talk to the director and the lights went out and I was alone and . . . and this happened. I stabbed him, though."

"You killed him?"

"You really are bloodthirsty; you know that?" I tried to smile. He didn't respond.

"If you didn't, I'll take care of it. Who was it?"

"It's not as though I don't appreciate the macho posturing, Sailor, but I don't actually know who it was. If I did, my first call would have been to the SFPD, not to you. I'm crazy and law-abiding like that."

"I wouldn't exaggerate your law-abidingness if I were you."

"In any case, I don't know who it was. I was able to escape. . . . They had me from behind and I cut his arm—or her arm. . . ."

"You don't even know if the attacker was male or female?"

I shook my head, then swayed on my feet.

"How could you do something so dangerous without me?"

"I didn't really think about it that much. I guess I'm used to doing things on my own."

"And where did it get you?"

"I'm not about to start asking your permission, Sailor."

"It's not about asking permission. It's about being smart, keeping yourself safe, and most importantly, letting the man in your life know what's going on."

"I guess you're right. I didn't really stop to think. I considered calling you, but then since I was going back to the museum where they were having a party and just speaking with Nina—I never thought it would go wrong. I was just trying to . . . to figure this all out. And to find Oscar."

There was a pause, and I felt something I hadn't for quite some time: Sailor was trying to read my thoughts. He'd never been able to, but maybe he thought our relationship would change that. I sincerely hoped not. I wasn't sure I wanted anyone that much in my head. Even Sailor. *Especially* Sailor.

"What's the real reason you didn't call me?" he asked.

I swallowed hard and confessed. "Sometimes . . . when I'm around you, it's hard for me to be sensitive to other people's vibrations. To sense anything much, as a matter of fact. You fill up my senses."

"I think there's an old song about that," he said in a very quiet voice.

Sailor moved into the kitchen, took the bottle of tequila off the shelf, and poured us both shots. I cut open a lime; the tangy aroma wafted and hung in the already spice-laden air of the kitchen. Oscar's continued absence combined with the comfort of my things, this space, to bring the horror of what had happened—or *almost* happened—home to me.

So I let myself collapse against Sailor's broad chest. After a brief hesitation, he wrapped his arms around me, cocooning me in his warmth. He stroked my hair with his rough hand, kissing the top of my head as his other arm squeezed me tight.

"Do you have any idea how it feels to know the woman I love is in danger," he rasped, his voice rough with emotion, "but not be able to get to her?"

"I'm sorry. This whole relationship thing, learning to rely on someone else and ask for help . . . it's new to me."

"You think this is new for *you*? I've got news for you: You're in this with the champ. We've both got a lot to learn."

I nodded, my nose still pressed up against his shirt. I couldn't get enough of his scent, his warmth, his aura.

"So, are you going to tell me what happened?"

"Could we just . . ." I didn't want to relive any of it right at the moment, or think about Oscar, or worry about Conrad. I felt overwhelmed and depleted of inner resources. Right now, there was only one thing I wanted. "I know this is boring of me . . . but could we just go to sleep?"

"My aunt Renna told me there are legends about that tree. It's hosted death at its roots before, but she doesn't know why," said Sailor the next day after breakfast. "She also didn't say much about Crowley's murder, other than that he had a lot of enemies. She agreed to ask around, but I think my time would be better spent checking out this Lance character."

I had told Sailor what happened while lying in the co-coon of his arms in my comfy brass bed. It seemed unreal to talk about it there, in such a safe and comforting context. We agreed I wouldn't meet folks without backup anymore, though truth to tell, I was glad I hadn't exposed any of my friends to danger. But I took his point.

"Lance? Good idea." I said. "Just . . . don't do anything violent."

"You think I'm the type to be violent?"

I chose my words carefully. "I think that if you think Lance is the one who hurt me, who may have been trying to do worse, yes, you might be moved to violence. Just as I might be moved to some crazy witchcraft when my friends are threatened."

Our eyes held for a long moment and he let out a long breath. "Okay, I'll try to keep a lid on things."

"Thank you. I've got a whole lot going on, and having to get you out of jail would short-circuit my already overloaded senses."

He gave me a crooked grin. "Nah, you'd just call your buddy Carlos and have me released."

"I think I've used up that marker already, getting myself out of custody."

We shared a smile, and I saw him out of the store, then opened the shop as usual. Unfortunately, since Oscar's disappearance, it wasn't business as usual anymore. Instead, within an hour of opening, it had once again become Lost Piggy Central. I tried to keep a lid on my impatience; I was so grateful for everyone's support, but it nearly drove me clear 'round the bend, knowing that none of it would do any good.

I pined desperately for Oscar, but I also longed to have normality restored, especially after the events of last night. I still wasn't able to wrap my mind around that nightmarish chase through the basement of the Academy of Sciences.

A few hapless folks wandered into Aunt Cora's Closet looking for clothes, but between Maya's extended family, Bronwyn's coven sisters, and Conrad's gutterpunk friends—all looking for Oscar—it was a chaotic scene. There were people staffing the tables and handing out flyers, food piled on the side table, and Maya answering the incessant ringing of the phone with people calling to report mostly erroneous pig sightings.

I took advantage of a brief lull in phone calls to try the hospital and was able to speak with Conrad; he was feeling better, but had to stay another day to be sure all the poison had passed from his system and wouldn't cause secondary effects.

"Dudette, I have to tell you ... I had the craziest dreams while I was under the influence. They reminded me of a book. You ever read that play about what happened in Salem, Massachusetts?"

The back of my neck tingled. I just happened to have a copy of it next to my bed. "*The Crucible*, by Arthur Miller?"

"Yes! About the witch hunts, right? And it was like an allegory for McCarthyism? And then Miller was cast with suspicion himself, which was pretty ironic. But, you know, at least he got to marry Marilyn Monroe."

Conrad never ceased to amaze me. "When did you read *The Crucible*?"

"Back in eighth grade, I think. But now I find books all kinds of places. Usually paperback romances, but whatever. The Con reads what the Con reads. I've got a good mystery right now; one of my friends brought it to me so I could read in bed."

I made a mental note to bring some books down to the shop to share with Conrad and his friends.

"So, anyway, when I was high or poisoned or whatever," continued Conrad, "I felt like I was there, in that play. In Salem, during the witch hunts. *Dude*. Not a nice place to hang out."

Indeed. Not a coincidence, either, I was sure.

Before signing off, a nurse came on the line and said Conrad's many sisters and brothers and cousins had been crowding his room and urged me to ask folks to drop by only a few at a time. I promised to see what I could do, but privately I was willing to bet that all those "relatives" were kin of the fictive variety.

"Good morning, Lily," said Bart Woolsey as he walked into the shop.

"Good morning. Are you ... ?" I trailed off. "I'm sorry, but I haven't made much progress in what we talked about."

That was a bit of an understatement. I hadn't made *any* progress. Frankly, finding the remedy for Bart's love curse hadn't been at the top of my to-do list. But then again, perhaps it should be. If it was truly cast by Deliverance Corydon, perhaps breaking the curse could help me figure out the rest of the puzzle.

"Oh, I understand. I know these things take time. Good morning Duke, Maya ... Sierra."

I followed his gaze. It didn't take a genius to see why Bart had returned this morning: Curse or no curse, he had his eye on one of Bronwyn's coven sisters, who called herself Sierra Sempervirens. Sierra was a plump, strong-looking woman in her midsixties, with a ready smile, warm brown eyes, and a can-do attitude. I decided Bart showed good taste.

I asked Maya to help me print the e-mail from Inspector Romero. True to his word, he had sent photos of the wood scraps that had once been a box, some of which still showed carved symbols. Plus, he had scanned in the page of Sebastian's ledger that referred to the trunk.

I stared at the printouts for several moments, but the sad truth was that they couldn't tell me anything more than I already knew.

One of Conrad's friends was taking part in the Oscar search while also continuing to collect signatures for a reprieve for Ms. Quercus. She was an unkempt young woman with tangled red hair and incongruously beautiful straight, white teeth—showing obvious orthodontia. Last night, during the ride in the ambulance, I realized I had no idea if Conrad had family, and if so, how to contact them. How could I know so little about someone I cared about? *Friendship fail.*

I asked her if she knew anything about all of Conrad's visitors in the hospital.

"We're his family," she said as she handed the clipboard to Bart for his signature. "We gutterpunks are all the family Conrad's got."

"A rotten tree is a danger to the community," Bart said to the young woman, handing her back the clipboard.

"But it still provides a home—"

"A 'home' to whom?" Bart interrupted. There was no vagueness to him now as he fixed the young woman with a stare.

She took a step back. "Not to, uh, 'whom,' but to birds and squirrels and . . . never mind. Everyone's entitled to their own opinion. I'm gonna move along now. . . . 'Bye, everybody."

After she left, Bart looked a bit chagrined. "I didn't mean to chase her out. It's just . . ."

"No worries," said Sierra, passing a plate of blueberry muffins to Bart. He took one with a nod of thanks. "The young people have their minds set on saving that tree, as though there aren't hundreds of others in the park that could use some looking after. There's no particular logic to it, but it gives them something to work toward."

Bart just nodded and ate his muffin in silence. His occasional flashes of temper, followed by sullenness, weren't going to go very far in helping Bart find romance, I thought to myself. But then, perhaps true love would see beyond the obvious.

"Oh my *Lord*," said Susan Rogers as she burst through the door. "I just heard the news! That darling little oinker is *lost*? How could that *be*?"

"Oh, Susan, it's *awful*!" Bronwyn responded in kind. "Can you even imagine such a thing?"

Several of the other women joined in, with much clucking and *tsk*ing and shaking of heads.

"What happened?" asked one apparently well-meaning woman who had actually come into Aunt Cora's Closet in search of clothing, not a pig. She got an earful about Oscar before I could intervene.

"May I help you find something?" I asked.

"I hope so. My son's graduating from college—he had to go to summer school, so he's a little late, but that's not the point. . . ." She let out a loud breath. "Even though I've moved on, I want my ex-husband to . . . um . . ."

"See how great you're doing?" ventured Bronwyn.

"Eat off his own arm in a jealous rage?" suggested Maya.

The woman laughed. "Exactly. I can't afford anything special new, so I was thinking maybe vintage . . . ?"

"You've come to just the place!" Susan jumped in before any of us actual staff had a chance to respond. "Now, let's see. . . . You look about my size, maybe a little more voluptuous. You simply must play up that impressive cleavage—or is that inappropriate for a son's graduation? Depends on what he's graduating from, I suppose. . . . Have you seen the designer dresses over on the rack in front of the window? You know, Calvin Klein dresses don't look like much on the hanger, but you should try them on. Oh, here, let me show you!" She tucked her hand under the woman's arm and started to lead her around the store, as on a tour.

Bronwyn, Maya, and I exchanged amused glances.

It was typical of Susan to step in and help a customer, but she wasn't the only one who felt the impulse. Several of the coven sisters did the same when they were in the store, and it wasn't unusual to see customers helping one another find just the right belt or a hat that would finish off an outfit. The communal dressing room was more often than not the scene of dress swapping and encourag-

ing words among women who had previously been
strangers to one another. I couldn't take much credit for
it: It was something about the magic of the shop and all
the good energy within it.

And speaking of magical energy . . . I had a question
for Bart. I grabbed him for a moment when he was alone.

"Bart, did you ever talk to a man named Aidan
Rhodes about your . . . problem?"

He turned beet red, and when he spoke, his voice was
so low I had to lean toward him to hear. "You promised
me your discretion."

"Yes, of course." I looked around the shop; no one
was paying us any attention. "I don't think anyone's listening."

"You'd be surprised. The walls have ears."

"Um . . . okay. But—"

"Lily, the dress looks perfect on her, but it needs some
alteration," said Susan, interrupting our discussion. She
was right; the customer stood smiling in front of the
three-way mirror, admiring herself in a simple emerald
green sheath that fell too far below the knees, topped by
a gold brocade jacket that hung too low on her arms.
"Do you think it could be done by next weekend?"

"Let me take a look," I said, grabbing my wrist pin-
cushion from behind the counter. "As long as it's nothing
too drastic . . ."

Only later, while I was kneeling at my customer's feet
and pinning up the hem, did I realize that I'd never gotten an answer from Bart about whether or not he knew
Aidan.

Late in the afternoon, the bell on the front door tinkled
and I heard several squeaks and a quick little scream.

A huge black dog trotted into the shop.

He didn't seem aggressive; nor was he made nervous
by all the people and activity. Rather, he appeared almost

preternaturally calm and focused as he passed through the crowd to come stand near the register—near me.

"Oh, look at the sweet little thing," said Bronwyn as she came out from behind her herbal stand and stroked the dog's anvil-sized head.

"He might be sweet, but he's sure not little," muttered Maya, who was wrapping up a young woman's purchase of an orange crocheted jacket.

"Wait," I said as realization dawned. "I think I know that dog."

The tag on the collar read Boye, but there was no phone or license number listed. Normally I know better than to gaze into the eyes of a dog—especially one of this size, which could do serious damage if it so chose. But this animal's eyes were different. There was something about it. . . . I had met this dog before.

And unless I missed my guess, this was no ordinary canine.

After asking everyone in the shop if they knew where the dog came from, Bronwyn checked outside on the street. Nothing. The animal just sat by the counter, as though waiting patiently for something.

"I'm going to bring him upstairs," I said. "He might be hungry."

"Want me to call the shelter?" asked Maya. "I know the receptionist there by name by now, since I've called so many times about Oscar, and then Miss Nelly."

I was pretty sure no one would have filed a claim for this particular missing pet, but just in case I was wrong, I thanked Maya for thinking of it as I called for the dog to follow me. It trotted right past me, toenails clicking on the wood floor, through the drapes that hung over the access to the back room.

He stopped at the bottom of the stairs and looked over his big black shoulder, as though asking permission. I nodded and he ran up the stairs.

By the time I reached the second-floor landing, there was a man sitting on the top step outside my locked apartment door. Sleek black hair and sooty eyes, olive skin, very buff. Unsmiling. Wary.

"I take it Aidan sent you?" I said.

He nodded. I had met this man—and this dog—a couple of months after I first arrived in San Francisco, when I was investigating the disappearance of a child involving a terrible demon called La Llorona. The adult sister of a long-ago missing girl, Katherine, had a strange assistant and a big black dog. I had never seen the man and the dog in the same room, and there was something extraordinarily intelligent about the dog and unusually loyal about the man. I hadn't been sure, but I'd suspected that the rather taciturn assistant might be a familiar when in his canine form.

I remembered he wasn't much of a talker.

"Thank you, but I'm not in need of a familiar," I began, my stomach clenching, as usual, at the thought of Oscar. "I already have one."

"Yes, ma'am." He spoke with an accent I couldn't quite place—I was betting Eastern Europe.

"Then why are you here?"

"Just following orders, ma'am."

"Please, call me Lily." His "ma'ams" made me feel like we were in the army. "And it really is very nice of you to come here, but this is my place, and I don't much cotton to Aidan ordering me around."

Still with the staring.

I sighed. Clearly this wasn't going to be easy. Like so many things with supernatural folks, there was protocol involved, a series of unspoken rules and methods that I almost always managed to bungle.

From downstairs, I could hear Maya come into the back room. Might as well deal with this in the privacy of my apartment.

I stepped around the man, unlocked my door, and went inside. He followed.

"Your name's Boye?"

He nodded.

"I'm Lily."

"I remember."

"How is Katherine?"

"She is much improved. You were a great help to her, ma'am. I am very grateful."

I wished I could take more credit for having helped, but the fact is I sort of muddled my way through figuring out what had happened with La Llorona and the missing children. But if I had been instrumental in relieving Katherine's mind, so much the better. And I remembered I *had* been able to tell her an important fact about her mother, so at least some good had come from it.

As I crossed into the kitchen, another thing dawned on me. Katherine wasn't a witch, which was one reason I'd doubted my assessment of the dog/assistant familiar when I met them. Unless . . . "How did you come to be with Katherine? Did Aidan send you to her?"

Another slight inclination of his sleek dark head.

Huh. Just when I was about to throttle Aidan, I found out something like this. He wasn't such a monster, at least not all the time. He had done what he could to protect Katherine from La Llorona. Just as he had given me Oscar, to help and protect me in this surprisingly murderous City by the Bay.

"Could I get you a drink?" I asked. "Or something to eat?"

He didn't answer, but I noticed his gaze wandered to the loaf of fresh-baked bread I had made the other night when I wasn't able to sleep.

"I was thinking I'd make some toast with jam—home-made preserves, homemade bread," I said. "Maybe some peanut butter. It would be rude to refuse."

I headed into the kitchen and Boye trailed me obedi-
ently. I sliced a couple thick slabs of bread and put them
into the toaster, then brought butter, preserves, and peanut butter out of a refrigerator stuffed with supplies for
spells: Louisiana swamp water, fresh gizzards, fresh
herbs and resins. Back in the pre-Oscar days, my fridge
had been surprisingly free of edibles, given over instead
to casting ingredients. But ever since that little porker
had come into my life, I kept it chock-full of food as
well.

Sadness wafted over me again. It really was funny:
After struggling against having a familiar at all, and certainly wary of the attachment to Aidan that Oscar's presence implied, I would never have guessed I would yearn
for him so. But that was the way with life: You rarely
knew what you were missing until it stumbled into your
realm . . . and then back out again.

Boye waited, shifting silently from one foot to another, until I told him to take a seat at the kitchen table.
I brought down two floral-painted china plates that I had
picked up at a garage sale and set them on the counter.
When the toast popped up, I buttered the thick slices, put
one on his plate and the other on mine, and joined him
at the table. He placed a huge gob of peanut butter and
apricot preserves on his toast and downed the whole
thing in about two bites.

"Sorry," he said. "Force of habit. I have appalling table manners, I know."

I smiled and shook my head. "You're fine. Don't worry
about it. Would you like another piece?"

"Truth? I'd love one. I'll put it in, though, ma'am. You
relax."

"Nonsense. You're my guest." He continued to rise.
"Sit."

He sat.

"So . . . how does it work?" I asked as I sliced another

two hunks off the loaf and put them in the toaster. "Are you a human who shifts to a dog, or the other way around . . . or not actually human at all?"

He stared at me a long moment, blinking.

"Didn't Aidan tell you I'm a witch? It's not like you have to keep any of this sort of thing secret around me."

"I'm both."

"But your natural form . . ..?"

"As you see."

"Man, then."

More staring. I had the distinct impression I wasn't going to get much more out of him. Either he was a different creature entirely from Oscar, who had his given form but morphed into a potbellied pig; or perhaps he was so old and had been living his double life for so long he truly had forgotten. Or maybe he just wasn't willing to tell me. I was used to that last, at least. Oscar treated me as though I was on a need-to-know basis, and in his estimation I generally did *not* need to know.

So maybe playing one's cards close to one's chest was just a familiar thing.

"So Aidan told you to watch over me?" I asked as I slid the plate with buttered toast on the table in front of him.

He nodded, added more peanut butter and preserves, and dug into the fragrant slabs.

"I appreciate that," I said, "and you're welcome to stay here for a bit if you have to make it look good for Aidan, but I'll be getting my old familiar back soon, and he's the jealous type, so it will have to be temporary."

Boye stared at me again, crumbs decorating his otherwise handsome mouth and a dab of apricot preserves glistening on his chin. "Aidan says I'm your familiar."

"I already *have* a familiar."

His dark eyes shifted as he looked around the apartment.

"He's not here exactly at this very moment," I said. "But he's my familiar and I don't need another."

"Are you saying you're sending me back?" Boye said this with the same trepidation I remembered from Oscar back when he first arrived and I told him I didn't want him.

"I'll fix it with Aidan. Don't worry. I *told* him I didn't need a new familiar. I just wanted help finding my old one. He ignored me, of course, because that's what he does. A glass of milk?"

He nodded.

"Do you know Oscar?" I asked as I retrieved the milk from the refrigerator. It was raw milk I kept on hand for spells, but it was fresh.

He shook his head.

"Could you help me find him?"

"If Aidan sent me to you, your other familiar must be lost. For good."

I slammed the glass of milk down on the table in front of him so hard a dollop of white liquid jumped out and splashed on the table. Boye reared back.

"Sorry," I said as I handed him a dish towel. "But don't say that. Oscar is *not* lost for good. I will get him back if it's the last thing I do."

"Yes, ma'am."

"You really don't have to call me ma'am."

"Yes, ma'am."

"Could I ask you something? Do you know anything about . . . ? Well, would Aidan keep something on Oscar, maybe you, too, to keep you beholden to him?"

"I don't understand the question."

"Well, I mean, why do you do what Aidan tells you to do?"

"He's the boss."

"Why? I mean, what makes him the boss?"

"I don't understand the question."

I supposed Boye followed the pack leader, loyal and doglike. Aidan was the alpha, end of story. I decided to try another tack.

"Do you know where Aidan lives?"

"His office is at the Ferry Building. You can find him there most days, unless he's unable to see clients."

"Yes, I realize that. But I was wondering where he actually lives."

"Ma'am?"

I clamped down on my impatience. "Do you know where he might keep something? It would be all right to tell me," I said, feeling like a heel. But I couldn't think of any other way. "Does he have a warehouse space, something like that?"

Boye just stared at me. He might be obedient, but he was no fool. And Aidan was his master.

I went into the bedroom to use the phone to call the hospital again and check on Conrad. By the time I came back out, Boye was asleep on the couch.

He was still in man form. I studied him for a moment, thinking how it was funny that such a well-built, handsome man could hold absolutely no attraction for me. I wasn't sure whether it was because I was so enamored of Sailor, or whether it was because Boye was not a regular human man, or what, but it was intriguing. Asleep like this, dark eyelashes against his olive skin, muscled arms crossed over his chest . . . he was adorable. Very much like a dog.

Back downstairs in Aunt Cora's Closet, I found my employees closing up for the night. Maya was adding up receipts, and Bronwyn was carefully storing her herbs in their jars and sealed bags for freshness.

"The shelter hasn't had anyone call in, but I left them the information and our number in case anyone comes looking," said Maya.

"Oh good, thanks." I looked over Maya's tally of the day's receipts; the numbers were abysmal. Missing Pig

Central had not been good for sales. The store was jammed with people all day, but with a few exceptions, they weren't buying clothes.

Done attending to her herbal stand, Bronwyn started straightening the racks. "Where's the puppy?" she asked.

Maya snorted. "Some puppy. That dog has a few pounds on me, I think."

"I fed him a snack," I said. "And he lay down for a nap. I think I'll let him rest."

"My mother always said if he stays the night, he's yours," said Maya. "You might just have found yourself a dog. Hope he likes pigs."

"You're not allergic to dogs?" asked Bronwyn.

"A little, maybe," I said. "Not like cats."

"Poor little sweetie," said Bronwyn with a sigh. "I wonder how long he's wandered out in the streets, lost and confused, not knowing where his people are. Doesn't it just break your heart?"

"He looked well fed and healthy," pointed out Maya. "He probably hasn't been lost all that long. And if he was so well taken care of, he probably has a loving family out looking for him. I guess I should make up some flyers tomorrow."

"Well, we know the drill by now," said Bronwyn. "It's ironic, isn't it? We're looking for a pig, but we find a dog. Perhaps someone out there has our pig, and we can just make the switch."

We finished up, and I ushered my friends out with hugs. The bell rang out with its sweet tinkle. I double locked the door, cast a protection spell, and switched the sign to CLOSED.

Back in my apartment, I stood over the dozing man on my couch.

"Here's what I don't get," I said aloud. "If familiars have the ability to transform into people, how come Oscar chose to be a miniature potbellied pig?"

"Ma'am?" said a sleepy Boye.

"Nothing. Sorry." I patted him on the shoulder. "Go back to sleep."

I went in the bedroom, stripped, and got in the shower.

"Why is there a man asleep on your couch?" Sailor demanded when I came out ten minutes later, wrapped only in a towel.

Chapter 19

"I wouldn't say he's a man . . ." I replied.

"Excuse me?"

"I mean, sometimes he's a dog."

A careful look entered Sailor's dark eyes. "You mean, in the sense that all men are dogs sometimes?"

"What?"

"What?"

"Sorry—I should back up. Boye is a, um, well . . . Aidan sent him."

"I'll just bet he did. What, is he supposed to replace me?"

"No, he's supposed to replace Oscar. He's a familiar. He's a dog, much of the time."

Ah." Realization had dawned in Sailor's dark eyes. "That explains why I picked up on dreams of Milk-Bones. He's pretty good-looking. For a dog."

"You're missing the point. Apparently, Aidan doesn't th-think we'll get Oscar b-back." I ended with a hiccup.

Sailor wrapped me in a hug.

"Aidan doesn't know everything, despite what he thinks. We'll figure this thing out, one way or another.

You and I are good together, power-wise, and unless I miss my guess, Oscar will move heaven and earth to get back to you. With the three of us working together, we'll sort this out."

"Did you see Lance? Was his arm hurt?"

Sailor shook his head. "He didn't show for work today. I checked out his apartment, but he wasn't there, either. I did, however, find quite a library of books on the witchcraft trials in Europe and the Americas. Massachusetts, especially. And there was this."

He handed me a drawing of a box with symbols on it. The one Carlos had found under the tree, the one Will had shown me, drawn by a minister in Dathorne.

"Mean anything to you?"

"It was the box that the Ashen Witch put Deliverance Corydon's ashes into."

"Let's back up a minute. Ashen Witch and Deliverance Corydon?"

I realized I hadn't kept Sailor informed of everything I knew. I gave him the rundown, as best I could figure out.

"It sounds to me like you need to take another trip in that magic cape. The problem is, with Oscar missing . . ."

I nodded. "That's the problem. I don't know how to control it. With Oscar by my side, I felt I could handle it. But without him . . . I'm not sure what will happen when I put the cloak on. What if I can't control it, or . . . can't get back?"

Sailor nodded, and our eyes met for a long moment.

"Okay, let's try a different tack," he said. "Renna tells me she knew Sebastian well. It's very possible he was killed just for being a jerk."

"I could easily believe that, except for the fact that someone deliberately brought him to the tree, or he brought them there—in any case, he died there. This was no random fit of rage. Also, there's something creepy go-

ing on with the tree, as you know. And then the attack on
me at the Academy of Sciences last night . . ."

"Is there . . . I'm sorry to interrupt," said Boye, "but is
there anything to eat?"

In this, at least, he reminded me of Oscar. I fixed him
a sandwich and offered Sailor one as well.

He shook his head. "No, thanks. I'd rather go talk to
Herve Le Mansec."

"Herve? My Herve?"

Sailor gave me a crooked smile. "How many Herves
do you know? Renna says Sebastian came to her looking
for a cure for a love curse on behalf of a mysterious client he wouldn't name—Bart Woolsey, no doubt. She refused to deal with him, but she told him he should try
Herve."

"Okay, that's a great idea. I'm supposed to pick up
some supplies from him, anyway. Let's go."

Having inhaled his sandwich, Boye stood to go with
us.

"Boye, you stay here."

"I'd like to remain by your side, ma'am."

"Sailor will be with me."

"Even so."

"No. I'm sorry. You'll have to stay."

He continued to stare at me.

"*Sit*. And stay."

He sat on the couch and stayed.

Sailor was looking down at me, amusement in his face.
I refused to meet his eyes.

As I drove across town, we talked it through.

"Bart asked me to try to cure him of the curse," I said.
"But Herve's probably a better bet. If he hasn't met with
him already, I should probably send him to talk with
him."

"Why are you worrying about some old man's supposed curse? He paying you?"

"He's a sad old man. Besides, I can't help but think this might have something to do with the fix we're in— according to what I can figure out, Bart's ancestor was cursed by the witch he had sentenced to death. And that cape brings me back to that exact death scene. And anyway . . . Can you imagine having to go through life believing you have no possibility of finding true love?"

I was looking ahead, tending to my driving, but I could feel Sailor's gaze on me. "Yes. I can imagine that. Okay, I'm in. Let's fix this. What do we do?"

Amused at his sudden "get this done" attitude, I gave him a smile. "It's not like there's a step-by-step process laid out in a handbook somewhere. At least, I don't think there is."

I realized I hadn't yet looked this up in my Book of Shadows, the tome that held spells, stories, and quotes, which my grandmother Graciela had passed down to me when I was still a child—a young, unskilled witch. I knew my Book of Shadows held a series of love spells, but love curses . . . ?

"Love spells play on a person's fantasies, simply attaching them to the desired object. But love curses are more complex: The hexed person can never find true love because of the crushing inability to truly care for themselves."

"But a lot of insecure people are married or in relationships."

"True, a lot of people are in fair, ho-hum relationships and they make them work, building a life together, raising children, supporting each other. But the cursed won't settle for that. They're not satisfied with anything but the ultimate, true, deep and abiding love."

"That sounds like a true curse," said Sailor. "But would one of your kind be able to cast a curse strong enough to survive the ages? To pass on from one generation to the next? That seems like a bit much, even for you."

"I don't think *I* would be capable of it, but I think we're dealing with something beyond the common everyday witch here. I think Deliverance was much more than that — *is* much more than that. Besides, last words are powerful, no matter who you are. That's why witches were often denied their last words when they were facing execution: for fear that they would curse their prosecutors. A curse cast by a dying witch is pretty tough to repeal."

"Unless you're a pretty determined witch yourself," Sailor said, his hand cupping my head.

We arrived at Herve's shop and set about finding a parking space. Not an easy feat in this part of town, especially in the evening. The neighborhood was hopping.

Herve and Caterina Le Mansec ran a voodoo and spiritual supply store in the neighborhood of San Francisco referred to as the Mission. I loved this part of town; it had a decidedly Latin flair and was full of immigrants from Spanish-speaking countries, lately joined by young professionals seeking rents cheaper than downtown, along with the nightlife and good food that often accompanied immigrant areas. Tonight was no exception: Though it was still early, music blared from car radios and clubs, young people crowded the streets, and the shops were open late.

I still closed Aunt Cora's Closet at six, though lately I'd had some pressure to stay open later. It would be nice to accommodate people who work normal hours for a living, true, but I enjoyed having my evenings to myself. And being open evening hours also invited more trouble, what with people drinking and feeling rambunctious.

We found Herve pulling small votive candles out of a large cardboard packing box and placing them on a shelf near the door.

"*Lily*, how nice to see you," he said as he greeted me. We hugged. "You know Sailor, don't you?"

"Of course. Hello, and welcome." They shook hands, doing one of those manly, assessing handshakes.

I said hello to Caterina, who was tallying receipts. She gave me a polite greeting, but I knew she wasn't crazy about me. I feared she thought I led Herve into trouble, and she might be right. I know she associated me with the vandalism their shop fell victim to not long ago, when a local group lashed out in fear and anger at us magical types. I had helped Herve and Caterina clean up and get the shop back on its feet, but she still held a grudge.

"Your supplies are ready," she said, hauling a cardboard box out from behind the counter.

"Thank you. The shop looks great. That whole shelving unit is new, isn't it?"

Herve nodded. "The insurance money came through, so I had an unemployed friend build a few items. Upgraded a bit. Looks good, doesn't it?"

"Very." A couple of teenage girls came in to try out the essential oils. "Could we speak in private?"

"Of course. Follow me."

The beaded curtain clacked as we passed through it. We continued down a short, narrow hallway to his office, a decidedly utilitarian space with featureless beige office furniture. The first time I'd seen it, I had been disappointed by the quotidian surroundings. One might as well be at the DMV for all the personality it showed. On the other hand, when a person lived in the kind of world Herve and I operated in, a little boring was sometimes a good thing.

And speaking of boring . . . as soon as we were out of earshot of the other customers, Herve dropped his lilting Caribbean accent. He was born and raised in LA. The lovely accent was part of the show he put on for his clientele.

"What can I do for you?"

"Did you hear about Sebastian Crowley?"

He nodded.

"Any idea what's going on with that?"

He shook his head again, a broad smile slowly spreading over his face. "You've taken it upon yourself to investigate?"

"Well, I . . . not investigate per se . . ."

I realized Sailor was nodding by my side.

"You are awfully willing to insert yourself in such affairs, aren't you?" Herve asked.

Sailor nodded again. I was getting a little impatient with the "wow, she's so crazy" model of dealing with Lily.

"Once again, this is an issue that has implications for many people," I insisted. "It's not just finding justice for Sebastian. There's a wicked tree, a love curse, an enchanted cape. . . ."

Herve was grinning by now.

"And most importantly, I'm missing my pet pig. So okay, here's what I need to know," I snapped, now thoroughly irritated. "Did Sebastian Crowley come to you for help with a client in overcoming a love curse?"

"Of course."

"He did?"

"Of course he did. Madame Decotier's is the first place people turn when they need help lifting curses. You should know that by now. Especially since"—he paused, his eyes flickering over to Sailor's. He nodded in recognition of the family—"since Sailor's aunt was attacked. There are only so many of us in the area with that kind of power. How is Renna, by the way?"

"She's doing well, thank you. Almost fully recovered physically. Emotionally . . . well, that's harder. But she's a tough nut, and she's got family around her. She'll be fine."

"And your uncle?"

"The same. Healing."

"Please give them my regards."

"I'll do that."

"So, back to Sebastian," I urged

"Yes. A couple of weeks ago . . ." He thumbed through an agenda on his desk. "On the thirteenth, Sebastian requested a private interview. He told me a client of his was suffering under a love curse passed down through generations and asked if I could help."

"And did you?"

"As I'm sure you know, curses laid upon generations through time are very rare."

I nodded.

"And it was Sebastian. . . ." He met Sailor's eyes.

"What does that mean?" I asked, looking from him to Sailor.

"Sebastian had a way of exaggerating things," said Sailor. "He wasn't the most reliable of characters."

"There are a lot of people who wouldn't have minded seeing Sebastian dead," said Herve. "I'd say it's much more likely his death was connected to a business deal gone sour rather than the result of some alleged love curse."

"Thanks for your advice. I'd really just like to know what you did for him."

Herve shrugged. "I sold him a kit to remove love curses."

"Does that work?"

"Not in Sebastian's hands it doesn't. First I quoted him what I would charge to remove such a curse and told him I would have to deal directly with the client. He balked, of course. Cheap bastard. He insisted I sell him the ingredients to do it himself. But as you know very well, Lily, the success of any spell or curse has to do with the intent of the practitioner. The materials, the incantations might be exactly the same in a blessing as in a curse, but the intention is what results in magic—or not.

There aren't that many people able to instill that kind of intention in a spell for a stranger."

True. But for a family member or someone we loved, it was more plausible. Perhaps if Sebastian passed the items on to Bart, the cursed man in his desperation would have had enough intent to work magic. It was known to have happened: the parents of a sick child, the enamored of her love.

I glanced at Sailor again. He had asked me once if I had cast a love spell upon us both. Of course, I denied it. Yet what if I had done it by accident just because I wanted it so badly?

Stop it, Lily, I told myself. As Graciela had taught me, there are no accidents when the practitioner is well trained, the spell is well cast, and one has faith in one's helping spirit.

"Could you tell me what you gave him?" Perhaps Sebastian had been killed before he could pass on the items to Bart, for a small fortune, of course. Much more than he had paid Herve.

"Ti plant, Syrian rue, devil's pod, eupatorium, galangal. Storm water from Hurricane Katrina, cemetery dust, vervain-infused beeswax for the poppet, straw from a fallow field, a suffering root."

"Sounds like quite a care package," said Sailor.

Herve smiled again. "Only the best from Madame Decotier's. Oh, and the most important thing, of course: the words."

He took a large leather-bound tome from the shelf, flipped it open, and then handed it to me.

"The ancestor who was cursed was a Christian, so I kept it in the faith."

It was the Book of Common Prayer.

"Just prayers?"

"That and the protective incantation against historical influences. But again . . ."

"It's all about the intent."

He nodded. "The only other thing was the blood sacrifice."

Sailor and I both froze as we looked up from the book.

"Come on, Lily. Don't look at me that way. This sort of thing doesn't come easy, as you know only too well." He smiled. "Nothing focuses intent quite like a blood sacrifice."

"Did you have anything particular in mind?" Sailor asked. "Are we talking about a drop of blood, or a chicken, or . . . ?"

"Lily's able to use a drop of her blood as a substitute, but most of us don't have that kind of advantage. I don't, and Sebastian certainly didn't. Much less a civilian."

There was a momentary pause as we all pondered this one.

"Anyway, it seems to me it's a moot point," said Herve. "Sebastian was killed before he could perform the spell, or before he gave the ingredients and instructions to the client, right?"

"It seems so." I realized I hadn't specifically asked Bart about this.

"So . . ." continued Herve. "Could the perpetrator have been trying to keep Sebastian from sharing the information with the cursed man?"

"I suppose it's possible."

"It seems like a weak motive for murder," said Sailor. "Trying to keep an old man from finding true love?"

"In my experience, it doesn't take all that much for some people," Herve said. "So who would find it in their interest to keep the curse upon Bart? Perhaps someone who is set to inherit an old man's fortune, who didn't want him finding happiness and sharing it with a wife?"

That was certainly something to think about. I thought Bart had spent his fortune trying to dissolve the curse, but I could well be wrong. One man's spare change was another man's fortune.

"Here's one thing I don't understand: Bart said he had looked everywhere for a cure. Why didn't he come to you directly?"

"He doesn't share my faith. He didn't know the questions to ask. Or he simply didn't have the focus of intent."

"So you're saying . . . ?"

"Maybe he's scared of voodoo. A lot of people are. Especially if he was raised in a Christian tradition, he might have been wary. Or I was just never in his scope of thought."

"Any idea why Sebastian would have been killed under an oak tree rather than in his shop?"

"Not really."

"Okay." Sailor and I rose to leave. "Thank you for your time, Herve. I appreciate it, as always."

"Except that particular oak tree has had more than its share of death at its roots."

That brought us up short.

"What?"

"I think if you look into the history of it, you'll see it's taken more than its fair share of souls over the years. There's a ghost story about it. Like the traffic cop."

"The one who gives tickets?"

He nodded.

"I've heard that one. But what about the tree?"

"Just that a lot of people have died under its branches. Druggies, mostly, eating the mushrooms and inadvertently killing themselves."

"Are trees usually malevolent?"

He smiled again. "Of course not. You going to believe that sort of nonsense?"

"Then . . ."

"But whatever's *inside* the tree, that's a different story entirely."

When Sailor and I left the shop, I couldn't stop thinking about what Herve said about that tree. It had been on the tip of my tongue to ask him about Oscar, but Herve's magical system was different from mine. I wasn't sure to what extent Oscar was "out" to people. Sailor knew, of course, but I imagined that was through their work with Aidan. It didn't seem my place to tell Oscar's secrets.

Outside on Valencia Street, the smell of spices, corn tortillas, and grilled meats wafted by on the warm evening air.

"I'm starved," said Sailor. "Let me buy you dinner. I know a great place for tacos."

It turned out to be the same place I'd come with an old boyfriend, what seemed like ages ago. Max Carmichael was a myth buster who had doubted me, then romanced me, on my first supernatural case in San Francisco. It was earlier this year, but it seemed like a decade for all the things I'd been through since then.

The fling with Max hadn't lasted long because I couldn't stand being doubted and second-guessed. I realized now, though, glancing over at Sailor, that I couldn't think of Max without a pang of longing for what I could never have: ordinariness. I simply wasn't normal. And that was okay, I thought to myself. Normal wasn't all it was cracked up to be, after all. Especially with Sailor by my side, I was happy to remain my true, weird self.

After a beer and some food, I felt myself relax. Outside, the Mission neighborhood was as raucous and joyous as ever: people vying for parking spaces, folks selling jewelry and begging for change, a man pushing a little cart with Mexican fruit ice pops, another carrying a tall stick displaying fat bags of pink and blue cotton candy. Music— rap, salsa, and R & B—blared from cars and clubs.

"So do you really think someone's trying to keep Bart from finding true love?"

He shrugged. "I've heard of crazier things."

"But Bart doesn't have a fortune for anyone to inherit. At least I don't think so."

"He owns that apartment, right? In that building on Broadway? You know real estate prices around here—that place might bring in close to a million bucks. That's reason enough to kill somebody."

"You make me nervous when you say things like that."

He chuckled. "It's not reason enough for sane people like you and me. But if you're willing to kill for money, then that old man's property would be plenty of motivation."

"You're right. I guess that's a real possibility. I guess Hannah would be the obvious suspect, then? Maybe she wants to give it all to her snakes."

"Excuse me?"

"Hannah's a snake lover."

"Yet another reason not to trust her. And she was there at Cal Academy that night that you were chased through the basement, wasn't she?"

I nodded. And she had met with Sebastian the day before he was killed.

Chapter 20

"So, what now?" asked Sailor as we walked back to the car. "Might I suggest you go back to Aunt Cora's Closet and keep Boye with you for protection while I try to track down some information on the heir apparent?"

"No. If Hannah really is involved, it's not up to us to bust her. I should call Carlos, fill him in on our suspicions. I owe him a call anyway—I was supposed to tell him what I found out during my talk with Will."

"Will?"

"The professor from Berkeley—you met him briefly at Bart's apartment that day." I pulled out into traffic and headed home. "He's the one who told me about the Ashen Witch and Deliverance Corydon."

"Does he know Bart's nieces well? Maybe he'd have some insights for you."

That wasn't a bad idea. Will had attended the cocktail party with Hannah and Nina; maybe he could shed some light on the family dynamics. But then I reminded myself, again, this wasn't my role. I still wanted to know what was going on with the visions, and the tree, and I wanted my familiar back. But the murder part of this mystery? I would very happily hand that over to the professionals.

"I'll call Carlos as soon as I get back. I'll tell them what you found on Lance, as well, and let them follow up on it all. Let's just concentrate on getting Oscar back."

Sailor nodded.

"You know, there's something about Lance. . . . Tell me if this is crazy, but could he be . . . a familiar?"

"A familiar?"

"Yes, it occurred to me. This witch, Deliverance Corydon, was said to have a frog familiar."

"But Lance is a man."

"Maybe he's a man like Boye's a man. Would that be possible?"

"At this point, anything's possible. Though I'm not sure where that leaves us."

"True. So," I began, trying to sound casual. "How have your, um, meetings been going? About the psychic stuff?"

"Is that what we call it now?"

"I'm not sure how to ask the question. But you seemed able to read the oak tree pretty easily. Are things feeling easier?"

"A bit."

Clearly he wasn't ready to talk to me about this. We arrived at Aunt Cora's Closet, parked, and Sailor walked me to the front door. Boye was standing just on the other side of the glass, in canine form. He was shifting from one foot to another, appearing eager and happy to see us. I imagined he'd been waiting.

"I don't think you should stay here tonight," I told Sailor. "It feels sort of . . . I don't know, funny, with Boye sleeping on the couch."

"Just what a man likes to hear, that another man is sleeping in his girlfriend's apartment."

"It's not like that. You know that."

He smiled. "That's fine. We both need rest anyway. And as strange as it sounds, I feel better knowing Boye's keeping an eye on you."

"Really?"

A muscle worked in Sailor's jaw, and he let out a loud sigh. "Aidan is many things, but there's no faulting him in this: He's protective of you. Almost as much as I am."

Our eyes held for a long moment. There wasn't much to add to that.

The next day Aunt Cora's Closet was, once again, humming with activity. Maya had found a permanent home for Miss Nelly—a customer had a small ranch in Petaluma with two goats and a small herd of sheep—and folks were still coming in and out of Missing Pig Central.

I knew I needed to put on that cape one more time to see what it was trying to tell me. But without Oscar by my side, my powers were lessened, my intent clouded, and my intuition dulled. And, quite frankly, I was afraid. Afraid of what I had seen and what I might see if I tried again. And that I might not be able to control the situation and come back to the here and now.

But it seemed the only real connection to that tree, and thus to Oscar.

"What's wrong, Lily?" asked Bronwyn. "Is it Oscar?"

I nodded. I was glum, no two ways to see that.

"You know, I was thinking," she said. "I know you can't see anything in your crystal ball. But . . . what if you tried again, with the backing of the coven?"

"How so?"

"What if we formed the circle, called down the moon, and added our energy to yours? We've been able to help you before, a couple of times."

That was true. Bronwyn's friendly Welcome coven had surprised me more than once, and helped me realize that I had made unfounded assumptions about them.

Since they weren't "real" witches—born with the kind of powers I had inherited—I tended to write them off. But that was foolish. Witches weren't just born; they could be made. With enough study, practice, and concentrated intent, anyone could call on the powers of their ancestors and have an impact on the course of reality. And Bronwyn was right; the Welcome coven had saved this particular witch's backside more than once.

Could they help me understand what the cape was trying to tell me?

"Bronwyn, you're a genius. I think that would be just perfect. But I don't need help reading my crystal ball; I need help with the cape."

"The, um . . . the velvet cape from the other day?"

"The very one."

We made plans to gather that evening. Bronwyn set about contacting the coven sisters, several of whom were checking in frequently with Oscar Watch. The only problem was finding an appropriate location. My apartment was too small, and Aunt Cora's Closet too crowded, to accommodate the full coven—which in the Welcome coven's case amounted to more than twenty women. There would be fewer tonight because of the late notice, but Bronwyn still expected at least the full thirteen to form a traditional coven. Wendy offered the use of Coffee to the People, but it was too exposed, too public. This needed to be private, a closed coven event, as anathema as that was to the usual philosophy of the Welcome coven, which, as its name implied, welcomed just about anybody of good intent.

Outside in the forest might have been perfect, but again I wanted to be able to control our situation and exposure to others. Just in case something untoward happened with the cape—after all, I couldn't be sure what lurked within the fibers of that velvet.

Maya made a call and announced that we could meet at her mother's workshop.

"You're sure it's okay with her?" I asked Maya. Lucille was a church-going Baptist; she was quiet about her faith, but no less devout for her discretion. "She understands that it's . . . that we're . . . that it's a coven of witches?"

"Well, when you put it like that . . ." Maya trailed off with a laugh. "No, seriously. I told her what you're up to. She lives in San Francisco, after all. The whole pagan thing isn't exactly new to her, or unknown. She doesn't go for it in terms of religion, but she knows you, and she has no problem with anything you might be up to."

That was awfully trusting, I thought. Perhaps too trusting. After all, I wasn't sure *I* didn't have a problem with some of what we might be up to.

In the meantime, I called Carlos and talked to him about my suspicions with regard to Hannah and her uncle. He sounded noncommittal, but promised to check it out. I also filled him in on what Will had told me about Dathorne and the witch trials, as well as the love curse under which Bart supposedly suffered. As I heard myself say it out loud, I realized just how outrageous it all sounded.

One other thing had been bugging me, niggling at the back of my mind. It was Sebastian's ledger. I had found it neatly stowed away, but someone had tracked the trunk to Aunt Flora's Closet. So . . . they must have read it, right?

"Is there any way to tell what time Sebastian's Antiques was broken into on the day of the murder?"

"Not an exact time. We have some basic parameters, and a clock fell over and broke; its hands stopped not long after you called in Sebastian's shooting. But you've seen the state of that shop. There's no reason to believe the clock was telling the right time to begin with, so it might well have been a coincidence. Why?"

"The shop was a mess when I first saw it, true." But it had been ransacked even more when I'd gone back there that evening with Sailor. "What if the murderer returned to the store after killing Sebastian, looking for something? Maybe Sebastian refused to tell his assailant where the trunk had gone? So ... the killer might have gone back to the shop, searched for the ledger, looked up the transaction involving the trunk, and then ..."

"Okay, this would be the part where I read you the riot act for interfering with a crime scene. Where exactly did you find this ledger?"

"Um ... if I tell you, won't that be incriminating myself?"

"How about if I promise not to arrest you until after this case is solved?"

"Oh wow. You'd do that for little ol' me?"

"Just spill, already."

"That's what strikes me as odd. It was on a shelf, sandwiched between old novels."

"So why wouldn't he have just taken it with him?"

"Him or *her*," I pointed out. I had a hard time imagining Hannah as a cold-blooded killer, but I'd been fooled before.

"Or her," Carlos said. "Whoever it was, wouldn't this person have just taken the damned book to peruse at his or her leisure? It's not like anyone was going to notice it was gone."

True. Except for Aidan Rhodes, who might well have noticed it was gone. Could the killer have known of Aidan Rhodes's association with Sebastian? Was he—or she—afraid of taking the ledger, for fear that Aidan would be able to track it down? Maybe Aidan really did have some sort of witchy LoJack device, and the killer was afraid he'd find him—or her—out?

*   *   *

By late afternoon I retired to my apartment to prepare for the evening. Boye watched my every move, as silent as Oscar had been garrulous. His presence didn't boost my powers or smooth the portals like a real familiar would. But given what had been happening, it felt good to have some company.

I brewed. Paramount tonight was the safety of the coven members. I didn't want to bring anything back this time. I used the water with the ashes that had come back with me last time; I had saved it in a jar. It was a physical connection to the Ashen Witch. Incorporating it with my brew would allow me to maintain some semblance of control.

While the water was heating, I gathered herbs, centering myself by breathing deeply of the cool afternoon air. There would be a crescent moon tonight. I could see it already against the blue afternoon sky: a harbinger of struggle. I dressed carefully in the oldest clothes I had. A simple cotton shift covered with a long muslin overdress, old-fashioned-looking leather lace-up boots, and a cap.

I gathered several beeswax candles: brown for justice and stability, red for protection and luck, and purple for personal power. I "dressed" them by rubbing them with pure olive and almond oils while chanting. Finally, I packed smudge sticks and saltwater to be sure we left no residue of anything behind in Lucille's workshop. On the contrary, if I knew the Welcome coven, they would leave only a trace of easy, warm energy, as they always did. This was the way they were winning over the community at large, even among those who still feared witches. They were so loving, so dedicated to good works, and so fun to be around that they knocked people's objections out of the park.

Boye and I picked up Maya and drove to her mother's new warehouse space, located on the second story of an old brick factory with big multipaned windows. The other office spaces were occupied by edgy designers or scrappy up-and-coming fashion-related folk.

By the time we arrived, there were already a dozen women milling about, chatting excitedly. Some of these brave souls had helped me before, even at risk to their own safety. This time I felt less afraid of what would happen; though I was unsure of what portal the cloak was offering, I felt the risk was more for myself than for them. There was no demon on the loose, for example — at least, not that I knew of.

Or if there was, it was trapped in that tree.

Several counter-height worktables filled the space, many of which couldn't be moved, but we would work around them. There were threads and scraps of material all over the broad plank floors and a row of sewing machines in front of the windows. The Wiccans had already set up a steaming Crock-Pot of cider, plates of homemade cookies, and more tofu dippers. Where these women found the time to cook as much as they did while working regular jobs and attending to their families, I would never know . . . but cook they did.

I wouldn't allow Boye to enter the room. Instead, he guarded the door, brawny arms crossed over his brawny chest. The women were curious about him, and a few threw out flirtatious hellos, but he stared straight ahead.

"Hey, Lily, check out my new T-shirt," said Starr. "I didn't have a chance to go home and change, so I hope it's okay."

The T-shirt read: UNLEASH THE FLYING MONKEYS!

"Get it?" Starr asked. "It's from *The Wizard of Oz.* . . . The Wicked Witch of the West says it when she's had just about enough of Dorothy and her friends."

I had been so tense, but now started to laugh.

"Oscar loved that part," I said, biting my tongue as soon as I realized what I had let slip.

"Oscar the pig?" asked Starr. "Oh, that's so sweet! He watches with you?"

"He's *so* smart," said Bronwyn. "He always watches with us, and I swear it's like he's understanding what's going on! After watching *Cast Away,* he kept wanting coconut!"

The others laughed.

"I'm serious! Isn't that true, Lily? Don't you think he understands more than we think he does?"

"I think he might," I said. "And, believe it or not, that pig really does love to watch movies."

It was good to be reminded why I was doing this. It helped me focus. This was all for Oscar. I had to figure out what was going on, so I could get him back.

We began the ceremony by lighting the candles and forming the circle to draw down the moon. As the women clasped one another's hands, then touched their hearts, each in turn, I let myself soak up the feminine energy. I had been spending so much time with men lately that I had forgotten the connectedness, the perfection of this sensation. The calm, soothing vibrations. Together we were daughter, mother, and crone: the sacred triad. We were sisters. We were a coven.

My athame in one hand, my medicine bag in the other, I entered the circle and began the chant. The women joined in, and I allowed myself to dance to the beat with a building abandon that ended in a crescendo of chanting.

Then, while still in a semi-trance, I donned the cloak.

And just that fast, I was thrust back to that other time. This time there was no fuzziness, no difficulty in hearing or seeing. Everything was crystal clear, as though I had stepped through a portal in time. I was in a village made of humble houses. The road was lined with animal pens, and my feet sank into the muddy road.

People were running past me, shouting. They were afraid, angry.

Harlot! Wicked woman! Witch!

I followed the direction of the crowd, arriving at a clearing by the ocean. A bonfire had been set up. A woman was atop it all, tied to a post.

It was a horrifying scene.

I looked around at the faces in the crowd: shouting, anticipating, afraid and angry.

I stood up to try to defend her, to try to stop it. She just looked at me and smiled. And then I realized, she was chanting.

Chanting is power. Witches were sometimes called mumblers because of their incessant recitations, the words that, repeated, help to open the portals and establish the connections with the ancestors, with our sources of power. She was timing her words to the croaking of a frog. I couldn't see it, but I could hear it.

A man stood and declared his name to be Jonathan Woolsey. White with fear, he read the proclamation condemning Deliverance Corydon to death by fire.

"Stop," I heard myself saying.

But then I realized . . . I wasn't trying to stop her death. On the contrary, I had been pursuing Deliverance Corydon myself and had been on the verge of destroying her. This was no witch; she was something more, something evil. She had to be gotten rid of the right way, not by fire. The flames would only add to her strength.

I tried to stop it, but I couldn't. I was reviled, shouted at. Two men held me, one on either side.

And they lit the pyre.

All I could do was watch. Deliverance's strange smile eventually ceded to screams. The shrieks seemed to enter my body, my mind. I wondered if I would ever get rid of them.

Afterward, I gathered the ashes. I put them in a box

with special markings to keep Deliverance at peace, inside. It had to be disposed of properly: by lightning. It was the only way. I singed my hands, burned my fingertips as I grabbed at the ashes, but I didn't care. Time was of the essence. I had to dispose of her ashes properly. I . . . I had to hide my cape before . . .

The anger and fear of the townspeople turned on me. The next thing I knew, I was being brought to my own gallows. The noose was placed around my neck. It was scratchy, heavy. It felt like death. The floor dropped out from under my feet. . . .

I awoke.

As before, I was flat on my back on the wooden floor. This time, instead of a gnarled gobgoyle face over mine, however, was a ring of worried women.

"I think maybe we should call an ambulance," I heard one woman say.

"She's been out almost twenty minutes," said another.

"Lily?" Bronwyn asked, as though from far away. "Lily, can you hear me?"

"Let's call someone—"

"No, no, I'm all right," I said with a croak. "Thanks."

"Here. Have some cider," said Starr.

"I'm just . . . I had a really strange vision," I began, sipping the warm cider. The sweet tang helped bring me back to reality. "Did I say anything?"

Bronwyn shook her head. "You twitched a lot, but you didn't say anything intelligible. Were you able to see where Oscar is?"

"No. No, not really. But . . . I have an idea. I have a better idea than I did before."

Despite the fact that it was the middle of the night in Texas, I made a rare phone call to the woman who had raised me from the age of eight. The woman who had tried her best to train me not only in witchcraft, but in life. The woman who had also raised my father but lost him to raw ambition and greed.

My grandmother Graciela.

"*M'ija*, I was expecting your call. What is going on?" Graciela didn't spend a lot of time on niceties. Like me, she wasn't at her best over wires. I wrote her old-fashioned letters and cards from time to time—and sent her a monthly check—which she much preferred to the phone. Besides, I didn't like to call because just the sound of her voice filled me with strange, mixed-up feelings of longing and regret and homesickness and guilt.

She knew that if I was calling, there was a problem. An urgent problem.

I gave her the rundown of what had happened. She made a few grunts in response, but mostly just listened. One thing about Graciela: She was never fazed by anything. I do believe I could tell her a flotilla of dragons was invading San Francisco Bay, and she'd start to talk me through the appropriate magical response.

"As I'm sure you know," she said when I wrapped up the tale as I knew it, "the curse cast by a dying witch is the most powerful curse of all. Perhaps she used herself as the sacrifice; and of course, blood sacrifice is *lo mas importante*—it is the key."

"She . . . I mean, it's hard to say because it's not as though I was very near her. But Deliverance seemed truly wicked. Not a witch. Something else."

"Witches can be as evil as anyone else. You've always had a hard time accepting that."

"I just . . . I don't understand how you can feel the connection to the ancestors and not take the responsibility seriously. I mean, I understand how easily power can corrupt, but to actually set out to do evil . . . ?"

"Silver will blacken and tarnish when an evil witch is near—keep a piece in your shoe or around your neck."

"Okay, thanks," I said, tamping down my impatience.

I loved and respected my grandmother, but her little quirky superstitions—spin around three times and spit if you fear the devil is near; put slices of onions in your shoes to get rid of warts—had always driven me a little crazy. It was hard to tease out the real from the silly.

And right at the moment, after having seen—and *felt*—Deliverance Corydon, I didn't think a piece of silver was going to do the trick. I decided to try a different angle.

"I would like to help out Bart Woolsey, but frankly, ridding him of his curse is not my top priority. I just want to get Oscar back, and I want to make sure that tree doesn't hurt anyone else."

"Brew page three eleven or twelve, I forget. I am getting forgetful in my old age."

Forgetful, she called herself. Graciela was in her late seventies, and she hadn't seen the Book of Shadows since I left town when I was seventeen. And yet she remembered the location, give or take a page, of a specific spell. She was a wonder.

Cradling the phone with my shoulder, I flipped through the aged Book of Shadows, looking for the spell she mentioned. When I got to the page, my heart sank.

"It says . . . it says I need a part of him. I don't suppose . . . I mean, I have his blankets?"

She mumbled a dismissive phrase in Spanish.

"I don't have any nail clippings . . . and he has no hair. I don't . . . I can't think of anything else."

"If he is trying to get to you, too, the energy will be there. You might have enough power, but not without a tangible connection. You need part of his being, his *anima. . . .*"

"DNA."

"Whatever you call it. Our people knew what it was long before science came up with a picture and a name."

"All I can think of is . . . there is someone who might have his wings."

"Use those. But you will have to destroy the wings in order to save your creature. *Es una lástima*. It's a shame." I could practically see her shrugging. "But *asi es la vida*."

Such is life. It was one of my grandmother's favorite sayings, and she meant it. I wondered whether I would ever reach that level of acceptance, her ability to calmly deal with whatever came her way.

"Isn't there any other way?"

"No. Who has them?"

"Aidan Rhodes. He might be holding them, like a marker."

I heard a little sigh on Graciela's end of the line. "And you say Oscar's mother was one of the cursed gargoyles? If I were you, I would look for wings with the appearance of stone. That would be fitting, and easy enough for someone like Rhodes. But *cuidado, m'ija*—you will be making an enemy of Aidan Rhodes."

"Yeah . . . I'm afraid that might be unavoidable."

"*Está bien*. If you cast properly, when you take the wings into the circle, they will shift from stone to feathers, but they will have the consistency of a butterfly's wing. And you know what happens to a butterfly's wing when you touch it?"

"It turns to powder?"

"*Así es*. Just so."

"But then . . . will he ever be able to get them back?"

"No."

"And this is really the only way?"

The only response was silence. Graciela didn't believe in wasting her breath by answering silly questions. I tried again.

"Will he forgive me?"

Graciela laughed, a cackle truly suited to an elderly witch. "That's the least of your worries, *m'ija*. You are proposing to go up against a witch strong enough to cast through the ages, and you are worried about whether your familiar will be angry?"

I blew out a breath and accepted the inevitable.

"One more thing," I added. "I'm not sure how much help I'm going to have on this end. Can you help me?"

There was a long pause, and I remembered why I hated the telephone. Was she thinking? Looking into her crystal ball? Playing solitaire? I reminded myself to be patient and closed my eyes, trying to call up her face in my mind: wrinkled and leathery, with near-black, intelligent eyes and a rare smile that made me glow when she graced me with it.

"I will call the coven together."

"Really? Your local coven?" This was rare for her. Like me, she was usually a solo act.

"We will need the power of the thirteen. I will use your hair."

I had left a braid behind with her when I fled Jarod, for just such an occasion. Still, it was jarring to hear she needed to use it now.

"Will it be enough?"

She cackled some more. "It will have to be, *m'ija*. It will have to be."

Chapter 21

I left Aunt Cora's Closet to Bronwyn's care and returned to the Ferry Building the next morning, just as
soon as it opened for business. I pushed through the
throngs of folks at the farmers' market in front and the
food trucks. Up the stairs, past the "security" guard to
Aidan's door.

I knocked. No answer.

I knocked again, expecting those smiling, sparkling,
lying blue eyes to greet me.

"He's out," said the security guard.

"Any idea for how long?" I asked.

She shrugged, her attention already shifting back to
the smartphone in her hands. "Said he was leaving town
for a while."

I'll bet. I fumed. How could I find out where Aidan
lived?

But then I spotted Noctemus strutting down the hallway. If she was here, I was willing to bet her master
wasn't too far away. My anger helped me concentrate. I
rarely did this sort of thing, especially not in front of po-
tential witnesses, but I was in no mood for finesse. I put

my hands flat against the door, leaned into it, closed my eyes, and started chanting.

After several minutes, Aidan flung the door open.

"Enough already!"

"You don't seem happy to see me."

Aidan glared at me. This was rare for him; his happy-go-lucky, smiley facade was so much a part of him that it was disconcerting—and rather gratifying—to be able to make him lose his cool.

On guard, I watched him carefully as he took a seat behind his desk. I closed the door and faced him; only then did I realize that his glamour was shifting in and out. I could see his scars, terrible shiny, melted-looking burns.

I had once walked in on Aidan in his cloister at the Wax Museum, a tiny room with five walls that was devised to increase the magical vibrations. He hadn't been expecting me, and I saw that he carried deep scars on one side of his face. These he kept hidden from public with a glamour spell, which kept him as beautiful as always in the eyes of others.

Watching now as he strained to maintain the subterfuge, I wondered whether Sailor was the only one who was struggling with his powers lately. Could it be that Sailor's abilities were tied to Aidan and that Aidan himself was fighting to maintain control? And could this be related to Aidan's inability—or unwillingness—to help me get Oscar back?

"I need Oscar's wings," I said without preamble. I glanced around the office, but there wasn't much to see. No obvious gobgoyle wings—that's for sure.

Aidan seemed to read my mind. "Be my guest. Look in the closet. I think you'll be disappointed to see nothing but the accoutrements of a normal, everyday man."

I accepted his invitation and peeked in. He was right; his "accoutrements" consisted of nothing more exciting

than a filing cabinet, a raincoat and umbrella, an extra
suit jacket, shirt, and pants, and a pair of shined shoes.

"I'm serious. I want those wings."

"Oh yes, I'm sure you are. Who told you about them?"

"Just never you mind. I need them to get Oscar back."

"Familiars are a dime a dozen, Lily."

"Like you wouldn't move heaven and earth to protect
Noctemus."

"You know Oscar's not like a regular companion animal, don't you? Maybe it's time you graduate to a real
witch's familiar—you're certainly developing well, power-
wise. I have a nice crow. . . ."

"Stop it already with the replacements. Speaking of
which, I want you to take your dog back."

"He's a loaner. Just for the interim. I'm not sure Sail-
or's up to the job of protecting you at the moment."

"Sailor's none of your affair. And anyway, this discussion is about Oscar."

"Lily, be reasonable. You aren't even sure Oscar's
trapped in the oak tree. What if you're wrong and he's
with the Good People? He might emerge at any time
only to discover you have destroyed his wings. I guarantee you he'd latch on to the next little witch who would
feed him. You seriously think he's loyal to you?"

Aidan really knew how to push my buttons. I tried to
swallow my fear and uncertainty. "Listen, Aidan. I want
only two things from you. First, you were supposed to
talk to the woodsfolk for me to be sure about Oscar. You
know perfectly well they won't talk to me. And second,
give me Oscar's gol-danged wings."

"The only way a witch like you can save Oscar at this
point would be to sacrifice his wings."

"There's no other way?" My grandmother wasn't in-
fallible, and I had held out hope there was another option.

He shrugged. "You think this stuff is easy or without

sacrifice? Come on, Lily. You know better than that. That's just the way it is."

"You said 'a witch like me.' Are you saying someone else could do it? Someone like you?"

He just stared at me, that slight smile hovering on his lips as usual. I felt something close to hatred for him in that moment.

"I will get Oscar back, Aidan. I don't really care who I have to go up against to do so."

"Well, that's good, then. Because mark my words: You will have to sacrifice more than just Oscar's wings if you carry this through. If you go up against Deliverance Corydon, she won't cave in that easily."

"I didn't think it would be easy."

"No, I know that. But I'm saying it could be something more."

"Could we be a little less cryptic, please? I've had just about all I can take. I'm a fixin' to have me a hissy fit."

He chuckled. "Even when you're beside yourself, you talk Texan?"

"I talk Texan all the more when I'm upset. It's . . . well, it's natural, is what. So what will I lose? Will my friends be at risk?"

"I don't know exactly, Lily. But she won't be vanquished without consequence."

"Aidan, what are you trying to say?"

"I'm saying that this witch—or whatever she is—who appears to have been able to curse through the centuries, to survive fire and take refuge in the core of a tree . . . she is one hell of a witch. Personally, I'd want to get her on my side, not go up against her."

"Is that why you're not helping me with this?"

"Just take my advice. I know about these things. You can use this situation, Lily, to add to your own powers. Leave her in the tree. With her power added to yours, it will be easy to protect it so it isn't taken down—and she can boost your powers enormously. And her familiar will work for you."

"That witch took my pig."

"Enough with Oscar! I won't give you his wings, for your own sake."

"That's bullpucky. You won't give them up because then he wouldn't be beholden to you anymore."

"Well, according to you, he's about to be killed in a tree, so why would I care if he's beholden to me or not? Be rational."

A book flew across the room, barely missing Aidan but landing smack-dab on poor Noctemus's tail. She yowled and flung herself at me, scratching the back of my hand.

"Ow!" I said, leaping back. As I held my bleeding hand to my chest, a lamp fell from the desk and crashed to the floor, the lightbulb smashing. "I'm sorry! It's not intentional."

Aidan grabbed his furiously spitting familiar. I backed away.

"I think you'd better go," he said quietly.

"Yeah, I guess I'd just better."

My hand was red and swollen even before I made it back to my place. A cat scratch is always nasty; an injury from a familiar is worse. I cleaned it out and applied a special mustard-and-honey poultice, then went back down to Aunt Cora's Closet just as Carlos Romero walked in the front door.

"What happened to your hand?"

"Cat."

"I thought you were allergic to cats."

"I am."

"Nasty."

"Yup. So, was that ledger of any help to you?"

"No fingerprints—at all—and only undecipherable

symbols. The only thing that served as any kind of clue was the notation of Aunt Flora's Closet and the connection to the Woolsey family. Could we talk in private?"

I led him to the back room. He refused my offer of something to drink, but sat at the jade-green linoleum table and traced invisible lines with his finger.

I was no mind reader, but I'd always felt an interesting kind of kinship with Carlos. I knew that right now, for instance, he felt as though he shouldn't be talking to me about this case ... but that he wanted to.

"I don't think it's either of the young women," said Carlos. "Their alibis check out. And, frankly, I just don't like them for this crime. It's just too complicated a scheme—that they killed a man for trying to help their uncle find a spell to remove a love curse? Why not just kill Bart if they wanted to inherit? Now, if Bart had been poisoned, I might have bought it."

"Why's that?"

"Poisoning is a time-honored woman's method of ridding themselves of folks, especially troublesome male relatives."

"You're saying poisoning's a woman thing? Adding sexism to our list of faults now, are we?"

Carlos smiled. "The real reason I stopped by ... I wanted to let you know the oak tree is scheduled to be razed tomorrow."

"Tomorrow?"

"I did what I could to delay it, but the crime-scene folks wanted to release the scene the day after the murder. I've kept it open for a few extra days, but I'm afraid that's all I can do. SFPD doesn't really have jurisdiction over the actions of the Parks Department unless there's a crime committed."

Can I get Conrad and his crew to stop it? I felt as though I was grasping at straws. Anything I could come up with was temporary, at best.

"But I thought you might be interested to know that there's someone who has been harassing the Parks Department to take it down. He's the one who started them worrying about it; he threatened them with a lawsuit, claiming the tree was endangering the public."

"Who?"

"One Bartholomew Woolsey."

"Bart?" Dear, sweet, vague Bart?

"Apparently, according to what he told them, his family Bible has a note in it, claiming that tree holds 'the remains of evil.' Any idea what he's talking about?"

"Maybe."

Carlos rose. "I'm sorry I couldn't do more."

"Thank you for trying, Carlos."

That evening, I cooked dinner for Boye and Sailor in my apartment. As I had for the past few days, I tried to ignore Oscar's empty nest over the icebox. *Tonight is the last night I won't know,* I thought to myself. After tonight, I would have Oscar back—or I would be without him forever. No matter what, I would have some answers.

As we were finishing up our enchiladas—both men ate several servings, making me realize that I needed to shop more just to keep us in food—I decided to try Boye once more.

"I spoke with Aidan today," I said. Both men stopped chewing and looked at me. "Boye, do you know where Aidan keeps Oscar's wings?"

"Ma'am?"

"You heard me."

"You can reach Aidan during normal business hours, in his office at the Ferry Building."

"Yes, thank you. You've already told me that." This was reminding me of soldiers who were allowed to release only their name, rank, and serial number under enemy interrogation. I fixed my gaze on Sailor. "Did you know this about Oscar, that Aidan kept his wings?"

Sailor shrugged. "Not about wings *per se*. But Aidan always keeps a marker. That's how he makes things happen."

"He doesn't have one from me."

"Doesn't he?" he asked.

"What is he holding over *me*?"

"Oscar. Me. Your father. Any number of people he can get to whom you care about. Friends and family are dangerous to have while in Aidan's orbit—they give him leverage. Oscar and I are loners, so he had to come up with something else."

"Until now?"

He gazed at me a long moment; then his voice dropped as he said, "I think we both knew our relationship has made us vulnerable. Love is dangerous."

"Okay . . ." I really couldn't think about *that* at the moment. I had to keep focused. "So, how can I find out where Aidan lives?"

Both men gawked at me.

"Seriously, I have to find those wings, *tonight*. And you boys are going to help me."

Sailor turned to Boye, who had red enchilada sauce on his chiseled, bewhiskered chin. "You know where Aidan lives?"

Boye shook his head, wide-eyed and speechless.

"Well, neither do I. What's plan B?"

"There must be some way to find out."

"I wouldn't be so sure. In fact, I'm not all that sure Aidan lives anywhere. Maybe he turns into a bat, or sleeps in a tomb somewhere."

"He's not Dracula. He's a witch. A plain old mortal witch like yours truly. He has to sleep *sometime*."

Sailor shrugged. "And anyway, what makes you think he'd keep precious items at his home?"

"I don't know. . . . I guess just because that's where I would keep something like that."

"Aidan doesn't think like normal people," said Boye, before ducking his head and downing an entire glass of milk.

Sailor seemed as surprised by Boye's contribution as I was. Not that it told us anything new, but it did put me in mind of something Calypso had said. That Aidan likes to hide things in plain sight. And Graciela said the wings might have the look and feel of stone when they were bewitched.

"Wait . . . maybe . . . Could Sebastian have kept things for Aidan at his antiques store?"

I thought back. Didn't I see a pair of stone wings in the crowded shop, right next to a sculpture of Diana?

"Sailor . . ." I began.

"Uh-oh."

"I need you to help me break in to Sebastian's shop again."

Chapter 22

"If Aidan has cast a protection spell over the wings, or some other alarm device, there could be trouble," said Sailor.

"Like I care." I was already up and gathering my magical tools.

"Lily, listen to me. I admire your zeal, and far be it from me to try to keep anyone from trashing Aidan. I think you know I'm happy to jump on that bandwagon. But this is serious stuff. You've benefitted from your relationship with Aidan so far. You sure you want to take him on as an enemy?"

"I'm a woman on a mission, Sailor. I'm going to get my pig, and if that means making an enemy of Aidan, well . . ." As the significance of my words began to sink in, I lost my breath for a moment. I drew myself up to my full five foot five inches. "Then so be it. Maybe it's time this witch grew up and accepted the challenge."

Now Sailor was grinning. "There's a new sheriff in town?"

"Maybe."

"Okay, tiger. May I suggest you work a little more on

things like, say, divination and not losing your magic when you get angry before trying to unseat the most powerful sorcerer on the West Coast? But I do like the way you think."

"Does that mean you'll go with me to get Oscar's wings?"

"Do I have a choice?"

"Not really." I turned to Boye. "You, sit and stay. But answer the phone if it rings—I'll call if I need you."

At least the crime tape was no longer sealing the door of Sebastian's Antiques. But the fog was thick tonight, the alley dark and mysterious. The streetlamp was on, but the light was murky, as though it had lost most of its wattage. A rat scurried by, squeaking slightly.

"Land sakes, it's like a creepy movie," I whispered, squinting as I tried to look through the grimy windows into the shop.

"Yeah, and we both know how these movies go. The perky heroine always survives—it's the handsome helper who gets it in the first reel."

"I would hardly refer to myself as 'perky.' You are quite handsome, though, it's true. Hey—there they are! Oscar's wings."

"You sure? They couldn't, for example, be some random, worthless antique like everything else in this shop?"

"Or maybe everything that seems worthless is really a valuable 'marker' of some kind."

The doubt was clear in Sailor's eyes.

"Come on," I urged. "I don't know anything for sure, but it's the best I've got."

Sailor managed to jimmy the lock and we brought the dolly with us into the store. Unfortunately, the wings were clear on the far wall of the shop, and there was no path to them. In fact, they seemed to be trapped in a jumble of furniture, rolled-up rugs, lamps, and decorative items.

We set about clearing a path, but no matter how much stuff we moved, there was more in the way. I had no more shoved an umbrella stand aside than I was tripped by it when I turned back to grab a cherry end table. It was incredibly frustrating, like a dream where no matter how much you run, you never get any farther.

"Clever," I said, breathing hard. "Aidan set a spell to keep people from getting to it."

"How do we beat it?"

"Move fast."

We developed a method of removing one piece at a time, inching ahead with the dolly, and then moving the next. It took us a long while, but we finally arrived at the wings.

I circled them, trying to feel for vibrations. I've never been gifted in reading stone, but if these were not true stone, I thought I might stand a chance. Finally, feeling nothing, I laid my hands on them.

Sailor's eyes were on me. I shook my head. I couldn't feel anything.

"Let me take a shot," he said. Slowly, he placed one hand on the top side, which came up to his thighs. After a moment, he placed the other hand on the other wing, then ducked his head and half closed his eyes. He remained absolutely still for several minutes. Finally he stepped back and shook his head. "They're cloaked. By Aidan. It doesn't prove they're Oscar's, but they sure aren't ordinary old stone wings."

"And look at this," I said, showing him the price tag hanging from one wing. "This is clever: The price keeps rising."

"Were you planning on paying for them?"

"No—it's an enchanted price tag. No one would want to buy them at this price, and if they did, the number keeps rising. How does he *do* that? You've got to say one thing for Aidan: He's good at what he does."

"Oh sure, I give him all sorts of credit. So much so that I'm happy to give him a wide berth for the rest of my life." Sailor leaned over and picked up a small bookshelf, along with all of its contents of dusty porcelain keepsakes, which now blocked our path. "Do me a favor: Don't go asking him to teach you how he cast such spells over Oscar's wings, will you?"

"I won't. I'm just saying, he's impressive. Professional respect, is all."

"Okay. Let's get this thing out of here."

Easier said than done. The wings were heavy. Abnormally so. After all, Oscar often leaped into my arms and I had carried him without a problem; surely his weight couldn't support this kind of burden. I checked to make sure they weren't somehow attached to the floor, but the wings were freestanding. Just wildly heavy.

It took everything we had to tilt the pair of wings ever so slightly so we could shove the edge of the dolly's platform under their base. We finally managed it, both of us grunting and swearing. By now all of the items we had moved to get to the wings were sitting in our way, of course, blocking our exit. We modified the method we used to get to the wings: I would drag one piece of furniture out of the way, and Sailor would move forward incrementally with the wings. It was a torturously slow process.

I didn't even want to think about how we were going to manage to get the wings up to my apartment; I could only hope that the spell would dissipate when we got the enchanted piece out of Sebastian's shop.

We were panting and sweating by the time we'd progressed the twenty feet across the store and neared the front door. We paused again as a hat stand fell over in front of us, blocking our progress.

"Other women might want a nice Tiffany lampshade, maybe a pretty little antique vanity," grumbled Sailor.

"But my girlfriend? Oh no. Nothing but two-ton enchanted wings will do for her."

I laughed softly as I leaned over to pick up the hat stand, blowing at a strand of dark hair that had escaped from its ponytail. "Well, think of it this way: I'm pretty sure we got the right wings. After all—"

Two things registered at the same time: the frozen look on Sailor's face and the sound of snarling behind me.

Chapter 23

A huge black dog stood in the now-open doorway, its head low, snarling, showing yellowed teeth in the dim light. His eyes seemed to gleam unnaturally, putting me in mind of the famous Black Dog Ghost people thought was a demon.

But this was no demon. This was Boye. Sweet, obedient, hungry Boye.

"Boye, sit!" I commanded. *"Sit."*

He ignored me. His eyes were fixed on Sailor, who was standing stock-still behind the dolly with Oscar's wings.

"He's working for Aidan now," said Sailor quietly. "Not you."

"What do I do?" I asked.

Sailor lifted a shoulder, just barely, in a semblance of a shrug, as one hand moved slowly toward a carved walking stick. "You have any way to call for backup?"

"Boye *was* our backup."

"Then grab a weapon."

Moving only my eyes, I searched the area around me but found nothing more sinister than a thick volume of

Encyclopedia Britannica. My hand had no sooner reached for it than Boye lunged for Sailor.

Sailor swung his cane to keep the snarling, snapping dog at bay, but the powerful canine advanced relentlessly, forcing Sailor to retreat farther into the store.

"*Run*!" Sailor shouted to me. "Lily, *run*!"

"*Boye!*" I called again, refusing to believe he wouldn't listen to me if I could just get through to him. "Boye, I command you! *Stop!*"

He lunged again. This time his powerful canine jaws clamped down around Sailor's leg. Sailor fell to the floor with a thud, swinging the cane down on the dog's head with no apparent effect. The ferocious growling was all I could hear as Boye flung his head to and fro, yanking Sailor's now bloody leg, saliva flying.

"Lily, get *out* of here!" Sailor shouted again.

I smashed the heavy encyclopedia over Boye's head. He hardly flinched. Desperate, I tried to grab the old cash register, but it was bolted to the counter. Finally, I picked up a small side table and, swinging as hard as I could, cracked it over Boye's skull: once, twice, three times.

With a whimper, the great muscled dog finally collapsed, jaws still locked around Sailor's bleeding leg. Sailor gripped the upper and lower jaw in each hand and tried to pry them open, but they were still locked on. Finally, he jammed the walking stick between the teeth next to his leg. He and I both pushed on it, using leverage to force the canine's jaws open.

He scuttled back, out of Boye's reach.

The leg wound was deep and bleeding.

"Take off your shirt," I told Sailor.

"I do like the way you think," said Sailor, his voice hoarse with pain. "But this is no time for such things."

I gave a little laugh and helped him with the white shirt he was wearing over a black T. I used it to wrap his leg as best I could to stanch the flow of blood.

"Can you walk?"

"I'm sure I can manage to limp my way out of here, but I don't know about those wings."

I blew at the hair in my eyes again and looked at Boye's still body. He had transformed and was now lying facedown, naked, on the floor. He was breathing, which I was thankful for, but I sure didn't want to be here when he awoke.

Still, he didn't deserve this. He was loyal to Aidan, probably bound to him through some sort of marker, just as Oscar was.

If I left the wings here, I would never find them again. Once Aidan realized how close I was to recovering them, he would no longer hide them out in plain sight.

"Go," said Sailor with a grimace. "Get those wings out of here. Use magic if you have to. I can't help you carry them."

"I'm not leaving you here," I said.

"Seriously, Lily, listen to me. Get those out of here; then call nine-one-one. I'll say it was a crazy dog, or a street brawl, if Boye remains in human form, and we'll both be taken care of at the hospital."

"I'll do that for Boye, but not for you. Let me think for just a minute."

Quickly, I ran down my mental list. Often I called Aidan for help, but clearly that wasn't an option this time. Oscar was missing, Sailor was with me, Bronwyn and the coven sisters . . . well, I supposed I could include them again, but brute strength wasn't their strong suit.

Still . . . maybe if I cast, I could get the wings out the door, and it was likely they wouldn't be nearly so heavy after that. I found some twine behind the register and tied Boye's hands behind his back, ignoring Sailor's wisecracks about bondage. He was pale, and I worried about the effect of his injury. A dog bite was bad enough; the injury from a familiar animal was worse. I still had

the throbbing cat scratch on the back of my hand to
prove it.

I brought out my magical tools and started to cast
over the wings. I could feel—almost *see*—Aidan's magic
resisting mine; it was swirling in a cone around the wings.
I hadn't wanted to cast before because I knew Aidan
would feel my magic going up against his. But no doubt
Boye already had checked in with Aidan, so the jig was
up. If Aidan felt my magic going up against his now, what
did I care?

Just make it intense, Lily, I thought to myself. Give him
a little taste of what he's up against. I had grown stronger, more focused since I first met Aidan. I was getting
better at using my anger and fear to focus my intent.

I brought out the mason jar of brew and cast a circle,
then marked the five points of the pentagram. Earth,
wind, fire, water, and spirit. As fast as I could, but careful
not to hurry. There was no way to speed up the process.
I fell into the casting with surprising ease, and finally realized: The wings were helping me. Oscar's wings were
still a part of him. They were casting with me, as he would
be if he were here.

My power slipped through the portals. I called on my
ancestors, and an image of the Ashen Witch came to me
in a flash of light.

I came out of my mini trance to find all as it was a
moment ago, but Boye was stirring.

I jumped up, shoved my things back in my bag, and
tried the wings: They were heavy as stone, but no heavier.
With effort I could push them on the dolly.

"Can you walk?" I asked Sailor, ignoring Boye's
grunts.

"I can hop at least," he said. "Just help me up?"

I grabbed him under his arms and lifted. He was a big
man, I realized as I felt his weight. All those beautiful
muscles. Good thing I was no waif myself. And hauling

around the dead weight of clothing—especially when wet, on wash day—had built up my upper-body strength. Still, if I was going to keep up this sort of thing, I might want to consider a gym membership.

Once on his feet, Sailor was able to half hop, half limp out of the store.

"Back in Jarod, they'd say you had one heck of a hitch in your giddyap," I said as I followed him, straining to push the dolly.

Sailor chuckled and held the door for me.

I turned back to Boye. He looked so helpless lying there, prone and naked. "I'll send help. Try to relax. Are you okay?"

"My head hurts," he managed to answer.

"I'll send someone. Just . . . try to relax." I repeated, praying I hadn't caused him lasting damage.

As I closed the door, I noticed several dusty antique frames sitting on a shelf near the front window. What caught my attention was not the frames per se, but what was in them. They each showed the same stock photo: two dogs, one a goofy-looking golden retriever, the other a smaller dog of unknown heritage, grinning widely, tongues lolling. It was the photo Will had shown me in his office.

I didn't have time to process this little tidbit at the moment. It took all my strength and concentration to guide the dolly with its burden to the van. When we arrived, I realized that spell or no spell, the stone wings were still too heavy for me to lift into the back of the vehicle by myself.

"I can help," said Sailor.

"Are you sure?"

"I can't walk well, but my arms are still functioning," he said. "Get it as close as you can here, and we'll lift together, on three."

We dented the bumper, but finally succeeded in shov-

ing the wings into the back of the van and slamming the
doors.

"Let me use your phone," I said after I helped Sailor
into the passenger's seat.

"Why?"

"I have to call someone to help Boye."

He snorted. "Excuse me if I'm not feeling all warm
and fuzzy toward that particular canine."

"He was only following orders," I said. "It wasn't his
fault."

"You're using the Nuremberg defense?"

"I'm just saying. There are no bad dogs, just bad owners."

He gave me a slight smile as he handed over his cell
phone. "I didn't realize you were such an animal lover."

I shrugged.

"And you do realize, don't you, that he's not actually
a dog?" continued Sailor. "I mean, you just saw the
man...."

I blushed. "I know. In his altogethers."

Sailor smiled but leaned his head back against the
bench seat, blanching. I had to get him back to my place
and work some healing magic on him before infection
set in. Luckily, I had the perfect honey-mustard plaster
recipe in my Book of Shadows. I had used it before
against dog bites—though, since this was a familiar's
wound, I might need to ratchet things up a bit.

Still, I sat for another moment, phone in hand, trying
to think of whom to call. Finally, I dialed the number for
a money-market-manager-turned-private-investigator I
met a while back. His number was easy to remember as
it spelled out his name, which itself was easy to remember because, after all, Sam Spade was the name of San
Francisco's most famous private eye. I met Sam a while
ago, and while he wasn't the best private eye in the world,
he was eager to learn and keen to make money.

"I'll pay you to pick up a man from Sebastian's Antiques in Jackson Square and take him to the emergency room. He . . . hit his head."

"Um . . ." I could hear shuffling in the background, and I imagined he was looking up pricing in his private eye handbook. "Is it . . . Would I be breaking any laws?"

"No," I said, thinking that while there might be a little trespassing going on, it was minor and, after all, he was on a rescue mission. "You're just helping out a stranger you happened to notice as you passed by the store. Sebastian's Antiques, near the corner of Gold and Balance Streets."

"Okay. Is it dangerous?"

"No. He's unarmed. In fact, he's naked."

"Naked?" The sounds of pages flipping intensified, and I could only imagine he was searching his handbook for extenuating circumstances.

"Sam?" I asked after another long moment of silence.

"Okay. I'm gonna have to charge you time and a half because of the hour. And there's a surcharge for nakedness."

"Seriously?"

"Says so right here in my book."

"Just out of curiosity, would that nakedness surcharge hold if the person in question were a woman, or only for a man?"

"You want me to do the job or not?" Sam asked, sounding cranky. "I'm perfectly happy staying home and watching old movies. Last time I helped you out, I was nearly thrown over a balcony."

"I think that's exaggerating, just a tad. But anyway, yes, please. I will pay you if you go help this fellow out. He really does need to see a doctor."

And then I took my sullen psychic home, hauled him up the stairs, cleaned up his wound, applied a poultice, brewed from my Book of Shadows, cast a salt circle on my living room floor, and stayed with him until he fell asleep.

And then I took stock. Oscar was missing. Sailor and Conrad were both out of commission. Even Sailor's aunt was still down for the count. Aidan was, I supposed, an enemy, as was Boye.

I was running through magical allies like so many gorse blossoms.

All I could think to do, at this point, was brew.

Sailor slept on, drugged by the brew I had urged him to drink. This was good; the sleep would help his body to garner all its forces to mount an immune response to the injury. If I brewed well—and I almost always did—he should be up and around by later today, and within a week would have nothing but faint pink scars to show where he had been bitten. The poultice would heal from the outside, the brew from within.

It took me three trips to take all my supplies down to the van. It didn't help that I was looking over my shoulder the whole time. Not only afraid that Aidan or one of his minions might be coming after me, but also aware that in the middle of the night on Haight Street, even under ordinary circumstances, it paid to be on guard.

I climbed into the back of the van and shut the doors, then began to light the candles. I could feel a heavy weariness settle over me like a mantle. I was physically exhausted from too little sleep and the night's Herculean effort with the preternaturally heavy wings, then helping Sailor up to my apartment. Every muscle ached. Plus, my neck still hurt from the attack at the Academy of Sciences, my hand was still sore from the cat scratch, and I'd been casting so much lately, I feared my caster was all tuckered out.

As they said back in Jarod, I felt tore up from the floor up.

Unfortunately, feeling sorry for myself made it even

harder than normal to get to the semi-trancelike state that was necessary to concentrate and focus my intent to cast an effective spell. But I forced myself to think about Oscar, and sure enough, within a short period of time, I could feel the wings aiding me. Helping me cast in order to attain their demise.

Guilt washed over me. And self-doubt. Was I doing the right thing? Was there any other way? I was destroying a part of Oscar, a part that he likely cherished.

While I was wondering this, and chanting, the wings began to transform. Graciela was accurate in her description: They looked leathery like bat wings but were made of individual feathers like a bird's wing. And if she was completely correct, then they would disintegrate like a butterfly's delicate wings if I touched them, and touch them I must in order to cast the spell properly.

But I had to save Oscar. The tree was slated for removal tomorrow.

This was the only way. I took a deep breath, swallowed hard, and let several drops of my own blood fall as a sacrifice.

I braced myself. A great cloud of vapor burst forth, streaming up to the ceiling, where it coalesced and took on the amorphous form of a face, looking down at me.

Looking into that face, I was now certain: The Ashen Witch was my helping spirit, my guide. I had always wondered about this guardian who appeared when I cast an important spell, when I brewed and added my own blood—it wasn't any known relative, and Graciela had always told me not to push, that her identity would be revealed to me in time. It was the Ashen Witch. We were connected through the ages. Through time.

When the casting was over, a single feather remained. Leatherlike, it did not crumble like the rest.

Mourning Oscar's wings and still plagued with self-doubt, I took the time to weave a delicate leather strap through and around the feather, threaded beads of orange, magenta, and cobalt blue onto the band, and consecrated the feather, soaking it in the brew while chanting a charm. As I completed each step, I hoped and prayed I would be placing it around his scaly neck soon. Aidan might be right; perhaps Oscar would never forgive me for destroying his wings. But even if he left me in anger, at least he would be alive—and free even from Aidan.

Then I hung the amulet around my own neck, packed my satchel with the wing powder and jars of brew, my sacred rope, and all the pertinent charms and herbs I could think of.

And prepared to go to the oak tree to get my gol-danged pig back.

And there I would give the Ashen Witch another shot—through me—at putting Deliverance Corydon to rest. For good.

Chapter 24

It was three in the morning when I proceeded on my rescue mission. The witching hour. This was the time between night and day when most are asleep and the spirits move most freely.

I brought my things to the clearing in Golden Gate Park, where Ms. Quercus stood.

I knew the crescent moon was above me somewhere, but it was not showing itself tonight. The clearing was lit only by the subtle gleam of a streetlight on the nearby road.

In fact, by the time I arrived at the tree, the wind was kicking up, and now gusts of rain were billowing through the trees. This never happened in July in San Francisco. Like the old song says, it don't rain in California—almost never from May to October in this part of the state. Not even the occasional passing shower.

This rare storm, of course, was courtesy of a group of witches in Jarod, Texas. I imagined the thirteen were cranky as all get-out, since Graciela had roused them before dawn and insisted upon the coven meeting. At least Texas was a couple hours ahead of San Francisco.

But if I knew them—if I knew most witches—their circle would end with sharing a lot of food, laughter, and fellowship. They would probably leave with hugs and promises to get together and cast more often. That's the way these things went.

But other than the group of witches working from afar, I would cast alone. According to Graciela, it was woman to woman, a very private battle. This was the way it was; this was the way it had to be.

Luckily, there were no witnesses tonight. Only fools stood outside during a lightning storm, or ran under a tree already weakened by rot. Then again . . . I searched the clearing, trying to see through the rain-drenched darkness. I felt almost as though I was being watched.

The trees thrashed about, and raindrops pounded down, stinging my face. This was no gentle shower—it was a true storm, angry and violent. I tried to ignore the cold and discomfort as I drew my circle around the tree and set up the five points of the pentagram. I began chanting, keeping low as branches swiped at me.

The storm rose, more and more intense. I chanted louder, matching its fury. I brought out some of Oscar's wing powder and began to strew it about, allowing the wind to catch it. It swirled around the base of the tree.

The oak's massive gnarled trunk seemed to contort, its broad, thick arms waving and shuddering in the wind. I heard a cracking sound and desperately hoped the branches weren't going. There was no way to know exactly what part of the tree contained Oscar. What if he was in a branch that fell? Was he able to think in there, to realize what was going on? Surely if he was conscious . . . he must know that I would never give up on him, that I would move heaven and earth if I had to in order to secure his release.

I had done my best to move earth, and now it was time to move heaven.

For the spell to be complete, I needed lightning. I could hear thunder rolling, but it was still far away. Was the coven strong enough? I wondered. Were they too far away in Texas? Was the braid of my hair enough to make the connection?

The storm whipped up further and further. I started to feel a hum that went to the heart of me, that helped me to connect to the power of my ancestors through the centuries. Oscar wasn't here to help me open the portals, but I felt him. He was near.

I needed to time things right. . . . I needed lightning to hit the tree.

Now or never. Without pausing in my chanting, I whirled the gold velvet cape around me and let it settle on my shoulders. I fastened the clasp at the throat.

The brew did its job. Rather than transporting me back through time, I brought the souls to me.

I could feel the Ashen Witch as if she were a part of me. But . . . there was something else, too. Someone else.

Lightning struck. Directly down through the branches to the heartwood.

I saw a white flash and felt a tremendous blast of energy. My hair stood on end, and I fell onto my backside in the muck at the base of the tree. My fingers and neck burned.

As though in slow motion, the tree split in two, the top of each branch bursting into flame. I scrambled up off the muddy ground and ran from the falling branches. They caught on themselves while falling, giving me precious seconds to escape.

When I turned back, I saw what looked like Oscar's batlike ears sticking up out of the split center of the tree.

"Oscar!" I cried, trying to make myself heard over the sound of the storm.

Oscar's head popped up, over the broken lip of the tree trunk. He was muddy and wet and covered in bark and seemed mighty riled. He tumbled out and scampered through the falling branches.

"*Oscar!*" I said again, opening my arms wide. He threw himself at me, tossing me back onto my butt, once again, into the mud. He glommed on, arms and legs wrapped around me so hard his scales dug into my flesh, and I could barely breathe.

"Mistress!"

"Oscar, are you all right?"

"*Mistress!*"

I started laughing. Oscar had one arm over my face and his hand grabbing my head so I couldn't see a thing, but I could feel his heart thudding wildly against mine. Oscar was *back*.

"Um . . . mistress?"

The tone in his voice warned me. I pulled his arm down out of my line of sight. I was instantly sorry.

Something else was crawling out of the tree.

I felt it more than I saw it at first; something crawling along my skin like an army of ants, up my spine and down my arms.

It was a woman. Or something like a woman. She was covered in bark, leaves, and sap; her eyes were burning black, her mouth a huge vacant void.

Deliverance Corydon in the flesh, so to speak.

Her gnarled hands held the sides of the tree as she pulled herself out, stepping almost gingerly, as though unsure of her surroundings. Disturbingly, she started to smile, a hideous awakening, as though realizing she was released at long last.

She moved slowly, jerkily, with a seeking, yearning sensation I could feel.

She opened her mouth and a sound came out. This was no human sound I knew of, more like the screeching of an owl, something ancient and predatory.

Lance came on the scene from out of nowhere, throwing himself to his knees in front of his mistress. I noticed that his right arm was bandaged.

"I have followed you, mistress. I have remained loyal. I followed your ashes across the country. I watched as they buried you here. . . . I searched for a way to resurrect you, but I failed. I know that. Kill me if you must. I tried to kill the Lily witch for you, and I failed even in that. My only happiness is that you are released from your wooden prison."

She kicked him as she stepped past him, still looking around at her surroundings, her movements strangely awkward, as though not used to her body. Finally, her finger rose and pointed directly at me.

"I accuse thee; thou hast bewitched me!" Deliverance cried, then started to laugh.

I felt strangely cowed by her words, as though we were still back in Dathorne, among the hateful crowd.

"Run, Oscar. *Run*," I whispered, setting him down abruptly so I could face her.

I stood, stroking my medicine bag to center myself.

"Give me the pig!" she demanded.

"*Deliverance*, this is between you and me. Leave Oscar out of it."

Her laugh was a rapacious, destructive shriek leaving her terrible mouth. It sent chills down my spine. Her eyes shifted, and I sidestepped to stand in her line of vision, determined to keep her attention away from Oscar. My familiar hadn't obeyed me, of course, and remained by my side, growling a deep rumble I could barely hear above the storm.

"Deliv—" I began again.

"*Stand back!*" cried a man's voice. I looked over my shoulder to see Will Chambers running toward us. He was smiling and excited, as though discovering some wonderful surprise. "Are you . . . ? You are Deliverance Corydon?"

She cast her terrible gaze upon him, cocking her head to the side in interest.

"I can't believe this!" Will gushed.

"Will, what in the world . . . ?" I said.

"When I couldn't find the cape, I gave her a sacrifice! That's what she wanted, wasn't it? That's her, right? Deliverance Corydon. I can't believe this!"

"You called her?"

"I gave her Sebastian. His blood soaked into her roots. Just as the legend said it would. You knew, didn't you? You came to me, asking all those questions. . . . I thought you knew. You helped bring her back by wearing that cape! I've been watching, and waiting, and hoping. Bart was trying to get this tree taken down, but he didn't manage it in time. I knew if I couldn't find that cape, a sacrifice was the next-best thing. . . ."

Deliverance came toward him, arms extended. Her gait was jerky, but she seemed sure and strong as she wrapped him in her embrace. At first Will smiled, but then he started screaming.

I began murmuring my spell words again and released the rest of Oscar's wing powder, which swirled around wildly in the wind.

"Run, mistress!" Oscar yelled, pointing over my head.

I ran, as a huge, burning oak branch crashed down—right on top of the pair.

Deliverance crawled out, the sound of her terrible laughter rising above the storm.

Will's leg was trapped. He cried out for help as the flames came near.

I was racked with indecision. Despite what Will had done, I couldn't let him burn—I had to help him. But I didn't want to go near Deliverance.

She extended an arm to point at me once again. "Harlot! *Witch!* I accuse thee!"

"*Yes*, I'm a witch," I cried out. "A proud witch. And I don't know what you are, but you are *not* welcome here."

I started to chant in earnest, yelling to be heard over the storm. I stroked my medicine bag, envisioned my helping spirit, and called on the strength and magic of my ancestors.

After a moment, I could hear Graciela murmuring with me. Then another voice, and another. All those women's voices—my grandmother's coven and someone else . . . Was it the Ashen Witch?—coming together within me. I could feel them under my skin, their energy reverberating through my veins: All of their courage, determination, and resilience supporting me, holding me up as I faced this terrible menace.

The storm swirled up around us. A deafening *crack* filled the air. I was blinded by a flash of light and knocked to the ground, flat on my back.

Dazed, I pushed myself back up and looked for Oscar, but my eyes were still adjusting: I couldn't see.

But I could hear: Deliverance was screaming. The terrible sounds echoed through my head just as they had in my vision when she stood atop the burning pyre. They continued for several moments, finally fading away with a wretched sob.

"What happened?" I croaked. "Where is she?"

"There," said Oscar, pointing to a pile of ash. "Struck by lightning. What were the chances?"

Will called for help again, and Oscar and I ran to pull Will out from under the branch. Thunder continued to boom, and lightning flashed around us, but the greatest ferocity of the storm seemed to have passed.

"What . . . what's going on?" Will look stunned. "What's happening?"

"Ashes to ashes," I said quietly. I couldn't believe that, after all of this, it was done that quickly and easily. "Will, do you have a cell phone?"

He handed it to me, apparently too stunned and hurt to think about the consequences of cooperating. I called Carlos Romero, told him where to find us and that Professor Will Chambers had confessed all. I hoped he would do the same for the police officers in a slightly more official setting.

Just as I was hanging up, a flurry of white caught my eye.

Dozens of white butterflies swirled around the base of the tree, their fragile wings batted about by the waning winds of the storm.

"What's this, now?" I asked, afraid it was yet another incarnation of Deliverance Corydon. I wasn't sure how much more I could take. . . . I felt weak as a kitten.

"That's a sign from the woodsfolk, mistress. Like the mushrooms—they were a clue that a frog belonged here. Anyway, I guess they like you, after all. They helped take down that wicked witch for you. Remember: Don't say thank you. They'll come to you for a favor in return when they're good and ready."

"Really? They came through after all?"

"I reckon they made that branch fall." Oscar nodded. "'Course, now you're beholden to them something fierce."

"Oh, goody," I said. As I watched the butterflies fly away, I noticed one goggle-eyed, sad-looking toad crawling out from under the burning rubble of the oak tree.

Poor Lance.

Chapter 25

Oscar gazed at me, his green eyes huge and crumbs on his snout. "You want me to *go*?"

We were back in my apartment, after yet another exhausting chat with Inspector Carlos Romero. I was still soaked through from the rainstorm but had finally managed to unpeel my clingy familiar from my body so I could at least towel dry my hair. Oscar was sitting on the counter with the open cookie jar in his lap, and I had just been trying to explain to him the bad-news, good-news situation: I'd destroyed his wings, but he was no longer beholden to Aidan. In fact, he was free to go wherever he wanted.

"Why do you want me to *go*?" he whined as he stuffed another chocolate-chip oatmeal cookie in his mouth. He'd been eating since we'd walked back through the door of the apartment. "Are you mad at me?"

"*No*, of course not. I meant what I said. You are my family. This is your home as well as mine. But I don't want to *force* you to be here. I'm not your mistress anymore. I feel so bad about your wings, Oscar, but now you are your own pig. Or whatever. You are your own *Oscar*."

"Where would I go?"

"I don't know . . . visit your family, maybe?"

"My family's a little . . . dysfunctional."

"I thought you were searching for your mother."

He shrugged. "I always look, but let's face it: There are a lot of gargoyles to track down. Unless you want to go with me?"

"I could manage a trip or two, of course. I would love that. But this is my home, and I don't want to leave it, or Aunt Cora's Closet, for very long. But . . . I have an idea. I'd like to give you this."

I held out the Ashen Witch's gold velvet cape.

"For me?"

"You said you could use it to 'travel' around, didn't you? Now that everything's happened, it doesn't seem to have the same visions attached to it. Anyway, I destroyed your wings, so I thought . . . I know it's not the same, but I'd like you to have it. And you can keep it safe, so it doesn't fall into the wrong hands."

He gaped at me for a moment, but finally took the cape, cuddled it for a brief moment, then scampered up above the icebox to hide it in his cubby. I wondered whether he would use it as intended, to travel and look for his mother, or just as another of the blankets he slept with.

Oscar jumped back down, seeming embarrassed by our display of emotion.

"So, that professor tried to follow the old box, which he thought was maybe still in the trunk, because he was looking for"—he dropped his voice to a whisper—"Deliverance Corydon? But the box with her ashes had been buried at the base of the tree?"

"Seems like it. Will first heard the legends when he grew up back East. Through his research, he came to believe that Bart had the box with the ashes, but the truth was they had been buried at the base of the tree generations ago by the Woolsey relatives when they came here by wagon train. They thought she'd be trapped; they never realized anyone would work to release Deliverance from the heartwood. But Lance, as Deliverance's familiar, kept an eye on the Woolseys through the years and finally wound up with a very apt job—working with frogs—at the Cal Academy, alongside Nina Woolsey."

Oscar shook his head. "Some familiars are bad news, I tell ya."

"Will became obsessed with the stories and with Deliverance Corydon. When he found out Hannah had sold the trunk, he confronted Sebastian. I guess Sebastian had sold it to me on purpose, to keep it safe. He knew I had worked with Aidan Rhodes in the past. I wish he'd just talked to me about it."

"Doesn't work that way."

"So I gathered. Anyway, Sebastian refused to tell Will who he'd sold the trunk to."

"I guess Sebastian wasn't so bad then, right? He probably only kept the secret because he was afraid of Aidan, but whatever."

"Either way, I'm grateful. If he'd told Will I had the trunk . . ." I trailed off with a shrug. "Maybe *I* would have been the blood sacrifice."

"Excuse me?"

"Sebastian tried to convince Will of the truth, that the box with the symbols had been buried a long time ago at the base of the tree. Bart knew about the tree from the family Bible. Will took Sebastian there, and they looked around for it, but of course the box had mostly disintegrated years ago. Will got frustrated, and it occurred to him that if Deliverance really was part of the tree, he could offer her a blood sacrifice."

"To make her stronger," said Oscar.

"Is that why she abducted you?" I asked softly.

Oscar shrugged one bony shoulder. "I think she did it

first as a distraction. She thought it would throw you off track, keep you from nosing around too much. She thought Will would manage to free her. All he needed was to make a few more blood sacrifices . . . and once he'd killed, I guess it gets easier."

And Lance had tried to stop me as well, I thought, chasing me through the basement of the Cal Academy. I still wondered whether poisoning Conrad had been deliberate, or an accident—after all, Conrad had slapped Lance on the back. But I doubted I'd ever have the chance to ask him; Lance was nowhere to be found, and Carlos had informed me that he was not putting out an APB for a missing frog, no matter what I said.

I let out a loud sigh; Oscar did the same.

"Maybe Will realized there was something else valuable in the trunk—"

"The cape?"

"Maybe. Or maybe he just didn't believe Sebastian about the ashes, so he traced the trunk to Aunt Flora's Closet. He put the ledger back where he found it, though, because he knew of Aidan's association with Sebastian. Aidan probably would have been able to track the book."

"How'd Will know so much about this sort of thing in the first place? Most cowans are clueless with this stuff."

"It was his field of study. He taught at UC Berkeley."

"They paid the man for that? His classes must have been a little cuckoo."

"I guess so."

"But . . . *why* would he do it? Why would you want to bring back that . . . *thing*?"

"I don't know if we'll ever know the answer to that. I think people can easily be seduced by magic, whether it's for good or evil. That's why it scares even me, sometimes."

"Even *you*?"

I nodded as I poured him another glass of milk. We hadn't even had breakfast yet, and Oscar had gone through nearly a dozen cookies. But I was feeling extra indulgent; my heart swelled, just watching him eat. "What was it like, in there?"

"It was mostly . . . just dark. And damp. And I was sort of in a different dimension, so I couldn't really tell what was going on. But . . . I was scared that she would absorb me, somehow, for good. Maybe find a way to use me to increase her power."

"Didn't you know I would come for you?"

He nodded vigorously and bit into another cookie. "You said old-man Bart had a love curse on him, too? Did that disappear when *she* died?"

"As far as I understand inheritable curses, it should continue despite her demise—that's the point of a death-bed curse, after all. But Herve gave me a spell—once I get my strength back, I'll cast it and see if I can help Bart out. That is, if he even *needs* my help . . . He's been getting along well with one of Bronwyn's coven sisters. It's possible it wasn't a curse so much as a self-fulfilling prophecy."

"Hey, wait . . ." Oscar glanced at my moon calendar, then turned and gaped at me. "Do you know what today is?"

"What?" Dread swept over me as realization dawned. "Today's . . . *Saturday*?"

He fixed me with a suspicious glare. "*I'm* the one who's been stuck in a netherworld for a week, and you can't remember which day it is?"

"I guess I've been a little busy saving your hide," I said, feeling put-upon. All I wanted was a long shower and a longer nap.

"You're no quitter, mistress, I'll give ya that. Hey! I'll go with you if you want! I could pass you notes on the algebra questions!"

"I don't believe in cheating, but . . . you know algebra?"

"Sure; it's easy."

"Thanks, Oscar, but I think I'll try to pass on my own."

"I was wondering. . . . What did you have to do to destroy Deliverance Corydon?"

"I'm sorry?"

"What did you have to sacrifice to defeat her?"

"I sacrificed your wings."

"That was to get me back. But defeating her . . . It was something more than that, wasn't it?"

My fingertips tingled. I remembered that vision I had at the tree, when I was back in time. I was back, and Deliverance held out her hand and took me onto the pyre with her. I knew now that I was connected through time to the Ashen Witch. But as for Deliverance, in the end she had been defeated almost too easily. I wasn't yet certain whether she was gone for good, or would continue to haunt me. But as Graciela would say, *así es la vida.* Such is life. I would deal with it if and when it became a problem.

"I'm starved," said Oscar, interrupting my thoughts. "How about some French toast?"

Sailor was moving around in the bedroom, no doubt roused by the smell of coffee. Downstairs, I could hear Bronwyn, Maya, and Susan coming into the shop—I had forgotten I had invited them to come to breakfast this morning before I went to take the GED.

I pulled out a dozen eggs, milk, and bread. I had friends and family coming for breakfast and a ridiculous test to take. And then a well-deserved nap.

The many other items on my to-do list were just going to have to wait.

Don't miss the new release in Juliet Blackwell's
Haunted Home Renovation mystery series,

KEEPER OF THE CASTLE

Coming from Obsidian in December
wherever books and e-books are sold.

I wrapped up my day a little early and headed to Pacific Heights to pick up my ex-stepson, Caleb, whom I had talked into joining me, my dad, and our friend Stan at Garfield Lumber's annual barbecue.

"I don't know why I have to go to this lame barbecue," grumbled the seventeen-year-old. His chestnut hair fell so low over his forehead, it almost covered his near-black eyes, which was probably the idea. I tamped down on the urge to push it back so I could see his expression.

"It's . . . fun," I said. Which was sort of a lie. "Anyway . . . it's tradition."

"Not the same thing."

The truth was, Garfield Lumber was old-school. The nails were still kept in the same bins they had been in since 1929; the long wooden counter was scarred and gouged; the slower-selling items on the shelves had acquired a thick layer of dust. And if you stepped into Garfield without knowing what you were doing, the staff could be downright rude. There was no Helpful Hardware Man here; "Don't Waste My Time" was Garfield Lumber's unofficial motto. And if you valued your life and all your body parts, you didn't mention a certain huge store that catered to the DIY crowd. On the other hand, once they got to know you, the folks at Garfield would go the extra distance to make sure you had what you needed to get the job done right. In a rapidly growing and ever-changing region like the Bay Area, Garfield Lumber was untouched and entirely predictable.

I loved it. Probably because it was a place I always had been—and would always be—"Bill's girl, Mel."

"Besides," I continued, "you have to eat, right?"

"Stale hot dogs? Oh, yum," Caleb said in a snarky tone that reminded me a little too much of myself.

There was no denying the barbecue was no great shakes; at Garfield Lumber, even their hot dogs tasted like they'd been around a while. But no one seemed to mind. It was a rare chance to mill around with folks who were normally in a rush, to chill out and knock back a beer or two while swapping jokes, tales of construction mishaps, and the occasional delicious bit of gossip.

"Besides," I continued, "it's important to Dad. He wants to show you off, introduce you to his friends."

I glanced at Caleb. That got him. Caleb was sullen as all get-out lately, but my dad's opinion mattered to him.

It had taken a little while, but my dad had finally welcomed Caleb into the Turner clan. There were no blood ties between us, but I had married Caleb's father, Daniel, when Caleb was five and had been his official stepmother for eight years. I adored him, and the absolute hardest thing about leaving Daniel had been realizing that I would no longer have any legal tie to Caleb, who felt like my son. My heartbreak was lessened when I realized that Caleb was as loath to give me up as I was to let him go. Caleb's mother, with whom I had always gotten along well, was happy to allow Caleb to spend time with me, especially when she had to travel for business, because Daniel's new wife was not thrilled with the idea of being a stepmother. As a result, even after the divorce, Caleb had spent a lot of time with me, including numerous overnight visits at my dad's house, and so we had remained close. Now that he was seventeen—a difficult age—I was in the peculiar position of being able to speak to him not as a parent, but as a concerned, trusted adult. Despite his apparent disdain for all adults, he confided in me more than in his parents.

We headed over the Bay Bridge, which connected San Francisco to Oakland and the East Bay. The bridge was made of two spans that met at Yerba Buena Island, and the eastern section was brand-new, the old one having failed in the last serious earthquake to hit the area. Its single tower soared skyward in a dramatic sweep.

I enjoyed the novelty but held my tongue. The last thing Caleb wanted to talk about was architecture.

"So we'll just pick up Dad and Stan at the house and then head on over to the barbecue. I'll take you back after, or your dad says you can spend the night if you want."

"Whatever."

But his interest was sparked when we turned the corner onto the street where I lived in an old farmhouse with my dad and Stan.

"Who's *that*?" asked Caleb as we both spied a shiny black stretch limousine pulled up to the curb.

This wasn't the kind of neighborhood where you saw a lot of limousines. It wasn't prom season, and unless my dad had become a high-rolling drug dealer while I wasn't looking . . .

As I drew closer, I could see Ellis Elrich—flanked by two unsmiling muscle-bound men, who could only be bodyguards—standing on the sidewalk, talking to my father. Dog was barking wildly and ineffectually while wagging his tail, as was his wont.

Dammit.

When Dad asked me last night how the trip to Marin

had gone, I'd kept it vague, and soon enough his attention had turned back to the football game and his attempts to program his new smartphone.

It wasn't that I had been keeping McCall's murder a secret, exactly. But I was a little tired of having to explain why people seemed to die wherever I was on a construction project. It was downright eerie when I stopped and thought about it.

And since I hadn't been planning to sign on to the project anyway, it seemed an unnecessary worry.

I climbed out of my Scion with caution.

"Here's my girl," said Dad in the kind of booming, cheerful voice he reserved for important clients. My father wasn't easily impressed, but he did feel that the client was king and took that to its logical extension.

Dad wasn't a large man, but even now he retained the muscles of a life lived on a construction site, though he now had a prominent beer belly and thinning gray hair. Today he was wearing his usual outfit of worn blue jeans and a formerly white T-shirt.

Ellis Elrich, for his part, was wearing what I was certain must be a very expensive suit.

"Ah, the famous Mel Turner." When Ellis Elrich turned his attention to me, I understood why everyone was so gaga over him. Charisma. The man had it in spades. There was an intensity to his eyes, a keen intelligence that was apparent from the start. Or maybe it was just his aura—I never used to believe in such things, but now that I was in the ghost business, it was getting easier for me to imagine that we all put out energy, some more clearly than others, and that other people sensed and reacted to that energy. "May I call you Mel?"

"Of course. But what—"

"And let me introduce my driver, Buzz, and this is Andrew and Omar."

"Hello," I said. Buzz nodded in greeting, but Andrew

and Omar remained silent and stoic, flanking Elrich, their eyes hidden behind sunglasses.

"And who's this young man?" Elrich asked.

"I'm Caleb."

Elrich put out his hand, and to my surprise, Caleb shook it, standing up straight and nodding in a sort of hail-fellow-well-met stance.

"Nice to meet you, Caleb," said Elrich. "You look like you play soccer."

"Yeah, and baseball." Caleb nodded. "Too short for basketball."

"Ah, well, soccer's more poetic, anyway. And remember what Satchel Paige said: 'Never let your head hang down. Never give up and sit down and grieve. Find another way.' There's always another way." Elrich gave Caleb a warm smile before turning back to me. "Mel, it is *such* a pleasure. I was so disappointed we weren't able to talk yesterday."

"Well . . . it was understandable. Under the circumstances, it would have been awkward to keep the sherry hour going."

He held my gaze for a long time, then nodded. "In any case . . . I know this seems sudden, but in fact I spoke with Graham previously about whether Turner Construction might take over the Wakefield job, or even work together with Pete Nolan. Now, with what happened yesterday . . ." He trailed off, sadness in his eyes. "Anyway, we're in a real race with time here, and I hear you've done joint projects in the past."

"Only one, and it was a highly unusual project."

"I think you'll agree that this project is pretty unusual too," said Elrich. "Not only will Wakefield serve as a retreat center for the Elrich Method, but also as a pilot project for incorporating green techniques in historical renovations. I understand that's of particular interest to you."

I shrugged and nodded. Clearly, Graham had been talking.

"Graham also mentioned you're an anthropologist, which is perfect for this sort of project, which combines history, culture, and architecture. It's an archaeologist's dream."

"I'm not really that kind of anthropologist."

"I can't just let this project grind to a halt. Nolan's workers don't deserve to lose their jobs over this. And combined with your own staff, you can employ all those people and get a great job done as well. Keep Graham Donovan working on the most exciting project of his career and be an essential part of a fantastic project yourself. I don't have to tell you that this is the kind of building that can make history, and you'll have the resources you need to make it happen, do it right."

Stan and Dad were watching the proceedings with avid interest, but they kept mute. I appreciated the way they were standing back and letting me make this decision, as head of the company. When I'd stepped in to take over Turner Construction "for a few months" after my father fell apart following the sudden loss of my mother, I'd assumed Dad would pull himself together and step back in to run the company he had built, and I would take off for Europe. But it had been years now, and I had come to accept that my dad was permanently retired. The company was now mine, for better or worse. I should have gotten used to it.

But still, Dad and Stan were both invested in the future of Turner Construction, and they were as nervous as I was about the lack of work in the pipeline. Here stood a fabulously wealthy client with a project seemingly custom-made for Turner Construction, and I was balking? Since I hadn't filled them in on the details of what happened yesterday, they were bound to be confused by my attitude.

Elrich reached down to pet Dog. The canine wagged his tail and leaned his considerable weight against the billionaire's leg, leaving long brown hairs on his fine suit. Buzz looked annoyed on his boss's behalf, but Elrich didn't seem to mind; on the contrary, he seemed determined to make everyone like him, and he appeared to be doing so.

"I don't know anything about reconstructing an ancient building," I said. "I do historical reconstruction, but that's in a San Francisco context—we're talking a hundred years, not six hundred."

"Not a problem," said Elrich with a confident shake of his well-coiffed head. "I have a special consultant on the job, Florian Libole. Have you heard of him?"

No one in my business didn't know the name of Florian Libole. So it really had been his inscription on those drawings Graham showed me.

"Of course," I said, "Libole's internationally renowned."

"That's right. He's very anxious to meet you."

"To meet *me*?"

"There aren't that many firms that specialize in this sort of thing here in California, as you know. If you refuse me, I'm afraid I'll have to import someone from back east or, worse, from Europe. They would take time getting their bearings, not to mention that a job of this magnitude should be dealt with locally as much as possible. Don't you think so?"

"I don't know. I have several other jobs going, and with the commute . . ."

"You're welcome to stay at my place," he said. "It's huge, built to house plenty of folks. I've got several people staying there now, and I've invited Graham as well. In fact, according to my assistant, the house could use some sprucing up. It's a sort of Spanish-revival, mission style, lots of hand-painted tile—you didn't get a chance to look through it yesterday, but I think you'll like it. Don't forget your bathing suit; we have a beautiful pool. And please bring the dog—he'll love running free on the fenced grounds."

I looked at Stan's face, my dad, Caleb, even Dog. They all seemed to like Ellis Elrich. And Turner Construction needed a job like this.

But then, only Dog knew all the facts of what we'd seen yesterday, and he wasn't talking.

"I'll think about it," I said. "I'm sorry. I can't commit without thinking it over. I hope you didn't come all the way here just to talk to me about this."

"I had some business in San Francisco anyway, and I rarely take time to explore Oakland. Florian tells me I simply must stop by and see the Chapel of the Chimes while I'm here. He says it's a hidden gem. Oakland really is a beautiful city."

That was very politic of him. My dad's house was no-where near the Chapel of the Chimes; instead, we live in the Fruitvale section of Oakland, a neighborhood once chock-full of orchards but now jammed with small bun-galows all in a row, with the exception of the old farm-house. Working class, to be kind; "gritty" was the adjective most often applied to the area by outsiders.

"Just in case you decide to join us." Elrich signaled to one of the burly men next to him, who reached into his breast pocket and extracted a plain manila envelope. He handed it to Elrich, who offered it to me. "This contains documents that will fill you in on a few of the details and, most importantly, a check with a deposit."

I peeked in at the figure he'd written and gulped. The check was huge. It didn't take an accountant to realize the sum would keep Turner Construction—and all the people we employed—solvent for a full year. And this was just his "deposit."

"You think about it," said Elrich. "And let me know

by tomorrow morning. I'm sorry to rush you, but we don't have much time to lose. Even with yesterday's tragedy, it's essential we keep on schedule to the extent possible."

"Do you have the go-ahead from the police to start construction again already?"

"That won't be a problem."

"Okay, I'll ... think about it," I repeated. I wasn't promising anything, but I'd be lying if I claimed the size of that check hadn't swayed me.

We watched the limo glide down the street. The appearance of the luxury vehicle had coaxed several of our neighbors out onto their porches, and a trio of laughing kids chased it for a block before giving up.

"A limo like that's even more exciting than when the garbage truck fell into the sinkhole right there. Remember that?" observed Stan. He explained to Caleb: "It took three industrial tow trucks to pull the lumbering truck out of the hole, and it forced the city to finally fix the problem for good."

"Seriously?" said Caleb.

"Yup."

We waved at the neighbors, and when the limo turned the corner and zoomed out of sight, Dad turned back to me.

"I thought you said the site meeting in Marin yesterday didn't result in anything."

"I wasn't planning on taking the job."

"Why the devil not?"

"It's sort of a good-news, bad-news situation," I explained.

"I can't wait to hear this," he said, and I imagined he was mentally rolling his eyes.

"The good news is, someone died at the Wakefield jobsite yesterday. Was killed, actually."

Dad, Stan, and Caleb looked at me like I'd lost my

mind. Dog looked at me as though waiting for me to drop food, but that was his typical stare.

"Someone *died*?" asked Caleb. "Who?"

"No one you know," I said. "A building inspector."

"Well, no one likes building inspectors," Dad observed with a grunt.

"Even so," said Stan, "I would have thought a murder would count as the *bad* news."

"Yes," I said. "Well, obviously, if you were the one killed. Or his family or . . . Okay, clearly it's tragic. Horrible. All I'm saying is that in terms of *me*, at least the place is now predisastered."

They still weren't following my logic. I tried again.

"You know how lately I have a tendency to stumble across dead bodies on my jobsites? Well, this jobsite has already had one dead body. What are the chances I'll come across another one?"

"We sure could use the work, babe," said Dad with a shake of his head. "But I don't want you on yet another job with yet another murderer running around."

"That's more good news, actually. The killer's already in custody. He was the general on the job: Pete Nolan. Graham said you know him."

"Sure, I know Pete," said Dad. "They say *Pete's* the one who killed this guy?"

"He's a loose cannon, all right," said Stan. "That SOB sucker-punched me once when he didn't like what I said about the chances for Oakland Raiders to win the Super Bowl. Remember that?"

"That was back when he was still a drunk," said my dad. "He hasn't had any problems like that for years now."

Stan shrugged, apparently unconvinced.

"Anyway, he's in custody," I continued. "So I guess that's the end of that. That's what I mean about the place being predisastered."

"Okay, so if a dead guy on site is the good news," said Caleb, "what's the *bad* news?"

Ghosts. I thought to myself, but did not say aloud. Just the thought of whatever it was I saw hovering over Larry McCall gave me the shivers, but my family had enough to keep them preoccupied as it was; no need to pile on the worries. Besides, in the case of Wakefield, I couldn't imagine the ghosts had anything to do with McCall's death. Whatever spirits those stones held—with the exception of the newly departed Larry McCall—belonged to another land, another age. The building inspector's demise was a senseless crime of passion, a case of testosterone run amok and tempers flaring out of hand. Period.

"The bad news is, it's really too far for me to commute. Raul can take over the day to day on the current projects we're finishing up, but I'll have to take Elrich up on his offer to stay up there for a while." This, of course, was good news for me. I adored my father, and his friend Stan, and this old farmhouse. But there was no denying I could use some time away. As the guest of the stinking-rich Ellis Elrich in a beautiful old Spanish-style hacienda with a pool and a view of the ocean? *Yes, please*.

"Well, you gotta do what you gotta do, babe," said Dad.

I had to admit, he didn't appear exactly broken up over the news. I supposed it was possible I had become a bit annoying, what with nagging him to eat organic vegetables and to stop watching so much TV.

Probably we could both use a little time apart.

"But I don't know . . ." Dad trailed off, his attention seeming as divided as Caleb's usually did. He kept staring at his new smartphone. "Maybe if you're gonna go on up and stay at Elrich's house, you should take a gun, just in case. You're a good shot with that Glock."

"Um . . . okay."

He looked up, surprised, a slight smile on his face. "You're getting smart, now, are you? Change your mind about gun control?"

Stan, who had a few decided opinions about gun control, gaped at me.

"No, no, it's nothing like that," I said. "I just . . . Just in case, it might not hurt to have a little extra protection."

"You think you'll be in danger?" asked Stan. "Mel, no job is worth putting yourself at risk."

"No. Not really. Not at all. I'm just . . . I thought it might be a good idea. Considering my track record. Besides, Graham will be there, so I'll have plenty of protection."

"Still . . ." Dad trailed off again. This was not like him.

"What are you *doing*?" I demanded, annoyed.

"This *smart*phone isn't near as smart as a person would hope." Dad had only recently upgraded from his old-fashioned flip phone. He explained that he had been waiting to make sure it wasn't just a fad. Now that he had broken down and bought the newfangled device, he appeared to be enamored with its many features and apps. "I'm trying to look up directions to the barbecue."

I felt a sudden stab of worry. I knew Dad was getting older, slowing down, but he wasn't *that* old, was he?

"Dad, you've been going to Garfield Lumber for thirty years. You need to look up the directions?"

"I just want to hear the voice tell me how to get there. See if she's right. I like her voice, sounds like a real nice gal."

Caleb rolled his eyes, but smiled and held out his hand. "Here. Give it to me, Bill. I'll show you."

"Okay, everybody ready?" I asked, wanting to get the show on the road. "Shall we take the van?"

Stan was in a wheelchair after a construction accident years ago. It was easiest to take the specially outfitted van so he didn't have to get out of his chair.

"Sure," Dad said, tossing me the keys. As we were all climbing in—he and Caleb in back, Stan riding shotgun—he added: "Hey, when are you and Graham gonna make me a grandfather again?"

Stan hooted with laughter.

Wow. That was out of left field. I was just beginning to move past my I-hate-all-men phase; that didn't mean I was ready to move on to procreation.

"You've got Caleb," I said, trying to ignore the strange sensation in the pit of my stomach. "That's about all I'm guaranteeing at the moment."

"Well, now, I guess he'll do just fine," Dad said.

Caleb pretended to be absorbed in programming Dad's phone, but when I glanced at him in the rearview mirror, I could tell he was smiling.

"Hey, Bill," Caleb said. "What do you call a ridiculous old man?"

"I give up. What?"

"A fossil fool."

Dad chuckled.

Garfield Lumber's stale hot dogs had never tasted better.

Unfortunately, construction workers are big on lame jokes; after Dad blabbed about what had happened at Wakefield, I'd been forced to listen to a million funny stories that culminated in dead building inspectors.

Maybe it was just too soon, but I didn't find them amusing.

About the Author

Juliet Blackwell is the pseudonym for a mystery author who also writes the Haunted Home Renovation series and, together with her sister, wrote the Art Lover's Mystery series. The first in that series, *Feint of Art*, was nominated for an Agatha Award for Best First Novel. Juliet's lifelong interest in the paranormal world was triggered when her favorite aunt visited and read her fortune—with startling results. As an anthropologist, the author studied systems of spirituality, magic, and health across cultures and throughout history. She currently resides in a happily haunted house in Oakland, California.

CONNECT ONLINE

julietblackwell.net
facebook.com/julietblackwellauthor
twitter.com/julietblackwell